SAILOR'S WELCOME—
OLD SAN FRANCISCO STYLE

"Mister Moran," called out one-armed Timothy Wiley as he slithered down the stairs. "It's a clipper, sir. My, aren't we ready for a pretty ship?"

'Whale Whiskers' Moran put his cue stick down on the billiard table. "Please excuse me," he said to his opponent and several spectators, then followed his "runner" up the stairs and onto the roof of his establishment.

Taking the telescope from Wiley, Moran put the eyepiece over his ruddy cheek and studied the semaphore signal mast on Telegraph Hill. He slapped the leathered spyglass together and tugged on his whiskers.

"Timothy, my boy, line up a dozen prospects," the older man said. "Go to city prison and bail out Hurley and Stewart. Keep 'em sober enough to tend to business this week—and get word around to Carrie and her girls. There'll be a crowd of Jacks who ain't seen shore in four months."

"As you say, boss—and I'm looking forward to giving them a real California welcome when they come in this afternoon." Timothy Wiley pulled his boot pistol out and examined it. "Poor Timothy junior," he lamented sadly, pulling back the horned hammer and inspecting the tiny copper percussion cap, "hasn't had any real exercise in weeks . . ."

CHINA CLIPPER

by John Van Zwienen

Exclusive Distribution
by
PARADISE PRESS, INC.

Printed in the United States of America

For
Ilsebuddy

Ships are but boards, sailors but men;
there be land-rats and water-rats,
land-thieves and water-thieves.
                              —Shakespeare

PROLOGUE

On the fifth floor of a gray cast-iron mercantile facade, one of many that looked out on a forest of wooden masts that lined South Street, a groping hand laid its palm on a dusty windowpane. Blood trickling from its fingers sotted a ruffled silk shirt-cuff as the hand clawed at a window lock, then slipped down and left behind a red streak on the glass.

Preceded by a bloomered majorette, a five-piece military band strutted lively on the cobbles below the jib-boom arbor that stretched from the Battery all the way up to Jackson Street. A mile and a half of packets, coasters and clippers. Following the band was a roisterous entourage of scraggly recruits under banners that proclaimed:

SAVE THE UNION
*****
1776
1863

TOTAL BOUNTY FOR NEW RECRUITS—$677 PLUS U.S. BOUNTY OF $100 TO VETERANS!

and

$15 HAND-MONEÝ PAID ANY PARTY WHO BRINGS IN A RECRUIT!

A figure waited in the shadow of a pier shack for the procession to pass, then ran across South Street and up a short flight of stairs into Number 67, just off Pine Street. The caller's rough index finger traced across the pneumatic bell labels in the vestibule: Dove's Chandlery, 2d Fl . . . Dunham & Dimon, Commission Merchants . . . G.A. Johnson, Liquors, 4th . . . W. R. Bertram, Ballast . . . Gibbs & Co., Montebianco, 5th. The seaman yanked briskly on the bell pull. Sucking air inside a long tube, it struck a clapper in a cluttered fifth-floor office.

No answer came through the voice tube.

He tried again, then shrugged and left.

Two days later, summoned by the next office's proprietor, the New York City Police broke in. With gloved hands over their noses they found a stocky, dark-complexioned man in his late forties sprawled across his open roll-top desk by the front window.

Diffused light glinted on a metallic shape in the dead man's back—on polished steel, steel worn smooth by generations of nimble hands, steel burnished by the calloused palms of seafarers.

David Montebianco had been dispatched with a foot-long marlin-spike, driven in almost to the palming hilt. He was identified by his neighbor, the liquor merchant.

Missing, according to Montebianco's part-time coloured handyman, were the office keys, a gold nugget finger-ring inset with a diamond, and a page from the accounts ledger. Monroe Lawrence described the page as containing the names of people who owed money to his employer.

A subsequent search by the police of Montebianco's holdings turned up a safe-deposit box at the Knickerbocker Trust Bank which contained many packets of small diamonds and a duplicate copy of the debtors' page in the accounts ledger. At a value of $1000 per carat, the diamonds, which weighed about two pounds, would have commanded a market price of more than $300,000—enough to build or buy four one-thousand-ton clipper ships.

An investigation of the diamond import records showed that the deceased had declared only a tenth of his diamonds for import duties. The case was turned over to federal authorities and assigned to the newly organized U.S. Secret Service under the command of Major General John Dix.

The New York agent was Colonel H.C. Whitley, who, in turn, assigned the case to a deputy, Detective John Nettleship, a specialist in smuggling as well as murder.

The duplicate ledger page listed nine accounts outstanding, with a marginal note to increase the interest from seven to nine percent for the second quarter, which would commence on the first of April, just two weeks away. As a bookmark in the ledger, a theater ticket was found for a benefit performance of *Julius Caesar* at the Winter Garden Theater, featuring the Booth Brothers, Edwin Junius, and John Wilkes. The performance was to provide funds to commission and erect a statue of Shakespeare in Central Park.

The names, listed in careful handwriting, were:

William Hadley, Shipbuilder	Portsmouth, NH	$12,300.35
John Wilson, Theatrical Agent	New York City	$ 4,500.62
Miss Cleopatra Smith	Portsmouth, NH	$ 3,789.05
Jack Renfrew	New York City	$14,320.11
Mrs. John Dixon	Mobile, Ala.	$ 6,351.75

James Dance,Merchant	Galveston, Tex.	$ 4,903.20
Edward K. Collins, Shipowner	New York City	$19,461.33
Hiram Currier, Importer	Baltimore, Md.	$13,005.71
Hien Chi, Importer	New York City	$ 6,872.14

Detective Nettleship, noting the name "Edward K. Collins" of New York City on the list, recalled the famous Collins Steamship Lines of the fifties. He remembered, too, the colorful posters from his school days: P.T. BARNUM . . . JENNY LIND . . . THE CRYSTAL PALACE of the International Exhibition in London.

The Collins Lines were long bankrupt; the remaining ships, after several catastrophes, had been auctioned off at a fraction of their original costs in 1858. The economic panic of the year before had put an end to the once-thriving business started by Isaac Collins: the regular Atlantic Packet service to Liverpool.

It wasn't difficult to track down Isaac's son. Failed enterprises marked the path, and Nettleship found the former shipping magnate in a small room at Farrar's Hotel overlooking Burling Slip, several blocks east on South Street. Edward Knight Collins, amidst a clutter of ship models and dusty manifests, looked even older than his sixty-four years.

He acknowledged his indebtedness, taking Nettleship to be a collection agent despite the detective's introduction of himself as a representative of the Secret Service.

"The Collinses have done it many times," he boomed between coughs. "First full-rigged packet service to Vera Cruz, then Tampico and New Orleans." He rubbed his sagging jowls. "Then Liverpool and the *Dramatic Line*. You remember my beautiful steamers, don't you, son? The *Shakespeare* . . .

and the *Garrick*. Why, in 1834, she was years ahead of her time—the *Shakespeare*, that is—"

"That was the year I was born, sir." Nettleship twirled a mustache end and drew up a chair. He pretended not to notice the ripped upholstery.

"Well then, son, how about my Atlantic queens? The *Pacific*—queer name for an Atlantic boat, eh? And the *Baltic* . . . and the *Atlantic* . . . and . . ." The portly businessman tugged at his tight shirt collar and heaved deeply as he rocked back in his swivel chair. "And the *Arctic*, sunk."

"All the nation was sorry for your loss."

"Thank you, son." Collins turned an easeled photograph on his strewn desk to better advantage. It was of a woman and two children. "And poor Brownie—he lost *six* of his family. That's why I sold out so cheaply. I gave it all to Brownie. It was the least I could do . . ."

"It was almost twenty-thousand dollars," Nettleship prodded. "What was the loan for?"

"You know damn well."

"Really, I don't. But I'm sure I can find out." Nettleship got up, paced a few steps and then spun around. "Mister Collins, when was the last time you were out? I mean out of this room."

"Now you're beginning to sound like a policeman. Why?"

"Try to believe me. I'm not a bill collector. And what have you got to lose in answering such a trivial question?"

"All right." The old man stacked up some loose papers on his desk. "Haven't been out since noon yesterday. I've got to get together my ideas for an iron-hulled steamer. Got some rich people interested in a confidential venture as soon as the war is over. Right here, son." He shook a sheaf of paper. "Right here is the way I'm gonna pay off Montebianco—in spite of his damned nine percent."

"Your last boat was named after a sea in Europe, as I remember. Large one, wasn't it? Something like the *Caspian*?"

"No, goddamn; it was the *Adriatic*. Sixteen knots she went—and the government had to cut back the mail subsidy. The creditors tore me to shreds."

"And Montebianco was one of the harpies?"

"He was decent—at first. Then after the war started . . ." Collins righted his chair. "Look, Mister Nettleship, lots of people owe money today—and I'm only a month or two in arrears . . ."

"Montebianco was found dead this morning. Murdered."

Silence and heavy breathing.

The Regulator wall clock ticked like a hammer.

Collins's chubby fingers dug into his lapels before extracting a handkerchief from the breast pocket. He dabbed at his forehead as he collected his thoughts, then spoke waveringly.

"And you think I did it?"

"I just came here to question you."

"How did it happen?"

"Stabbed in the back."

"He didn't get a chance to use his pistol?"

"Pistol?" The detective flinched.

"He showed it to me once. He was proud of it. Kept it in one of the desk slots. A bone-handled Derringer. Two barrels."

"Apparently not." Nettleship sat down again and took out his vest pocket watch, then wound it. There had been no pistol found in Montebianco's office.

"Most of us have defensive weapons on this street. One never knows who gets off those boats down there. Some of those pack rats think nothing of killing a man—especially the Irish and Sicilian. It's a way of life where they come from. They all carry knives in spite of the regulations." Collins reached into a drawer and pulled out a half-empty bottle of bourbon. "If you'll excuse me, son, I need a drink right now. Will you join me? I've got another cup somewhere under this mess."

"Not today, thank you," the Secret Service man demurred. "Can you tell me anything about Montebianco—what he was like, his eccentricities, anything that comes to your mind?"

With a drink warming him, the entrepreneur smiled and lost some of his grayness. "It's very difficult for me to discourse with an opponent who does not abide by the rules of the game." Collins held up an empty tin cup and polished it with his coat sleeve, then shook it upside down and set it on his desk.

"Very well." Nettleship gave in and his host poured.

"Son," Collins waxed authoritatively, "David—that's what I called him during our frequent conferences—David, God rest him, and I both have—had—the same maker. He was an admirable adversary. We respected each other in our professions. He a financier, and I an expert in the art and practice of nautical commerce. I shall miss him. For all our differences we were closer than many men of the same trade. Mind you, I wouldn't have him to my family's table because they would not relate—he being what he is. Or was."

"What *was* he, if I may ask?" Nettleship took a small package out of his coat pocket and drew from it a thin white cylinder which he placed between his lips. "*Cigarette*," he drawled through his prominent teeth. "French word. These are made in a factory in London. Tobacco from Latakia."

Collins started to look for his friction matches, but he was stayed by Nettleship who took a small box from his pocket. "Newest thing—from Sweden." He struck a tiny splint against a side of the box. "Safety matches; the phosphorus is in the striking surface on the box, not in the match head. Good for traveling." He blew out a cloud of smoke. "Now, about the deceased, if you will."

"Perhaps it was that he was different."

"In what way?"

"He was a Jew. He told me that his father was one of the rare few of his persuasion who was allowed one of the twelve licenses issued to Jews as brokers on the London exchange. His father amassed a fortune, then retired and was even elected Sheriff of London, as well as being knighted. Of course, it helped that he had married a sister of Baron Rothschild."

"Why did he leave London?"

"I believe his brothers got on better. He certainly had a sense of adventure to go off on his own."

"Aside from his pistol, do you remember anything else about him? His habits, his friends. Hobbies?" The agent toyed with his match box.

"His hobby was women."

"Can you name one?"

Collins leaned back and closed his eyes. "There's a man, a former seaman in my employ, who introduced him to me. He's now a manager at Bill McGlory's Armory Hall over on Hester Street."

Nettleship licked the point of his pencil. "Name?"

"Patrick Dooley." Collins riffled through his papers. "Paddy knew them all—sail and steam, bad and good."

"Many thanks for your help, sir; I trust you'll be available. Formalities, you know. We'll need verification of your whereabouts over the last twenty-four hours."

"But how can I prove that I *didn't* take a quick walk down South Street at some odd hour?" The older man shrugged.

"Then we'll have to prove you did."

"By the way, son, to whom shall I send the next quarterly interest payment? It's due shortly."

"It seems there is no Gibbs." The agent pondered.

"Montebianco bought him out, but never got around to hiring a sign painter. Besides, Gibbs was well-known and respected. The name lent credibility to David's business."

"Send a draft to General Dix's headquarters for my attention. Make it out to 'Estate of David Montebianco.' At least it will show good intentions." Nettleship smirked.

"I was afraid you'd say that."

"Don't worry, Mister Collins; it will be some time before the draft is cashed—plenty of time for new ventures and iron hulls."

A black silk top hat stood on the lone chair. Trousers and a worsted coat with velvet collar hung over the back like a scarecrow in a sparse room over McGlory's raucous Armory Hall. Across the dim room, a customer rolled over next to one of McGlory's dancing girls, spent and drunk. The girl, knowing what to expect, lay quiet, bedcover drawn over her nakedness.

A panel jiggled on the wall behind the scarecrow chair, then slid aside as a deft hand emerged from the aperture and searched the coat pockets. The customer's billfold was taken into the wall, then returned to its original pocket.

"Paddy," a girl's hushed whisper in the service corridor beyond the wall startled the panel game virtuoso as he counted the greenbacks, "there's a *bloke* downstairs, wants t' see ya. His name is Nettleship.''

"Christ, that's no ordinary bloke." Paddy peeled off a greenback from his take and handed it to the girl.

"I'd rather have silver," she moaned.

Paddy obliged reluctantly with a silver dollar, then descended cautiously down the curved staircase.

"I swear I've gone straight, chief." Dooley elbowed up to Nettleship at the crowded bar. "How about a beer—on th' house?"

Nettleship turned his eyes right and left.

"I get it, chief." Dooley led the detective past the bar into a corridor, then ushered him into a private office. He signaled a barmaid to bring in some whiskey and glasses.

"Sarsaparilla for me," added Nettleship.

After the barmaid had left and closed the door behind her, Nettleship set his wide-brimmed black hat on one of the vacant chairs and lit a cigarette. Dooley nervously accepted one.

"How long's it been, Paddy?"

"You were just on the force—five, six years ago."

"Have you given up cigars?"

"Too much trouble, and not worth it—better for younger men to swim after the bags in the bay," Paddy joked, then turned serious. "I don't know anything about the racket anymore, what with goin' to sea again.. . .''

"Since I got a promotion, I've been after bigger game myself," Nettleship said. He pulled back his lapels and Paddy noticed the black, blunt handle of a holstered pistol. Paddy's hands went up instinctively as the agent reached for an inside pocket. Nettleship laughed as he drew out a photograph and slid it onto the green felt-covered poker table.

"Ever see this man before?" He sipped his sarsaparilla.

Paddy screwed up his gnome-like face and loosened his enormous silk tie. Playing with the garter on his shirt sleeve, he snapped it and shrugged. "There's many a man looks like this and might have come into the establishment, so I can't say I have."

"Too bad, Paddy. I guess I'll have to tell Sergeant Brady to go ahead with his panel search. He's waiting outside. There've been some complaints lately . . ."

"In that case, I'll take another look at the picture."

"Paddy, I know you worked for the Collins Line back in fifty, and I know this man was aboard on one trip that you made from Liverpool. Edward Collins showed me the manifest—an August crossing. Arrived in New York on the first of September."

"I remember it well. We brought the Swedish Nightingale to our fair shore. All kinds of excitement. She gave a concert in the middle of the ocean, and the proceeds went to crew's benefits. Lovely lady, Jenny Lind. I can still hear her when the wind pipes up. Captain shut the motor down and we put up sail before she sang."

"As an Able Seaman you didn't have it too difficult aboard a steamer." Nettleship blew smoke rings over the table lamp chimney glass.

"There was still a lot of wood to care for, and when there wasn't, I helped out at the game tables. That got me some experience for my present occupation. I would have stayed with Collins but for his bad luck."

"Then you tried smuggling Havanas—"

"Then I picked up with my old boat again. The Hadleys had given me my first job when I came over with my family back in forty-eight, and a sweet, sharp ship she was. The old *Cathay*, Hadley's first clipper.''

Nettleship held the photograph closer to the lamp. "Sure, I've seen 'im. Used to come around. He was soft on one o' the girls here—my girl.''

"Used to? Where's he gone?

"Well . . . I mean—" Dooley hid behind his beer stein.

"Come on, Paddy, you knew.''

"The *Dead Rabbit* boys always get the news first.'' Dooley dribbled whiskey from his thin lips. "Nobody was surprised when he did the toes-up act. Comin' in here with his fancy ways and all that money to turn girls' heads. Never left a tip either. And that cape—you'd think 'e was a duke the way he carried on. I had enough o' his kind back in Liverpool. Queer name for an Englishman—Montebianco it was.''

"Any idea who might have shot him?

"I heard 'e was stabbed.''

"You heard right, Paddy. Anything else?''

"A marlin-spike it was, they say.''

"Who says?" Nettleship stiffened.

"Might have been th' mortuary boys.''

The detective slumped back. "Paddy, I want you to tell me everything you know about Montebianco. From the beginning. I want to know who his friends were—and his enemies. I've got to get some leads.'' Nettleship took a scrap of paper from his vest pocket and set it on the table next to the photograph. "Here's how I got on to you. A list of people who owed him money.''

"Ah, yes. Mister Collins is among them I see . . . and Bill Hadley. Even Miss Cleopatra. Yes, I have had the pleasure of meeting several of these individuals.''

"Go on—and don't worry about McGlory.''

"Well then, let's start with the Penhallows. Captain Penhallow—'e was from Portsmouth, New Hampshire, as were the Hadleys—was Master of the *Cathay*, the clipper I mentioned earlier, when I signed aboard. My brothers bade me to go to sea, as they would look after my mother after our poor, ailing father died in steerage coming from the famine in Ireland.

"I might say I met the Penhallows about the same time as the Hadleys. It was winter in New York City; South Street was digging out of a February blizzard. The spars, as far as one could see up the street, were an icy forest, and those of us who had time between passages found itinerant employ at odd jobs below decks and among the commercial houses . . .

"One bright afternoon, Sam Hadley—the Hadleys had built The *Cathay* in Portsmouth—came aboard with a right fancy-dressed foreigner, a Swedish Baron, no less, and gave 'im a tour of the boat. When they went off several hours later, they seemed to be in accord, agreeing and nodding as they got into a carriage and headed up Pine Street . . ."

BOOK I
1849

CHAPTER ONE

Baron Louis Gerhard de Geer ran his aristocratic fingers over the alternating mahogany and white pine layers of Samuel Hadley's creation. The miniature half-model of a clipper hull, mounted on a black ebony backboard, stood proudly on a Louis Quatorze coffee table, where its hand-rubbed and vertically doweled horizontal woods glowed with a rich, warm, satiny sheen.

"Exquisite," the nobleman son of a mercantile family that had moved from Brussels to Sweden several centuries earlier whispered enchantedly. "It is like caressing a beautiful woman." The velvet-coated Swede rose from the divan and walked thoughtfully over to a window from which he looked down on the afternoon bustle of Broadway. Sleighs on the snow and boys cavorting past the white-marbled Hotel St. Nicholas. "Marvelous view. The snow makes me homesick. Interesting how snow can make all cities in the world seem similar."

"You're welcome to stay here, if you want", offered Sam. "I usually spend nights aboard the *Cathay* when she's in port."

"I'll take your offer up if I run out of funds.

Talking about money, how soon will you need the first sum?"

"Figuring backwards from the opening of the London Exhibition, I'd want the keel laid six months earlier. That means ordering the timber and fittings. Timber has to be cut in the winter for proper seasoning through the spring . . ."

"Then, aside from your own fee, which, of course, is forthcoming from Baring Brothers within a month, you'll need the first third by the end of this year."

"Twenty thousand in gold by November. If we wait any longer, the large shipyards will buy before us and deplete the available labor and services. McKay, in Boston, builds five or six ships a year." Hadley poured more coffee.

"I'm planning to come again to New York in September. Might you have sketches for the figurehead by then?"

"For an additional hundred dollars from Baring along with my fee." Sam picked up an envelope from the table and drew out two daguerreotype portraits of a woman.

"Agreed." The Baron eased back onto the divan and sipped his coffee. "Perhaps, if the woodcarver could do one sketch based on each picture, I could make up my mind. One seems too prim, and the other a bit daring."

"I'll have a contract prepared within the week."

"Don't forget—all oak. My father's solicitors will insist on oak as an investment. And they will demand that Lloyd's underwrite the boat with an A-1 sixteen-year rating."

"It will stand a thorough survey; I'm including a clause for escrow to guarantee our work."

"Very well." De Geers raised his china cup. "A sober toast to Jenny Lind . . . and the extreme clipper, *Nightingale*."

"I suggest we celebrate by having supper at Delmonico's," Sam said, as he wrapped the ship model in soft cloth and put it into a cabinet. "I'll show you the town." He picked up *The New York Daily Tribune*. "Here's a good way to see the town." He chuckled over an advertisement. "There's a carved wooden model of New York City on display at the Minerva Room, just a few blocks' walk. Every tree, building, shed and fence in the city. Built by over 150 craftsmen, sculptors and artists. Over 200,000 buildings with a quarter-million windows and doors, 30,000 trees, 20,000 awnings and lamp posts—and 5,000 pieces of shipping . . ."

"How exciting—and to have a ship designer as a guide . . ."

"And look here," Sam read further. " 'A Special Attraction . . . Colonel Beale is exhibiting a twenty-four-pound solid-gold nugget at the Minerva Room. Found in Calavaras County, California, by a member of Colonel Stevenson's Regiment, the nugget is worth over thirteen thousand dollars . . .' "

Baron Louis Gerhard was the first one through the door.

> *Ship* Cathay,
> *Pier 15.*
> *March 11/49*

My dear uncle,
Do not be alarmed at this change of plans. I have decided to go to California. The agreement with de Geer is signed, and I herewith forward a copy and instructions regarding the preliminary work (including a request for sketches from Woodbury Mason).

Slate and Olyphant are in accord with a plan of mine to carry passengers and gold-mining equipment to San Francisco. I am refitting between decks and should be ready to sail by early May. Hadley's share of the boat will return an excellent profit, perhaps enough to buy a steam saw and hoisting engine and to build a larger shop. Five-dollar barrels of flour will bring tenfold in California. Shovels and pans are all needed desperately and we will supply them.

I have just purchased one thousand decks of playing cards at twenty-five cents per deck and expect to sell them at three dollars each. All in all, the cargo will exceed fifty thousand dollars as loaded in New York. It is a pity that we do not own a larger share of the cargo as well as of the boat.

But that is the reason I am going. If I don't strike it rich in six months after arriving, I'll have to come back anyway to supervise the construction of the Nightingale. If I do strike it rich, Hadley's will be the biggest yard north of New York City.

Captain Penhallow is not averse to hiring on Matthew and Mark as mates. I think it will be excellent experience for them, especially Mark. He will make a fine supercargo under the wing of yours truly. Order your studious son to join his robust twin around the Horn before he grows roots in the shop. A dose of salt air will help strengthen him and prolong his life.

By the way, the owners, in capitalizing on the times, have voted to change the name of Cathay to Alchemist—a better choice than an earlier consideration of Olyphant's: Philosopher's Stone. For my own part, I would have preferred something more to the point . . . like Golden Quest.

In view of the rush, we have contracted with a New York shipcarver to alter Woodbury's mandarin into an alchemist.

Please advise about your boys by the next mail.

Yr. Affec. Nephew,
Sam, Jr.

P.S. It is possible that Alchemist will load copper ore at Santiago instead of returning in ballast.

CHAPTER TWO

Bows plunging and sharp stem knifing into the long swells between the Falkland Islands and Tierra del Fuego, *Alchemist's* oak frame groaned as the prevailing westerlies came roaring down off the Patagonian highlands. Twenty-nine days below the equator and fifty-seven days out of Sandy Hook, the clipper was well into the dangerous fifties, the latitudes that have for centuries been the seafarer's consummate challenge.

Ten years earlier, the captain of a Brittany-bound merchantman wrote concerning his passage: "Such was the malevolence of Cape Horn that the winds around her blew west against those attempting to reach the Pacific and east upon those sailing on the opposite course."

July third was midwinter, and the fiftieth parallel in the Southern Hemisphere corresponded with its northern twin in distance from the pole and consequential frigidity. The southern tip of the Americas was subject to the same extremes in temperature as the coast of Labrador—with the addition of hurricane-force winds. The "malevolent" cape, still two days' hard sailing away, rose like an ominous spectre in the minds of those who had been there before—the Captain, the first mate, and maybe a quarter of the crew. And not a one among the passengers.

Already, hardly past three, the cold sun had dipped into the western horizon and evaporated in a haze broken only by a solitary albatross, riding the wind, soaring and dipping without a tremor of its gigantic wings. The sea, taking on the grayness of sky, became pitted with frozen rain; rollers were now breaking and pitching *Alchemist's* bow deeper until a spray of sea erased the fine lines of bowsprit and headstays, and the glint of ice shivered in the wake. The painted and gilded pine figure reached ever forward under its protective spar and, cradling a cauldron from which spumed fluted fire and smoke, seemed to incant the formula for transmutation of his elixir into gold. His flowing cloak flared into the trailboards in a shower of stars and wizard's symbols that glinted through the spray. With each dip of the bow another sheathing of ice clung to the polychrome wood figure, to its heavy brows and broad nose, its chiseled hands, its flames and fumes.

Aloft on the foretop, mast reeling like an inverted metronome gone mad, young Seth Mason mumbled an inaudible prayer as he inched out on the fore-topsail yard, his boots clawing on the foot-ropes and knees feeling for the security of the inboard stirrup.

The sixteen-year-old son of a Portsmouth shipcarver leaned into an iron parrel band and bent his body over the ice-encrusted spar. One hand for the man; one for the ship. It wasn't enough. Seth looked starboard and saw Paddy Dooley using both hands for the ship. It took two hands to grab the stiff canvas and haul it up to the reef points. Just a matter of balancing one's body on the boom. Seth pushed himself up, lost contact with his foot-ropes and grabbed a handhold of iced topsail. Sleet pelting his face, he glimpsed roiling surf eighty feet below. The jackstay knots pressed into his young ribs painfully, and the iced yard pressed through wet oilskins to his very privates and shriveled them to frigid nothings. One boot, clawing, caught the foot-rope as Dooley sang out, "Together boys . . . haul away . . ."

Six pairs of fleeting hands in desperate unison clawed at the ponderous sail, pulled the canvas up to its buntline thimbles and secured the reef points. Then it was scramble down the ratlines from all three tops. Eighty rope-steps down on the weather side. Better to be pressed into the shrouds than be blown from them into the roiling waves. Now only the courses were full, t'gallants and royals were already furled.

"Brail in the spanker . . . lower away on the outer jib . . . trim the fore stays'l an' hop to it or—" Harry Taggart swung his brass speaking-horn at a scampering seaman. The brawny first mate cast an eye aft for the telltale light from the poop hatch. Yes, Penhallow was there—quietly watching. Taggart, late a bosun in His Majesty's service, was of the old school: discipline by way of violence. And the ship's Master, who had not the crew's respect, would close his eyes to the mate's methods. Harry had seen Penhallows on frigates and ships-of-the-line. They were of a mold.

The shortening of sail had righted the 760-ton clipper and she gained headway once more, its yards braced at an efficient, yet cautious angle to the gale's teeth.

Now crawling out between the knightheads on the ice-covered headworks and onto the bowsprit doubling to the foot-ropes, the shipcarver's son glanced down at the ghostly figurehead. Once a benevolent Mandarin prince in warm hues, as cut and lovingly finished by his father in Portsmouth, it had been transmuted into a cold, unforgiving sorcerer. Such was the way of gold—the enemy of beauty and craftsmanship for some, the patron for others. Woodbury Mason's words crackled over the squall's wail:

"Go, Seth; get it out of your system, but hear my words. . . . The Masons are landsmen and always have been. Generations of artists and craftsmen. There will be a time between leaving New York City and, God willing, arriving in San Francisco when you'll know that I speak for your good. There are many boys who would be grateful for the chance you've been given to pursue a decent profession. I have no alternative, being blessed with only one son, but to hire an apprentice in your place . . ." Seth winced as a heavy sea boot crunched his own on the foot-rope.

"Up with ye, lad, before Taggart comes along." Paddy Dooley lent a hand and they slithered forward up the spar, past the martingale band to the inner jibstay where they wrestled the flailing canvas down to the boom. Freezing rain had turned to stinging hailstones, pelting ship and crew alike.

Hands scurried fore and aft, securing the deckhouse portlight shutters, lashing down the fowl and sheep pens, covering the compasses. Hatches were battened and spars secured, the six-pounder signal guns double-lashed and covered, the quarter boats skidded in, turned and secured inboard—all to the shouts and threats of the first mate.

And then, as quick as it was done, it was over.

Taggart had gone below—a signal for the crew. The
weary, drenched men and boys—except for the lookouts and helmsmen—staggered to their quarters in
the forward deckhouse, where the cook was banking
a welcome coal fire, and to the forehatch, the access
to the fo'c'sle.

Samuel Hadley, Jr., enjoyed one of the staterooms
in the quarterdeck trunked cabin. Aft of the Master's
stateroom on the starboard side, he shared it with a
wealthy Mexican merchant, Don José Figueras. The
merchant, refined and dressed like an Eastern banker,
was immersed in a volume of French poetry as Sam
searched through his locker and trunk for Sunday
clothes to wear to the Fourth of July celebration
dinner the Master and his wife were giving on the
next day. Penhallow and his wife, Cleo, always dined
privately in their well-appointed cabin, and this promised to be an unusual shivaree from more angles than
one. A sheep had been slaughtered that morning and
was soon to cast its savorous spell from the galley
funnel. From the looks of the glass, the weather
would clear by morning.

Sam found a proper fancy shirt and hung it carefully in his wall locker. Next, a blue silk neckerchief,
and . . . He lifted a leather packet from the trunk. It
had opened partially, and a small, framed daguerreotype
had almost slipped out. It bore the imprint of a
London photographer, Fox-Talbot. Hiding it from
Don Jose's view, Sam studied it for a moment. Well-
practiced handwriting in the oval across a summer-
frilled white blouse worn by a striking young woman
proclaimed:

Always,
Cleo

Sam, in closing the packet, noticed a folded note in the sleeve which he laid on his bunk. He brushed and hung up his Sunday suit, then polished his good shoes. Kicking off his boots, he swung himself into his upper berth; he had graciously given the lower to Don José after noticing the gentleman's limp upon meeting him in New York. Past nine by his pocket watch; he hung it by its fob on the wall, then tucked the watch between the wall and the mattress as the boat took a broaching wave. He opened the browned note carefully and read it to himself:

"Witnesseth this Indenture, That Samuel Hadley, Jr., now aged fifteen years, eight months and five days, with the consent of his father, Samuel Hadley, hath put himself, and by these presents doth voluntarily and of his own free will and accord put himself, apprentice to Messrs. Smith & Dimon of the Co. of New York, ship carpenters, to learn the art, trade and mystery of the business, and after the manner of an apprentice, to serve from the date hereof, for and during and until the end of four years, six months, and eleven days next ensuing, during all of which time the said apprentice his master shall faithfully serve, his secrets keep, his lawful commands everywhere obey; he shall do no damage to his said masters, nor see it done by others without telling or giving notice thereof to his said master; he shall not waste his master's goods, nor lend them unlawfully to any; he shall not contract matrimony within the said term; at cards, dice, or any other unlawful game he shall not play, nor haunt ale houses, taverns, dance-halls or playhouses. And said masters shall use their utmost endeavors to instruct said apprentice in

the trade and mystery of ship's carpentry and shall pay to said employee the sum of two dollars and fifty cents per week.''

The indenture was dated February 18th, 1839, and signed by Sam, Jr., his father and the shipyard partners.

Another shipwright, indentured at Isaac Webb's yard some years earlier, had, at the age of thirty-four, started his own thriving yard in Boston. Sam Hadley's dream was to do better, but there were obstacles. Unlike Donald McKay, Sam saw little prospect of marrying rich, and the chances of meeting another shipping magnate like Enoch Train, as McKay had done, who backed unproven designers was slim. Perhaps the *Nightingale* would do for him what *Rainbow* had done for famed John Griffiths and *Joshua Bates* for Donald McKay. Despite the slashing of seas on the deckhouse and the shuddering of his creation's innards, Sam fell asleep even before Don José extinguished the whale-oil lamp. Sam dreamt of *Nightingale*. His next boat would be better than *Cathay*. The new name had not altered her deficiencies. Designed for the light airs of far eastern doldrums, she proved no match in cargo capacity to the conventional packets. She was a tender boat, having to shorten sail drastically in heavy weather. The answer, as McKay already knew, was a larger boat built on the same lines, larger than the packets and Indiamen. *Cathay*, as *Alchemist*, still put its rail awash with reefed tops'ls in a moderate blow. Sam dreamt of *Nightingale* rounding the Cape in record time, doubling in seven or eight days from 50° Atlantic to 50° Pacific, under more than bare poles and a stays'l. He'd learned his lesson as a designer: any departure from the tried was fraught with danger, regardless of theoretical and test procedure. All the components had to merge at one time to prove the value of a boat, and not the least of these were men and money, ingredients that were impossible to include in the plans and specifications.

He dreamt he was sitting on a driftwood plank, high and dry on a white beach, a sliver of land with ocean on both sides and not a sign of civilization— except for a large, black slate chalkboard mounted on an oak frame. On it was a diagram of an East Indiaman, the conventional heavy-hulled boat that had not changed in design for several hundred years. Superimposed on the white chalk hull was a green chalk drawing of a strange fish, and below, the caption:

A CODFISH HEAD & A MACKEREL TAIL

It was a recurring dream, stemming from John Griffiths' first lecture to him at Smith and Dimon. Griffiths stood impatiently by the blackboard as the scene was dominated by an unkempt old man with long white hair, dressed in a black frock coat and a blue velvet knickered suit. Sitting on a gigantic iridescent conch, his silver shoe buckles tarnished, Sir Isaac Newton glared suspiciously down at his audience of two. Taking a glass prism from his vest pocket, he held it up to the noon sun and projected a rainbow onto the white sand below his dangling legs. Satisfied, he blew on the prism, rubbed it on his sleeve and slipped it back into his pocket. He clapped his hands and a mulatto boy emerged from the shell's opening. He carried in one hand a codfish head on a string and in the other a mackerel's tail section. Another resounding clap and he laid them on a small plank, head section to tail section as if they were one complete fish.

The prism rainbow was cast down once more, this time upon the composite fish. A puff of pink smoke rose from the fish and it was made whole. The boy ducked back into the shell and came out with a polished cherrywood spindle; round in section, it tapered along its eighteen-inch length from six to three inches.

"My spindle shape is derived from mathematics. It is the solid of least resistance. I have inserted and sealed in lead shot, so it weighs the same as the hybrid cod as well as displacing the same amount of water. Actual experiments have shown it to be even more efficient than the cod-mackerel." Newton clapped once more and the mulatto—after attaching the fish and the spindle to fishing lines, which in turn ran off separate spools to which were attached spring mechanisms to determine the resistance in water—waded into the calm sea until it was up to his mouth. There he waited, with fish and spindle poised in his hands.

"Mister Griffiths," the scientist groaned annoyingly, "you seem to disapprove of my demonstration?"

"Only with the reason for it, sir." The gray-eyed designer revolved the blackboard on its stand and drew a fish. Above the fish he sketched a clipper's hull, then a waterline through the hull, extending fore and aft. "Because most species of fish are largest near the head and have their greatest transverse section forward of the center of their length, it need not necessarily follow that a ship must be so constructed. I can discover no analogy between the ship and fish in their evolutions through the trackless deep. The ship must contend with the buffetings of two elements, while the fish knows but one, AND THAT ONE ALWAYS TRANQUIL."

"Can it be, young man, that my predecessors and contemporaries did not see the woods for the trees? Your theory is valid."

"Credit must first be given to an Englishman, Colonel Beaufoy, who experimented with towed floats over seventy years ago. The results were only published at his death in 1834. I merely repeated what he had done, then built *Rainbow*."

"At least he was an Englishman," Sir Isaac said, as he slipped nimbly from his perch atop the shell. "I'm sure he tried to persuade the shipbuilders of his time, but it took an energetic new atmosphere to depart from tradition—such as is here in America at this time." Newton shuffled over toward Samuel Hadley. "And you, my boy; undoubtedly you will surpass your teacher. What have you in the box?"

Sam reached in for the half-model he had carved, then, aghast, drew out his hand and closed the lid. "I have nothing to add, sir. Perhaps in time I shall contribute in other ways, with improvements in rigging or with knowledge of wind and tide." Sam was perplexed. Instead of warm wood, he'd felt cold metal within the box—and strange appendages on the model. Bulges on each side . . .

Paddlewheels.

CHAPTER THREE

"Mark me words, men; Penhallow has all the signs of a Captain Carney." Paddy Dooley gestured aft with his white clay pipe.

"You've been talking to your astrologer again?" Lars Norberg wedged a piece of scrap canvas between two forward bulkhead boards to stem the occa-

sional surges of sea water from the hawse-pipes. Seth
Mason set about bailing the trapped water in a bucket.
As an apprentice "boy" he'd been assigned to the
fo'c'sle as orderly for the able seamen quartered there.

"Avast ye miserable squarehead; don't besmirch
me dear mother, for she's taught me all I know of the
art. But of late I've taken to reading up on a method
that gives one an insight into the character of men.
Practiced by the ancient Egyptians, the Greeks, and
the Chinese as well as in India, it is called chiromancy.
None other than the great philosopher Aristotle wrote
that 'the hand is the organ of organs, the active
agent of the passive powers of the whole system.' "

"Not with me it isn't," able seaman Wayne Devers
drawled from his lower bunk.

"Ach, he has his organ in hand again," Klaus
Spielhagen guffawed, as he whittled out the center of
a lignum vitae cringle, oblivious to the pitching and
yawing of *Alchemist's* bows.

"Stow it, you hopper-arsed piss-makers, or I'll not
let you in on an astounding divination."

"*Si, habla por favor* . . ." Miguel Ortiz swung out
of an upper bunk and added, "please."

"Well now, that's better." The diminutive Irishman
held his left hand up to the swaying whale-oil lantern,
casting a five-fingered, giant dancing shadow on the
white cabin walls. "See these bumps on m'hand.
They're called mountains; this is the mount of Venus."
He touched the ball of his thumb with his right index
finger. "And this is Jupiter, and Saturn, and so on.
Notice how well-rounded my mounts are . . ." Paddy
turned his palm slowly in the light. "Roundness such
as mine stands for charity and love. Now, I've had
occasion to study the palm of our Captain—and what
d'ye think I found?"

"Not some of his wife's doodle-sack hair?"

"Mister Devers—" Paddy cautioned, then continued. "Our brooding Master has a left-hand palm that's as flat as a flounder. Do you know what that means? Love of gain and dishonesty, that's what—and improvidence as well."

Lars Norberg shook his massive head. "Love of gain is common to many men, and who among us can claim to be honest at all times? Besides, how can one see the man's hands when he is below so much—if there be something to bumps on the hands."

"Ah, but there is more to tell." Dooley rubbed his palms in delight, then held his right hand out before him. "Notice my thumb in its natural state. At a right angle to my hand . . . like a carpenter's square—right, Miguel?"

"*Si*, she is like carpenter's square."

"Now, if I try real hard, I can flex my thumb backwards."

"Like thees?" Miguel displayed his ruddy hand proudly.

"You do it well." Paddy stared in disbelief. "Is that your natural position?"

"I have always had the double-joint." Miguel's large teeth flared in the lamplight. "What she mean, eh?"

"Captain Penhallow's thumb bends backwards . . ."

"That's true," Seth said, as he wrung water into his bucket. "When he stands on the quarterdeck with the sun behind him. I have seen it."

"Then, according to the ancients, you have seen a killer."

Klaus stopped whittling. All in the cabin turned and looked at the Mexican. The gale seemed remote.

"So, maybe I keel somebody in self-defense." Ortiz put his hands between his knees and feigned a fiendish laugh.

"I hope it wasn't any of our boys at the Alamo,

outnumbered as they were ten to one." Devers sneered. Ortiz ignored the comment.

"Come on, mates; we've still got two more months on this tub. Have yer fights when we get to San Francisco."

"I hope you're wrong, Paddy—especially for his wife's sake."

"Now, now, lad, that's what I like to hear. A little concern for others, especially the weaker sex . . ."

"Weaker?" Klaus tied up a sack of sail cringles. "She looks like she could take on any man. Have you noticed how she looks at some of us 'more handsome' sailors?"

"Aye, Klaus—and I've read a word for the affliction. A feminine disease characterized by morbid and uncontrollable sexual desire goes by the term *nymphomania*."

"Is it catching?" Seth held his breath.

A rattling of the deck hatch and rush of cold air aft was followed by a shout: "It's after ten, boys."

"Aye, sir, so it is." Paddy blew out the lantern flame. "It's the third mate. Lucky for us that it wasn't his brother who was on watch, not to speak of Taggart."

Mark Hadley braced himself against the foremast bitts as *Alchemist* rolled steeply. He thought of the old adage: "Good sailer, bad roller." As the deck leveled once more, he was about to go aft when the forward lookout cried out. Mark turned and saw a mountainous shape against the dark sky. He dove between the fife rail and the foremast as a thousand tons of icy ocean tore over the bows. It seemed a cold eternity until the torrent subsided and he could once again breathe. Bruised and numb, Mark staggered up and surveyed the damage. The longboat had

been torn from atop the seaman's deckhouse and
jammed against the midship pumps in a tangle of
spars and lines. Forward, a door had been ripped
from one of the heads and the pigpen was missing.
Mark crawled over rigging debris and strained into
the darkness to assess what damage had occurred to
the bowsprit, then realized the worst had happened:
the forward lookout was gone.

A sprit could be repaired, but a man could not be
replaced. There was no point in shouting "man
overboard;" he would make his report to Taggart,
who was, no doubt, roused from his bunk by now.
Clawing his way aft, Mark saw the quarterdeck hatch
spring open and the silhouette of Taggart against the
cabin light.

"Damnation," he roared as he charged to the
quarterdeck rail and looked down on the devastation.
A bolt of lightning flashed and the first mate swore
again upon seeing the mangled longboat. Climbing
irately down the ladder, he tripped over a splintered
crate. Pushing it out of the way, he suddenly realized
that it was the pigpen—and it was empty. With a
handful of wet straw he climbed back up on the poop
and stormed aft to the helm. "Now look what you've
done, chimney chops; I shouldn't have expected a
sambo could hold the helm to a quarter point—"

"It was a big wave, sir; I did my best . . ."
Decatur Hill's ebony face shone wet in the binnacle
lamplight as he leaned into the heavy wooden wheel.

"God knows what damage you've caused, but
here is reason enough to throw you overboard!"
Taggart slammed the handful of wet straw into Hill's
astonished face and pushed him away from the helm.
Before Taggart could grab the wheel, it spun out of
control, almost broaching the boat and flinging Decatur across the quarterdeck where his head struck an
iron bollard. Mark scrambled up the ladder and scur-

ried aft of the companionway, where he found Taggart struggling with the wheel. Together, they brought the helm over and eased the boat back on course.

"Take the wheel, I'll get another helmsman."

"What happened to Decatur?" Mark saw a crumpled form lying near the rail.

"Lousy seaman, that sambo. He slipped. Watch your helm; we'll have Lavender look at him."

"Benson is missing," snapped Mark.

"The bastard probably ran below, Mister Hadley."

"No—he was atop the head before the wave hit."

"He should have lashed himself to the boat," Taggart said, as he backed down the ladder. "Just wait till Penhallow finds out that his pig is lost. Somebody's in for it, that's for certain."

The first streaks of midwinter dawn hung low in the east as the second dogwatch ended. Matthew Hadley, second mate and twin brother of Mark, stepped wearily out of his oilskin trousers and hung them on a peg in the cabin door. After wringing out his skivvies in the wash bowl, he sidled over to the bunks and, in one swift movement, yanked the blanket from his brother's sleeping form. "Happy Fourth of July!" he hollered, laughing, as Mark sputtered and shivered on his upper bunk, then swung his thin legs out. Even in long woolen underwear, his legs looked as narrow as rails. For a moment, he watched his brother dry himself. Matthew had a strong, muscular body, unlike his own. Mark felt a pang of jealousy. What must it be like to have the body and face of a classic Greek warrior—and the strength, the seafaring ability of his fraternal twin. He shook off his envy, as usual, by reassuring himself that he was better off with his mental ability than with Matt's body, if it was impossible to have both. Mark jumped lightly to the deck, grabbed the washbowl, opened the porthole, dumped out the water and refilled it from a pitcher.

"Any word about Decatur?"

"He's still unconscious, but he took some laudanum. Lavender's got him bunked by the galley stove over the coalbin. No bones broken; just a bruise on the side of his head. Old Lav said he nearly came to. Said some nonsense and fell off again. Talking of bruises, how are the ribs?"

"Couldn't sleep on my left side . . . besides, I kept on thinking of Benson. Taggart was more concerned with the Captain's pig."

"He doesn't really mean it. Taggart's seen many men lost and he's hardened to it. There's hardly a ship goes 'round the Horn that doesn't lose a man or two, especially in winter."

Mark didn't reply. He washed and dressed as his brother put on dry clothes. Then they went out into the dining saloon, where a Chinese steward was setting breakfast before Taggart and the passengers. Exactly one-half hour was allowed, for at 8:30 the Captain and his wife were to be served, in privacy. The Captain's wife preferred the later breakfast in these latitudes because of the lateness of sunrise. There had, during the past fifty-eight days since leaving New York, been occasions when the Captain joined the others at the table by himself. It was assumed that his young wife was taking a nap, though it was well known that the ship's menu was not as complete as she would have liked it. Her favorite food was chicken, but as Joe Lavender, the Haitian cook, pointed out, two dozens of poultry were better kept for their eggs than meat, and if one chicken per week were cooked, as she demanded, there would be none for the passengers and crew as well as a declin-

ing production of eggs. Cleopatra Penhallow pouted
at his reasoning, and napped through those meals that
were not to her liking—until she got hungry enough.

Cleopatra lay back on the divan as if on her royal
barge and petted her cat, a magnificent star Burmese
named Antonius. The daughter of a Portsmouth
clergyman, Jabez Smith, she was whispered about by
folk of Pleasant Street and Old Puddle Dock alike.
There were even hushed rumors about her soirées
among the fungus-encrusted slate headstones at Point
of Graves. It got so that her father preferred that she
wasn't seen in the vicinity of North Parish Unitarian
Church on Sunday mornings.

"Wib," she cooed to her husband, "do you think
my blue gown too daring for the dinner this evening?"

"If I did, you'd wear it anyway." Captain Wiburd
Penhallow rolled up a chart of the Horn and opened a
volume entitled *Illustrations of Ornithology* by Jardine
& Selby. As he turned its pages, he noted those
colour plates that did not have an embossed stamp in
the margin—an indication that the specimen shown
had been collected by W. Penhallow. One of the
fifty-three plates that was not stamped was that of
Diomedea exulans, wandering albatross of the Southern Ocean and largest of all sea-birds. The Captain,
in a stark black suit with a gray satin vest and full
bow tie, popped a dried apricot in his mouth and
rolled it within his side-whiskered cheeks.

"Curious," he observed, as he cocked his prema-
turely balding head at an illustration, "that man is
one of the few species in which the male is less
decorative in appearance than the female."

"Wib, you *could* have picked a more cheerful
necktie."

"It is also a day of mourning."

"I'll miss poor Benson."

"I didn't know you were that close."

"He played so nicely with Antonius." Cleo got up with the cat in her arms. "Antonius, you'll just have to go out and find a new friend." Cleo let the cat out of the cabin and stretched out on the divan again. Wiburd came over and sat near the low table in front of the divan. "Thank God we're alone again," he sighed, knowing it would amuse her.

"Then you won't mind the blue gown?"

"I'm sure that Sam Hadley won't mind." Wiburd poured some souchong tea for himself after offering his wife a cup. "You're still fond of him, aren't you?"

"I'm fond of many people, but I married a Penhallow."

"For what, my dear? Was it for my family's position, their wealth? Certainly the only thing that Sam didn't have was money."

"Wib, didn't I agree to make this trip? Isn't it what you wanted—like most other masters—a wife to share your cabin? Isn't it a victory? Especially with Sam aboard?"

Wiburd stirred his tea slowly. "But you've always preferred Sam Hadley."

"Not any more." Cleo swung her smooth legs off the divan, letting her lounging robe fall open.

"You don't know how long I've been waiting to hear you say that," Wiburd said, as he reached for her amorously.

"Later." Cleo slipped from his grasp and vanished into the private bedroom. A frown crossed the Captain's long face as he heard the latch slide.

"Sail hoooo," came a cry down from the fore t'gallant shrouds.

"Where away?" called Matthew Hadley through the brass speaking-trumpet, as Penhallow emerged from the companionway and the duty watch put down their tools and squinted into the noon sun.

"Dead ahead," a relay answered from the foretop.

"Mister Hadley," said Captain Penhallow, as he buttoned up his long watchcoat, "do you think we can overtake her?"

"I'll do my best, sir . . ."

"You misunderstand me, Hadley," murmured the Captain, as he trained his glass forward from the weather side of the quarterdeck. "I meant that as an order."

CHAPTER FOUR

London

The club attendant yanked the trap string, pulling an old hat off a hole, and a bird fluttered skyward. Almost instantaneously, a 12-gauge shotgun erupted in a cloud of blue smoke. The impeccably attired marksman shook his head disconsolately and stepped back, allowing his competitor, a distinguished gentleman in his sixties, to take the mark.

"Are you ready?"

"Yes, your Lordship." The puller took firm hold of the second of five strings that trailed out to the ground traps, twenty-one yards from the shooter's mark.

Baron Montebianco raised his Lefaucheux breech-loader and cocked the right hammer. He leveled his sight over the second trap and slowly squeezed the trigger.

"PULL!"

A crumping detonation and a puff of smoke.

The blue rock pigeon hung for a moment against the clouded summer sky over Uxbridge Road, then plummeted to the green. There was a round of polite applause for the popular gentleman, who acknowledged it modestly, then addressed his youngest son:

"David, you're improving, but I didn't ask you out here to beat you in trapshooting. Let's have an ale." The elder Montebianco handed his gun to an attendant, and he and his son strolled across the green, turning back occasionally to see the results of a shot or volley, and went into a public-house, the outside sign of which featured a battered brown hat and the inscription:

OLD HATS

Seated at a table by an open leaded casement, they quickly downed the first ale, then sat quietly over the second. "Frightfully hot day for a shooting jacket," David said, as he loosened his necktie. "I much prefer the autumn for shooting."

"Perhaps you'll get your wish—in Canada. The hunting is reputed to be extraordinary."

"Father, I appreciate your offer, but I'm too accustomed to civilization and its comforts. There is only one place that I would consider."

"New York is out of the question. The House of Montebianco has no influence there." Sir Moses Haim stomped his foot.

"Father, look . . . I know that my excesses are a detriment to the business, that I'm too visible and flamboyant, that old Rothschild doesn't like me, that Mother is ashamed of me. I know that Levi and Jacob can run the business better without me . . ."

"You know a lot, my son. But we need a solution."

"I want to go off on my own. No Montebianco."

"With no money?" Sir Moses rubbed his chin.

"My inheritance is still the same as my brothers'?"

"You are still my son, but I am alive."

"Of course, but may I bargain with you, Father?"

"David, I should be happy if you can bargain well."

"Very well; I have given it much thought. If I can have but one-half of my intended inheritance, I will happily leave England on the next boat, never to darken the name of Montebianco again. I will deed the other one-half to Levi and Jacob."

"In front of witnesses?" Sir Moses' eyes opened wide.

"If you so require."

The father pursed his lips and studied the ceiling, the walls and the plank floor of the Old Hats public-house. "So you will go to New York and invest in a business?"

"My own, yes." David held up his stein proudly.

"What happens if you have trouble? Our name will be in the newspapers then, so who is to gain?"

"I will buy a partnership. An American name. There must be someone who will sell his name and reputation."

"Two pigeons with one barrel."

"Correct, Father."

"What kind of business will you buy—providing you don't gamble the money away on a ship getting there?"

"America is building ships and railroads, and build-ers always need money."

"David, you can start with ships; they're cheaper.

If you get the money, when will you leave for New York?''

"I didn't say I was going directly to New York; I said I'd leave England on the next boat. Perhaps a few months in Italy . . . then Athens . . ."

"My son, you are old enough to know what you want and I am old enough to know what I don't want. I'll see my solicitors within a fortnight and you'll have your money."

CHAPTER FIVE

A carved wooden Liberty Bell with tricolor ribbons and the inscription, *Our Republic—July 4, 1776–1849,* stood on a platform in the center of the dining saloon table. Little but bones remained of the succulent sheep that had been roasted earlier, and the boiled turnips laced with onions was a welcome change from potatoes. The cook was most proud of his turtle and yam soup, though the accolades were for his baked breadfruit with rum.

"Good night, gentlemen," Cleo Penhallow said, and managed a mock curtsey. "I know that you'll all want to be left with your Havanas and brandy." The drawn-out curtsey was done behind her husband—

and gave the guests an awesome exhibit of her décolletage.

"I'd like to propose a toast," Don José Figueras said, raising his wine glass. "To the great republic, Los Estados Unidos . . . and to the most beautiful señora ever to sail to San Francisco . . ."

"Don José, you flatter me so much that I'm tempted to stay. And such handsome men! When has a woman ever received so much attention and so many compliments? I will be spoiled if I stay, so I'd best retire."

Jim Dance, a suave hardware merchant, exchanged knowing glances across the table with Ferris Greenslet, an obese businessman.

The empty chair next to Matt Hadley belonged to Taggart, who, accustomed to the separation of upper and lower classes aboard His Majesty's ships-of-the-line, had gone for a look topsides rather than betray a lack of conversational ability. Taggart also knew that Penhallow was nervous about leaving the deck in charge of the bosun, regardless of his qualifications. The quietest soul at the dinner, Nicholas Miles, was hurriedly finishing a portrait of Cleo which he had started without the expectation of her leaving so abruptly.

The artist, slim as a scarecrow and attired in patterned toggery befitting a harlequin, turned toward Mark and whispered: "Such a frivolous bitch; a born actress." He put away his portrait and watched with rapture.

"Dear . . ." Cleo leaned over her husband's shoulder as he was sipping his wine. "I'm going to take a bath; will you have Wu Sing prepare it? I'm so tired."

The Chinese steward, on cue, picked up a heavy iron pot of boiling water from the saloon stove and followed Cleo into the captain's cabin. While she was in the bedroom, Wu Sing poured the steaming water into a cast-iron tub aft of the day room, then pumped in fresh tank water until the level was adequate and the temperature comfortable. When finished, he knocked once on the bedroom door and left the cabin, closing the door behind him.

Cleo waited a moment, then excitedly turned down the bedroom lamp flame. Quickly undressing, she dipped into the tub, then toweled and applied aromatic oils to her body. She combed her raven hair out and long over shoulders and breasts, then lay down on the bedroom berth and waited breathlessly. Within minutes she heard a scratching sound on the other side of the forward mahogany paneled bulkhead. Next, two distinct and equal scratches, as if by a cat.

The signal! She deftly drew a slide bolt aside and lifted out the mahogany panel nearest the berth from its channel.

"Hurry," she whispered, as young Seth Mason slipped through the opening and replaced the panel behind him. Cleo turned up the oil lamp and latched the bedroom door. It was her room anyway, since Wiburd, tall as he was, preferred the day-cabin divan.

"Seth," she moaned, and embraced him—only her chemisette between her body and his bare, soft-downed chest. "Your Liberty Bell was a great success. Some day you'll be a great sculptor and I'll commission you to do a statue of me; perhaps reclining—in the nude."

The sixteen-year-old blond boy sat hesitantly on the berth, barefooted, wearing only snug white duck trousers. A frightened animal, he listened to the hearty voices beyond the cabin walls.

"Don't be afraid; they'll be at it for hours," Cleo said, as she pushed Seth down on a bank of pillows. "Just relax and think about beautiful pictures and statues. . . . Close your eyes. . . . That's the way."

Cleo turned up the oil lamp flame and studied the boy's chaste body. It excited her to know that he had not yet become a man, that he had agreed to let her teach him the proper way—her way. He'd been nice to Antonius, had played with him when poor Benson was on watch. Now they would share two interests. It had first happened a week earlier: the cat had heard scratching noises behind the bedroom wall. It was then that she found the movable panel. Secured by an inconspicuous ironwood bolt, it opened on a narrow space between the cabin wall and the 'tween deck bulkhead aft of the quarterdeck hatch companionway. How Antonius loved to hunt rats behind the panel! Bored one evening, while her husband was on deck, Cleo crawled into the space and discovered a second door, locked from the inside. Her first impulse was to ask Wiburd why he had not shown her the exit, which, in the emergency of fire or mutiny, made considerable sense. Then it occurred to her that he was either afraid to tell her or didn't know about it himself. In either case, she couldn't lose by not telling him. Lying alone in her berth, she let the possibilities of the covert panel take wing, and the winged image she imagined was not unlike certain silver pendants worn by the daughters of joy as indicative of their profession. The prospect of ninety more nights with a candle was dimmed when she found out that all the ship's candlewax was mixed with rat poison. Cleo then surveyed the ship's company and decided to compromise on that seaman who would give her most pleasure. She decided on the loneliest and youngest.

Now she would be the aggressor—releasing the animal that was in woman and that had been repressed for all time by strength, society and role. She would be the person her husband couldn't be. Kneeling before the berth, she untied the square knot in

Seth's rope belt and drew his trousers down, tugged them off with ecstasy at the sight of her quest. Pushing his knees apart at the edge of the divan, Cleo took a firm, clawing hold of his hips and tenderly found him with her lips. Whirling her head round and round, covering his body with her swirling long tresses, he responded with squirming spasms that, in turn, fired her passion so that she drew from him the last iota of energy he possessed before falling, spent, onto the divan with him. Hardly had they finished when a loud, sharp report echoed amidships and catapulted the young man out from under his benefactress.

Seth undid the panel and, grabbing his ducks, abruptly disappeared from whence he had come.

Another explosion and the Captain shouted, "Mutiny! Break out the weapons," as he stumbled aft toward the armory. The startled guests had flung themselves under the table, fearing an attack from the quarterdeck hatch. James Dance had magically produced a large-bore derringer from his coat and had it leveled at the ceiling skylight.

Suddenly, the pantry door sprang open and the merchant, wheeling, fired both barrels as a grotesque, flailing apparition charged out, covered with a putrid substance and propelled by yet another explosion that sprayed the saloon with the contents of a tin of rancid *bouef boulli*. A mutiny of exploding tin cans!

"Not to shoot, please—is Wu Sing," screeched the steward as he slipped and fell to the deck, where he lay looking like a human jellyfish. "Missy Penhallow give me cans of meat for the pantry, and they fall in the storm las' night and Wu Sing fix nice like before and . . ." The steward looked up blankly and wiped some *bouef boulli* from his eyes. The dining saloon was empty and the quarterdeck hatch and skylight were wide open, despite the biting cold of a starless polar night.

CHAPTER SIX

Alchemist leapt into the waves as the royals and lower stuns'ls were braced up and began drawing. The wind had veered from west through south and was blowing lightly from the southeast. It was rare that stuns'ls were set below the fiftieth parallel in winter, just as it was that the wind would back to southeast. Ahead, the stranger maintained its lead as it had since the previous afternoon.

Sam Hadley had come to the quarterdeck to oversee his cousin Matthew in handling the boat in variable light airs, conditions that it had originally been designed for. As *Cathay*, it had responded well enough to heavy weather under shortened sail, but its talents lay with the tropical trade winds. Born and built for the China passages by way of Africa's cape and the East Indies, it had proved itself in the doldrums off Sumatra on its maiden voyage two years earlier. But like *Rainbow*, John Griffiths' experimental ideal, she had proven deficient. As larger clippers came off the ways of Webb, McKay and others, *Rainbow* and *Cathay* became young anachronisms—revered by design purists but scoffed at by businessmen. While these sharp-bottomed boats could sail rings around the later full-bottomed craft in close-hauled and light weather, it was another matter in heavy squalls and following gales. The newer clippers were a blend of proven packet and sharp hulls, and in gales they would travel three miles for every two that the experimental boats could manage, and they carried sail, too, long after the others were reduced to bare poles.

Samuel Hadley, Jr., was possessed of a basic flaw; he was a purist. Younger by fifteen years than his mentor, John Willis Griffiths, Sam had his own ideas about hull design, stemming from the fast Baltimore clippers and New York pilot boats. While he agreed with Griffiths regarding concave bows and sharp cutwaters, he regarded flat packet-type bottoms as left-overs from the British Indiamen. After finding that Griffiths' next boat after *Rainbow* had a flatter bottom, Sam ascribed it to encroaching senility and proceeded with his assumption that the solution lay not with keel revisions, but with a heavier boat and a more powerful rig.

And *Nightingale* would prove him right.

But there was something gnawing in his gut. Fewer and fewer new clippers were being laid down with the extreme dead-rise he had planned for *Nightingale*. Even *Witch of The Wave*'s half-model, shown in Portsmouth, and to be built by his deceased father's friend and competitor, George Raynes, was shorter in dead-rise.

Why was he aboard a ship bound for the gold fields? Sam told people that it was for the good of his family's yard, but he knew it was not true; whether he was running away or just needed a temporary change of surroundings he was unsure.

Sam winked at Matt when Taggart, nursing a mug of tea, most probably laced with rum, peered out of the deckhouse galley. Taggart, while he was indeed first mate, and had been for a year under a previous master, knew that Matthew Hadley was aboard for a reason, and that was for his skill in all weather, particularly in the variable airs they were experiencing at the moment. Penhallow had explained it all to him. The Captain's family background was one of storekeeping—ledgers, orders, deliveries. What they wanted, they bought and sold at high profits. What they didn't want, they unloaded on unsuspecting buyers. Volume and speed were utmost—and so was cunning. Penhallow & Co. was the largest purveyor of hardware north of Boston.

Wiburd was merely following his father's formula. He had ordered what he needed, and that was Matthew Hadley—in spite of past differences with Sam.

Regardless of his motives, it was a day for Sam and for his boat. At first imperceptibly, the distant sail rose higher on the horizon until the black speck of hull became visible from *Alchemist's* deck. Soon the word spread and anxious heads looked up more frequently from their tasks.

Lars Norberg, assisting the ship's carpenter in repairing the stove-in longboat, set his adz down and shaded his eyes. "If this wind stays, we catch her before the sun goes down."

"I'll bet you your albatross foot that Cape *Stiff* is just playing with us," full-bearded "Chips" Swasey cautioned. "Last I looked, the deckhouse glass was dropping . . ."

Steadily, *Alchemist* gained on the stranger. By noon she was off the starboard bow without changing tack. Her lines, those of a large clipper low in the water could be easily made out. Beyond her rose the hills of Tierra Del Fuego, and the sea took on a short chop as they were entering the LeMaire Strait, between Cape San Diego and Estados Island, one hundred-twenty miles from the Horn.

All hands came topside as the distance shortened.

Cook Lavender's fishing line off the stern was unattended and hauling a hooked dorado dolphin that was being torn apart by swooping albatrosses.

Captain Penhallow braced against the forestay on the bow, leveled his glass at the smart ship's transom and focused on its gilt lettering:

AGAMEMNON NEW YORK

A contented look on his face, the Captain tucked his glass under his arm and strode aft to the quarterdeck. There was a chance that he could collect the ten-thousand dollar bonus offered by Slate and Olyphant as an incentive to reach San Francisco before *Agamemnon*. Even more important would be the accomplishment itself. A victory over Griffiths' pride and joy, which ship, a year earlier, had set a record for the Liverpool run by passing the crack steamship *Europe*, of Samuel Thompson's Line, at better than thirteen knots. Fourteen days and seven hours for the crossing.

Agamemnon was owned by a corporation that represented merchants who were in direct competition with Penhallow & Co. Cyrus Penhallow, the Captain's father and founder of the firm, had bought a warehouse of miners' equipment from a bankrupt manufacturer in Poughkeepsie and shipped it down the Hudson River on barges to New York Port rather than to Portsmouth. Since Cyrus Penhallow was the man to watch, a group of New York merchants chartered the clipper and sent her off a day before *Alchemist*, loaded with equipment for the gold fields and supportive enterprises of California. It was logical that the first ship to unload its cargo in San Francisco would receive the highest prices, perhaps as much as a five-fold return on many items, while each succeeding ship, in diluting the frantic gold-fevered market with goods, would receive less. The only other ships to have cleared for California earlier were *Architect*, a small clipper out of Baltimore, and two others, of yet less tonnage, out of Philadelphia, and none of them had carried very much in the way of hardware.

To Wiburd Penhallow, a triumph over *Agamemnon* meant more than a feather for his family's business cap. It would bring him fame of his own—not as much as a Captain Bob Waterman or a Nat Palmer, but enough to gain the admiration of Portsmouth and indeed, he hoped, of his wife. The passage was almost half-completed, and now his ship was in sight of the adversary. What quirks of fate, tide and weather were responsible, he didn't know or care about.

Captain Deliverance Gordon had cleared Sandy Hook on the fifth of May and made a fine passage of barely nineteen days to the line. In thirty-two days *Agamemnon* was off Rio, then put into Montevideo "with all hands refusing duty." Gordon lost two days going off course to deposit the mutinous instigators ashore and to sign on competent replacements. In addition to crew problems, he had the added handicap of a score of 'tween decks hammock passengers, rowdy forty-niners who had to be rounded up from the Montevideo brothels before sailing.

The ruddy-cheeked master from Maine recognized the rig behind him as having a Portsmouth character in cut of jibs and headworks. A fair man and not one to deny praise where praise was due, he marveled at the lines of his pursuer, then gave the order to crack on more sail.

As *Alchemist* drew up on the larger boat, a cheer rose from its crew and increased to a crescendo that drove even the crustiest bilge rats into their lairs.

In the deckhouse galley, Decatur Hill stirred and mumbled on his jury bunk over the coal bin. He raised his bandaged head and painfully tried to comprehend the clamor outside. Eyes glazed and lips quivering, the Negro mumbled, then raved. "Don't . . . don't, Mister Taggart," he repeated, "don't hit me again, sir . . . I did my best, sir . . ." Then he screamed and lapsed into unconsciousness once more. Standing by the galley door, Seth Mason, come to fetch coffee for the quarterdeck saloon stove, had been listening.

Matthew Hadley was everywhere, calling out sail trim and helm adjustments. Taking a suggestion from his cousin, he ordered the off-duty watch into the hold and had them move what cargo they could to windward in order to lessen thereby *Alchemist's* heel angle and gain an extra knot. The Captain, content and cross-armed, stood behind the azimuth binnacle, forward of the mizzen, and occasionally glanced at the compass lubber line.

First mate Taggart, alone, was disgruntled, though he dared not show it. Jealous of the ability of another man better than himself at the sailing master's position, he still counted that his time would come—a time that demanded more than the bracing of yards and making good board. There would be a time of driving men and of bending their very wills. It was still a long haul to California.

Alchemist bore gradually up until the ant-like figures in *Agamemnon's* rigging grew pink faces and showed expressions of awe at the sight of a smaller ship overtaking them. Crews climbed up the ratlines and set stuns'l booms on the tops'l yards, then shook out the extra wings—but to no avail. *Alchemist* was already on their windward quarter, easing up and blanketing the southeast breeze until the larger clipper's courses and topsails fluttered, sagged limply, and allowed the Portsmouth clipper to spurt ahead, abeam and a pistol shot away.

Penhallow, exchanging his glass for the speaking-trumpet, hailed the other quarterdeck: "This is the ship *Alchemist*, Wiburd Penhallow, Master . . . bound for San Francisco . . . fifty-nine days out of New York . . ."

". . . Captain Gordon," came the reply, "also bound for San Francisco . . . sixty days out of New York . . ." A cheer went up from *Agamemnon's* crew at the same moment that Cleopatra Penhallow, wearing a bright yellow dress under her coat, appeared on the quarterdeck beside her husband. She waved merrily and threw raking kisses as *Alchemist* drew steadily past and showed her transom plate and bubbling rudder.

"Heave the log," called Matthew, and bosun Spicer flung a line over the lee quarter, watching intently as it paid off a spinning reel held aloft by a crewman. Noting an affixed red pennant striking the water, Spicer shouted, "Turn!" A second seaman replied, "Done," as he turned a half-minute sand glass in hand. With the last grain running out, the turner cried, "Stop," and the reel-holder braked the line from running further.

Next, the bosun hauled his line back aboard, counting the equally spaced knots tied in it: ". . . four . . . five . . . six . . . seven . . . eight . . ."

*   *   *

Cleopatra, cat over her bare shoulder, minced across the cabin as Wiburd struggled on his chart table with a plethora of books and instruments. She reached over his head for the vertical brass barometer that hung in a gimbal on the paneled mahogany, and tapped the glass lightly. "Wiburd," she exclaimed, "I'm worried. I can't even see any quicksilver."

"I've told you many times, dear . . ." Penhallow did not bother to look up. "Ships are not a business for women, much less the art of navigation. Don't you think it about time that you worked on your needlepoint, like other women?"

"But Wiburd, I'm not in Portsmouth, and I want to do something useful on this voyage. I only brought the sewing along in case I got bored."

"And are you?" Her husband rolled up his charts.

"And just what do you mean by that?" replied Cleo defiantly.

"Nothing, my dear. I'm sorry there's not more recreation aboard, other women to chat with . . ."

"Wib," she changed her tone, "couldn't we stop somewhere, after we've rounded the Horn? I've read that Valparaiso is a delightful city. It even has fashionable European shops. And it would be just wonderful to walk on land again; I so desire to."

"We'll see. It depends on our progress."

"I heard the bosun call out eight knots, and we're on course. Shouldn't we be off Cape Horn by morning?" Cleo slipped into a robe and started toward the bedroom.

"The wind has changed; we're standing to southeast."

"Going backwards?" she chided. "Well, should we stop at Valparaiso, the Negro could be put ashore if he's not better by then. He can only get worse at sea. What if he died?"

The Captain scoffed, "Many people die at sea; accidents happen all the time."

Cleo bit her lip. "Was he the helmsman who was blamed for losing one of the pigs during the last storm?"

"Who have you been talking to?" Penhallow became concerned. "Certainly not Taggart." Not expecting an answer, he stretched out on the divan, content that she'd taken the damn cat to the bedroom.

The helmsman struck the small bell atop the binnacle three times. Half past nine and a low winter sun just cleared the eastern horizon. Petrels and albatrosses, sharp-eyed for scraps, glided over *Alchemist's* meandering wake.

In response to the binnacle bell, the great forward bell on the forecastle deck rang out for all the ship to hear. To the west, Tierra Del Fuego was a gray ribbon woven into the horizon mist.

"Good morning, gentlemen," said Cleo, as she emerged from the companionway, flashing lemon yellow ruffles and a matching cap in contrast to her coat and the somber surrounding picture. Captain Penhallow, startled, fumbled with his sextant, then handed it to the first mate.

"Where are you off to?" He stared at the cat, its sienna head protruding from Cleo's fur collar.

"If you want to join me, I'm taking Antonius for a walk around the deck. If I'm not back in half an hour, you can send someone after me," she quipped, and descended the short stairs beside the quarterdeck trunked cabin. Noticing the main deck companionway hatch open, she looked down and could just make out the sack she had placed behind the stairway earlier by removing and replacing the bedroom panels.

With Antonius tugging on a yellow leash, she promenaded primly toward the bow.

"Mister Taggart," snapped the Captain, as he leaned on the forward poop rail and watched his wife, "have you noticed, at any time, Mrs. Penhallow talking to any particular crewman aboard this ship?"

"Not since Benson was lost, sir."

"What is the condition of Seaman Hill?"

"Last I saw today, he was still unconscious." Taggart handed the sextant back to the captain.

"What is all this about a pig—and Seaman Hill?" Penhallow squinted as he lined up the horizon glass of his instrument and tightened the index bar thumbscrew.

"Pig, sir?" Taggart became flustered. "Oh, yes; there was a pig lost overboard. Just one, sir."

"Why wasn't it reported to me?" asked Penhallow brusquely. "Do I have to find out everything for myself? How many do we have left?"

"Two pigs, sir, and four sheep and one goat. Didn't lose any poultry. With all the damage—especially the longboat—it slipped my mind."

"And Seaman Hill?" the Captain persisted.

"I'm sorry that he wasn't up to the job, but a good helmsman would have taken that wave sharper, and there'd be not nearly the damage." Taggart looked up. "I've seen a lot worse weather, sir."

Penhallow paced several times, then sat down on the skylight bench and recorded his observations and the time of day from his pocket watch, which he had set from the ship's chronometer prior to leaving his cabin. "Mister Taggart, before we get caught in a blizzard, I want you to catch me an albatross. There are to be no injuries or marks on the bird. It's for my collection. There's no telling when I'll have as good a chance as now."

"You'll stuff the bird, sir?"

"I've brought my taxidermic equipment, yes," the Captain said, rubbing his hands excitedly. "It will make a fine project for the voyage north."

The blue and white cliffs of Estados Islánd were receding off the port quarter as Joe Lavender and his helper, Bruce, a somewhat retarded boy, came aft carrying an assortment of fishing gear. "Now mind you, cook," boomed the first mate to Lavender, "not a mark on the bird that nature didn't give him, or ye'll be out here all day and night 'til ye do it right."

The Haitian stiffened and threw a brisk salute which delighted the first mate. Bruce sat cross-legged on the holystoned deck, cradling a large block of cork into which was set an open wrought-iron triangle, with one of the points facing away from the block. The boy stuffed a large piece of "salt-horse" beef fat into the triangle and packed it against the metal, but left a hole in the middle of the assembly. He handed it proudly to the cook, who, after inspecting the tackle, patted the boy on the head and complimented him as one would a faithful dog. Joe then tied his fishing line to a heavy wire leader on the block, heaved the contraption over the lee quarter rail, and waited till the float was fifty yards aft of the stern. "You watch now, Bruce, and holler when we've hooked one of those loony birds."

"Mrs. Penhallow, ma'am," the cook apologized, as he closed the galley door behind him, "I am extremely sorry, but the first mate requested that I catch him an albatross. It is very charitable what you do for Decatur Hill."

Cleo had washed and re-dressed the injured man's

head wound and covered him with a woolen blanket she had concealed under her coat. "He must be kept warm and in dry linens. I have hidden a sack under the quarterhatch stairs which contains another blanket, some linen nightshirts and a box with medicines— camphor, vitriol and fever powders. Hurry and fetch it while I wait here."

"Very good, ma'am. I have already used up the medicine allowed by the first mate for this poor soul's pain." Lavender ducked out, leaving the top of the galley half door unlatched.

The ship rolled sharply as the wind changed and the galley half-door swung outward to let in a frigid blast. Leaving the unconscious seaman in his make-shift bunk over the coal bin, Cleo crossed athwartships and was alarmed by a figure framed in the door opening. A stark, terrifying portrait, it was the sailmaker, Juho Kokko. His albino eyes glared into the galley and his pure white hair was ringed by a backlighted halo. A smile on his thin, colorless lips, he leaned on the door and tried to get a glimpse of Decatur before he spoke.

"Excuse me, but ay was looking for th' cook." His voice was high-pitched and he hardly opened his mouth. The crew referred to Kokko as both 'the ventriloquist' and 'the Finn.'

"He'll be back . . . He went—He's fishing," Cleo lied.

"Ah, yes. I saw his helper making up an albatross hook. I wish," the sailmaker lamented, "that they would not do this. I have a very bad feeling about it—to kill an albatross on this day when my muzzuk spoke to me about grief and misfortune." Juho closed his eyes dramatically, as if recalling a vision, and held on to the half-door as the ship rolled again. Cleo grabbed for a handhold, and when she'd caught her balance again, Kokko had disappeared from the doorway.

A short time elapsed before Joe Lavender returned with the sack of clothes and medicine. "Joseph," Cleo asked, as she buttoned up her collar and picked up her cat, "what is a muzzuk?"

"I see you have conversed with the ventriloquist. Muzzak is the Bombay word for bottle. Mister Kokko likes his bottle so much that he talks to it. He claims it once belonged to a renowned Indian prophet and retains the power of divination. If this is so, the spirit within must be mellow for all the rum it lives with."

"Do you believe it bad fortune to kill an albatross?"

"Mrs. Penhallow, on my island there is a belief that the spirit of a murdered man haunts his killer in the form of a bird. I believe that it can be so. The white man, who knows about the sea from thousands of years upon it, has seen the albatross always come before the storm and before the fog. For myself, I would not tamper with my people's warning. The birds are thought by some to be the spirits of seamen swept overboard in gales. Mister Kokko, like most sailors from Finland, believes in such things. It would be sacrilegious indeed if Mister Benson . . ." The cook didn't finish. "Let us talk instead of good. If Mister Hill survives, it will be because of the Captain's lady and her generosity."

"No one must know of this."

"I understand, ma'am."

The giant white bird, a Royal Albatross, descended in diminishing circles, its black wingtips gently wavering ten feet apart as it watched the plume of foam skipping along in the clipper's wake. Named *Diomedea* by Linnaeus, the classifier of species, there was reference to the mythical metamorphosis of the Greek

warrior Diomedes' companions into birds. The first
seamen to encounter these huge birds were fifteenth-
century Portuguese, who called them "alcatraz," their
term for large sea birds. English sailors corrupted the
name to albatross.

Dull-witted Diomedes glided down for a close look
at the moving object. Swooping, he braked his webbed
feet on the water and snipped at the white substance
attached to the float, then kited off once more into the
wind to relish his morsel.

Savoring the unusual taste of beef, Diomedes
wheeled and dove again, this time grasping the cork
float and flapping and snapping voraciously at the
bait until its beak, having a large bone protuberance
on the top, became snagged in a corner of the metal
triangle. Screeching furiously, Diomedes fought against
the tug of the trap and only succeeded in becoming
more securely wedged. Its strength sapped, the once-
proud bird was pulled along the surface and drawn
clear of the water by its beak. The weakly struggling
creature, stark white against the clipper's black hull,
rose hand over hand as an ominous gray cloud bore
in from the west and obliterated the ribbon of Tierra
Del Fuego.

Abruptly, the ocean's color changed from blue to
ashen green and then to cold gray. The long rollers
broke into whitecaps as the first mate's shouts sent
both watches scurrying aloft and hauling the clewlines.

By noon, the wind had increased from a light
breeze of fifteen miles per hour with a pressure of
one-half pound per square foot of sail area to thirty-
five with a sixfold increase in pressure. The stuns'ls
had been stowed, and the t'gallants and flying jibs
taken in. Two reefs had been taken in the tops'ls and
the flywheel pumps were manned 'midships. The

Alchemist was now racing at full hull speed of fifteen knots, considering the shortened sail and rising seas. The lee rail was under and a torrent of cold sea ravaged and tore along the decks, then cascaded in great spumes over the deckhouses, hatches and poop. This was the weather that spawned speed records to Canton and Liverpool, providing it blew from the beam or abaft the beam. But Cape Horn, a contrary spirit by most accounts, was apt to blow in the opposite direction of most ship's headings, whether easting or westing, despite the prevailing westerlies. The average passage plot chart in doubling the Horn from 50 Atlantic latitude to 50 Pacific looked like it was covered with broken glass—such were the jagged tacks and backtracks. A good doubling would be two weeks, but with adverse weather some ships took as long as six weeks. The Horn, affectionately referred to by seamen as "Cape Stiff," was the ultimate challenge of its kind.

As the wind piped up further, it was accompanied by hail and sleet that brought darkness on before its time. The fresh gale, with winds of fifty miles per hour, required that the fore and mizzen tops'ls be triple-reefed, the main courses furled and jib and spanker taken in. Running under scant top'sls and close-hauled stays'ls, *Alchemist*, in flashes of lightning, appeared as bare, white bones, bobbing and tossing, with shards of slatting flesh on the yards.

The helm was manned by two strong men, both lashed to the wheel. Hail and sleet pelted down on the deckhouses, the clatter of which testified to those below of the storm's fury.

High aloft, a sharp report preceded the tangle of spars and rigging as the foremast came tumbling down. On deck, the gig was torn off its skids and dashed aft against the cabin before another wave boarded and carried the boat over the side, and took a piece of rail along with it.

Under reduced canvas, the ship had come back to even keel, but still rolled violently and made scant headway in the mountainous seas. Decks awash, the galley stove had been inundated and the cook had done all he could to save his stores from being carried away by the torrents. Joe Lavender hung on. He lashed Decatur Hill to his bunk and fanned some coal to life in a tin pot to warm the patient.

As it became evident that the storm would last indefinitely, the inevitable order was bellowed by the first mate to stow the shortened sail, now only temporarily clewed up to the yards lest the rising gale break them out of the buntlines and tear them to shreds.

Harry Taggart was in his element—sloshing on the pitching deck and shoving the slow to their tasks. "All hands aloft, you sons o' bitches, and secure the tops'ls!" Groups of shivering men clambered up the ratlines, while others hauled, hip deep in water, on the clew lines. Paddy Dooley's crew gained the fore topyard and inched out on the icy foot-ropes where, leaning into the cold yards, they loosed the sea gaskets. The Irishman, with an eye for his mates, passed his gaskets about the furled sail, caught turns and hove in. Suffering broken fingernails and bruised limbs, the five seamen hung onto the yard as the boat heeled to its beam ends and almost dipped the yard ends to the roiling waves. The stress on the rigging was imparted as vibrations and shock tremors through the men's oilskins and into their very guts. The mast doublings creaked and groaned as if they were splitting, but after an hour the job seemed done.

Then, suddenly, a gasket parted and a billow of sail pulled out and slatted violently. Paddy, hearing a wail above the storm, called out the names: "Spielhagen . . . Devers . . . Ortiz . . . Norberg!"

There were three cries of "yo" in reply.

Paddy called out once more: "Nooor-berg!"

No reply came through the sleet and darkness.

The Swede was lost. There was no thought of putting a boat over, for a seaman overboard had but one chance in four of surviving in a storm. It had to be daylight, and it had to be summer—and it was neither.

The misfortune was reported to the first mate, who set to replacing the lost rigging hand before sending Dooley's crew up the mizzen. "Here's a man who wants to become an able seaman, eh, Greek?" The big mate grabbed little Angelos Vlachos by the collar. "Go on up there an' secure the mizzen tops'ls."

Vlachos, a deckhand, could not speak English very well, but he understood what the mate wanted. Terrified that he, too, would fall and having little experience nor love of rigging work, he broke from the mate's grasp and ran toward the quarter hatch. Taggart, furiously cursing, overtook him and dragged him to the weather rail and flung him against the ratlines. "Now you scum, get aloft before—"

The Greek collapsed into the swirling lead-lined scupper and sobbed.

"There's ways to handle the likes of yellow-bellied cowards," boomed Taggart. "Get back to yer duty and report to me as soon as the watch goes below. I'll teach ye a lesson about goin' aloft that ye'll never forget . . ."

The gale persisted and Captain Penhallow called for the ship to heave to and lay a-hull under a triple-reefed tops'l and a backed storm jib. This done, *Alchemist* put her head into the wind and fell off into the deep troughs, wind abeam and drifting to leeward—a precaution in heavy weather.

The gimbaled brass oil lamp swayed over the dining saloon table as the Hadley clan gathered for coffee.

"A steamboat wouldn't get into a fix like this," Mark said, setting his steaming mug down with a thud. "The *California*, for instance, would have taken the Straits of Magellan, regardless of wind direction, and trimmed two weeks from the voyage. Now, look at us: hove-to and making no westing—in fact we're being pushed backwards."

"I wouldn't want to pay for all that coal, not at fifty dollars a ton," replied his brother, stopping his cup from sliding.

Cousin Sam gripped the table as the ship rolled. "Mark is right. Once there are coal depots at South American ports, the price will come down and more steamers will make the passage."

"It may not be necessary for steamers to round the Horn at all in a few years," Mark spurted excitedly. "Howland and Aspinwall are examining the practicability of running a marine railway across the Isthmus of Panama."

"You mean for *passengers*?" asked Matthew.

"No, the entire ship would be hauled out and carried on special railroad freight cars. No need for transferring cargo."

"Or making a connection with another boat on the Pacific side." Sam whistled in amazement. "You can't fight progress."

"I thought you were on my side, Sam. After all," Matthew laughed, "you built this boat and I don't see any steam engine on it."

"Would I surprise you if I said the next boat I build—that is, after *Nightingale*—will have auxiliary power."

"Paddlewheels," scoffed Matthew.

"No, I'm thinking of the Ericsson screw propeller.

He's perfected a new one that can be handily shipped and unshipped. It's abaft the rudder and can be disconnected from the engine shaft and raised above the waterline—so there's no drag when under sail . . .''

"Gentlemen, may I join you?" Cleo surprised the trio.

"Of course," Sam said. He struggled to his feet and drew a chair up behind her. "Where's Wiburd?"

"He's skinning his albatross."

"During a storm?" Mark was amused.

"He started before, when it was calm. I'd rather he finish than have the creature lying around the cabin." Cleo sniffed the air.

"Another good reason to lie a-hull," observed Mark. "Taxidermist's knives are like scalpels. You'd best keep an eye on Antonius when Wiburd applies preservative. It contains arsenic."

"Yes . . . I know," Cleo lied and wondered why her husband had never told her—especially after acquiring the cat.

They talked well into the evening, with Wu Sing keeping the coffee pot filled. They talked of gold, steam, sail and money. Sam felt a pang of jealousy as Cleo's attention was centered on Mark Hadley, whose knowledge of topics Cleo was interested in far exceeded his own. Was she deliberately ignoring him, or had she indeed lost her love for him? Wiburd was an occupation, she had told him facetiously after the wedding—and after giving him the photograph he kept in his locker. Or was she merely playing with him?

Even handsome Matthew became uneasy with his brother's mastery of the table talk. This was the first time that he felt inferior to his fraternal twin brother. Cleo and Mark had hit it off as if they were of one mold. When they exchanged phrases in French, Matthew felt particularly inept. Cleo was well aware that

Matthew had not done well at school, though he'd been given the same chances as his brother. She had been educated at a fancy school in Boston, then had studied in Paris and London for a year.

But she had always been Sam's girl, at least as far as the Hadleys went. It was understandable, Sam being five years older and a man of the world. He'd been considered the hope of Hadley's Shipbuilding yard, the one destined to be rich and famous. Portsmouth's Donald McKay, they said. But then Samuel, Sr., died and the business saw bad times. William Hadley, his older brother, took the reins of the faltering yard and began investing money and assuming a larger percentage of ownership. He brought his sons, Matthew and Mark, into the business, though Matthew preferred to be at sea, and by default he'd got his wish. Sam Hadley, without his father, had lost his earlier drive and ambition—as well as control of the business. It was then that Cleopatra Smith had turned to the wealthy Penhallows.

Covering a yawn, Matthew bid goodnight.

Sam lingered, catching Cleo's eyes several times, and decided that he'd best retire and try again when they were alone. His greatest hope was that Cleo would leave absurd Wiburd and accompany him to the gold fields when they reached San Francisco. She was a daredevil; perhaps a mutual hunger for gold would re-kindle their old relationship—what they had enjoyed at Point of Graves when she was sixteen and he twenty-one.

Shortly before ten o'clock, water streaming from his oilskins, Harry Taggart clomped down the companionway. "It's pure hell out there," he roared and looked curiously at Cleo and Mark before pouring himself a mug of hot coffee from the stove pot. "Ain't my cup of tea, but any pot in a storm." He

guffawed at his own joke and lumbered into his
private cabin.

Once inside, Taggart pulled a bottle of brandy out
of his locker and poured a healthy dollop into his
coffee. After several more, he crawled into his berth
and thought about Decatur Hill and wondered how
the Captain found out about the lost pig—unless Decatur had regained consciousness. But no, he would
have found out from his foc's'le friend. His trusty
spy. He stretched out and felt for the reassuring
hardness of his Colt Navy revolver. Try as he did,
there was something he had meant to remember, but
couldn't because of the grog. Something on deck
he'd meant to do. It would wait till morning.

Dawn came, and it was still blowing hard, though
intermittently. Lying a-hull, the ship's pulse slowed
down. Crew and Captain alike took advantage of a
day of rest—a respite from duty on deck. Many
preferred sleep to breakfast, which often consisted of
porridge made from moldy oats or biscuit dust with
occasional vermin boiled in.

Matthew, a lighter sleeper than his brother, bolted
out of his bunk at a sharp knock on his cabin door.
"Sorry to wake you, sirs," bosun Spicer apologized,
"but can you come up on deck?"

The husky second mate, by faint port light, stumbled into his foul weather gear and followed the
bosun aft and up the companionway. Spicer, leaning
into the wind, led Matthew over ice-encrusted spars
and tangled lines to the ship's waist. "I came up
early, sir, to survey the damage, and . . ." He shook
his head and pointed up toward the foreyard. There,
on the weather end, was what seemed to be a clump
of canvas fouled around the lift.

"I went up, sir, and took a look. It's the Greek

lad, Angelos. 'E's frozen stiff, and what's more, lashed to the yard and lift. What business a green lad like 'im had aloft in a blow escapes me. I thought you should be told first, sir . . .''

As several seamen mutely looked on, Matthew climbed carefully up the ratlines and stepped onto the foreyard foot-rope. He edged out slowly; then, leaning on the icy spar and braced on a stirrup, he reached out to the odd mass of canvas and ice. It was hard to his fingers and he crawled closer, gripping the gaskets lest he, too, be claimed by the surging waters below. He leaned over and brushed the snow from the frozen clump, and a pair of ashen eyes appeared, staring and glazed over with ice. Icicles glinting the dawn dangled from the head's nostrils and withered lips. Frost edged the eyelashes and an earful of polar white . . .

Matt Hadley recoiled in horror at what he saw beyond the encroachment of nature. Surely it wasn't a caprice of the God of Winds, noble Aeolus, that had bound the seaman's wrists to the halyard. Instinctively he clawed at the bindings and ripped the knots loose before calling for aid. "Mister Spicer, let's get some men up here. Hurry, man, he may still be alive."

Tucking the cold form into his own cabin bunk below his astonished brother's, Matthew covered it with stove-warmed blankets while Spicer set to massaging. It was too late. Angelos Vlachos's spirit had flown.

The clipper cracked on sail and got under way in a moderate gale. Full and by, she carried double-reefed courses, trebled tops'ls and shortened fore and aft canvas. Late in the afternoon, the storm abated to a fresh breeze and the sun appeared dimly. Reefs were shaken out and the black hull cut smooth and swift to make fair westing. At sundown *Alchemist* backed its mainsail and hove-to.

Juho Kokko tugged the coarse thread tight and set his needle into the next awl hole. He had sewed up the body neatly, from foot to head, in worn canvas. "As good a job," he mumbled, "as the Egyptians used to do."

All hands had gathered midships for the ritual and Captain Penhallow, Bible in hand and followed by his wife in black, descended from the quarterdeck. Ned Swasey had found a proper wide board and a new American flag, as well as a rusted chunk of pig-iron ballast which he had Seth Mason lash to the corpse's wrapped feet.

The Finn cursed to himself, disgruntled that he would not be paid for his craft, as in the British Navy. A guinea was not easy to come by, and equal to half a week's wages. Noting the impatient mourners, he raised his curved needle high over the body's shrouded head and, with his other hand, groped for its nose. Pinching the canvas about the nose and setting his needle firm in his palm thimble, the Finn pierced both canvas and nose in one thrust and drew out the waxed thread taut before reeving it snug and snipping the needle off.

There had been no scream nor wince from the thrust so it became final that Angelos Vlachos was entirely dead.

With two crewmen steadying the corpse on the board and holding down the flag over it, the Captain read aloud from his Bible:

". . . And we therefore commit this body to the deep, to be turned into corruption, looking for the resurrection of the body, when the sea shall give up her dead, and the life of the world to come . . ."

Matthew looked askance at Harry Taggart. He had yet to tell Penhallow of Angelos' bound wrists; neither, apparently, had Spicer noticed it in the dim dawn light.

The first mate, cap over breast, stood in the rear ranks, prosaically propped on the rail. Penhallow's words were all but lost in the wind's wail and slatting of sails.

Matthew's fists doubled at the thought of the wanton death—at Taggert's lack of remorse. It was the first mate's watch and his responsibility, but he claimed that all was well when he went off. It was not uncommon of a sailor to lash himself to the wheel or a spar rather than chance going overboard in a storm, but why had the Greek, an inexperienced deckhand, gone aloft? Certainly his mates would not have forgotten him, considering his station. However, it was not impossible, especially in the fury of a midnight blizzard. But those bound hands—it amounted to murder. He vowed that, should he command a ship of his own, such tragedies would never be allowed to happen, that he would have the respect of his crew and mates to the degree that there were no secrets, excluding the aberrations that might occur, and no matters that would not be dealt with openly. He felt a glimmer of suspicion, felt that the first mate knew more than he was saying, but then there was no proof and it was important to keep confidence in the quarterdeck. What motive other than discipline could have brought on such an end for a gentle soul? The baffling knot was whether to report his observation of the bound hands at all. If reported to the Captain first, it would be insubordination. If he told Taggart, he too, might be in danger, providing his suspicions were correct. A puzzle, it would have to be discussed with Sam and Mark first.

The body slipped from under the flag. Everyone was hushed, waiting for the final splash. But there was none—only the dirge of sea and wind.

Decatur Hill succumbed a week later, despite the good care of Cleo and Joe Lavender. The ship, lacking a surgeon, had scant way of knowing that the Negro had not died of his injuries, but of arsenic in his first meal after regaining consciousness—a bowl of pea soup. Nobody noticed the candle tallow floating in it after it cooled.

CHAPTER SEVEN

The first days of August saw *Alchemist* plying the roaring forties of the Pacific Ocean. She had doubled the Horn, but at considerable expense. Persistent storms had whittled her spars and she was a concoction of jury rigs. The mainmast had cracked and was "fished" below the lowest yard; both fore and mizzen had spouted makeshift tops'l masts; and a new jib boom had been fashioned from a stuns'l spar. The starboard anchor, fully two tons, had been ripped from its lashings and stove in the starboard toilet and part of the fo'c'sle while mangling the windlass as well.

Nevertheless, Captain Penhallow pressed on. If the boat conquered the Horn it could go the rest of the way. Once north of the fortieth parallel of latitude the ship would take advantage of the celebrated Humboldt Current, thereby gaining some fifty miles for a day's run. Her damage, more cosmetic than functional, had not noticeably affected her speed. Celestial observations and log calculations showed an average of almost two hundred and forty miles per day made good since crossing the fiftieth parallel.

Slashing through heavy seas on a beam reach off the port of Valdivia, the hold suddenly shipped water so quickly that the pumps were barely able to keep up. Ned Swasey found that the starboard hawsehole stopper had come loose and was letting water into the fo'c'sle. Since this forepeak accommodation deck was on the same level as the main deck, the carpenter was perplexed when he, in testing, noticed that a great deal less water ran out of the fo'c'sle into the overboard scuppers than was shipped through the hawsehole. He then went into the hold and saw a stream of water pouring from the ceiling under the crew's quarters and into the 'tween decks and cargo areas. Upon examining the fo'c'sle deck, he found, under a lower bunk, that a section of plank had been deliberately augered and chipped out. Advised of this, Captain Penhallow immediately ordered the first mate to find the culprit and throw him in irons.

That evening Taggart hauled Wayne Devers forcibly from his bunk, even though the hole had been bored under another's bunk. First denying guilt, he was confronted with the fact that "someone" had seen him carrying an auger out of the fo'c'sle the day before. He then maintained that, if he did cut through the deck, it was for the purpose of comfort, since the cabin drains did not empty fast enough in rough weather. Penhallow ruled that Devers' intention was to flood the hold and force the ship into a Chilean port. Chips Swasey stood over Devers and had him fix the damage until it passed thorough inspection, then assured Penhallow he'd be personally responsible for the Alabaman's behavior and that he would chain him to his workshop vise at the first sign of infraction. Devers was a good carpenter's assistant and worthwhile of Swasey's confidence. Besides, everyone in the crew was convinced that Devers' motive was as much the comfort of the fo'c'sle as anything else.

More than two thousand miles west, between Pitcairn and Easter Islands, a pulsing seafloor rift emitted clouds of steaming bubbles as molten lava and fire-hot gases exerted tremendous upward pressure. A fault line extending a thousand miles shifted and undulated. Then one side heaved and, abruptly, a quarter million square miles of ocean floor sagged and slipped along the fissure, displacing a billion tons of water. The movement caused a surface drop of almost two hundred feet—a thousand-mile trough. The rush of the displaced water returning to the surface carried it above equilibrium by a hundred feet and created a gigantic oscillation that produced radiating ocean waves, focused along the epicenter axis and directed at the coast of South America along the thirty-second parallel of latitude.

Preceded by an underwater shock wave traveling at one mile per second, huge surface waves built up and rolled toward the land—waves of seventy-five feet in height and speeding at four hundred fifty miles per hour.

The first wave to reach Easter Island was heralded

by a swift recession of water that bared a mile of ocean floor beyond the low tide mark, leaving millions of fish and crustaceans wiggling and burrowing frantically in kelp, sand and reef, and exposing, for the first time, numerous species of multi-hued flora to the dry, alien world above. With an immense roar, the first *tsunami* wave crashed into the sprawling void and swept all before it onto the mysterious island that had been discovered by a Dutch naval admiral in 1722 on Easter Sunday.

The wave inundated a fishing village, catapulted over an ancient stone wall and tumbled asunder a circle of mammoth stone sculptured heads from their bases.

The shock wave reached Selkirk Island within sixteen minutes of the eruption, striking the copper-covered bottom of *Alchemist* with such force that all hands came topside to abandon ship. It was thought that a reef had been struck.

"Man the pumps!" shouted Matthew, as canvas was hastily shortened and the ship's boats made ready for launching. To the surprise and relief of all, the boat was not taking water. The crew and passengers, with what possessions they could carry, waited at the boat stations for orders that were not given, though they fully expected the boat to sink within minutes.

An assessment of damage below showed that the only casualties were objects made of glass. In the social stores area, wine and preserves bottles had been shattered, looking glasses and signaling mirrors cracked, and china plates were in shambles. In the dining saloon, drinking glasses and decanters lay in shards among splintered glass chimneys from the overhead lamps.

On deck, Nicholas Miles clutched his sketching portfolio and packet of drawing materials while squinting through his cracked spectacles. Passengers and crew alike talked of the Captain; how peculiar it was that he'd not been seen on the quarterdeck during the entire emergency. It was most certainly a situation that merited his presence. Had the ship gone down quickly, they would have made for the nearest island without him. Mas Atierra, or Robinson Crusoe Island, was just visible on the starboard horizon.

Under canvas again, Matthew put the boat back on course. According to Maury's Abstract Logs, brought aboard by Mark, the best winds were to be found by veering westward upon approaching the equatorial doldrums. The passengers and crew had all gone their ways when Cleo Penhallow emerged from the hatch, a look of horror transforming her usual mien and complexion. She implored Mark Hadley to accompany her below, an action that was noted by Harry Taggart. Cleo led Mark through the dining saloon and entered the Captain's cabin, where they were confronted by an extraordinary sight.

Wiburd Penhallow sat at his chart table before his stuffed and mounted albatross. Bottles and vials lay smashed and scattered about the table and the cabin. The odors of oils and preservatives permeated the room as tiny balls of quicksilver from the shattered barometer rolled to and fro on the deck, several caught up in the sienna fur of a Burmese cat in its last death-agony spasm. The white bird's beady eyes were locked onto those glassy counterparts of the Captain, hardly a foot away.

"Captain Penhallow," Mark called softly, then louder, as Cleo looked on in disbelief. He walked over to the Captain and passed his hand several times between Penhallow's face and the albatross's long beak.

"He's in some sort of trance," Mark said, and backed up.

"I wasn't sure; sometimes he plays strange games,"

Cleo grasped Mark's arm. "What shall I do? Does he need a doctor?"

"My albatross," the rigid man spoke like an automaton, "please don't let them take my albatross away from me . . ."

"Oh, Mark," Cleo gasped at the child-like voice.

"Who are *they*?" asked Mark.

"Look at all my broken toys. Will you buy me some new toys? Please . . . Mother?" He got to his feet and reached for Cleo.

"Come, Captain," entreated Mark, "you need rest." He gestured and Cleo opened the bedroom door. She watched with hands to lips as her husband was put on the berth with comforting words: "Tell me, Wilburd, what happened to your toys?"

"Oh dear," he tremored, "I was playing so nicely with the wings when the bad lightning came—and bad thunder. I'm afraid of lightning; it broke all my toys . . ." Penhallow fell back on the berth sobbing as Mark closed the door.

"Perhaps if we leave him alone, he'll get over it. It seems that he's gone into shock as a result of hitting that reef. It's almost as if his mind were made of glass, too. I don't understand why that reef was uncharted. Certainly we are on the trade route."

"Could it have been something floating?" Cleo attempted to shake off the situation. "Perhaps a whale? That would explain why we were not stove in."

"You could be right, but normally our lookout would sight a whale with enough time to avert a collision."

"Not if the whale was mad," answered Cleo.

"Whales are dumb creatures and do not attack without provocation. In any case, if your husband does not recover, we will have to get him to a proper doctor."

"But where? We've already passed Valparaiso."

"Callao is four to five days away. I suggest we continue, giving your husband time—and then, if necessary, go into Callao. It's very near Lima, which is a civilized city. They even have a telegraph line to Callao. If, in Lima, we find that your husband should go back to New York for treatment, we can go on to Panama City on the isthmus and hire a coach to transport him to Chagres, and then he could be put aboard a steamer for New York. I'm confident that we can complete the trip to San Francisco, should you have to . . ."

"Let's not plan further than Panama City for the present." Cleo studied the mute albatross. "We will continue as you say, but as the Captain's wife, I am responsible for him, his assets and his debts. As such, I am responsible also for his command; it is no fault for the mates to bear. I shall expect that you and your brother will serve under a woman's command as well as a man's, should Wiburd not get well. I will not pretend to *run* the ship any more than my husband did—probably much less, since it is not right for the crew; they wouldn't understand seeing a woman on the quarterdeck. The *Alchemist*, because of my husband's lack of personal involvement and his unfortunate dependence on medieval discipline, has already shown evidence of turning into a hell ship. The Negro helmsman, I'm told, was injured as a result of the first mate's brutality, and seaman Benson was less mourned-for than a common pig. There's no telling how many injustices have already been committed by Harry Taggart in the name of my husband, and I intend to do what I can to give this ship a good name before it reaches its destination. Do you think there will be any problems?"

"I think I can speak for my brother. We're signed on for San Francisco and have promised our father that we will return."

"How do you know that you won't catch gold fever? It seems to run in the Hadley clan." Cleo cornered the slim young man against the cabin divan and pressed her supple body to his.

"Excuse me, Mrs. Penhallow, but—" Mark didn't finish.

"No excuses, Mark. You feel the same way I do; I can tell. That night when we talked, the night of the storm when Taggart came off watch, I felt it then."

"I was tired . . . and the wine . . ."

"Are you tired now?"

"I don't think so."

"Do you have any idea why I called you, rather than anyone else on the quarterdeck?"

"Mrs. Penhallow, I ought to go up on deck. Your husband . . ." Cleo took Mark's hand and pressed it against her breast. "But your husband," he protested. She pulled him down on the divan.

"You're so brilliant, Mark—so different from all the others." She embraced him and kissed him on his cheek. Deftly, she snapped open her blouse and pushed down on her whalebone corset to expose a breast, and encouraged his hand to explore it, to cup and manipulate it. She thrust it close, and he slid down and ravished it with his lips while his hand found her knee and moved up her thigh between her rustling petticoats.

"Oh my God, what am I doing?"

"You're doing very well," she giggled, as he turned his body away to hide his physical excitement. "But you're absolutely correct; you'd best go up before they come looking." She thought of Seth Mason. With Wiburd occupying the bedroom, there would no longer be the trysts with Seth. The panel would mind its secret.

"I'll send in Wu Sing to tidy up—and take . . ." He pointed to the dead cat lying on the Oriental rug.

"Not Antonius, he was almost a person to me. He deserves a burial at sea. I'll tend to it." Cleo went into the bedroom and collected her things. It was time to move into the captain's cabin.

The *tsunami* wave tore completely over Mas Afuera Island, and its long roll picked up *Alchemist* on its broad shoulders, raised the boat precipitously and played havoc with the normal sensations of gravity and motion. Many a stomach was upset and the deck livestock raised such a bleating and clucking that it might have portended doomsday.

The enormous wave, at four hundred fifty miles per hour, broke its seventy-five-foot high crest on the beach rise of the larger of the two Juan Fernandez Islands, Mas Atierra, raking along its fourteen miles and carrying a dozen human inhabitants and scores of domestic and wild animals to a watery grave in the shark-ridden seas beyond.

The first order of Cleopatra Penhallow was to land at Mas Atierra Island to take on fresh water, vegetables and fruit. *Alchemist* wore round to the north coast to Cumberland Bay, where, after some difficulty due to great depths, it anchored and lowered a boat. The landing party, which included the quarterdeck passengers and officers—but for Matthew Hadley and Ferris Greenslet—and some picked crewmen, separated into three groups to scout the island. They found the remains of several houses, with clothing, furniture and possessions strewn about the land and snagged in rocks and scrubby trees. The island looked as if it had been demolished by a storm at first, but analysis of the course of events and the disposition of artifacts indicated the dreaded tidal wave.

Cleo, in seaman's attire, tricked Mark into getting separated with her from their group. She led him toward a series of high rocks covered with rich vegetation. "If there was a tidal wave," she reasoned, "the surviving animals would be in the high rocks." Cleo climbed vigorously toward a massive height that had been observed from the sea. It was a landmark called *El Yunque*—The Anvil.

After climbing for an hour they could go no further. Only the bulbous summit loomed above, a thousand-foot-high knob of volcanic rock. Finding a flat area with a view of Cumberland Harbor, they rested in the shade of El Yunque. Mark handed Cleo his water flask.

"But I have my own. You forget that I am not a lady but part of the crew. Nor am I a captain who does not do his share." She imitated a rowdy sailor drinking. "When we first saw El Yunque from the boat, it was so small and far away. Now it's the other way round. It feels so good to get away from the boat after three months of dampness and cold, and the incessant rolling, and the maggots and the awful odors, and that albatross . . . and poor Wiburd. It would be enjoyable to remain here for some days. If Robinson Crusoe managed, I'm sure a resourceful man like you could."

"Even though you jest, Crusoe was a fiction. While Defoe based his book on the mariner Alexander Selkirk, who spent more than four years on this island alone, it was by his own request after being insubordinate to his captain aboard *Cinque Ports*, a galley of sixteen guns. The island itself had been inhabited just before Selkirk was put ashore. He didn't have to build a house."

"How do you know this?" Cleo took her boots off and stretched out on a sunny part of the ledge.

"The Portsmouth seamen have told me many tales

of castaways and deserters. Mister Selkirk was fair game."

"Portsmouth is so far away," Cleo reminisced. "Tell me about your brother Matthew. Is he still infatuated with the girl from Kittery? Her father is a naval commander, I believe."

"No, she got married to an officer who served in the Mexican War with Commodore Perry's fleet at Vera Cruz." Mark moved into the sun and lay next to Cleo. A sea breeze had made the shade too cool.

"I've often watched lizards sunning themselves on flat rocks," Cleo said, as she propped herself up on her elbows and studied Mark's slim body. She reached over and playfully unbuttoned his trouser front. He didn't move; instead closed his eyes and smiled.

"You aren't afraid anymore?"

"There's nobody around, I hope."

"Don't move," she ordered the young man. "Keep your eyes closed." Cleo drew herself over him and reached inside his trousers to liberate the object of her desire. Stroking it tenderly until it rose, she quickly stripped off her bell bottoms and undergarment. Like a mountain wildcat, she pounced upon Mark and kneaded him with intensified dispatch, this time enlisting the aid of her passionate lips and sensuous raven tresses until his body arched violently. In a trice, she was straddling him, knees pressed into warm rock, rhythmically undulant, her warm breath exciting him.

Finally, spent, Mark opened his eyes. Still quivering, her head was buried into his shoulder and her milky back silhouetted as twin hills on the cerulean blue sky. Mark looked about and up; he marveled at El Yunque's majestic presence and observed a cinnamon-hued tropical bird cavorting with its emerald green mate, darting and diving . . . as was their wont on this, their eternal island.

* * *

Alchemist took on fresh drinking water in barrels that had been taken apart and newly coopered by Ned Swasey with the help of Wayne Devers. A she-goat, captured by Jim Dance, was brought aboard and named Juanita after the island's discoverer. The anchor was catted and a new course charted that allowed for the contingency of Captain Penhallow's stop for medical treatment.

On August 22d, the clipper dropped anchor off La Punta in the sprawling harbor of Callao, Peru. Captain Penhallow was taken ashore, and, after inquiries, boarded the new steam railway for the seven mile ride along the left bank of the Rimac River to the capital city of Lima. *Alchemist*, to the displeasure of a superseded Taggart, was put in command of Matthew Hadley for the replacement and repair of rigging in the port's shipyards.

CHAPTER EIGHT

A cold winter drizzle fell on the Plaza de la Exposicion, outside the offices of Doctor Ignacio-Mariano Vivanca, a specialist in the treatment of mental disorders. Wiburd Penhallow had entered the examination room in late afternoon. It was dusk when the doctor appeared and stated his confidential opinion to Cleo and Mark. The distinguished physician stood by a white marble fireplace mantel that was dominated by a brass English skeleton clock in a bell jar. Putting one hand on his vest, he cleared his throat and found the proper tone of voice and cadence. He was proud of his English.

"There are two basic forms of trance. First, we have the ecstatic trance. It is characterized by joyful contemplation. The subject seems to lose touch with the world of things and people around him, owing to the extreme concentration of attention upon some image or train of imagery, which in most cases is hallucinatory. The ecstatic patient normally remembers, in returning to his normal state, the nature of his radiant vision.

"The other form—the mediumistic trance—most fits Captain Penhallow. He exhibits no memory of any experience during his trances, as you related earlier. Most indicative is the fact that those parts of his body not directly concerned with my verbal interrogation remained in a completely lethargic condition, the eyes being closed, the muscles of neck, trunk and limbs relaxed, and the breathing stertorous—that means the patient snored. The mediumistic trance, essentially, is one that allows the possession of the body by some other soul or spirit; for, not infrequently, the speech or writing produced by the organs of the entranced subject seems to be, or actually claims to be, the expression of a personality quite other than that of the entranced. It is noteworthy that in almost all past ages the possessing spirit has been regarded in the great majority of cases as an evil or non-human spirit, whereas in modern times the possessing spirit has usually been regarded as, and often claims to be, the soul or spirit of some deceased human being.

"Whether the patient's condition is a result of

simple quiescence or the coma produced by defective cerebral circulation due to toxic substances in the blood or by mechanical violence to the brain, I cannot say.

"I strongly recommend that the patient be exposed to those surroundings and stimuli that seem to be of a positive nature in his formative years as soon as possible, so whatever demon has gotten within him can be cast out before it gains a permanent hold. Unfortunately, the science of human behavior lags far behind that of astronomy and physics. We can observe, we can prescribe, but the most important thing we can do is to act . . ."

Jury spars replaced and a new ship's boat on her skids, *Alchemist* heeled to a fair trade breeze and set a course to Panama City. A new spirit evident from stem to stern, she sailed smoothly and briskly. No longer did the duty watch shirk brightwork chores, but pressed resolutely to the task at hand whether it be aloft or below, whether it be varnishing, holystoning or cleaning out the livestock pens. It would not be long, Ned Swasey proclaimed, till the boat would be as dainty and trim as the day she first cracked on canvas and glided past Cutt's Eddy into Portsmouth Harbor for all the townsfolk to see and acclaim—the first of the Piscataqua Clippers, born upstream, like the shad and the salmon, and come to the sea.

Paddy Dooley no longer sang alone:
". . .Then up jumped a mermaid covered with slime.
We took 'er below and had a good time . . .
Stormy weather, 'm boys, stormy weather,
When the wind blows our barge will go boys . . ."

*   *   *

"Mister Taggart," Cleo addressed the first mate, "I called you below to explain the new order of command, and to have you read and sign an agreement. The note is for legal purposes and states that you are aboard the *Alchemist* in the capacity of third mate, and that you accept the demotion after being given the option of leaving the ship at Callao where other employ was available. It states also that you will receive full wages only as long as there are no reports or evidence of mistreating the crew or insubordination to your superiors.

"In the event of such conditions, you shall be relieved of your position and transferred to the fo'c'sle until being put ashore in Panama City." Cleo pushed the document across the cabin table and uncapped the ink pan.

The coarse Englishman's eyes gleamed quickly as Cleo leaned over and dipped the pen. A plan was forming in his monomaniacal mind, and Cleopatra Penhallow was to be part of it. He smiled benevolently and assumed a docile manner and soft voice.

"There be ways I have only done what has been taught me—methods of handling men that have been in practice as long as ships have been on the sea. If I have done wrong, then so have others who have not been called to account. We only do the bidding of our masters, and who can find fault with that, lest mayhem and mutiny occur on the ship. I thank you for your offer and will gladly sign as it is m' fondest desire to 'ave a good look at San Francisco and find a ship that will appreciate a mate of my experience."

Taggart sat down and feigned reading the agreement, as he was afraid of revealing his deteriorating vision, a result of his social behavior. He scrawled his first initial and last name below the fuzzy writing.

"And might I ask about the Captain's condition?"

"He's quite ill and will be sent back to New York when we reach Panama City."

"Of course, you'll be going with him?"

"That will be all, Mister Taggart."

Alchemist plied past Taboguilla's treacherous reefs under jib and spanker and headed toward the company of masts off the promontory of Panama City. Making toward the anchorage, she was besieged by a swarm of dugout native bungo canoes offering their services in debarking or embarking as the case might be. Miguel Ortiz explained that the *Alchemist* was not a ship for hire and that it had come by way of the Horn. After threatening the bungo hordes with the rail swivel guns, Matthew Hadley eased the trim clipper between a side-wheeled steamer, *Oregon*, and a listing schooner of about five hundred tons, the *Humboldt*. Accepting the *Humboldt's* signal to board and exchange information, Matthew Hadley, in his new position as first mate, lowered the gig and pulled alongside the steamer.

Captain Tobin voiced his condolences for the condition of Wiburd Penhallow and gave Matthew a tour of his boat, all the while extolling the profit that could be had by using his method of berthing. At $200 per passenger he'd managed to create accommodations for 401 gold-seekers that had come across the isthmus after arriving by steamship at New Chagres on the Caribbean shore. Tobin had arranged tiers of bunks in the hold so that each six-foot cubicular space held nine people, and the cubicles in toto grossed the owners the piratical sum of over $80,000 for a trip to San Francisco beset with rotten, wormy provisions and intolerable water, as described later by the passengers, some of whom got off at Acapulco and waited two months for the next boat.

Later, the gig delivered the Penhallows, Mark Hadley and baggage, including a boxed albatross, to the concrete-faced seawall and ramshackle piers of Panama City.

Inquiring at the tiny steamship agent's office of Zachrisson and Nelson, they found that the *Falcon* was due to arrive at Chagres in four days, and because it was the rainy season, the chances of crossing the isthmus in ample time were excellent.

Hiram Nelson, the Pacific terminal agent, balanced his chair on its back legs and placed a book of tickets on his desk. "We do keep a few extra berths for emergencies such as yours; in fact, we have a perfect first-class cabin at only double what we normally charge for reservations. First stop is New Orleans, and then on to New York. Now, if I were you, I'd let us handle the isthmus crossing. Better to get skinned by us Americans than by the savages—if you know what I mean. Some 'o the Negroes are all right and some are not. We've had cases where the bungo boatmen have gone crazy and killed their passengers. They can be a strange lot, especially the ones whose families came over as slaves back a couple hundred years. They still act like they're in the Congo. For forty dollars extra I can get you a good guide and a couple of trustworthy bungo paddlers. Now, you say that you, sir, will return. I advise you to let us hire you an extra bungo man because you'll be buckin' the Chagres upriver. We'll have you stay at the Hotel Americano tonight so you can get an early start. Our guide will be outside in the street with mustangs and mules at daybreak."

Nelson got up and looked at the baggage near the door. "Yep, two mules'll do it." Then he looked at Wiburd Penhallow, mutely seated. "I hope he can ride better than he looks. There are some sharp turns and rough trails gettin' to the river. Eighteen miles of 'em.''

"We can tie him on and lead his horse." Mark picked up the steamship tickets. "How much for all this?"

"I'll need a ten percent deposit on the tickets, and another two hundred for the crossing. There is no reimbursement on the animals if any of 'em die on the way. That'll come to three hundred dollars." He handed Mark a bill which Cleo snatched from his fingers. She set the amount in twenty dollar gold pieces on the table.

"Here's yer receipt, Ma'am," the agent said, trying to look in Cleo's handbag as she drew it closed. "Now you ain't riding in that fancy dress, I hope, Ma'am. You'd better wear men's duds. There's an emporium next to the hotel . . ."

After checking in at the hotel, Mark went down to the waiting ship's boat and told Bosun Spicer to expect him back in six or seven days. Meanwhile, he added, the Captain's wife had ordered that all the spars be scraped and varnished to the first mate's satisfaction before any of the crew would be given time ashore.

Ancient stone houses and ruins overgrown by the jungle soon gave way to deep mud, the salt-tinged air to musty rain forest. Through swamp and thicket, beset with clouds of mosquitoes, they followed the old Cruces Trail. Overhead, the fluttering and screeching of vultures pointed to Cruces—the birds waiting to descend once more on the dead mules that littered the trail. The guide, a swarthy *mestizo* named Hector

Gardos, signaled back to Mark whenever a particularly dangerous gully or obstruction lay ahead. Mark then pulled up alongside Captain Penhallow's mount, which was tethered to Cleo's, and took the reins to ride cheek by jowl past the hazard. The chattering of spider monkeys and cawing of parrots seemed to ridicule the procession as they slid in the mud and ducked under vines, the Captain swaying precariously despite being lashed to the back of his mustang. Eerie green light filtered down from the high, dense growth, coloring all and fusing man, mount and mud trail into an undulating serpent.

Now and then they contested for the right of way as a raucous procession of westbound forty-niners splattered at them on the narrow, glutted trail. One group, claiming Alabama as their own, shouted in passing: "Don't go to Cruces . . . Cholera . . ." Hector Gardos, upon arriving at a way station called Paraiso, needed no other inducement to change to the Gorgona Trail. It would take less advantage of the river, but, cholera was nothing to tamper with. He explained that the beer included in the provisions carried by the second mule would assure them, in barter, a room with hammocks and precautions against the dread vampire bat.

Once in the town of Gorgona, on the Chagres River, they were welcomed by the mayor and a Mr. Miller, the local store owner and only American resident. As evening fell, several fleets of bungos, westward bound, pulled up on the Gorgona banks, and the wooden drums of the village proclaimed a fandango. The aristocracy of Gorgona turned out and the natives set up bazaars and roasting fires on the mayor's lawn. The alcalde, a white-bearded Spanish widower, was happy to show his virtuosity with the guitar in company with two violins, as his attractive daughter implored the guests to join her in dancing the fandango. Spit-curled Dolores Vásquez twirled her skirts past Mark, daring him to dance with her, to the infuriation of Cleo Penhallow. The clergyman's daughter hurried to her luggage and changed in the brush from her sailor's togs to her party dress in time to claim Mark Hadley as her partner in the fandango.

Alcalde Vásquez, amused at *los Americanos*, invited them to be guests of his patio for the night. It was the first time in many such celebrations that he forgot his plight as a widower, put down his guitar and danced with a woman.

That night, one of tropical magic, with the blinding moon high and the *ko-ki* call of mating lizards in the pulsing jungle, Mark slipped out of his hammock and undid the cloth wrapping from his feet. There was little danger of being drained of blood by the vampire bats while awake, though he wondered whether his intake of the chicha drink at the fandango had put him in a state equal to sleep and, as such, vulnerable to the fanged night raiders. He shook his hands and feet vigorously, then lit a cigar stump with a stalk of dried grass flared up from the embers of the smoldering fire. Suddenly there came a clatter of footfalls as a dark shadow dashed and stumbled, catching the moonlight as it climbed over the vine-covered patio wall.

Hector, awakened, caught Mark by the wrist. "Señor, we do not chase him. It is his land and we are the intruders. They follow us by day and steal by night." The guide made a slashing gesture at his throat.

Early the next morning two bungoes were ready for boarding; one for the Penhallows and Mark, the other for the trunks, provisions and albatross crate. Hector's boat, with him as stern poleman and one native paddler, cast off first. Wiburd Penhallow, in the second bungo, was lashed in, between his wife and Mark. Two glistening Negro boatmen manned the pole and paddle.

"When you come back, Mister Hadley, you will need three boatmen because the river will flow against you," Hector reminded him as his boat pulled away.

As they passed the way-station of Mamei, a rainstorm pitted the swift-flowing river and drove the bungoes to the bank's shelter with the occupants under India-rubber ponchos, courtesy of the isthmus agents. With the downpour ended, the river became a steaming paradise; blossoms opened fresh and wide till the summer growths were mingled in one impenetrable, eternal mass of green. Clumps of tall cane and giant lilies changed to storybook cities and interconnected castles—thickets of brown and lime shrubs with curling, grasping tentacles reaching out to snare the gliding dugouts. Beyond the crowded banks rose gnarled and tortured, vine-entangled trunks of mango, ceiba, cocoa, and grandiloquent palm. Sunlight's rays fanned down on the jungle bounty: the purplish zapote fruit, large as a man's head, and the gourd tree, with its seven-foot-long fruit. Darting past blossoms of unearthly crimson, purple and yellow were flocks of paroquets and luminous butterflies. Creepers and parasites dropped leaf-bedecked trains and streamers while, deep in the musk of a towering tree, glowed a solitary pearl orchid. There was no trace of soil or rock; all outline of land was lost under the deluge of vegetation and all was one verdant continuum. The sublime mystery of growth and decay was forgotten, overcome by the lush, ever-unfolding torrent of deep jungle.

*   *   *

In the afternoon they encountered a Pacific-bound bungo fleet, the last one turning out to be a heavy wooden barge, with a crew of eight paddlers, upon which was balanced a curious machine. In passing it was recognized to be a hand-powered printing press, as tall as a man and cast in heavy iron. The owner proudly shouted that he was from Baton Rouge and going to California to mine not gold, but the affairs of man by starting the first newspaper in the territory. With that proclamation, he raised a bottle of wine, took a deep swig, and passed it on to his naked boatmen.

A half mile downriver, in a clearing behind a vine-covered native hut, a towering Negro raised his massive arms to the darkening sky and cried through his file-sharpened white teeth *"Ahorca Lagarco . . . Ahorca Lagarco . . ."* With each exclamation, an Indian dropped a potion into the raging fire to send the flames exploding higher and higher. On one side of the fire sat a black-robed high priest named Father Boco, holding up a wooden doll for the gathered tribe to see. He shouted, *"Ahorca Lagarco,"* then drove a steel dart into the effigy's squarish torso. The priest rose and picked up a woven twig cage and held it up to the firelight as the celebrants danced past, each one nodding at the sight of the little bright green snake inside. In the manner of a cobra, the snake reared up and hissed, darting its forked tongue in and out.

Still incanting, the high priest handed the cage to an aide and submitted to a horned mask being placed over his head. Red in the firelight, he stepped out of his robe to reveal a body glistening with exotic paints and dyes. His *wangah*, or incantation, was intended to please the tiny serpent. The priest wailed his lament and changed his pitch every eight drum beats. From the darkness emerged a naked woman—the high priestess. She pointed at a native who sat alone, and all converged on the man, whose appearance was that of a zombie, mechanically staring into the fire. The priest slipped a loop of hide about the man's ankles and, at a signal, the long thong was thrown over a tree branch and pulled taut. The entranced victim was hauled up feet first till he swung clear of the ground, his belly level with the high priest's head. Taking a curved blade from a proffered golden tray, Father Boco set the glistening razor tip at the base of the man's penis. With two aides restraining the unfortunate victim, the priest cut a quick gash up the torso to the neck, where he plunged the blade in. Scream gurgling in blood, the priest embraced the trembling body and buried his face into the wound to drink deeply of the warm spurting fluid.

The priestess took her turn, and so did the dancers, still shuffling to the drums' rhythm. Once again the priest wielded his knife, laying open the torso and cutting out the vital organs. Carefully severing them into small pieces, he handed them to his aides who distributed the pieces to the gathering to eat raw. Keeping the heart, the priest diced it on a flat stone and fed it to the snake.

The high priestess had her servant slip the entranced and severed head into a boiling cauldron while the torso was let down and placed on a roasting spit over the fire.

Suddenly a messenger disrupted the ritual and spoke with Father Boco. The priest beckoned to the giant Lano, descendant of the infamous scourge of the conquistadores, Ballano. After some fervid discussion inside the priest's hut, the Negro giant emerged and, followed by a file of warriors armed with blow-guns and machetes, disappeared into the jungle.

"My Priestess," smiled Father Boco, "Lano is going to bring us another subject—a white man who is under the spell of *Rong-dah* and who returns from the gold fields with a cargo boat and a guide. Surely this will be valuable treasure for the use of our people. Let us, on this rare occasion, attain the success over our enemy that our ancestors did when the glorious Cimarrones killed Pizzaro's lizard soldiers. *Ahorca Lagarco!*"

"*Ahorca Lagarco!*" chanted the tribesmen in unison as the drums' intensity increased. "Hang the lizards!" echoed through the jungle.

Lano, the image of Ballano, a slave brought from the Congo by gold-crazed Spaniards three centuries before, tied a tough vine to his body and swam across the rushing Chagres River, where he attached the loose end to a sturdy ironwood root. The vine's end, brought downriver, made a diagonal trap, designed to snare and turn the bows of river craft toward shore. The trap completed, and tested, Lano and his lithe group hid in the foliage around the apex just as the bungoes came around a bend.

Hector Gardo's boat was in the lead. "This is the place of ladrones and murderers," he cautioned the boat behind him. "I do not like to hear the drums, especially those that count by eight."

The *mestizo* scoured the river and its shadows with wary eyes and a hand on the butt of his ancient belted pistola. The leaves swirling ahead were to be expected; he ignored them and looked instead for movement on the banks and in the low-hanging overhead branches.

Then he saw something unusual. The surface leaves

had gathered in a curve—like fish in a net. Too late. He poled sharply, but the overpowering current foiled his attempt to turn the craft. The square, wooden platform bow of the dugout slipped sideways along an invisible track, and the bungo was forced into the dense, overgrown embankment. With curdling shrieks the band of near-naked savages was upon the lead boat. Hector's flintlock pistola flashed and cut down one of the boarders, the half-inch lead ball tearing the Indian's bare chest a split second before a blowgun dart pierced the guide's left eyeball.

The bungoes were hauled ashore and covered with brush, and the three surviving boatmen tied to trees while Mark and Wiburd were pushed ahead onto a jungle trail.

"Come on, little one." The giant Lano grinned as he plucked at his one gold earring. "Hurry or I'll have to carry you." He tapped Cleo on the head and knocked off her hat. Her long black hair fell free. "Take them to Father Boco; I bring this one soon," ordered Lano of his warriors. He grabbed Cleo by the shoulders. "If you are woman, you should look like woman," he said. As he ripped her shirt off, she slipped from his grasp. Enraged, he lumbered after her and cornered her in a thorn thicket. Slowly he advanced on her, his huge hands reaching out—and then the giant stopped.

There she stood, nakedly confronting him, hands on white hips thrust forward—daring him. Lano, confused, turned away and docilely picked up her torn shirt. Looking away from her, he handed it over. "Put on shirt, please. Lano wait."

The procession was marched into the ritual clearing and the baggage set on the ground before the high priest. Father Boco, attired in his robe, bade the prisoners sit by the fire, except for Wiburd, who was given a ceremonial bench position a few steps away, under a tree. The priest, swinging his looped thong, walked around Captain Penhallow and studied him intensely. Then he clapped his hands as a signal to open the trunks. The high priestess examined the contents, shook her head and pointed to the wooden crate. One of the warriors came forth and pried at the crate boards with his machete as Bocos waited breathlessly, the dancers and warriors craning for a look as well. As one of the boards came loose, Lano dismissed the machete wielder and, with his immense strength, pulled the covering boards from the crate.

A forlorn cry rose from the tribe as Lano covered his eyes and sank to the ground in front of the crate. The high priest and priestess moaned in unison and threw themselves beside Lano, scraping in horror at the ground.

The giant white albatross glowed like a god inside its box and the drums were silent once more.

CHAPTER NINE

"That roast meat we were served last evening was the tastiest I've had since—well, ever, for that matter," Cleo sighed as she stepped into the bungo. "And such comfort—the royal quarters. I feel so invigorated."

"And now, even separate boats," Mark said. He watched as Captain Penhallow was assisted aboard his bungo by several boatmen, then boarded his own. Each bungo, including the baggage boat, was provided with a surrey-type canopy, under which the passenger reclined on hide and furs. In the baggage boat, the stuffed albatross looked forward out of its crate through an open woven-twig door as if it were the admiral of the fleet. Each boat was manned by a poleman, two paddlers and a servant who tended to the passenger's comfort with fruit, tobacco, intoxicants and a host of delicacies.

"Lano," implored Cleo as she stretched out on a bed of vicuna furs, "what was the meat that was served last night?"

"Ma'am," the powerful Cimarron said, as he poled against the current and steadied the boat as it rounded a bend, "the people from the big water call it 'the Long Pig.' In my village it is 'the Goat without Horns.'" Lano grew quiet, trying to avoid further questions.

"Well," Cleo said, as she set down her wooden tumbler of chicha and turned around to face the Negro, "is it pig or goat? Tell me."

"Ma'am," replied Lano with a grin, "it's not so much the meat, as it's how you cook it. A quick sear first, to seal in the juices, and, of course, the meat should be fresh. I'm sorry we arrived back last night too late for you to see how it was prepared."

The powerful renegade paddlers drove down the Chagres in record time and scattered westbound boats in their wakes.

"Lano," Cleo confided to the polesman, "will you do me a favor? I will pay you in gold."

"No gold; Lano is ordered by Father Boco to serve you."

"Because of the albatross?"

"Yes, but I like to serve you by myself, Ma'am."

"That's very sweet of you. I want you to wait in Chagres until Mister Hadley is ready to return to Gorgona. It will only be a day or two."

"Lano sorry you have to go, but I will do as you say. But we must wait upriver from city. My people not welcome in Chagres."

"Why is that?"

"People say we kill *Americanos* who go to gold boats."

"Do you?"

"Only sometimes."

"I understand." Cleo gulped, but quickly regained her composure. "If I say that I've hired you, and will be responsible, it might make a difference."

"Maybe, ma'am, but *Americanos* have many guns and get very drunk. We will wait upriver. We catch fish to eat, and maybe you give us wine. That help us wait better. Now Lano have question. Long time ago I go to Spanish school and I learn of queen from Africa. Mister Captain call you same name: Cleopatra. She have beautiful boat on big river, too."

"Mark," murmured Cleo, turning toward him in the moonlight streaming through the open window of the Crescent City Hotel, "is it wrong, what we're doing?" Their hands met and clasped.

"I'd feel better if he wasn't in the next room—and that goes for the loony bird as well." Mark looked at her body: stretched out on her back, it was a landscape on the Sahara—soft pyramids and dunes catching the moon's caress, and a glistening ebony oasis the apex of the warm and forbidden terrain.

"We can't help what happened, Mark. We're almost the same age. It was meant to be. I hope you understand that Wiburd and I—seldom—that is, we never . . . Do you know why we're here tonight."

"You're the new captain and I am obeying orders?"
—"Silly. That's not true."

"We're both animals?" Mark bit her on the shoulder.

"In a way," Cleo purred. "We both exude a magnetism. We're in harmony, yet we're in opposition, and that is to be desired."

"I admit," Mark sighed, "that in Portsmouth I often watched you walking with Sam, and I wished . . . I even daydreamed about you. What I would do if . . ."

"And now you have. Are you disappointed?"

"But you're married, and you have to . . ."

"Mark, what would you do if you had enough time—and money?"

He thought for a while before answering, then put his hand on her stomach, rubbing gently aloft and below. "I'd build a canal across Panama, and then another from the Red Sea to the Mediterranean—but first I'd build a steamship."

"And then?" Cleo reached for him. "First, we'll erect your smokestack." She played her favorite game as he continued.

"And there would no longer be reason to go round Cape Horn or the tip of Africa. Steamships would simply chug and be tugged through the canals, regardless of wind direction. And, most important, distances would be cut in half . . . to China . . . to San Francisco. The sailing ship has seen its best days. Oh, there will always be men like my brother, Matt, and they'll occasionally make faster runs than steamships, but not on a regular basis. A sharp clipper, with good winds, can make Liverpool from New York in fifteen days—but only once out of ten trips—whereas a steam packet can do it every time, barring storms or mechanical breakdowns. Man cannot stop storms, but he can perfect the marine steam engine. Look what's happened with the railroad in just a few years. Forty and fifty miles under steam in just one hour.

"And look at Mister Collins," Mark continued. "He's sold his sailing packets and is now building five steam packets under a government subsidy to carry mail."

"Was he the gentleman who owned the Dramatic Line? His boats I remember as having such names as the *Shakespeare* and the *Garrick*. Oh dear, we've been talking so much that your smokestack has fallen over," Cleo apologized. "But it's all so exciting. Can't you get your father to build a steamboat?"

"Sam and I have tried; at least we've discussed it, but just like Sam's father, he said he'd quit rather than do it."

"Is that one reason Sam is going to California—to strike it rich and build what he wants to?" Cleo rolled and put her leg over Mark's body.

There was no cemetery in Chagres, at least not in Yanqui Chagres, which was across the river from the old city. Presumably, all corpses were thrown in the river to be carried out by the tide. With many deaths occurring from cholera, malaria and gunshots, there were no questions asked and no law to answer. Homeward travel across the isthmus and through the terminal cities was lower than outbound, and those returning could well afford it. They had taken a hundred dollars, a thousand, five thousand a day out of the hills around San Francisco, out of the Trinity River, out of Dry Diggings near Coloma and out of Weber's Creek. These were the men who had picked up tree stumps and found gold nuggets hanging on the roots, and a fortune in yellow metal in a claim that was too small for a grave.

Leaving Wiburd sleeping in the hotel room, Cleo donned her liveliest dress while Mark put on a suit just bought at the emporium. After a supper of dried beef, beans and bread, followed by a dessert of fresh mangoes, they sauntered into the brightest and noisiest building in Yanqui Chagres. The Monte Carlo Casino had one objective: to fleece both west-and eastbound travelers. Roulette, faro, poker, *trente et quarante*, blackjack, craps—all with a two-dollar floor and no ceiling. Girls cost two dollars a dance and they ordered dollar "blue moons," pocketing a half on each drink of the colored water. A man who wanted more than a dance was referred next door to "The House of All Nations," serviced by black, white, yellow and brown girls from New Orleans and points east.

Cleo set a twenty-dollar gold double eagle on 20 *noir* as the tourneur called out "*Rien ne va plus.*" The fleet ivory ball careened and jumped, then clicked to a stop in the metal compartment that lined up with the numeral 20.

"*En plein* twenty," cried out the tourneur, and waited as a croupier raked in the losing bets and pushed thirty-six golden double eagles in front of an astonished Cleo. Mark started to gather in the coins, but was abruptly stopped. "I always continue if I'm ahead," she said, and pushed the stacks of coins forward, placing one on the cloth layout over the intersection of 3, 6, and *manque*. The tourneur gaped at her stake and spun the wheel. The ball stopped on 9.

"*Transversale* six," he called, and she'd won again by betting on six numbers with one coin. Only 5 to 1, but it was enough to stop the other boards as the players gathered up their holdings and crowded around the roulette table. The suspense mounted as Cleo surveyed the red and black squares. Dancing girls stood quiet and wide-eyed; sourdoughs and merchants waited keenly, cigars burning and drinks in hand. Eyes flicked from Cleo's décolletage to her stake.

"All of it," she said with a smile, "except my lucky gold piece." She placed coins on the intersections of 5, 8, and 9—two betting coins, both touching the eight *noir*. Just as the tourneur spun the wheel she replaced the coin between 8 and 9 with the original double eagle. The metal spokes at the center of the wheel crackled like close lightning as the ball took its contrary path. Even before the wheel slowed down, a cheer went up around the table.

Disbelievingly, the tourneur whispered, "*à cheval* . . . nine." One of the table croupiers slipped through the onlookers and hurried up the stairs to the balcony. Then the tourneur motioned that the roulette table was closed.

Shortly thereafter, a thin, hollow-cheeked man of about sixty limped down the stairs. Dressed in the manner of a southern planter, his salutation was as eloquent as if it were the Governor's mansion in Baton Rouge rather than a gambling house.

"I have not had the honor," he said, extending a manicured hand. "I am Cassius Claibourne, proprietor of this establishment."

"Mrs. Wiburd Penhallow, of Portsmouth, and the ship *Alchemist*, lying at Panama. My husband is the Captain, and this is the second mate, Mark Hadley."

"Welcome to our little casino. It seems that you've done well—in only three turns of the infamous wheel. While we're waiting for the, ah, bank to bring the cash from our safe, won't you both join me in my private room for a drink—and a little game of poker?" The white-maned gambler stretched his fingers.

"Thank you for the invitation," said Cleo, rising, "but my ability does not go beyond roulette."

"But you must—where is your spirit of contest?"

"Must I, Mister Claibourne? Your bank owes me almost sixty thousand dollars."

"There must be some mistake," Claiborne said, his voice changing from saccharine to sour. "The house limit on any one wager is one thousand dollars."

"But the sign said the floor bet was two dollars and there was no ceiling," Cleo replied irately.

The gambler grinned and looked around. "What sign? I don't see any sign."

"But that's ridiculous; then why didn't the tourneur reject the lady's bet of over three thousand in gold?" Mark slammed his fist on the table.

"Mistakes do happen, Mister Hadley. I am a reasonable man; perhaps we can settle on a compromise." Claibourne snapped his fingers and a croupier flashed a derringer pistol under his jacket.

"I'll call the police." Mark started toward the door.

"There *are* no police in Yanqui Chagres, Mister Hadley."

"Just a minute," a sharp, authoritative voice rang out, and a well-dressed gentleman came forward. "There was indeed a sign—and I saw a croupier remove it during the last turn. The lady is right, and I, for one, will vouch for her."

"And who the hell are you?" Claibourne screamed. "Do you want to go out of here feet first?"

A squad of uniformed soldiers stormed through the front door, carbines at the ready, and took positions around the hall. "I'm Major Blackburn, 4th Infantry, United States Army. Mister Claibourne, one of our functions is to protect our citizens and their property, no matter where. Shall we close up your establishment and send you to New Orleans under guard to stand charges of fraud and robbery, or . . ."

Claibourne bowed fawningly. "I'll just go to my office and have the amount taken from my safe."

"Halloran," snapped the Major to his corporal, "see that Mister Claibourne doesn't go out a window. Take a few men."

"Yes, sir."

"Miss . . ." Blackburn doffed his hat.

"*Mrs*. Penhallow; my husband is captain of a ship lying at Panama. He's very ill; we're putting him aboard the *Falcon* tomorrow morning to go back east for medical attention. This is Mister Hadley, the second mate."

"Mrs. Penhallow, you've won a great sum of gold, and this is a dangerous town. I suggest—unless you want to take your chances of getting murdered—that the winnings be put aboard the *Falcon* immediately. The purser will give you a receipt. It's the nearest thing to a bank in town. You may even want to go aboard yourself tonight—with your husband."

"Sir," Corporal Halloran saluted perfunctorily upon his return, some minutes later, "we've got it all in sacks. He weighed it before us, and it all came to something over two hundred and eighty pounds."

"Good." Blackburn glanced at Cleo, who nodded. "Take the squad and load up one of the mules. We're going aboard the *Falcon*. And Mister Claibourne is coming along to help us assay the nuggets and weigh it all on the ship's scale. Carson," he called out to one of the troops, "go along with these people and arrange for the baggage. We'll wait in the *Falcon's* boat."

Mark watched from the wood-planked pier as lanterns swung in the gig and the crew cast off the lines.

He had an empty feeling within, but they had decided it would be better this way. A clean break, no lingering confusion. Her place was with her husband. Perhaps another day, another place. If it was meant to be, it would happen. He waited till the lantern was but a firefly over the dark bay and flitting toward an indistinct shape in the mist. He heard the ship's bell clang faintly. Six times.

Mark walked slowly back to the hotel and upstairs to the flat he had shared the night before. At least the albatross was gone. The next morning, he would go down to the pier and wait till the *Falcon* had steamed away.

CHAPTER TEN

"Mark . . . Mark . . ." The screams routed him from his bed. It was just after sunrise, and at first he thought it was a dream. Then he realized that it came from the hallway. He slipped into his drawers and unlatched the door. It was Cleo—breathless and excited. She was carrying a Siamese cat.

"What on earth happened?" Mark let her in quickly and locked the door. "The *Falcon* sails at nine. You have less than one hour . . ."

"I'm not going, Mark; I'm going to California—with you."

"It doesn't make sense, Cleo." Mark poured water into his washbowl and splashed it in his face. "Where's your husband?"

"That's just it. He's still aboard, and everything's just marvelous. Last night, after boarding, I met this gentleman in the ship's lounge. He talked a bit, and he even bought me a cordial. I needed it so—after that episode at the casino, and all that money. I suddenly realized that we would not be together again for . . . Well, the gentleman—he said he was a financier—was on his way to California, but he was waiting for his cargo to be unloaded. The native bungoes he'd ordered earlier yesterday did not want to carry his cargo up the Chagres. They went, instead, to another steamer."

"What was he carrying? Gunpowder?"

"No." Cleo pouted and stroked her cat. "He had twenty crates on deck—all filled with cats. Twenty cats of all descriptions in each crate—at least, that's what he started with in New Orleans. A few of them died. He's taking them to California, to sell them to the miners. There is a plague of rats in the gold fields, and the rats are devouring the miners' food supplies. David—I mean, Mister Montebianco—is going to make a fortune. A cat brought in New Orleans at a dollar will bring fifty in San Francisco. He's doing this as a sideline. He's just come from England and he's investigating the business possibilities of American cities.

"When I told him about the *Alchemist*, and poor Wiburd, he offered me an exchange. He would have his trusted valet care for Wideburd and see that he got back to New York, and even to Portsmouth, if, in return, he could obtain passage for himself and his cats to San Francisco. I was only jesting when I mentioned that we, or rather you, have dependable transportation at hand. Then, when I thought it over, I realzed it solved my dilemma. He even found me a replacement for my cat. Meet Antonius the Second.''

Mark took the Siamese from her. "He's probably stolen.''

"Mister Montebianco wouldn't do such a thing. He's extremely distinguished. Oh Mark, it's all so fortunate. It was meant to be. With the many bungoes there'll be ample space, and our new guest can take Taggart's cabin. Taggart should be in the fo'c'sle anyway, for all his coarseness. It's either that or he stays in Panama City.''

Mark put the cat down. "Taggart's going to be furious—but we'll all be happy to have our acting captain back on board.''

"Thank you, Mark. I was torn between accompanying Wiburd and completing the trip. He didn't seem to mind when I told him this morning. He gets on well with David's man, who should be able to take care of him better than I. And he has his albatross. The valet has a letter I wrote, explaining everything to Wiburd's father. Mark, tell me that I did the right thing,'' she said, collapsing against him. "Please.''

"You have an extraordinary business sense. We could certainly use you at the Portsmouth yard.'' He laughed, then kissed her gently on the forehead. "But most of all, Cleo, you are kind—a rare combination. They will understand.''

Cleo took a sheet of folded paper from her dress pocket. "Here's the purser's receipt for the money. Major Blackburn handled it all for me. For a small fee the purser will transfer the gold, in my name, to the Mail Steam Line's bank in New York. He said it was routine because of all the gold coming across the isthmus.''

"Is this Mister Montebianco ready to travel?" Mark asked, as he tightened the straps on his luggage.

"He's waiting at the pier with his cats. I sent a messenger to have Lano bring the boats."

"Let's get something to eat and buy food for the trip back."

"Mark," she said, and stopped on the stairway.

"Yes?"

"How much does a steamship cost to build?"

CHAPTER ELEVEN

The polychrome figurehead glistened with fresh gilt and varnish as the sharp cutwater stem of *Alchemist* sliced through the azure Pacific. It was one of those rare days in tropical seas when the winds were moderate and the surface smooth, when the triangular skyscrapers were set as well as the stuns'ls, and the Master looked forward to entering his best day's log distance and thus compensating for the doldrum calms.

"Keep the needle as best you can on this point of the compass, but remember, Lano, first the ship has to be under control."

"Lano understand, Mister Matthew." The statuesque Negro gripped *Alchemist's* brass-trimmed wheel.

"First, ship feel good in water; second, keep arrow on point that say NNW."

"Lano," said Matthew Hadley, slapping the giant on his bare back, "you're going to make a fine helmsman."

"Thank you for chance to steer big boat."

"You have earned it. There's hardly a man among our ordinaries who's done as well as you in only two weeks. To boot, what other man is as strong as you? You'll not be needing help in a blow. It's the wheel that will break first."

"Maybe Lano learn from Chagres River. Many time I paddle bungoes in storms for my people. Catch many fish, go far upriver to the white waters and never lose boat. Maybe big water is same God as river. Many fish go from river to ocean."

"That is so, Lano." Matthew looked up proudly at the clouds of white canvas. "The river has its currents and rocks, but out in the ocean you cannot turn in to shore for shelter—you can not leave the ship if the devil is aboard. It is not a question of hours or even days to set foot on land. A seaman must be prepared to stay at sea for months without seeing land."

"God help seaman to be happy?"

"God helps me. Everything good comes from God, and why not happiness? God is the reason our ship will arrive safely in San Fransicso."

"Is that the God of Jesus?"

"The true God, yes."

"Lano have many Gods; one for food, one for storm. Even talk to Jesus when I see his pictures in Chagres church many years ago. Then Lano grow big; everyone afraid, so stay in jungle with Father Boco."

"You ran away because people were afraid of you?"

"White man want to fight Lano in city."

"From what my brother told me, your people are called outlaws by the New Granada government." Matthew checked the compass heading and nodded approval.

"Maybe that good reason for Lano to go California."

"The nearest I can calculate is that we must be off Guerrero." Don José Figueras looked furtively behind him as he leaned on the windward rail.

"*Si*, my *Generale*, I think I see the Sierra Madre del Sur this morning." Seaman Miguel Ortiz, on his knees, pressed the holystone against the oak deck and rubbed back and forth.

"We will have to act soon," said Figueras, looking landward. "Once we pass Acapulco, we'll turn further out to sea. I don't want to have more than a day's sail to the mainland."

"That is wise, Don José. We are only five, and they are more than twenty."

"Six. You forget Mister Taggart."

"Can we trust him?"

"He doesn't like the *Americanos* any more than we do—especially after his demotion. Besides, he has a clever plan. We will let him carry it out as a diversion—a flank attack."

"As we did in Los Angeles against the gringo *Coronel*."

"It is a small prize we claim, Miguel, but we must have revenge. So much of our rightful land has been stolen by the Yanquis: California, Utah, Arizona, New Mexico. And now they take our gold out of the land. Tell Carlos to be ready at dawn. I shall find out our exact position at supper and plot it further."

"*Commandante*," whispered Miguel. "We shall

sail proudly into the Rio Balsas with our prize. A victory for Mexico."

"I go, Miguel; someone approaches."

"Mister Montebianco," Sam Hadley said, as he stirred his coffee, "why did you leave England?"

"I wanted a challenge. London is stodgy and predictable."

"Then why not India—or Canada?"

"Partially a matter of climate. I am a lover of the temperate clime. Business has always prospered where there are constant seasonal changes, and in America you have that as well as a frontier. In addition, I admire the American spirit of enterprise, something England, at the present, is lacking."

"You're quite an entrepreneur yourself," Jim Dance chuckled, "considering the unusual cargo you brought aboard at Panama. I'm glad the crates were put forward."

"It seems a whim, but a return of forty or fifty to one is nothing to be scoffed at. If, as you say in the gold fields, 'it pans out,' all the stray cats in England will be shipped to California."

"But the price will have dropped," obese Ferris Greenslet said, as he lifted his bowl of oatmeal to his thick lips.

"I have no intention to continue in the livestock trade," Montebianco said. He got up from the table and stretched, then looked out a porthole. "Strange, I had a queer sensation that we had changed our direction."

"Variations in the Humboldt Current," replied Matthew. "Bosun Spicer knows what he's doing."

"What do you intend to do in San Francisco," Sam persisted, "after you sell your cats?"

"The development of any territory needs strong backs

and materiél—weapons, food, transportation. All these are not possible without money. I intend to sell money. I want to see whether it will be worth starting a California office." Montebianco took a card out of his billfold and set it on the table before Sam.

GIBBS & CO.
67 South St. N.Y. City
Brokers
David Montebianco

"I've heard of Gibbs." Sam put the card in his pocket. "Good firm, but it's seen better days."

"That's why I bought them out." Montebianco looked around the dining saloon. "Isn't it about time Mrs. Penhallow joined us?"

"Wu Sing," Matt asked of the steward, "see if Mrs. Penhallow is feeling well. She is usually out here by this time."

The steward departed for Cleo's cabin. He knocked on the door and, receiving no answer, let himself in and knocked on the bedroom door. He hurried out excitedly. "Missy Penhallow no answer . . . and door is locked."

Matt jumped up from the table and called his brother out of their cabin. "Have you seen Cleo this morning?"

Mark blinked sleepily as he joined his brother in the dining saloon. "I last saw her before I went on watch—about ten last night."

"Where?" The stronger brother asked anxiously.

"At this very table. We talked, and when I went on deck, she'd gone to her cabin."

"Well, there's no answer from her room—and it's locked." Matt ran aft, ship's keys in hand, and returned from the armory room with a boarding pike. "We'll have to break in," he said, as he stormed into the captain's cabin. He slammed at the bedroom door after slashing at the handle and prying the lock loose. The door swung open.

The bed was empty.

Mark ran in, but was stopped by Matt as he spotted the displaced wall panel and started to crawl through. "Sorry, but I'm the ranking mate here." Wielding the axe before him, Matt ducked through the dark opening, stumbled across the air space and out into the between-decks level behind the companionway ladder.

He caught a glimpse of a figure just in time to prevent a belaying pin from crashing down on his head. Dropping his axe, he grabbed the assailant by the shoulder and they both tumbled to the deck. "It's a trap!" he shouted, as he forced the pin out of the man's hand and pressed it against the intruder's neck. By the dim light of the deck hatch, Matt thought he recognized his attacker. But no, it couldn't be one of the crew. The man wore a soldier's uniform—epaulettes, glinting metal buttons; a cockade hat was lying on the deck. He raised the belaying pin as the soldier gasped for breath.

"Drop it, *señor*."

Kneeling over his adversary, Matt looked up into the barrel of a large bore revolver. Behind it was another soldier—an officer in full dress uniform, replete with gold braid, medals, high polished boots and a plumed hat.

Suddenly there was a flash of orange fire and loud report. Matt fell face-down over the sprawled soldier as the lead slug grazed his temple, then tore into the bedroom and drove Mark into the day cabin.

"Quick, Carlos," the officer commanded, as the soldier dragged Matt away and a rumbling six-pounder cannon was rolled up to the bulkhead opening and its muzzle thrust in and carriage lashed to the hatch ladder. "Gentlemen, this cannon is filled with chain and nails, so I advise you to stay in the saloon. We have another one on deck, aimed at the quarterdeck hatch, so do not try to escape.

"Mr. James Dance, are you listening?"

"What is it, *Señor* Figueras?"

"At last we meet. Our paths have crossed many times. I am not Figueras. Do you recall the battle of San Pedro?"

"Major Flores?"

"Yes. Tell your friends about Major Don José Flores of the Mexican Army and how we defeated the miserable *Americanos*, desecrators of our proud land of California del Sur . . ."

"The San Pedro garrison was outnumbered and short of powder."

"The *Americanos* are always claiming to be outnumbered when they are defeated. Yes, I am Major Flores, victor of San Pedro, and victor on this day. I claim the *Alchemist* as a prize of war for the Government of Mexican California. I must—according to the rules of war—advise you that, as my prisoners, you will receive humane treatment, providing you follow my orders. I warn you that I will stop at nothing in delivering this prize to my country and comrades-in-arms. If you value the lives of your first mate and Mrs. Penhallow, you will do as I command. When we arrive at our destination, the hostages will be released as will the crew and passengers—with a possible exception or two. Precautionary measures."

"And who might they be?" Mark shouted from the day cabin.

"*Captain* Dance, formerly of the gringo army, can answer that."

"You have no right to do this." James Dance edged closer to the bedroom, derringer in hand. "It is not an act of war, pure and simple, but piracy—and punishable by hanging. The treaty of peace between President Polk and General Anaya included all officers in the Mexican Army, regardless of their location, disposition or inclinations.''

''Ah, Captain Dance, you are correct, but in my case I was not under Anaya's command. In 1846, at the onset of hostilities, I was elected to the combined post of both Governor and *commandante Generale* of California del Sur. My constituents were not all military men, but landowners and businessmen whose stakes in California go back to the conquistadores. During the war I fought visibly as a Mexican, but my commission was from the proclaimed independent Republic of California. In effect, a state of war still exists between our two countries—mine being in hiding, but very much alive.''

''What do you want us to do?'' Mark called to Flores.

''That's much better, Mister Hadley. As ranking mate, you are now the captain of this ship. Your crew is under guard in the fo'c'sle. I want you to order them to handle the sails. You will be the only person allowed out of the quarterdeck cabin. I judge that we are about fifty miles off the coast of Mexico; with this wind it should take about six hours to reach shore. If you do not comply I shall not be responsible for Mrs. Penhallow, who is under custody of Mister Taggart, a sympathizer to our cause.''

''Where is she?'' Mark flared up. ''How do I know she's unharmed?''

''I will take you to her. Come through the passage—and no tricks.'' Flores ordered the cannon rolled back.

''What have you done with my brother?''

''He's resting; he'll be all right.'' Major Flores prodded Mark up the ladder and onto the deck with his long-barreled revolver. ''As you now see, the four Spanish seamen Captain Penhallow signed on in New York are all my comrades-in-arms, loyal to a man. Mexicans with a sense of honor. You cannot say you are outnumbered now, eh?"

Mark looked about the deck: Ortiz at the wheel, Zamora on the starboard swivel gun, Jorgé forward on the six-pounder, and Velez below. Of the four, only Ortiz was an experienced sailor, the others having been hired as deckhands. But who could have suspected?

There was a knock on the carpenter shop door in the forward deckhouse. Taggart cursed. He enjoyed just sitting and looking at Cleo, who was bound, hand and foot, to a chair across from the workbench. He enjoyed thinking of what he might do with her helpless to his advances—a lady in a fancy dress, with petticoats and perfume.

"Who's there?" he hollered gruffly.

"It's me; Bruce, sir."

Taggart unlocked the door and let the retarded boy in.

"The Major is coming—with the second mate," Bruce said. He cocked his head at the Captain's wife and looked down like a naughty child.

Taggart lunged at the workbench. "I've got you, you scroungy rat-eater." The cat screeched and clawed at the air as Taggart held it up like a trophy. "Mrs. Penhallow, you're going to give us no trouble now, are ye?" He pressed the cat's head between the jaws of the bench vise.

"You wouldn't," Cleo gasped.

Taggart turned the screw handle, and the cat howled like a banshee. "Oh, I wouldn't, eh?"

"Please—I'll do anything you say. Don't hurt Antonius."

"CLEO, ARE YOU ALL RIGHT?" It was Mark's voice, outside.

"Yes, I'm fine," replied Cleo.

"They've taken over the ship, and now Major Flores wants us to sail it for him. I cannot take it upon myself to obey."

"Mrs. Penhallow," apologized Flores. "Forgive me for this deception, but this is war. I still cherish the friendship I had with you in my guise as Don José Figueras . . ."

"Do as he asks, Mark. They've done me no harm."

"Very well, to Mexico it shall be."

Cleo bit her lip as the footfalls faded.

"Worse than rats in a trap, we are," Paddy Dooley lamented to the crewmen packed into the fo'c'sle. "Rats don't get trapped by their own kind. Here we are—seventeen strong men—and we've been taken by a half-dozen at the most. Shame on us."

"That's easy to say, Paddy," Ned Swazey argued, "but you didn't have to look into that cannon's muzzle. We mustered out of the deckhouse, and there it was—meaner 'n hell, and filled with nails and powder. They sure had the jump on us. And here we've been messmates around the Horn. Who would have thought that Miguel and Carlos . . . Taggart's in on it, too. I saw him with Figueras."

"The Mexicans, they forget about Lano," the Negro said. At six inches over six feet, he could not stand up in the fo'c'sle. "Lano no like to be caged like animal. He break hatch door now."

"And take a six-pound charge in the gut? You'll be cut in half, and most of us with you," seaman Devers winced.

"Maybe Lano break wall near anchor hole. Go front way . . ."

"Ahoy the fo'c'sle—this is Mark Hadley. Paddy," he shouted, "pick six good men to come out and brace the sails. We're changing course. The rest of the crew will remain."

"Is this a trick, sir?" Paddy called through the hatch.

"This is an order. Mrs. Penhallow is a captive, so we have no choice. On the double, now."

"Ah, there had to be some reason." Paddy faced the crew. "Now let's have the second watch follow me. Mister Hadley," the able seaman said, as he opened the hatch door slowly, "that cannon . . ."

"Don't worry, they won't shoot because they need you."

Lano's group stood aft to handle the mizzen canvas. But he had a plan. His jungle aptitude was no less useful in the world of the white man. Trees became masts, and vines were hemp. Serpents and vicious animals crawled between the decks as their cousins did in the swamps and glades of the tropical forests. After bracing the lower and tops'l yards to the new easterly course, Lano swung out and up on the ratlines as if to secure an errant mizzen halliard, then screamed and pitched overboard. Pepe Zamora, at his starboard swivel gun post, looked over the rail. "He's gone; the Negro has drowned."

"Just as well," called Miguel from the helm. "I didn't trust him anyway. We get somebody else from the fo'c'sle."

But Lano had not drowned. He had purposely dropped from the ratlines and caught the chainplate channel, seven feet below the rail, and swung himself up under it by clinging to the backing link against the hull—hidden from view. Hand over hand, he worked his way aft, dangling over the streaming water toward the brace block bumpkin, which was lined up with the wheel. Pulling himself up and peering over the quarterdeck rail, he saw that Miguel Ortiz was alone. How different his crewmate looked—with green tunic, white belts and red epaulettes, the eccentric high-plumed cap and purple Zouave trousers.

Pepe's attention was inboard, one eye on the two-inch swivel cannon aimed at the quarterdeck hatch and a weather eye on the main deck. Still hanging by his fingers, Lano moved along the rail and around the transom, past the gilded scrollwork, port-of-call letters and ship's name, then over the massive copper-sheathed rudder and around to the port fairlead. He pulled himself up again and noted that he was behind the helm and screened from Pepe's sight by the companionway hatch and skylight seat. Stealthily, the big Negro swung himself up and over the varnished rail. With a jungle hunter's silence he crept past the steering box and, before the helmsman could react, closed his powerful forearm about the neck. There was a grinding snap as Miguel collapsed to the deck. After quickly lashing the wheel with Miguel's white belt, Lano crawled past the hatch and waited behind the skylight seat, several paces from the swivel gunner's position.

When Pepe finally turned his gaze seaward, Lano sprung upon him, then lifted the astonished Mexican and flung him over the rail. Picking up the flintlock lanyard, he turned the swivel cannon's muzzle toward the ship's waist and crouched low against the rail as a figure strode aft. It was Major Flores. He stopped at the forward deckhouse, then appeared with Mark Hadley and, walking behind his prisoner, continued toward the quarterdeck. Mark ascended the short stairway first and, recognizing Lano, dove to the deck and left the Major staring into the swivel gun's muzzle above him. Lano, now looming up to his full height, held up the firing lanyard threateningly at the terrified officer. "Now," ordered Lano, "turn your back to this cannon, unbuckle your pistol belt and let it drop to the deck." Beaten, Major Flores complied as the sails started luffing and slatting aloft. "Now, please put hands in air and walk two steps forward."

"You do a foolish thing," the Major cajoled, "The *Americanos* make slaves of the Negro. Join me and live as a free man. I can give you gold and a position in the proud army of California del Sur—"

"Do what I say before I shoot another of Pizarro's lizards. It was the Spaniards who enslaved my people," boomed Lano. The Major stepped forward and Mark jumped down from the quarterdeck to pick up the weapon.

"Major, after you," Mark said, motioning to the quarterdeck.

"Thank you, Mister Mark." Lano ran back to the wheel and brought the ship back on course as Mark, pistol leveled at the crestfallen Mexican, opened the hatch and called below.

Taggart made sure that the sliding portlight shutters were secured, the carpenter's shop being equipped with a ceiling skylight. He whispered drunkenly to the retarded boy. "How would you like to play a game, Bruce?"

"I like games, sir; we don't play enough anymore."

"Good." The hulking mate drained his rum cup, then took a cloth from the workbench and tied it around Cleo's mouth. "We don't want any screamin' to spoil our fun, Mrs. Penhallow." Taggart felt a surge of excitement as the young woman squirmed in his grip. He was not one for ordinary pleasures and worried about his ineptitude with the ladies. It took drink to give him confidence, to turn him away from whores and boys such as Bruce. When he first tied her to the chair, after Bruce had dragged her through the panel exit, he'd had no thought of taking advantage of his prisoner. It was enough that Flores had promised to share the cargo and ship. But that was before the rum. It was Bruce who found out about the panel by watching Seth Mason one evening. Bruce, Taggart's informer and plaything.

Taggart's obtuse mind whirled. He would repay Bruce for confiding in him, for being his only friend, for doing his bidding on deck—and below, in the dark recesses of the ship's hold. It would be two birds with one stone: repayment to Bruce and revenge on this woman who despised him, who had broken him as first mate, and on all women who would not have him, as well as on all those he could not perform with. Now he would laugh at them.

After untying Cleo from the shop chair, Taggart sat and locked one arm around her waist as he forced her across his lap as if to spank her. Arms still bound behind her, she kicked and struggled, then fell limp as the mate applied more pressure.

"Bruce, m' boy," Taggart said, as he stroked his prisoner's rump and fingered the fine cloth of her dress, "in the Angus country of England, I once watched a prize bull jumping a cow. The breeder hi'self even put the bull's pego in—"

"It's the same in Tennessee, sir." Bruce's eyes lit up.

"You be the bull, Bruce, and I'll be the breeder. Now you drop your trousers, and I'll—" Cleo struggled violently and Taggart struck her on the rump. "If you want a thrashing—" He crossed a leg over hers and pressed her knees down against the chair, then forced her into an uncompromising position— jack-knifed her over his knee. He fumbled with her dress, clawing it up over her back and grappling with her petticoats, probing with his clammy hands as the sixteen-year-old mountain boy came closer and manipulated himself under Taggart's eager gaze. "Damn you," he shouted and pressed the fight out of her as he parted her petticoats and grabbed the boy's erect penis.

"TAGGART, OPEN UP—IT IS MAJOR FLORES COMMANDING YOU."

The voice staggered him. In a daze, he let the woman fall to the deck as Bruce tripped backwards over his trousers.

"Go to the devil," Taggart shouted. He stood and picked up a carpenter's adz. "I'm keeping my part of the agreement—"

"OPEN UP!" repeated Flores, in the iron grip of Lano behind him. "I FOUND A CASK OF RUM AND WANT TO GIVE YOU YOUR SHARE."

"Well now, that's a different story." Taggart unlatched the deckhouse door and Lano slammed it open, then rushed in, only to be struck a glancing blow by Taggart's adz. As Lano fell, stunned, Taggart dragged his hostage out, adz pressed to her neck. "Out of my way, or I'll do her in, I swear . . ."

The ship's company and passengers on deck backed away. Taggart, seeing the Mexicans in irons and realizing that he was now alone, and surrounded, climbed up on the starboard rail and swung out on the mainmast ratlines with Cleo over his shoulder. Belting his adz, Taggart scrambled up the rope ladder.

"Don't shoot," Mark Hadley warned, as Jim Dance raised his Colt pistol and tried to get a bead on Taggart. Up and up climbed the desperate mate, in drunken frenzy . . . past the main yard and onto the maintop. Resting for a moment and clinging to a mast stay, Taggart shouted down, "Leave me be—or I'll throw her into the bloody ocean."

Crewmen on both ratlines backed down at Mark's behest as Taggart climbed yet higher, to the topgallant doubling where he crawled onto the crosstrees, where he dropped Cleo across the spreader braces to which she clung in terror. " 'Ere, now . . ." He ripped the gag from her mouth. "Scream all ye want." Taggart brandished his adz for all below to see. "Tell yer friends that Harry Taggart means business." He shaded his eyes. "Tell 'em that I can see land from here, and if they don't turn east again, I'll kill ye . . ."

"You tell them—you maniac!" screamed Cleo above the wind rushing through the rigging. "You don't have my cat anymore."

"You call me that once more and I'll cut your cunt out. It's women like yerself have driven me daft," he spat, drawing back the adz as if to strike her.

"I'm sorry," Cleo pleaded. "You're right, I will tell them to do as you say." She averted her eyes so as not to give away a figure climbing the mizzenmast. It was Matthew Hadley, already on the royal mast ratlines and going higher.

Ninety feet below, on deck, all was tense and quiet as Matthew grabbed hold of the skys'l brace, a rope running diagonally down from the mizzen skys'l yard to a doubling of the mainmast, about ten feet over Taggart's head. Head bandaged from being grazed by Major Flores' bullet, he slid down the rope as several of the crew feigned going up the ratlines in order to keep Taggart's attention from what was coming toward him from aloft and behind.

At last Matthew was above his quarry. Hanging by his hands, he measured his distance, grasped a halliard line, and dropped—squarely on Taggart's back, knocking the adz from his grip and catapulting the bewildered Englishman from the tiny platform.

Screaming, Taggart plummeted through the main

shrouds to leeward, struck the cross-jack braces, tearing head from body, deflecting the latter into the sea, while the former hurtled to the oak deck and bounced overboard.

Alchemist turned north by northeast once more, in its wake a frothy patch of ocean beset by ominous black fins.

The next day, August 19th, a sail was spotted off the Revilla Gigedo Islands. It turned out to be a fishing schooner out of Mazatlán. On Cleo Penhallow's suggestion, first mate Matthew Hadley put a boat over and had Major Flores, his two remaining revolutionaries and the cook's boy put aboard the Mexican vessel.

With fair winds, it would be another two weeks before picking up the pilot outside of San Francisco.

CHAPTER TWELVE

An immense flag billowed seaward: the familiar red and white stripes, and a field of blue containing twenty-nine white stars. Wisconsin had been admitted to the Union as the thirtieth state only the year before, but the firm of Sweeney and Baugh decided to wait till California was admitted before bringing Old Glory up to date. There weren't many seamstresses in San Francisco, and, like every other service, moving old stars and sewing on new ones was very costly.

The flag was rigged on a semaphore mast atop a frame building overlooking the Pacific Ocean at Lobos Point. On the roof was a lookout platform manned by two men with powerful telescopes, each one continuously scanning the horizon. One of them jumped up and called through a trap door to the semaphore operator.

"CLIPPER SHIP STANDING IN FROM THE SOUTH!"

The operator referred to his signal code board, then pulled seven of his eight halliards down and cleated them, leaving only one wooden blade extended on the semaphore mast. It was one of the top grouping of four, indicating an approach from the south, specifically by a clipper ship. Two blades were reserved for a steamer, three for a schooner, and four—with a fully retracted bottom group— signaled a warship. A clipper from the south meant cargo and passengers from New York or Boston by way of the Horn—a voyage of four to five months. It also meant scarce manufactured goods were to be soon bid for. For some businessmen, there was the prospect of restocking their shelves with liquor to sell at 200% profit; for others, it meant fleecing the ship's crew of their accumulated wages. And there were also those who dealt in man as a commodity. They were called "crimps," and their business was to secure enough seamen to fill the rosters of ships that had been deserted in part for the gold fields, but not so many that they'd have to be abandoned in the mud off Rincon Point. These were the smart clippers and packets whose scheduled runs had demanded that their masters and mates, and at least half the crew, were dependable to make the return voyage. These were ships of considerable value and investment, sailing under stringent insurance agreements. Ships such as the *Agamemnon, Greyhound,* and *Alchemist.*

Another station built by Sweeny and Baugh, across from the old Spanish Presidio House, picked up the message and transmitted it to a high hill on the extreme northeast of the peninsula, upon which was built the third station. This station was visible to the town of San Francisco, nestled below Yerba Buena Island. The hill was known as "Sydney Town Hill," the center of a criminal settlement, though the businessmen referred to it as "Telegraph Hill."

"Mister Moran," said one-armed Timothy Wiley, as he slithered down the stairs. "It's a clipper, sir. The semaphore reads a clipper from the south. My, aren't we ready for a pretty ship?"

"Whale Whiskers" Moran pushed his cue-stick, striking the cue-ball deftly against the red ball, which, in turn, holed the white, before spinning off the cushion into a corner pocket and nipping another into a center pocket.

"Ten points, gentlemen," Moran said, and put his cue-stick down on the billiard table. "Please excuse me." He showed his opponent and several spectators to the door, then followed his "runner" up the stairs and onto the roof of his establishment, a saloon called "The Shades," on Pacific Street near Sullivan Alley. Taking the telescope from Wiley, Edward Moran put the eyepiece over his ruddy cheek and studied the semaphore signal mast on Telegraph Hill. He slapped the leathered glass together and tugged on his whiskers.

"Timothy, my boy, line up a dozen prospects. Go to the city prison and bail out Hurley and Stewart. Keep 'em sober enough to attend classroom this week—and get word around to Carrie and her girls. There'll be a crowd of Jacks who ain't seen shore in four months.''

''As you say, boss—and I'm looking forward to giving them a real California welcome when they come in this afternoon.'' Timothy Wiley pulled his boot pistol out and examined its percussion hammer. ''Poor Timothy junior,'' he lamented sadly, ''hasn't had any real exercise in weeks.'' He pulled the horned hammer back, inspected the tiny copper percussion cap, then eased the lock back in place and slid the pistol into the inside of his left boot. Then he held out his only hand, palm up. Whale Whiskers grunted once, and dropped the whiskey locker key into Timothy's hand.

The *Alchemist*, carrying full sail, wore a trifle north, due to a contrary breeze and lack of a harbor pilot, who had absconded to the diggings. Matthew gave the land wide berth as was sensible in entering any port for the first time. Hardly had he taken bearings off Point Reyes when a heavy fog slid up from the protected bay. Bell clanging and announcing its entry, the ship glided blind toward the Golden Gate as both watches were ordered to shorten sail and ready the anchor for an emergency mooring in the rocky bay. Matthew had just called for coming about when the heavy fog parted and bright afternoon sunshine broke through, to the crew's and passengers' hurrahs.

Clouds of thousands of pelicans swooped about the ship, and whales cavorted—spouting and diving within twenty yards of the rails. An exuberant James Dance and his obese merchant companion amused themselves by firing their pocket pistols into the air. Greenslet, however, after a few reloads, found it greater sport to put his pistol balls into the welcoming whales.

Gradually the fog dispersed along the shore and uncovered the most extensive maze of sailing rigging ever accumulated in one port. Spars, masts and shrouds—tangled, tipped at angles, enmeshed, yard to yard and sprit to sprit—obliterated all but the higher portions of the boom town. Over eight hundred ships were anchored in Yerba Buena Cove. Others had been run aground in the haste to abandon ship and lay opened from looters in the mud. Several of the larger ships had been hauled up close to the makeshift piers, stripped of their rigging and converted into hotels, stores and gambling houses.

Anchor catted, *Alchemist* wove its way into the mast forest under backed topsails. Aft, the stream anchor was readied since the crowded anchorage left no room to swing with the tide.

"Let go forward," called Matthew, as the vessel lost headway. The heavy bower caught in the mud and *Alchemist* swung round with the current until aligned and secure. Rope was then let out until the stream anchor could be dropped off the stern. Next, a crew of four manned the windlass and hauled on the cable to pull the vessel forward until the stream anchor also pulled taut.

The crew was still aloft furling the sails when a high-pitched shout cut into the late summer blue:

"HALLOOO, THE *ALCHEMIST*!" One-armed Timothy Wiley waved from the bow of a skiff, briskly rowed by a muscular Kanaka from the Sandwich Islands, as another islander tended to baskets of bottled whiskey and cakes. "Welcome to El Dorado . . . I bring gifts for a weary crew."

Bosun Spicer cast a glance at the quarterdeck, received a nod, and called for lowering the gang-board. The skiff was secured and thin Timothy, wearing a black suit and Sunday bowler, pranced up the rungs singing a familiar ditty:

"I'll be in San Francisco soon
And then I'll look around,
And when I see the gold lumps there
I'll pick them off the ground . . ."

Behind him, Fish, the Kanaka, carried a basket of green bottles up the ramp, to the delight of the crewmen leaning over the rail. "Where's the ship's master?" Timothy Wiley squinted fore and aft as he boarded at the waist gangway.

"I speak for the master," Matthew Hadley hollered down from the poop rail. "What is your business?"

Moran's messenger bowed graciously, then took a bottle from his aide's basket and held it high. "Gifts from a generous gentleman of our fair city. Mister Edward Moran, proprietor of the most elaborate refreshment palace on the peninsula, does hereby contribute one bottle of an original blend of whiskies to each and every man of your stalwart crew to show our esteem for their bravery and skill in rounding the treacherous Horn."

"And what about us passengers?" Ferris Greenslet twanged from the quarterdeck.

"You are all welcome to our establishment, *The Shades*, on Pacific Street near Sullivan Alley." Wiley made a grand gesture with hat in hand. "But first . . ." He grabbed several bottles and, tucking them into his coat pockets, jumped up on the rail and reached one out toward a crewman on the ratlines. Klaus Spielhagen had no choice but to accept the offering, so slick was its presentation. The runner handed out another to Paddy Dooley and one to each of the seamen as they came down from furling the last sail, despite the objections of Matthew from the quarterdeck.

Incensed, the first mate shouted: "There'll be no spirits aboard this ship. Take your wares back now and leave. Dooley, collect the bottles and return them at once."

"Now, now, young man," chided Timothy. "You're not back east. You're in God's country now, where one man is as good as the next." He took more bottles from the basket.

"Get off this boat, *now*," Matthew ordered, as he stormed down the ladder.

Timothy reached down to his boot and pulled out his pistol. Cocking it, he repeated: "God's country," and took pointblank aim at Matthew's astonished face.

A shot rang out, but not from the boot pistol. Wiley's hat sailed from his head and he dove for cover. A second ball splintered the harness cask a few inches from his ear. Terrified, he dropped his pistol and scrambled over the side and slipped from the gang-board into the bay. Fish gathered what bottles he could and hurried with short steps down to the waiting skiff, as bottles whizzed past him.

Cleopatra Penhallow stood frozen on the quarterdeck—her husband's naval Colt pistol extended in both small hands.

"Thanks," wheezed Matt, as he ducked from under her aim.

"Now we are even," Cleo said. Suddenly she felt faint and dizzy, and Mark took the pistol carefully out of her grasp.

CHAPTER THIRTEEN

David Montebianco, standing guard over twenty crates of cats, brandished a broom at the city's wild dog population, howling and yelping in front of the clapboard building upon which a sign proclaimed:

H. LABITTE & CO.
AUCTIONEERS

Help finally arrived—in the form of Seaman Lano, snapping a bullwhip that scattered the hounds in all directions. A crowd of jabbering miners and local businessmen milled about, examining the unusual merchandise and discussing the pros and cons of purchasing.

Montebianco had already been offered what he'd expected, but the excitement of the venture had impelled him to follow it to its limits—and what would bring the best price out of a crowd but a live auction? A far cry from his father's type of business transaction, but no less efficient and profitable.

The crowd grew as the auctioneer started his chant; gesturing at the crates, he chattered out a stream of unintelligible terms, every so often punctuated by an ear-splitting word. Young women with parasols looked into the wooden slat cages and prodded their escorts. Old women turned up their noses at fleeting odors, while merchants raised fingers, nodded and deliberated their next bids.

A young boy, shoeless and unkempt, five years old at the most, strolled casually over to the crates and toyed with the reaching cats' paws. Then he turned to the auction audience, bowed and climbed atop one of the crates. Unaware of the boy, the auctioneer continued his calling as the boy took a live rat out of his trousers pocket and swung it by its tail, just out of the reach of the voracious cats below him. Then, to the gasps of the onlookers, he held the rat over his head, lowered it into his open mouth—and bit off the rodent's head. "Poor child," called a spectator to the shocked, "his father was killed in a brawl and his mother works in a saloon."

The large, complex machines looked like cotton gins, washing machines and electric shock generators, but bore curlicued labels such as *Patented NUGGET DIVINER*, *AMAZING GOLD DUST SEPARATOR* (Guaranteed to separate the gold from the gravel with no water and a minimum of work), and *EUREKA MAGIC BELLOWS* (Just point it at the ground and blow—all the dirt blows away, leaving acres of clean gold).

"Cyrus Penhallow and company will realize a great profit from this shipment," Jerome H. Cogdill asserted, thumbing his striped silk vest as he surveyed the warehouse floor from the consignee's balcony. "According to the isthmus mail, we were expecting the *Agamemnon* with a similar cargo to arrive first. My congratulations, Mrs. Penhallow—and I must commend your supercargo for his superb manifest and its

condition. It is rare that a cargo such as you carried
was so little damaged in the Cape Horn passage.''

"Mr. Cogdill,'' replied Cleo, squirming uncomfortably in her best Boston dress, ''I am amazed that
the *Agamemnon* is not here. It is reported to be the
fastest clipper afloat. We encountered the ship off
Estados Island, just before rounding the Cape. My
first mate—Mark's brother—with masterful sailing,
passed Captain Gordon's boat, but in a light breeze.
Certainly it was only a temporary lead, since the rest
of the trip was mostly in weather that *Agamemnon*
excells in—strong breezes and moderate gales.''

"In addition,'' said Mark, deepening his voice,
"we lost ten days by stopping at Callao and Panama.''

"Perhaps,'' conjectured Cogdill with a shudder,
"they were lost.''

"And *we* were lucky,'' replied Cleo.

"Let us not forget that you have good mates in
Mark and his brother. One a fine sailor, apparently,
and the other a natural shipboard organizer. I can
understand why Wiburd hired them.''

"You know my husband?''

"We were classmates at Harvard before he decided to go to sea. I do wish Wiburd a speedy
recovery. What did you say was his illness?''

"We're not sure; he needs rest.''

"The important thing is that he is home and safe.
He will be delighted with the proceeds of his cargo.
We should do very well without competition from the
Agamemnon—wherever they are. Perhaps as much as
fifty percent more on the entire cargo. Such are the
rewards of winning. Now, Mrs. Penhallow . . .''
Cogdill looked over the long manifest, ''we shall
probably have sold everything within two days. Do
you prefer gold in payment, or will a draft from
Baring Brothers—less my commission, of course—be
more convenient?''

"A draft will do."

"As you wish. Gold at sea can be hell. Do you plan to stay in California for a bit?" Cogdill glanced at Mark.

"We're leaving as soon as possible."

"Of course; I do understand. Then you'll sail in ballast."

"We plan to load copper ore in Santiago," replied Mark.

"An excellent idea," Cogdill said as he filed the manifest, "with all the shipbuilding going on back east—copper for copper bottoms. Well, in your sojourn here, I must warn you of several things. Firstly, most every measure and weight in the Sacramento Valley is false. When purchasing or selling to strangers, bring your own set of balance weights. Nuggets and dust are the exchange medium and brass weights can be fashioned with lead interiors. Secondly, don't gamble. If you do, insist on your own playing cards or dice. I noticed on your manifest that you shipped a quantity of playing cards, but it's listed under a private owner. Perhaps you'd ought to buy from him."

"We've already gambled, in Panama. And we're stopping while we're ahead." Cleo raised an eyebrow at Mark.

"Good. Another problem will be the temptations to your crew. You're going to lose some of your men to gold fever. You will then have to replace them or sail short-handed. Beware of the San Francisco crimp. He has been known to put a corpse into the fo'c'sle after telling the captain it was a drunken, but experienced sailor.

"One thing more. If you have a good cook aboard, you may want to increase his wages, for you'll not find a replacement should he leave for the diggings."

"Where is the most gold being found now?" asked Cleo.

"Just beyond Sacramento there are many rich veins. The towns of Volcano and Columbia are being staked out and report the average daily find at a hundred dollars. Nuggets bringing from three to five thousand dollars are not uncommon. Were I more adaptable to the outdoors," said Cogdill, suppressing a cough, "I might have given it a try myself."

"I can't fault a sailor for leaving his ship when there's a chance to earn three thousand a month instead of thirty," mused Cleo. "Even I am tempted. Perhaps a woman's intuition would uncover sources overlooked by men. But, of course, my responsibility to the ship and to our investors precludes such escapades. Mr. Cogdill, we shall expect you aboard the *Alchemist* for supper this Saturday."

A lantern swung gently in the night breeze from a sloop's boom in the deserted cove north of the Sacramento River town of Martinez. The sloop's stern was secured to the remains of a wooden pier, while a kedge anchor kept the bow into the current. Tethered horses grunted and neighed softly under the waterside trees. James Dance puffed on a cheroot as he quietly watched the Indian brave lift the lid of one of the boxes that were neatly laid out on deck. The Miwok Indian's eyes flashed as he reached into the box and took out a rifle.

"It's a better gun than the first Hunt repeater," Dance said, as he picked out a second gun and demonstrated the action. "I bought the first two hundred from the New York manufacturer. Based on the Hunt gun, it can fire seven times without reloading. It will be many months before it goes into mass production. Even the United States Army does not have such a weapon."

"How much gold for this gun?" asked the Indian, known as Captain Jack, as he examined the rifle excitedly.

"Ten ounces for each gun." Dance splayed out both hands.

"How many pounds for all guns?"

The dapper merchant whipped out a pencil and scribbled on a box label that said: HIGH GRADE PICKAXES. "One hundred twenty-five pounds of gold for the lot." He peeled off the label and handed it to the brave.

"I get gold now. Bring braves to carry guns. Now we shall be stronger than miners who take our land and hurt our squaws."

"You're forgetting something, Captain Jack."

"What I forget?"

"You can't shoot without bullets."

"How much more gold?"

"Fifty cartridges for an ounce."

"I buy all you have." Captain Jack smiled anxiously.

"Pay for the rifles now, and take them. Tomorrow, send a couple of braves with an extra pony and twelve pounds of nuggets to the warehouse on Clark's Point. I'll be there with ten thousand rounds. You can buy more later."

"Very clever, Mister Dance. I see how you can survive in your business. You will become a rich man. What will you do with your gold?"

"Buy more guns."

"It is strange, Mister Dance. For all the years of the Miwok tribe, the yellow metal meant nothing to my people. It was everywhere. In the tree's roots, in the gray rocks, and shining in the swift streams as we speared the fish. Now it has made men into devils. I long for the years of my childhood, before the white man found this wicked, cold metal on our land.''

Seth Mason rowed as Nicholas Miles fumbled with his sketch pad. The dinghy plied between schooners and barks, steam packets and whalers, ships of every description and condition, riding listlessly at anchor, some with bowsprits fouled in a neighbor's rigging, some with hulls tilting on muddy shoals, their ports and hatches open and pelicans roosting on the deckhouses. A great silence clung to the armada of abandoned vessels in Yerba Buena Cove—the silence of a nautical graveyard.

"Over there—to starboard." Miles' shrill voice carried far and set a pelican to unfold one wing. "There," he pointed with his conté drawing stick, "a fine figurehead and a perfect composition against the island." It was the packet *Athena*, out of Philadelphia. The figurehead carving portrayed the Greek goddess, her spearpoint raised to the bowsprit as the silver-helmeted, robed figure held a calming hand over the water. The vessel was a frigate-built packet, with heavy knee head and gilded trailboards. Aft, it exhibited ornate quarter galleries, an arch board and stern windows. With the demise of this style of ship, in favor of lean, swift clippers, went the livelihood of many a talented shipcarver. Clippers, divested of extraneous and vain decoration in their quest for an image of speed, retained only the figurehead, as faired into the stem as possible, and a small carved piece on the stern.

Seth tied the dinghy line to an adjacent schooner's stern anchor rope and the small boat trailed off steady enough for Nicholas Miles to block in the scene.

"My father would have had the figure lean out

further and gotten a better sweep from the trailboard into the robe," Seth criticized the sculpture.

"I agree it might have been better integrated, but then I'll cover the fault with chiaroscuro—like *so*." Miles made a flamboyant stroke with his conté. "Seth, have you noticed how Mrs. Penhallow and Mark Hadley are getting on?"

"Should I have?" Seth feigned disinterest.

"No offense." The artist smirked and changed his tone. "Cleo is a remarkable woman, what with all her involvements. I understand that she even knew Sam Hadley before her marriage . . . Oh, I just love Athena's profile. Helmets do unusual things for women."

Seth ignored Miles' barb about Cleo. For some weeks he'd wondered why she no longer desired him. She'd told him they'd best stop the passage trysts for a while. Then she went to Panama with Mark and returned a changed woman, almost a stranger. In a way, Seth was relieved. It was wrong, and his conscience bothered him—not to mention the danger of being found out. The Captain would have had him in irons or shot him. But one did not say no to Cleo. Now it was over, and he was the better for it.

Now he was a man.

"May I see the drawing when you're finished?" The melodic young voice startled both of them.

"Oh my God," sputtered Miles, almost dropping his sketchbook overboard, "I thought it was Athena who spoke."

A girl stood atop the fo'c'sle deck, looking down past the gilded cat head beam. She had long flaxen hair and wore a simple cotton dress; the sunlight behind her silhouetted her charms—an image that burned its way into Seth's very core.

"Mother wants to know if you'll come aboard. You're from the clipper that arrived the other day?"

"We are, Miss—" Miles doffed his straw hat.

"I'm Anne Griswold; my father is Master. Come around to starboard when you are ready. Mother is so anxious for news."

". . . And so here we sit," Maude Griswold, a handsome woman in her thirties, said, as she sipped her tea. "Half the crew were over the side and into the boats before we were properly anchored. Then my husband went with the mates and the passengers, leaving us with just the bosun, bless him, and a steward. That was almost two weeks ago. And we've heard nothing. My husband said he was going to a place called Volcano, or was it a valley?" Maude shrugged despairingly and fiddled nervously with her graying blond hair. "The *Alchemist*, I assume, has cabin accommodations?"

"Fine cabins," replied Miles, "and mostly vacant now."

"Splendid. I so want to send my daughter back to Philadelphia. California is no place for a young girl. With Anne safely on her way, I could go ashore and join my husband, providing I can find him. If I don't, there's no telling when he'll return. We have to load a cargo of hides in San Diego and should leave here before the end of the month. If Anne could leave earlier, and on a fast clipper, she could be back in Philadelphia in time for her spring semester. She's already missed enough schoolwork."

"Have you considered the mail packet passenger service? The trip would be much faster by way of the isthmus." Nicholas noted that Seth was entranced by the sixteen-year-old girl sitting across the saloon table, with skylight sun caressing her hair like an angel in a Venetian golden-hued oil painting.

"I won't have Anne crossing that perilous jungle by herself. I would like to see the *Alchemist's* accommodations and meet her captain."

"The ship's master is Mrs. Cleopatra Penhallow. Her husband took ill and returned to New York by steamer out of Chagres." Miles scrutinized his sketch which lay on the table. "I'm sure it can be arranged. She will be on board this afternoon."

"I like your drawing, Mr. Miles. Are you staying in San Francisco?" Maude noticed her daughter smiling at an antic of Seth's.

"For a while. I shall make sketches of the city and the harbor before going to the gold fields. My plan is to continue on through the new territories ceded by Mexico, and then to New Orleans. I intend to see and sketch the canyon grande of the Colorado River." Miles sighed at the thought.

"What about you?" Maude interrupted Seth's reverie.

"Er, I'm part of the crew, ma'am . . ."

"And a fine Portsmouth family he comes from," Nicholas added. "I've spent most of the voyage telling Seth to give up the sea and follow his profession. He is a talented sculptor and should study under a master when he gets back."

Anne suddenly got up and rushed into the captain's cabin. When she came back, she had a book of plates in her hands. Sliding it in front of Seth, she waited expectantly for his reaction. Hardly had Seth glanced at the title when they immediately immersed themselves in the illustrations, she discussing her favorites and he his. The book was a superb edition of Giovanni Piranesi's engravings of Greek and Roman classical sculpture.

Maude Griswold hadn't seen her daughter so content and radiantly happy in months, if ever before. At least she hadn't noticed before. For a moment she felt misgivings about Anne going aboard the *Alchemist*, but remembered her first time alone with Thomas Griswold, aboard a Baltimore pilot schooner. Also sixteen years old she was, and Thomas, midshipman who'd claimed to be 'practically seventeen,' was no less a stranger than young Seth Mason. Maude chided herself for foolishness and rejoiced at the good fortune that had come into Buena Yerba Cove.

CHAPTER FOURTEEN

Dressed in fresh seaman's togs, convicts Ben Hurley and Rob Stewart sat on a bench in the yard behind "Whale Whiskers" Moran's saloon on Pacific Street. Below the ancient oak from which 'The Shades' saloon derived its name, was an assortment of nautical objects: ship's wheel, capstan, binnacle, knighthead. A lithographed diagram of a full-rigged sailing ship was nailed to the massive oak's trunk. To the right of the tree, a thirty-foot mast had been erected, complete with a yardarm, spanker spar, ratlines, halyards and a mahogany fife rail about the base.

Beefy Ed Moran took a cow's horn from a peg on

the mast and set it carefully down on the footworn grass. "Now, Ben, you go first and git up and walk twice around that horn—and be careful not to kick off the silver tip. Atsa boy, Ben . . . Now, come on, Rob, you'd ought to be sober enough to do th' same thing. Jest twice now, an' we'll set down agin and learn all about the parts of a ship. Got to have at least a couple 'o Moran's boys look like sailors."

"Ah don't savvy whut this here cow's horn is doin' on a boat, but if ah see one ahl sure walk 'round it," Rob said. He scratched his bald head, finished his second round and sat down again.

Timothy Wiley slapped his thighs, laughing. "You jes' wait, you ol' cracker. You'll find out on the *Alchemist* fer sure."

The blazing orange sun had dipped behind Telegraph Hill and the forest of mast tops appeared aflame, casting long, spidery shadows on the calm, darkening bay. *Alchemist* lay content, her water tanks brimming and pantry full. Her brightwork glistened and the rigging had been tuned. The crew, exhausted from a week of carousing ashore, and some days of holystoning and varnishing afterwards, were asleep to a man, except for the duty watch. There was hardly a dollar left of three month's wages. Chloroform Clara and her bevy of brothel beauties on Pacific Street had seen to that.

Cleo Penhallow had just taken a hot bath in the cast-iron tub aft of the day cabin. Snug in a robe, she was looking forward to a good night's sleep before weighing anchor at dawn. The dinner had gone well the night before and she was happy to have a companion aboard, even a sixteen-year-old girl. A change of conversational topics was indeed welcome. Still, there was a yearning within her, a flame fanned by the warm bath and coziness of her bedroom. There had been no time, no privacy with Mark. And Chips Swasey had fixed the panel. No longer was there any danger of being spirited off. She thought of the affair with Seth Mason, closed her eyes and imagined him sitting on her bed once more, and then became instantly jealous of Anne Griswold. She countered with her memories of the nights with Mark, in Panama. She dared wonder what it would have been like, had Harry Taggart and retarded Bruce . . . There was something about sexual violence that intrigued her. There must be a median where love can be pleasantly violent. But where? But who?

A knock came on the door. "It's Sam Hadley."

Cleo combed her hair quickly and, after a look in her vanity mirror, walked into the day cabin. "I thought you'd be at the gold fields by now. Did you change your mind—or lose your money already?"

"Let me in; I want to talk to you. Just for a minute."

Cleo unlatched the door and let it swing open, then waited across the cabin. "Come in, but you can't stay long."

"I promise." Sam, wearing buckskin, shut the door behind him. "I came on Ed Moran's boat. He's brought you some new sailors. Most of them are drunk . . ."

"What do you want, Sam?"

"Come with me, Cleo. There's no reason that it can't be like it was once. There's no point going back to Wiburd. Be sensible. You never loved him, and there's nothing you can do for him. Stay here and we can build a whole new life—an empire." Sam reached for Cleo, but she evaded him.

"I thought you were coming back to Portsmouth to build the *Nightingale*. You promised your uncle—"

"That depends on how things go. Besides, the

plans are complete and the money is being advanced. The yard can do without me. I've done a great deal of thinking since leaving New York. Cleo, you always were a gambler. What do you think of building ships on the west coast? Here, in San Francisco. Somebody's got to do it.''

"Sam, I'm not going back for Wiburd.''

"Then it's true—you and Mark . . .''

"No, Sam; it may look that way, but I'm going back for Cleopatra Smith. It's all over.''

Sam looked down into Cleo's green eyes and chucked her lightly under the chin. "Okay, Queenie . . . Good luck.'' He turned and abruptly left the cabin. Cleo listened to his footsteps as he went up the companionway to the quarterdeck. "Queenie,'' she reminisced. Sam used to call her that back in Portsmouth when the townsfolk whispered about them. She felt a tinge of fondness for those carefree years, then shrugged it off and got into her berth. When she was lonely, there was always one gentleman to share her bed. Cleo turned up the oil lamp and opened a book by the mathematician Nathaniel Bowditch. It was a treatise called *New American Practical Navigator*. It was Cleo's intention to surprise Mark on the voyage back by observing and determining the sun's altitude.

Mark, with his analytic mind, was one of the most skillful users of the nautical sextant of his time. It was the science of motion that fascinated him—the part that was measureable in finely engraved numbers and vernier calibrations on polished steel and brass. It was a precision that was coming to perfection in the machine rather than the effect of wind on canvas, and nowhere was it more pronounced than in the steam engine. Yes, she would have to prove that a woman could understand the mechanical principles of power and motion if her dream was to succeed. And she would start with the science of navigation, a practical pursuit.

As she studied the text and diagrams, voices filtered down from deck, and the gang board rattled against the hull. Matthew and Mark were handling the purchase of seamen to replace those who had run off to the diggings. And it was indeed "purchase," with the procurer, "Whale Whiskers" Moran, being paid with the advanced wages of his drunken charges. And it was "legal" since the procurer had documents to show that the seamen were only paying back what they owed by signing over their wages. The signatures or marks had been generally affixed after a glass or two of "Miss Piggott's"—a concoction of whiskey, brandy, gin and opium.

Five besotted men lay on deck near the gangway where they had been dumped by Moran's Kanaka musclemen. Two others were less pickled, having managed to stumble aboard under their own steam and brace themselves against the rail.

"You wanted bodies, here ye be. Swilled at the present time," drawled Whale Whiskers, "but hard workers by the mornin' light."

Striding back and forth at their feet, Matthew looked at each man in turn, until he saw a sign of life. A cough, a grunt, a movement. For a moment he was concerned with one of them. The body hadn't moved. He was just about to kneel down and examine the figure closely when the man's chest moved. Then his arm stirred.

"Take 'em forward and put 'em in fo'c'sle bunks to sleep it off," Matthew ordered the Kanakas, and handed Moran a quantity of gold coin. "And these two?" He referred to Hurley and Stewart. "They seem the best of the lot."

"The best to be had in all the city," said Moran, raising his right hand. "I swear by my mother's grave and all the Saints. May I be struck dead if what I say is not the truth. Both Ben and Robby have been around the Horn."

"Twice," stammered Rob Stewart proudly.

By midmorning, *Alchemist* had made fifteen miles southing, and was abeam of San Pedro Point. The Golden Gate and the peninsula hills had disappeared into a gray mist. Seaward, off the bow, a dark squall line was approaching. From the deckhouse and fo'c'sle filed the crew to their posts on the braces and clewlines for shortening sail. One by one, the royals were drawn up to the yards, then the t'gallants and the flying jibs taken in, as the black-hulled clipper heeled in the mounting breeze and pitched into a contrary sea that sent spumes of spray over the bow.

The recruits had been put to the simpler tasks—all but one, who still lay in his bunk, shivering and twitching. "There's no telling what the poor beggar had drunk before he was shanghaied," shouted Wayne Devers, as he passed the deckhouse and picked an apple out of a wooden tub, to the wrath of Paddy Dooley.

" 'Ere now, ye napper, the apples are for ducking. It's Hallowe'en. Don't ye 'ave no respect?"

"Respect?" Juho Kokko the Finn repeated as he looked into the galley. "You call this respect? Children's games. This is the feast day of Saman, Lord of Death, an observance of the day he called together the wicked souls that within the past twelve months had been condemned to inhabit the bodies of animals."

"Begone with your black visions, you swill-bellied prophet," railed the Irishman. "Tend to your canvas instead of the devil."

Joe Lavender, leaving his steaming pot of potatoes, ventured to the galley door. ''Is Captain Panhallow's soul in his albatross? It must have gone somewhere.''

''An albatross ain't an animal; it's a bird.'' Dooley's face reddened upon realizing what he'd said. The subject was squelched by a commotion on deck. Matthew Hadley, closely followed by boson Spicer, rushed past and went into the fo'c'sle.

''He's dead, but still he moves,'' Daniel Spicer lamented. ''There's no mistaking; his hand is cold— and that odor . . .'' The bosun held his sleeve over his nose.

Matthew reached into the bunk and threw the thin blanket aside, then unfastened the body's shirt buttons. The body twitched and its sleeves rippled. Suddenly a rat's head appeared from under the man's shirt and the rodent scurried out, ran over the body's face and behind the bunk. Another flurry of movement in a sleeve and two more rats slithered out. The two men shrank back, horrified.

Now the body was still; the tremors had stopped. There was nothing that could be said. Only man could conceive of such vile, irreverent deception.

Matthew felt sick that night—and for weeks and months thereafter as the image kept recurring. The rats, the body, the twitching. It appeared in his sleep and at the helm, in the mountains of Ecuador and the copper-rich ranges beyond Valparaiso.

Neither did the storms of Cape Horn erase or diminish the apparition. In the waves, in the clouds, superimposed on the familiar heights of Boston, and on the Piscataqua below Portsmouth—Matthew Hadley would be captive to these grotesque images for the rest of his days.

BOOK II

*Portsmouth-built ships and New York merchants—
the superiority of the one is equalled only by the
enterprise of the other. Possessed of the former,
the latter may safely defy the competition of the
world.*

—*Toast at a Portsmouth launching, 1851*

CHAPTER ONE

It was a time of deep snows in the Piscataqua valley of down-East New Hampshire—a time for felling the tall mast pine. Two hundred years of plundering the forests for this noble tree, the majority having been marked by British "timber cruising agents" with a three-pronged arrow symbol as "Reserved for His Majesty's Use," had pushed the foraged perimeters far upriver, into the ice-ravaged, swift tributaries.

The Revolutionary War had terminated the British contract with New Hampshire's forests, but not before the masts that carried Nelson's sails at Trafalgar had cleared the harbor. Such was the preference and dependence on Piscataqua mast pine that many a British man-of-war, during the revolution and after it, had suffered both in battle and storm for the lack. Though less strong when first cut than Norway pines, the American product retained its natural juices longer, and, consequently, its strength and durability.

Matthew Hadley had arrived home in time to accompany a timber gang to a remote stand of pine in the foothills of the Moose Mountains, near the headwaters of the Cochecho River below Merrymeeting Lake. He had brought rough drawings and specifica-

tions for the pine spars and white oak beams, and
pieces as a guide for cutting down trees of adequate
sections and proper bends which would be further
sawed and trimmed after curing. Dressed in leather
and homespun—more Boone than Hadley—he looked
up in awe at the two hundred-foot pine that had been
selected for *Nightingales's* mainmast. Branchless, until the top, it was capped by a green cone that caught
the afternoon sunlight.

So tall a "stick," without any limbs nearer the
ground than a hundred or so feet, was in danger of
breaking in the fall. With deep snow, the danger was
much less, as the rocks were covered and a natural
soft bed lay on the ground to receive the tree.

After felling, the pine was cut in the "mast
proportion": three feet in length for every inch of its
diameter. The base, measuring thirty-four inches, called
for a total lower mast length of one hundred two feet,
which allowed for adequate trimming to a final ninety-
two, as specified in the rigging plans. There would
be a total of about five hundred feet of spars thicker
than eighteen inches, and another eight hundred feet of
spars under eighteen inches needed for the rigging—
some sixty pieces to cut from Piscataqua pine. Once
felled, the trees were immediately stripped of bark to
prevent worms from getting in. Each piece was marked
and recorded before being put on sleds for the long
journey to the iced-in Cochecho. The task of pulling
was laid to the diligent and patient New England ox.
Well trained and handled, the powerful animal was a
mainstay of the deep-forest timber trade. The largest
mast sections needed teams of up to sixty oxen to
haul them on sleds, and great skill was demanded of
the handlers in descending slopes.

After a week of such work, Matthew was beginning to yearn for the sea again. He missed his brother,
who had raised their father's ire by suggesting that

Hadley's Yard build a steam-powered vessel. An argument ensued, and Mark had left for Boston.

Satisfied that the spars were in the best of condition once they were lashed into rafts on the ice and ready to be driven downstream upon the ice breaking in spring, Matthew joyously galloped back south along the Piscataqua. He rode thirty-five miles, through Dover and Sawyer's Mills, and over the bridge to Canney's Cove. Matthew was elated, being on the wrong side of the river, for he was not heading for the Hadley Yard below Mast Cove—he was headed for Portsmouth, the home of a young lady.

The gray-shingled saltbox stood proudly on the south end of Mechanics Street, far enough from the elegant Wentworth House to be inconspicuous to the socially prominent of the day, who turned up their noses at tar-barrel smells, joiner-shop shavings and the traffic around Emery's South End Mill.

To one side of the front entrance hung a wooden sign with raised and painted lettering within a border of scrollwork:

S H I P
C A R V I N G
Upstairs

Matthew tethered his mount to a post and rapped with a polished brass door knocker. In the form of a whale, and pivoting against a plate, the knocker had been fashioned and cast by Woodbury Souther Mason, father of Seth, Liz, and four younger children.

There was no response, so Matthew went around to a side stairway and up to the loft, the entrance of which was a double door. One of the doors was accessible from a platform, while the other, with a boom and tackle above it, was used for hoisting heavy blocks of pine and lowering finished figureheads to a wagon below.

Woodbury Mason had married very young and, soon becoming a father, applied himself to many pursuits in augmenting his earnings as a shipcarver. At various times he had managed a farm, run a livery stable, and carried mail twice a day from Portsmouth Pier to Dover and back. In providing for his growing family while perfecting his sketching and carving techniques, Woodbury started his workday at four every morning, save Sunday. It was rare that the lights in his loft went out before ten at night.

"Surprise!" shouted Matthew as he entered. "Where is everybody?" He walked through a maze of figureheads in various stages of completion. On the walls were billet heads, gilded trailboards and stern ornaments. At the far end of the loft, a cauldron of glue bubbled on a cast-iron wood stove.

Seth Mason got up from a work bench where he had been pounding gold alloy into small gilding sheets. He placed a finished sheet carefully between pages of a small book and greeted his friend. "Welcome back to civilization," jested Seth dourly.

"What's wrong? Where's Beth—and your father?"

"Beth drove him up to see Doc Paxon."

"Your father needs a rest."

"I feel responsible," Seth said, looking down at his hands. "I went away when he needed me. All that time at sea . . ." He picked up a mallet and slammed it on the workbench. "Sorry," Seth apologized and walked over to a newly carved figure of a bearded man wielding a primitive wooden club, hanging from a ceiling beam by block and tackle. He swung it round slowly. "It's for a naval frigate; I carved the bearskin and the club."

Matthew examined the piece. "If you hadn't told

me, I would have thought it was all Woodbury's work."

"Thanks, Matt. Shipcarving can be rewarding once you're working on the figurehead. I was getting tired of carving trailboards and quarterboards." Seth took a chisel from the bench and pried some chips from the rough-hewn mounting behind the warlike figure.

"I suppose you'll not be going to be apprenticed to the Philadelphia sculptor this year. Perhaps after Woodbury has finished his assignments . . ." Matthew looked out of the window facing up Mechanics Street and hoped that Liz would return soon. He was expected back at the yard after a week in the forest. William Hadley would not understand such a detour by his faithful son. Not after Mark had left.

Seth thought about Anne Griswold, the girl he'd met in San Francisco who sailed back aboard the *Alchemist* with him. No, he wouldn't go to Philadelphia this year. Perhaps it was better this way. He was still only seventeen. There was time yet. Yes, after his father finished his assignments. An odd feeling suddenly came over him. He imagined that the figureheads in the loft were laughing at him, talking with one another, chiding him. The wooden mouths were moving. Now and then a hand would point at him. He caught a whisper from the wooden tribunal . . .

"Woodbury Mason will never be finished . . . never be finished . . ."

Seth shook his head. He opened a window and let the cold air rush in from the river, from the "inalong" and the "outalong" of the harbor channels. He'd forgotten the grogging effect of boiling glue without proper ventilation.

South Pond, with Emery's Mill as a sentinel, was swarming with the town's young ice revelers.

Skates, sleds and shoes—there were no rules, each mode of sliding having its own charms and falls, bruises, sprains and wet consequences. The Badgers kids, the Blunts and the Goodriches, Hickeys, Laightons, Louds, Peduzzis, Sweetsers and Wendells were all there after school was out on a Friday. Snowballs, iceballs and snowdrifts were the weapons of the day, and narry a little girl of grade-school age dared to venture within a block of the pond.

A sky-blue wheelbarrow followed the snow ruts along Pleasant Street. It was pushed by a lean, wizened man whose vacant white face seemed always canted to the sky, eternally oblivious of everything, yet proceding with a heaven-borne instinct straight and unswerving toward his destination. So unconscious was the trundler that many a small boy would jump into the wheelbarrow, whether containing deliveries or not, and gain a ride without the proprietor's knowledge.

The barrow pusher was a man at least old enough to be the father of a skater. Appearing quite suddenly the preceding fall, with his sky-blue wheelbarrow, he was at first thought to be a prankster left over from Hallowe'en. But he persisted through the year-end holidays, carrying produce and goods on his barrow until his prominent family tightened the reins.

It became more and more infrequent that the unearthly wheelbarrow and its owner haunted the streets of Portsmouth. But when he did appear, the schoolboys of the town made the most of it.

"Wiburd, come on. The ice is great fun," they enticed him in unison, and he, clapping his cold hands in moronic glee, let the sky-blue barrow roll down the icy embankment and skid across the frozen pond, where it became at once the object

of a winter game in which Wiburd Penhallow was
the other team. He chased and slid and fell until
he was the image of father winter—and until the
Penhallow's servant, a freeman Negro called Primus,
rescued him.

CHAPTER TWO

The vertical, black, sparless bow of the Collins Lines'
steamship *Atlantic* cut through the late August swells
south of Newfoundland. The roseate sky ahead was
dimming and the wheeling Dipper jousted with a
waxing moon for dominance of the evening. With an
occasional porthole sparkling on her dark hull and the
long deckhouse ablaze with festivity, the wooden
vessel, displacing three times the tonnage of a large
clipper ship, was bound for New York City, out of
Liverpool. Her stark lines, high funnel and churning
paddlewheels were anachronously disjointed from the
three raked masts, two of which were stepped far aft,
away from the belching stack. Each mast was gaff-
rigged for spankers, the foremast having, in addition,
a main and topsail yard. No gilded trailboards or
stern pieces graced the long hull, though at the peak
of its bow, almost invisible because of its tiny size, a
bust of Poseidon looked solemnly westward.

"Half speed ahead." Captain James Wald, former master of the sailing packet *Shenandoah*, ordered his second officer.

"Half speed ahead," repeated Mark Hadley into the speaking tube of the engine room. He wore a smart uniform with brass buttons, as did the complement of Edward Knight Collins' new flagship.

On deck, Bosun Paddy Dooley called out orders to let fall and sheet home the spankers. As fore 'n aft sails filled and drew, the engines were eased down to mute the sound and vibration for the occasion of a gala concert by the Swedish Nightingale, Jenny Lind, who had been contracted by Phineas T. Barnum for a tour of America. The shipboard concert had been arranged by Barnum's agent, John Wilton, with the ticket proceeds to go toward establishing a merchant seaman's benevolent fund.

Mark Hadley, whose duties as second officer included keeping the ship's log, entered the following for Thursday, August 29, 1850:

> *6:00 PM, Lat. 44 54'N, Long. 48 27'W. Dist. 24 Hrs. 311 Miles. Coal Used, 39.2 T. Passed several vessels fishing off the Banks. Light airs SSW. 8:30 PM, 3/4 Moon and clear. Eased engines & set spankers for Miss Jenny Lind benefit concert. Light Breeze SSW 3*

Contrary to the austere mechanical outer appearance, the interior was a palace. Cabins and saloons were paneled in white holly, satinwood and teak, skillfully combined and inlaid. Gilded columns and pilasters reached up to high ceilings covered with mirrors.

Stained glass windows alternated with wall mirrors for scintillating effects within bronze frames emblazoned with ancient marine and mythological symbols. Scores of burnished gold oil lamp supports lined the saloons, sparkling by day as well as night. All around the cabin hung portrait paintings of the nation's founders and heroes, "in the very highest style of art," according to advertisements of the period. The drawing rooms were plushly carpeted and furnished with sofas and green marbled tables.

The grand saloon featured an allegorical oil surrounded by stars and eagles which depicted the "female figure of Liberty gracefully trampling on a feudal prince."

Aft of the spacious dining room was a gentleman's smoking cabin and a genuine barber shop, complete with bottles of colored tonic and a patent adjustable cushioned chair. Even the spittoons had been disguised as bronze sea shells.

Staterooms were steam heated and had hot and cold running water as well as call bells for the stewards, a far cry from the Cunard Lines' *Britannia*, of which Charles Dickens only eight years prior had written: ". . . an utterly impracticable, thoroughly hopeless and profoundly preposterous box," adding that his bed "was like a shelf" and "nothing smaller for sleeping in was ever made except for coffins." He later complained that he had expected the accommodations of the *Britannia* to be as spacious and comfortable as was depicted in the agent's highly varnished lithographic pictures.

The *Atlantic* was justifiably proud of its cuisine. The menu was a replica, in content, of New York's famous Delmonico Restaurant. It featured green-turtle soup, turkey in oyster sauce and goose in champagne sauce. Fruit and vegetables were kept fresh in ice stored in a special room. Each Collins liner carried forty tons of ice on every trip. The desserts, coffees and service were all of the most luxurious persuasion. While the British Cunard Lines had proved steamships reliable and swifter than sail under most conditions, Collins had made ocean travel comfortable.

Edward Knight Collins had been born on Cape Cod, son of a sailing captain and his wife, herself the niece of a British admiral. Upon his father's death, he carried on the family shipping business in South Street of New York's clipper row. After his success with the Dramatic Lines, he acquired a mail subsidy from the government, for which he agreed to build a fleet of steamships to compete with Cunard. The *Atlantic* was his prototype. Collins had sold his sailing fleet and changed to steam. New York City built more steam tonnage than sail in 1850 and so went the entire nation and the Navy.

As had Captain Wald of the *Atlantic*.

And Mark Hadley's dream was becoming a reality. He had discussed it with Cleo Penhallow in Boston. He would learn everything he could about the *Atlantic*, under actual conditions, while she was to find a convenient place to build a steamship in the city. Between crossings he was to accompany her and consider the options. It was Cleo's idea. She had the money.

Moon now high and sea shining, the side-lever engines idled softly and the long liner skimmed toward New York under a warm quartering breeze as the diminutive nightingale sang a mellifluous *Casta Diva*. Next, the Italian baritone, Giovanni Belleti, joined her in a duet with Rossini's *Il Turco in Italia*, and she closed with the popular Swedish ballad, *The Herdsman's Song*.

Sir Julius Benedict, acclaimed pianist and conductor,

was the accompanist on a splendid Broadwood pianoforte, bought in London for P.T. Barnum and Jenny Lind by Baring Brothers, the showman's financial representative in England. Sir Julius was to realize $25,000 for one hundred performances and the baritone $12,500, while Jenny was to receive $1000 for each appearance.

The curtain call ovations reverberated throughout the ship, muffling the massive ninety-five-inch diameter engine cylinders as they chugged faster with enormous nine-foot strokes and the thirty-foot paddlewheels bit into the sea. Spankers brailed against their masts and, with sparks flitting from the funnel, the reveling flagship raced into the veering wind at better than twelve knots.

Amused at the allegorical oil on the paneled wall behind the performers, a stocky, curly-haired gentleman in evening attire applauded politely among the clamorous ladies and escorts. Raising from his chair, he noted Barnum's theatrical agent, John Hall Wilton, as he tallied the concert's receipts. Turning his gold nugget ring playfully on his finger, David Montebianco slipped out of the grand saloon and walked pensively toward the first-class cabin stairway. Once in his cabin, he laid out his gold and silver coins in preparation for the nightly poker game in a secluded stateroom that was furnished for such occasions. The participants were all rich or at least capable of high stakes. It had taken several days to organize the participants, to discard the pretenders and obvious cheats and to come to a businesslike understanding.

He picked up a claim check that had lodged among his coins and set it aside. It bore a claim number, the claimant's name and cabin number, as well as a description of the baggage and its location in the hold:

Montebianco, David A-23
Coffin bearing deceased Male, embalmed
Destination: New York City

The card game of American poker had created a sensation when introduced into England by way of ocean packet travel in the 1840s. An offshoot of England's primitive game of *brag*, it was further developed by the Germans, who called it *pochspiel*, and brought to the Louisiana Territory as *poque*. The game traveled upriver on the Mississippi steamboats and was adapted to the fifty-two card deck from the original twenty-card game by 1837. It was a gambling game that traveled well, and the nation was on the move.

The midwatch had just gone off, and the game was still in progress. First officer George Adams stopped by in the deserted ship's galley for coffee, where, to his delight, he found Sally Baines, a former dance-hall girl who had been signed aboard as hostess for such occasions as demanded more than the Negro stewards.

"Who's winning?" asked Adams, ogling Sally's daring costume.

"Wilton."

"Again?" The first officer moved behind the shapely girl and slipped his hand around her hip as she arranged a tray of cakes. She pushed his hand away and filled a coffee pitcher from an elaborately decorated silver urn.

"You like people with gold and money, eh?" Adams was angry and forced her against the pantry counter. "If I catch you playing up to another man—I'll kill both of you." He gripped Sally with his weathered hands and kissed her harshly over her open bodice. She didn't respond and it made him more furious. "You're mine, damn you," he said, slipping his hand lower on her body until he found his way under her short, dancing skirt.

"Stop, George . . . I'm warning you," she pleaded.

The gruff seaman persisted, bending her back over the counter and clawing at her body. Sally's hand reached out blindly, and felt the serving tray . . . the coffee pitcher.

There was a loud scream as the first officer twisted away, rubbing his back in agony from the scalding coffee. A flurry of activity rose in the adjacent cabins and sent Adams into retreat as he muttered threatening oaths at Sally and ran out on deck.

When Sally arrived at the smoke-filled stateroom, there was a strange stillness. The boisterous New York merchant and the tobacco importer from Liverpool sat cardless, dejectedly watching the financier and Barnum's agent playing out the richest hand of the evening. Towers of gold coin and a mass of bank notes lay in the center of the round, green-velveted table. Purposely dawdling, the provocatively clad hostess gathered up the empty glasses and liquor bottles, then set coffee and cakes next to each player.

John Wilton smilingly set his five cards face down.

Montebianco had discarded two cards and laid his remaining three on the table, also face down. The octagonally framed Ansonia Lever wall clock ticked all the louder for the silence in the room, its second-hand flitting quickly around a tiny calibrated dial that intersected the upside-down Roman numeral VI.

John Hall Wilton had won heavily, amassing all the stakes of the two businessmen as well as a good part of Montebianco's. The financier, however, had come prepared. He had called for an all-or-nothing pot with which to end the game. Wilton had hedged, but after his opponent discarded two cards, he'd matched the ante and bettered it. There was over $2000 in the pot. Sally stood next to Wilton—and why not? she thought. He'd promised to find her a lucrative stage contract and make her as famous as Lola Montez. Pressing into the agent's shoulder with her hips, she encouraged unseen pinches as the attention of all was on the gambling son of London's Sir Moses Montebianco. Wilton picked up his cards and, fanning them out, showed Sally the corner symbols. Full house— aces over kings. Wilton pushed his last one hundred dollars into the pot.

Montebianco drew two cards and inserted them among the cards lying before him. He palmed the hand, then secretively examined it. Without emotion, he counted out one hundred dollars in double eagles, then added another five hundred dollars.

John Wilton's face turned to chalk, and the deposed players, sensing a turn of fortune, leaned over expectantly.

"But I don't have . . ."

Montebianco gestured at the businessmen. "Gentlemen, would you mind letting us play this hand . . . alone?"

"We understand," the merchant replied, as he rose, "but please don't keep us in suspense." Sally Baines picked up her serving tray and followed them out of the stateroom.

After waiting a few minutes, the stocky banker handed Wilton a pencil and slip of paper. "Just give me your voucher for my bet. You still have the concert proceeds, no?"

The suave-spoken Englishman stroked his blond side whiskers, then signed the $500 voucher. As an itinerant gambler, Wilton knew something about odds.

His opponent, in keeping three cards, most probably had three of a kind, queens at best. The established odds of improving on three cards were about nine-to-one against completing a full house or making four of a kind. The chances of the latter alone were yet much more extreme. Since a full house would not beat his own hand, it would have to be four of a kind. The chances of being dealt the latter were of the order of four-thousand-to-one, as against seven hundred for a full house. Wilton's mind reeled with numbers—numbers distorted through a veil of Kentucky corn whiskey from the county of Bourbon. He decided that nine-to-one were good odds in any game—or war. Wilton dropped the slip of paper into the stakes, then sat back and waited.

The financier called in the other players, then laid his cards out on the table. Four treys and a jack.

The black sheep had won. And it was more than mere money. He had also won power—over another man . . . another world.

CHAPTER THREE

Cracking sounds like pistol shots parted the late March afternoon serenity of the snow-blanketed Cocheco valley and scattered the otters and beavers along the river's banks. In the lowlands, the fox and ruffled grouse scurried into the brush, while on the rock ledges and mountainsides, the wily lynx perked up his ears and the timberwolf slinked back to his lair.

As the ice gave way to spring and the cycle of nature was rekindled, so was the work of man. Massive rafts of mast pine, white oak and hatmatrack plunged into the swift, cold rivers to be guided downstream to the sawmills and shipyards of Piscataqua. Past the town of Dover and Perkin's wharf on the Cochecho sped the rafts consigned to Hadley's yards. Turning into the Newichawannock and down by the Elliot Shore, the rafts were hailed by sawyers, carpenters and tradesmen who gathered their tools and went down to the yards of Long Reach and Kittery, for they were raring to hew and build once again, and to earn the shipbuilder's wages after a spare winter and an increase in family.

After hauling the rafts ashore, the timbers were trimmed on four sides and steeped in scalding water to remove the sap. Next they were stacked carefully to allow dry air to season the logs before being saturated with solutions of metallic salts and zinc chloride as a precaution against dry rot. During ten months of seasoning and drying, the timber would lose as much as forty percent of its weight and up to eight percent of its dimension.

Sam Hadley had built only a few boats, using the facilities that had been in his family since before the Revolution. His grandfather had assisted James Hackett in the construction of the first ship-of-the-line, *America*, ordered by Congress in 1776 for the United States Navy. Before designing and building the *Cathay*, he'd built several clipper schooners, the *Lamartine* and *Sacramento*, as fast sailors for the Mediterranean fruit trade. The repeal of the British Navigation Acts in 1848 opened for the first time a chance for American ships to engage in commerce of foreign origin with Great Britain. Consequently, there was a rush in America to build ships large enough to carry profitable cargoes over long distances.

Hadley's yard was one of many to discontinue building small vessels, such as coasting schooners and barks, in favor of the swift clipper ship, which was in great demand by ambitious merchants. The yard's scheduled work for 1850 was a pilot schooner and a brigantine of three hundred tons for the fruit trade. These were the only vessels for which William Hadley had seasoned wood. His nephew, Sam, had left for the gold fields almost a year earlier after completing a half-model and specifications for an 1100 ton extreme clipper to be called the *Nightingale*.

On September 11th, 1850, Jenny Lind, the "Swedish Nightingale," gave her first American performance in the Castle Garden Theater, New York City.

P.T. Barnum, her American promoter, had auctioned seats for the performance. It was sold out for a record sum. A hatter named Genin paid $225 for the first ticket and became a celebrity.

Baron Louis Gerhard de Geer looked passionately across the elegantly set table. "You were simply glorious this evening, my dear." He reached his lace-cuffed hand toward Jenny's. The eyes of Delmonico's after-theater patrons flickered at the corner booth. "After this marvelous success, there is no question that your fame will be greater than Mademoiselle Rachel's. The entire world will clamor for the Swedish Nightingale." De Geer nodded and the *maitre d'* poured champagne.

"I have great admiration for Mademoiselle Rachel," the diminutive brunette of thirty years whispered—conscious of the stares about her. "Her beginnings were as difficult as my own. The difference between us is that she can be splendid when angry, but she is unsuited for tenderness. I am desperately ugly—and nasty, too, when angered—but I think I do better in tender roles. Of course, I certainly do not dare to compare myself with so fine an actress. She is immeasurably better than I. Poor me, with my potato nose. I am plain by comparison."

"You are too modest." The Baron raised his glass. "Let me propose a toast . . . To the Swedish Nightingale—and to the American Nightingale . . ."

"The *American*?" Jenny lowered her glass.

"It's a surprise. I have invested in a business in this country. I'm having a boat built—that is, I'm financing the building of a clipper ship in New Hampshire. That's a state that borders on Massachusetts. I stopped off at the shipyard after arriving in Boston. The boat shall be called the *Nightingale*, and it is to be ready in time to attend the opening of the Great Exhibition in London next spring.'' He took her white-gloved hand in his. ''This is to be my wedding present to Baroness Jenny de Geer. Don't say anything yet, my dear. Let me tell you a little about it.'' He felt her hand tug away. ''This will enhance your career. I'm sure your Mr. Barnum will give you a month's leave. He may even want to accompany you to the exhibition. Everyone who is anyone should be seen there. I've read that the Crystal Palace will be a spectacle beyond parallel. A million square feet of glass and three times the space of St. Paul's Cathedral, with over twelve thousand exhibitors.''

''I wish you hadn't,'' the singer answered with distress. ''That we have had an 'understanding' should not have bound you to do something rash.''

''Nonsense, my dear. This is a worthwhile venture. The vessel will be constructed to Lloyd's specifications and finished in the most expensive fashion. It will have luxurious accommodations for fifty first-class passengers—a proper way for the rich and famous to attend the exhibition.'' De Geer untied the laces of a portfolio he had brought with him. ''Here are some drawings I had done in New Hampshire by an excellent shipcarver.'' He laid two sheets on the table before Miss Lind. The *maitre d'* strained his neck for a view and a reporter from the *Tribune* swooped by.

''Quite flattering,'' Jenny said, as she studied one of the drawings, ''but isn't it a little risqué?''

''But it is taken from my favorite daguerreotype of you, and the bow of a clipper ship demands a certain *élan*. We are not in the Middle Ages. Now, shall we toast the Nightingales—and leave it at that? Regarding my proposal—''

''It is a grand gesture, and I'm tempted to say yes,

Louis—but my commitments do not allow me. There are so many needy and unfortunate souls in this world.''

"At least I haven't been rejected," replied the aristocratic Swede elatedly. "Perhaps you will write me when you are ready.''

Jenny smiled radiantly, as she could when undecided. One hundred concerts in all, and she'd only given her first two. She'd be traveling to many cities, to Cuba and Mexico. Within, she was afraid. It was all too good, and too easy, to last. And could she withstand the stress and discomforts of so arduous a tour? The Italian baritone had professed his love for her, which posed an extra dilemma, and Barnum had shown excesses in promotion that were beginning to embarrass her as an artist. The day after the first concert, the hatter, John Genin, who paid $225 for an auctioned seat, had to close his shop early after being sold out of merchandise. Mr. Genin was a friend of Phineas T. Barnum.

She raised the champagne to her lips and saw in the sparkling wine the face of Otto Goldschmidt, the young pianist who had often accompanied her on tour in Germany and was considered as good a pianist as the late Felix Mendelssohn, whom she had known in Leipzig. "To all the nightingales," Jenny toasted and drank.

CHAPTER FOUR

The half-model measured sixty-seven inches in length, which was one thirty-third of the planned length of the *Nightingale's* hull. One hundred and eighty-four feet long, the vessel's thirty-six-foot beam was represented by thirteen inches, which in the half-model measured six and one-half inches. Any measurement of the model, made of alternating horizontal layers of dark mahogany and light pine, could be multiplied by thirty-three in order to determine the full size of the particular measurement. Designed for a cargo-hold depth of twenty feet, it was a simple matter to calculate the depth of the model without using a yardstick. Twenty divided by the constant, thirty-three, gave six-tenths of one foot as the height of the model, from keel to deck. Samuel Hadley, Jr., understood this well when he whittled the model. So did Mark, who had a way with mathematics. But both were gone, and it was up to Matthew to oversee the transference of the model's measurements to full-scale drawings on the mold loft floor. Matthew's ability with numbers was restricted to navigation. But now he had to learn, and he enlisted the help of Elizabeth Mason, whose intended vocation, before her mother died, was that of a schoolmarm.

By lamplight they practiced laying out chalk lines of the various components of the ship's hull, so that the next day Matthew would feel confident enough to make suggestions in the mold loft as the craftsmen enlarged and outlined the ship's curves on the broad floor and applied templates of soft wood strips as guides for the precise sawing and shaping of the complex oak frame.

Thirteen-inch thick timbers were adzed into curves and rabbetted to lock into the scarfed keel timbers, then double-checked against the loft templates before being mortised and doweled to succeedingly smaller sections to make the complete rib. These were then dubbed and caulked before they were stacked in precise order of assembly.

The fifteen-inch oak sections of keel and keelson were scarfed with intricate locking tenons and keys to insure a firm longitudinal strength and base for the frame.

While the major timbers were being assembled, thousands of wooden peg fasteners called treen'ls were handsplit and trimmed to a standard inch-and-a-quarter diameter, then slotted and boxed till needed to "nail" the inside and outside planks to the ribs.

In the mast shed, a team of adz-wielders chipped at the pine timbers, first for the thirty-inch diameter lower masts, till smooth and true, then the topmasts and t'gallants in turn.

Rigging, hardware and anchors had been ordered from New York, and services such as painting and complex joiner work was ordered in advance. In the absence of the designer, Sam Hadley, a Captain T.A. Miller had been hired to design the interior arrangements and decorations.

*   *   *

On a bright day in early February, a team of snorting, steaming dray horses strained under a timber derrick rigged with heavy tackle and lowered the first section of keel onto blocks that had just been swept clear of a light snow. One by one, the horseshoe-shaped oak ribs, each twenty feet high by thirty-two in breadth and cross-braced, were raised into position and secured. Each rib was doubled at the bottom and faired open from chine to top with doweled space blocks as the ribs decreased in measure from fifteen inches square over the keel to eight inches at the tops. In all, 128 ribs were set onto the keel, the forward units being faired hollow in degrees toward the missing stem.

"Grog-hooo," the foreman cried out, as cold night descended over Hadley's yard. The dubbers, the joiners and caulkers, weary from the week's work and proud of completing the rib frame, came down from their scaffolds and queued up at the rum barrel for half-a-pint, a Saturday ritual.

At midnight, the full moon tide reached up the canted slipway of Hadley's yard and licked at the platform footings under the newly laid frame. White in the winter moonlight, the frame was a gigantic whale's skeleton lying on its long backbone and casting symmetrical patterns on the snow. The unearthly silence was broken by a crunching of snow crust as a solitary figure approached the slipway. Nimbly it climbed onto the platform and crossed over to the backbone, then walked slowly into the yawning skeleton.

Matthew Hadley took a small gold coin from his vest pocket and held it up to the moonlight, where it glinted briefly. Then he sat down on a midships frame and reached down to the keel, feeling for a hook-scarf joint. After several tries, he found the lateral joint and pressed his slim three-dollar gold piece into the caulking. It was a practice that had its roots in the shipbuilding of Scotland and was adhered to by the Hadleys. Good fortune would befall the builder who secreted a gold coin in his ship's keel, and what better fortune could there be than the safety and success of the *Nightingale*? With this boat would sail the future of Hadley's yard, and possibly his own as a master. Matthew would some day be captain of a vessel, but due to his lack of experience, he would not be given command of such an investment. Aside from the voyage around the Horn in the *Alchemist*, in which he proved himself as acting master on the return trip, he'd only been in charge of coasters.

The *Boston Journal* had run an advertisement:

TRANSATLANTIC EXCURSION TO LONDON
The elegant new clipper ship, Nightingale, 1100 tons burthen, commanded by Captain T.A. Miller, now building expressly for conveyance of passengers on the GRAND TRANS-ATLANTIC EXCURSION TO THE WORLD'S FAIR, landing the same at the port of Southampton, England, will be despatched from this port about May 20th. In the designing and construction of this splendid specimen of naval architecture, intended for this great mission, nothing will be overlooked. Parties, families and all who contemplate joining the excursion are informed that the model and drawings of the ship with a plan of cabin, staterooms and berths may be seen and rates of passage made known at the office of
DAVIS & COMPANY, 76 STATE STREET.

May 20th. Matthew shook his head annoyingly. Already late. The original plan was to sail on the

15th of April and arrive at Southampton by the opening of the exhibition on May 1st, or shortly thereafter. The boat was then to act as a floating luxury hotel during the passengers' stay, and then was to be utilized as a cruising yacht—the first big ship to be built for that purpose. He blamed himself for the lag in construction. He was not a builder. He knew little of schedules and procurement of services. Not that it was his job, but he felt responsible as a Hadley, regardless of the hiring of Captain Miller as construction superintendent by his father. If only his cousin had returned from California. If only his brother had not gone daft over steam. There was only one thing to do. Pray . . . and perhaps trust to luck. Matthew would do both. And he would sail as first mate under Miller. He would gain the experience for a command of his own, and, if he had a choice, it would be the *Nightingale*.

"Almighty God," Matthew spoke to the moon as if it were a diety, "I ask your help that I may be worthy of command of such a ship as this. Give me the strength to learn and to become reputable enough to deserve to be master. I will do anything—anything for such a chance . . ."

For a moment he became embarrassed that someone might have heard him—ranting in the moonlight. Was this the effect of the rum he'd had earlier? Matthew walked slowly on the backbone of the *Nightingale*. The ribs felt solid and dependable. After the Sabbath the keelson would be locked into position over the frame, concealing for all time the gold coin and satisfying the ancient dictum that the builder's luck be dependent on the fact that he alone knew the hiding place.

Matthew slept deeply in his small room above the mold loft, a peaceful sleep without the specters of slithering rats and frozen corpses lashed in the rigging. Neither did he hear the slosh of oars, nor see the blue wheelbarrow that nestled between the moonlit thwarts of a small skiff as it left the slipway for the dark town across the Piscataqua.

CHAPTER FIVE

TO SHIP OWNERS AND BUILDERS:
Plans, Models and Moulds of
Sailing Ships and Steamers,
furnished by
JABEZ T. COOK
Naval Architect
Cunningham's Wharf—East Boston
Please address orders to the Wharf,
or to Charlestown Post Office.

Cleopatra Penhallow had the clipping in her hand as she stormed down the People's Ferry gangplank at the foot of Border Street. Cunningham's Wharf was adjacent to the ferry slip and Cleo, after inquiring in a chandlery shop, went upstairs where she found Mr. Cook's office and a panoramic view of Boston Harbor.

"With such an interesting view, I'm surprised that you can concentrate on your work, Mr. Cook." Cleo noted a wall covered with plans, elevations and half-models. Mr. Cook, a dapper young man of twenty-four and a connoisseur of lines and form, took note of his visitor's, then described the points of interest visible from his bay window. "Over there is the Otis Tufts Wharf, where Boston's first iron tugboat was built. The sheds near it are foundries and engine factories."

"That was the *R.B. Forbes?*"

"It was. You are well-informed, Mrs. Penhallow."

"For a woman?" She smiled.

Somewhat taken aback, Cook said, "You've heard, then, of Donald McKay. His yards are just beyond that packet in the dry dock, and Samuel Hall's yard is just before that marine railway. He built the *Surprise* and the *Gamecock* after my designs. I'm now working with Curtis, in Medford and H.O. Briggs, nearby. Let me show you my new designs." Cook rummaged through a flat file drawer.

Jabez Treat Cook was the son of Jabez Moore Cook, eminent Portsmouth Naval Yard constructor, who, with the son of Joshua Humphreys, builder of the famed *Constitution*, designed the heavy corvette *Saratoga* and then, separately, the *Plymouth.* Cleo could hardly contain her excitement at being in such illustrious company. They looked at his latest designs and discussed the Piscataqua, where Cook had graduated from Portsmouth Academy ten years earlier.

"Yes, I know of the Hadley twins. The athletic one and his friends liked to bombard the Academy schoolyard with snowballs. They are related to a little boatyard up on Elliot Shore."

"Hadley's yard built the *Alchemist.* It was originally the *Cathay,* a sharp clipper of seven hundred and sixty tons. It was my husband's last command. He took ill on the way to San Fransicso and we sent him home by steamer from Panama. The athletic one is a fine sailing master; he handled the boat for the balance of the trip. His brother, Mark, is the one who is interested in steam navigation. He is presently employed as second mate aboard a Collins Line steamer, the *Atlantic*.''

"Excellent experience for the future captain . . ." Cook vacillated a moment. "Does Hadley's have facilities for building a steam vessel?"

"Mark and his father had a falling out. William Hadley believes steam a tool of the devil and he's convinced that iron can do nothing but sink. Will Hadley took over the yard after Sam, Sr., died and Sam, Jr., went to California aboard the *Alchemist* last year. Will is not as adventurous as his brother was."

"There seem to be too many Hadleys. I've lost track . . ." The naval architect spread several ships' plans on his table. "This is the *Surprise*. It was the first large clipper built outside of New York City. It's owned by the Low family and commanded by Phillip Dumaresque—and on the London to Canton run."

"Why didn't the Lows build in New York City?"

"All the yards were swamped with California clipper orders. I wish I could say it was because my designs were better than Griffiths' and the other New York people, but I was lucky to have Sam Hall as a builder. He gave me my first assignment—that is, after the steam tug. It was the bark, *Race Horse*, ordered by Mr. Forbes for the China trade. I met Mr. Forbes while working with Otis Tufts on the steam tug."

"What boat is this?" Cleo was startled by a drawing that looked very much like the *Alchemist*. The dimensions, tonnage and rigging were almost identical, but the plans bore no name.

"Just an idea. I provide plans on speculation occasionally, in the hope that a builder might procure a backer who has a need for a particular vessel. In the event of interest, I would develop the plans further to fit the need and the destination."

"Have you shown these plans to anyone in the Portsmouth vicinity?" Something had occurred to Cleo.

Jabez turned the sheet around and looked at notations on the back. "Ah yes, here we are . . . one set of drawings to George Raynes of North Mill Bridge. Why do you ask?"

"Forgive me, but it seems I'm mistaken. I thought I'd seen a similar boat on the Piscataqua."

"It's difficult to tell, because so much of the design is in the hull. One would have to see the boat in drydock to be sure." Cook collected the plans, then set down another series. "Your proposition does interest me, Mrs. Penhallow. Here are a few sketches I've done for steam-powered vessels. As yet, I have not been commissioned to do one, but I'm very anxious. The future lies with screw propulsion. Paddlewheels are fine for calm waters and rivers without waves, but put a paddlewheel steamer in an Atlantic squall and half the time one wheel will be out of the water." Jabez got up and demonstrated with his arms. "Let's pretend my elbows are the bottoms of side paddlewheels . . ." He pumped his arms rhythmically back and forth as he scooted around his studio. "Now a big wave comes and I tilt over, like this." One of his arms increased its velocity and he spun around in a circle. "You see what happens? The paddlewheel that's in the water becomes a pivot and the boat goes out of control, frequently broaching with disastrous effects. Even if the steamer isn't destroyed or run aground, can you imagine the loss of way and waste of coal and time over an extended period—to say nothing of the passengers' distress?"

Cleo was thrilled by his appearance as much as by his performance. She loved his lank, sandy hair with its turned-in ends, his blue tail-coat and damson-flowered silk waistcoat, his pale buff trousers with green stripes and his flamboyantly careless royal blue scarf necktie. How different this man was from the others—Wiburd, Seth Mason and Mark. He was happy with his lot, and a product of talent and good breeding. Yet his hands were those of a worker rather than a dandy, while his attitude bordered on the mischievous.

"So . . ." Cook sat down at his desk across from Cleo. "What we want is a twin-screw steamboat." He twirled a set of brass dividers playfully over a drawing. "But to build a steamboat to compete with Collins or Cunard is quite out of the question considering the money you are prepared to spend. Sixty thousand may build a thousand-ton clipper, but it will take double that to build a steamer of the same tonnage. Until engines and boilers are made in quantity, the price will remain very high."

"I will borrow against my investment," Cleo replied. "What can I have built for a hundred thousand?"

Cook scribbled with a pencil. "One hundred and fifty feet overall, and about seven hundred tons."

"And you would recommend coastal passenger service?"

"I doubt that the Panama run will continue long enough. It will take eighteen months to build your steamer. And then, no matter what you decide, there will be great competition and vested interests. It will be extremely difficult for a newcomer in a declining market. Don't forget the railroad. It's growing faster than shipping . . ." Cook was sketching a world globe on his pad while talking. He suddenly drew a symbolic steamship on the globe. "There is one possibility, and a very lucrative one at that for a small steam vessel." He turned the pad to face his prospective client. Behind the steamer, he'd indicated a shoreline and labeled it. *CHINA*. "The proper boat could return its original cost in one year. I know of a merchant who would be interested in such a boat. If my own business were more profitable, I would think of backing the venture myself."

"Why can't you get the merchant to pay for the boat, if it's that good an idea?" Cleo primped her long raven curls.

"Secrecy." Jabez became very serious.

"The venture sounds illegal."

"Not in the least. It is simply good busines not to let one's business competition in on a profitable new idea. If this merchant were to build such ship, it would be plain to his adversaries as to the reason, and they might very well do the same thing. One can't build an invisible steamer in Boston."

"Mr. Forbes has offices in Canton."

"There are several companies in Canton," replied Cook.

"Can you tell me more? What cargos, or passengers—and which ports? I should discuss this with Mark when the *Atlantic* is in New York."

"I can tell you that there will be some risk from pirates in the South China Sea, but the steamer I would like to build will be able to outrun any craft in the area, even on one screw. The pirates sail small craft and depend on catching cargo schooners in the calms by rowing. A screw steamer will have an advantage over the paddlewheel in going from doldrum to monsoon. The boat now in use is a paddlewheeler, and it is underpowered. Should you be interested in a profitable application of your intended vessel in the China trade, I can arrange for you to discuss it first with the merchant."

Cleo picked up her sable muff and waited for Jabez to fetch her matching cloak from the entrance clothesrack. "Please do arrange a meeting as soon as possible, Mr. Cook." Cleo handed him a card. "I shall be at this address during the next week. Thereafter I have business in New York City, and will return on the first of March. I want you to design me a steamship."

CHAPTER SIX

Charleston, 18 March, 1851

My Dear Louis:

The tour has been marvelous beyond all expectations. All four concerts in Baltimore were to capacity houses. After the performance in Washington, President Fillmore left his card at my hotel. The next evening I spent at the White House as his guest, sharing with his family a most memorable experience.

Mr. Barnum has been extremely generous, and seems to have made it his first object to see me satisfied.

I know how you have been awaiting my answer, so please forgive this hasty note. I just can't pretend any longer. Your proposal has been on my mind before and after every concert, and I have given it great consideration. I must now confess that I cannot accept, as I have just pledged myself to another, a composer I have known for some years. It was only with our separation when I came to America that I realized my love for him.

His name is Otto Goldschmidt, and he is coming to New York to join the tour as my accompanist. Sir Benedict will leave to honor a commitment in London. I trust you will understand that it is better this way, for I cannot leave my career, nor ever subject you to it.

Of all the compliments, I will treasure yours the most, and will understand if you choose to change your mind. With songs, poems, gloves and whiskeys named for me—even a race horse and a deck of playing cards—I am fondest of lending my name to a clipper ship. Should you desire that I participate in the launching, I promise to practice with a bottle of champagne, since I'm sent so much of it.

How I do look forward to returning to Sweden and introducing you to Otto. We shall all become the best of friends. Thank you for being so gracious and patient.

Affect'ly,
Jenny

"I'm sorry to hear of your former husband's incurable condition, Mrs. Penhallow, but you did your best."

"Please call me Miss Smith; it is all legal now, especially in terms of contract. My transactions from now on will have nothing to do with the Penhallow family or name."

"Very sensible. One as charming and resourceful as yourself should act without encumbrances." David Montebianco handed Cleo a fountain inkhorn pen and pointed to a space on a prepared document. "I wish you a handsome profit on this venture, and I naturally look forward to financing, in part, your next vessel as well."

"I hope I won't need help after this."

"An astute approach." The stocky financier adjusted the spectacles on his sharp nose and observed his client's *en coeur* neckline. Her body was rippling and young—alive under a fashionable mauve basquined bodice and a matching skirt tiered with ruffled flounces. So feminine, yet so forward. He caught a whiff of lavender; never had the offices of Gibbs & Co. smelled so sweet. Montebianco's narrowed eyes feasted upon her, from her stylish coiffure down to a black patent shoe with a carmine rosette protruding from under her skirt. His heart thumped with fantasies born of being alone with an idol.

Flustered at being caught by her sagacious stare, he dawdled with his papers and stashed some into the pigeonholes of his roll-top desk. "You'll find no better terms in the entire city. I am independent and can set my own rates. Of course, you are a special friend. Your generosity to me aboard the *Alchemist* has earned you many favors. Now, enough of business; why don't we become better friends? Surely if you plan to stay a few days in the city, you will find time to dine with me—especially on the occasion of our transaction. Tomorrow evening?"

"I already have an engagement."

"Then tonight?"

Cleo Smith nodded curtly.

They went to the Astor and devoured aspic de canvasback, salad beans with truffles and a truffled ice cream. Encountering August Belmont, a client of mutual continental banking consorts, David was invited to attend a demonstration by the celebrated Fox sisters at the residence of Dr. Rufus Griswold, a leading New York literary figure. Originally promoted by the efforts of James Fenimore Cooper, William Cullen Bryant and Horace Greeley because of their reputed ability to contact the nether world of departed spirits in the town of Rochester, they had incited a craze for clairvoyants and mediums. The newspapers called it "Rochester Rappings."

The two young sisters, Margaret and Kate, sat on a sofa in Dr. Griswold's posh library. Shortly thereafter, rappings were heard from under the floor, then from the table and other parts of the room. No one among the dozen guests could deny hearing the noises. They formed a compact circle around the sofa, and each, in turn, asked questions of the rapping spirits. They were "answered" according to a pre-explained code. All the while, David Montebianco, abstinent as befitting his heritage, attended to Cleopatra Smith's champagne glass, as she, wide-eyed at the demonstration, drank more than she should have.

The next morning Cleo awakened under a balloon-festooned canopy in a bedroom lavishly furnished in French Empire style. Her head was hazy and she tried to recall the events of the previous night—why wasn't she in her room at the Irving House on Broadway and Chambers Street? Sitting up in bed, she could see out the full height windows: winter trees, snow-covered hills and skaters on a distant frozen pond. Below her window, on the avenue, prancing, snorting horses drew sleighs with entire families swathed in buffalo and black bear robes. Far in the distance, beyond the hills was a long, gray wall, similar to Egyptian mastabas, with strollers atop. This was certainly not New York City.

Suddenly Cleo realized that the nightgown she was wearing was not hers. She pulled the bedspread up modestly. If not her nightgown, then whose? What on earth had happened after the seance—after the champagne?

There was a knock on the paneled white door.

"Cleopatra, it's me: David. Are you awake—or hungry? It's almost ten o'clock. Breakfast will be served in half an hour. Do look in the dressing room closets. You'll find a selection of things to wear. The maid went to Stewart's early this morning and took a few dresses on consignment. Do pick one out."

Cleo ventured into the dressing room. Attached was a splendid marble bathroom. She had vague recollections of being shown the rooms before. Was it last night? It had to be. She opened a glass-faced closet and found an assortment of striking day dresses and coordinated accessories, even to petticoats and unmentionables. Taking her choice out, she held the dress before her and looked in one of the full-length door mirrors.

It was certainly her size. How?

"Mam'selle, it is the maid, may I prepare your bath?"

"Of course, come in," Cleo said, and busied herself with decisions of what to wear as the dusky French maid scurried by.

"What is your name?" called Cleo over the rush of water.

"Denise, Mam'selle . . ."

"Denise, was I intoxicated when I arrived last night?"

"I 'ave no idea, Mam'selle; I was not here."

Cleo cavorted amidst fragrances and bubbles in a capacious tub of Italian serpentine green marble as

Denise waited with cashmere towels in white and jade. Cleo stood up and brushed the clouds of bubbles from her body, then laughingly stepped out to be toweled by the French maid.

"I hope you don't mind me saying that you have a very beautiful figure, Mam'selle Smeeth."

"Why, thank you, Denise," Cleo said, taken aback momentarily. No woman had ever said that to her. "Where are you from?"

"Morocco. My father, he ees French. I am here two years. Would you now prefer a massage? That's what I do in Morocco."

"Do you only massage . . . women?"

"In my country, it is all the same."

"I have never . . ." Cleo was at a loss.

"Mam'selle, let me show you 'ow—ze standing massage." Denise drew the white towel from Cleo's grasp and draped it over a chair. Before Cleo could object, facile hands found their way over her shoulder from behind.

Cleo, quelling an impulse to resist, stood squarely before the mirrored doors as the lithe hands kneaded her neck and shoulder muscles. She watched the reflection as the hands, nimbly working, moved across her body, over her abdomen and down her sides. The touch thrilled her and she allowed Denise full reign, began sighing and flexing to the rhythmic motions, then writhed in pleasure and closed her eyes. The hands were around her, behind her—everywhere, as if an army had possessed her. Cleo let herself float in ecstasy, wanting not to break the spell. She felt herself being pushed backwards, but did not resists and relaxed like a rag doll when she felt the sumptuous towels under her. Grasping the velvet arm rests of the chair, she stretched her legs out and threw her head back, stared raptly at the carved marble ceiling and traced its convoluted contours and interlaced veins until she was nearly screaming in rapture.

On the other side of one of the mirrors next to the closet doors was a cubicle known only to the owner of the house. This room-height mirror had been specially prepared. A thin solution of silver reflected the bright dressing room, but was transparent when viewed from the lightless cubicle beyond. There was a second one in the bathroom and another in the bedroom.

Behind the glass, invisible to the intertwined women, sat David Montebianco on a high stool—nude.

CHAPTER SEVEN

Woodbury Mason turned the figurehead around slowly. Balanced at its eventual angle on the stem of the *Nightingale*, it hung from the ceiling on a block and tackle attached to a lug imbedded in the bow-formed timber of the carving's back.

"It's your best work, Father," Liz Mason said, as she approached the mute, painted effigy with awe. "I wish I had such a gown; the folds are so real, and her face and hair so life-like. She looks as if she were about to sing."

"Thank you, Liz. Yes, I have worked hard on this lady." The lean shipcarver sighed and wearily sat down on a block of pine. "Two month's work, and one bad piece of wood. By God, I'm glad this piece didn't crack as well."

"It's time you rested, Father." Seth wrapped the carving in soft muslin. "Can't take any chances with scratches. I'll put another coat of varnish on in the morning."

Liz stroked her father's graying head. "I think your price is too low. The Boston carvers are charging more."

"But Hadley cannot be blamed for inferior pine. I chose the wood myself. The important thing is that it's finished. At least I'll not be responsible if the boat's not launched in time enough to go to the Great Exhibition."

"I don't see how the *Nightingale* can be put in the water before the middle of June." Seth turned a corkscrew into a bottle of port wine. "The bottom copper hasn't arrived from Boston yet and the passengers' cabins have only been roughed out."

"And the *Boston Journal* is still running the advertisement that lists May 20th as departure date," Liz chimed in and set four wine glasses on the workbench. It was a ritual upon finishing a figurehead. It was Sarah's idea, going back some years. As children, Seth and Liz would be given a sip each. Now they were old enough to have their own glasses. But Sarah had been taken from them, in the winter when Seth was coming back round the Horn. And Liz, at eighteen, had become the woman of the house—caring for her ailing father as well as for young Tom and little Caroline.

Seth poured carefully, and each took a glass in hand, leaving one among the chisels and shavings on the workbench. First, they raised their wine toward muslin-swathed Jenny Lind—and then to the brimming blood-red glass that was Sarah Mason's.

* * *

The black hull loomed high against bright white thunderhead clouds in the western sky. Workmen plied the ramps on either side and carried tools and joiner-work up to the deck. Ladders were propped on all quarters and sheets of copper glinted as they were fixed to the bottom planks. Standing on the stemhead, Woodbury Mason proudly watched his masterpiece being fitted into the bow below the bowsprit. He had personally supervised the figurehead's raising by tackle fixed to the spar and he could hardly wait to rush aft to the ramp and down to the ground to view the union.

Notebook in hand, and followed by Matthew Hadley and his father, a city-dressed gentleman stepped gingerly over discarded beams and planks in his tour around the hull. He stopped under the bow and glowered as he looked up. "Mister Hadley, I find everything in reasonable order below decks, on deck and on the exterior. Everything except one item—and an important one it is. Before I can advance you capital to complete this boat, I must insist on an agreement to be added to the document."

"Name it and we'll do it," replied the elder Hadley.

"That figurehead. It's totally wrong. Much too bare; why, it reminds me of a dance-hall wench. Jenny Lind, in the eyes of the world, is a consummate artist. What you have now on the bow of this ship is a sacrilege of her art. I want to see new drawings immediately—and a proper carving."

"But," argued Matthew, "Baron de Geer received approval from Miss Lind on this design. We have it in writing."

"Baron de Geer is no longer financing the *Night-*

ingale." David Montebianco grinned. "It's a shame that Miss Lind didn't wait a few more months before rejecting his hand."

"We're already a month behind schedule," William Hadley said and, seeing Mason approaching, led the trio away from the boat.

"I am a busy man, Mister Hadley. Shall I leave for New York now, or will we come to an agreement?"

"You win; Matt will talk to the shipcarver."

"Very well. Tell him to change her hair. I want to have her wearing a bun, not frivolous curls. The gown should be something that could be worn in church. Her face should be more classic—and absolutely no lipstick. Too much bust showing . . ."

"What you ask will require a whole new carving," said Matthew. He looked back at the boat to see that Woodbury Mason had climbed a ladder and was overseeing the joiner work of his figurehead to the stem.

"If your man cannot do it, I'll get someone in New York," Montebianco said, closing his notebook with finality. "One has to be firm with services; tell him that he will not be paid for his first carving until the second one is ready—that it's a matter of financial procedure. That will set him to work. And remind him of the acclaim his work will receive on such a prestigious vessel. I suspect that the competition for services in a city like Portsmouth is not as keen elsewhere. Mister Mason is probably the only shipcarver in town. Am I right?"

"But he's as good as any in Boston."

"Of course he is, Matthew. Are you good friends?"

"We grew up together," confessed the elder Hadley.

"Friends and profits are often bad bedfellows. I suggest you have your attorney add the condition we have just discussed to the document. Meanwhile, I shall be in my rooms."

* * *

On May 7th, the following advertisement was inserted in the *New York Commercial Advertiser*:

TRANSATLANTIC EXCURSION TO THE WORLD'S FAIR

Rare opportunity for a cheap and delightful trip to London. Captain Miller, so favorably known to the public on both sides of the Atlantic as a noble navigator and gentleman, goes out in command of the Nightingale. *To sail from Boston on or about June 10th. Rate of passage to London and back: First class staterooms, $125. Ladies' cabin, berths, $125. Saloon staterooms, $110. Saloon berths, $100.*

For tickets apply to Adams & Co, 16 Wall Street.

Winsome Captain Miller was a celebrated ship's master, and though named to superintend the *Nightingale's* construction, he was neither a builder nor a contractor. Sam Hadley was the moving force, as had been his father. But they were both gone and Uncle Will had done his utmost to fill the void. As the days grew longer and the work crews smaller on the lagging hull, William Hadley ascribed the delays to financial difficulties resulting from Captain Miller's rejection of work and materials that did not meet his high standards. In actuality, the blame lay on the lack of funds due to haggling among the several owners, all of whom had come to realize that *Nightingale* might well be renamed the *White Elephant* because it had missed its cue. The rich and influential travelers had already left for the Great Exposition aboard the Collins and Cunard steamers. At best, *Nightingale* would sail in late summer and arrive in Southampton only a month before the fair closed—a stale fish with empty cabins.

At a hasty meeting, the creditors all agreed that the clipper should be finished and towed to Boston to be offered at a public sale to satisfy the mortgages held against the vessel.

On the afternoon of June 16th, 1851, the *Portsmouth Journal* set type describing the launching:

> . . . *another beautiful clipper ship, of 1100 tons, called the* Nightingale, *was put afloat on the waters of the Piscataqua, from the yard of William Hadley. She was modeled by her builders, is a real clipper, and is constructed in the most substantial manner.*
>
> *Hundreds witnessed the N's graceful debut upon our waters, and cheered enthusiastically her first performance. . . . Her frame is all oak, and for strength and beauty of construction it is believed she is not surpassed by any merchant ship built in the U.S. As a specimen of American naval architecture, she is to proceed direct from Boston to London. Her cabin is to be finished in an entirely new style, at a cost of $6000, to accommodate 50 passengers. Her deck also will be finished in a superior manner, a pretty and graceful moulding being run completely around the inside of her rail. She has a commodious house on deck, for officers and stewards, as well as smoking and bathing rooms. Her cordage is from the manufacture of Mr. Jeremiah Johnson of this city. It is made of the best Russia yarn, and pronounced by judges fully equal to any that can be obtained. Her interior*

arrangements and decorations were designed by Capt. T.A. Miller, under whose superintendence she was constructed.

Named for Jenny Lind, the "Swedish Nightingale," her bow is ornamented with a figurehead of the popular singer, while the same lady is portrayed reclining at the stern with a nightingale perched on her finger. . . .

In dire need of funds to start on its one other commission, William Hadley sold the family's interest in the *Alchemist. Gemini*, a clipper schooner planned for three hundred tons, was to sail to Canton China, and engage in the opium trade. George Raynes, the Portsmouth builder responsible for the *Witch of the Wave* and *Wild Pigeon*, was also constructing vessels for the "poison trade," the *Minna* and *Brenda*. These boats were designed more as yachts than merchant vessels, with long, raking masts and forty-foot sweeps to run out of the gun ports and row if attacked by China Seas pirates while becalmed. As *Nightingale* rode at her mooring in the Piscataqua, Matthew Hadley set to work on the moulds for *Gemini*. He was anxious to describe to Liz Mason his idea for a small figurehead that her father, or perhaps Seth, would enjoy carving—twins, with trailing stars on the boards to the hawse holes. And Matthew and Mark would be on the bows: gliding past the Irrawaddy delta and down through the Strait of Malacca— brothers, working together.

But a day after the launching of *Nightingale*, Woodbury Mason's heart gave out. The work light in his loft flickered and the familiar second floor window became dark. The carver was found expired on the plank floor the next morning by Seth. He lay before a squared-off column of white pine, upon which was sketched the form of a male figure putting a giant sea-shell up to his mouth as if to use it as a horn. The carver's mallet and chisel lay nearby among a scattering of chips. Evidently Mason had no intentions of resting, even after the ordeal of reworking Jenny Lind. There were debts; there was a family to clothe and feed.

When Matthew went to the house to pay his respects, he was met with disdain. There was not a word from the girl whose hand he sought. He was a Hadley, and it was a Hadley ship that had killed her father. Whatever dreams and hopes he had were gone. The very streets and buildings of Portsmouth seemed to recoil at his approach. Children stopped their games and faces appeared in the shop windows.

Rarely had a burial been attended by so many. The hillside cemetery overlooked the Piscataqua, where lay serenely the black hull of mastless Nightingale, its copper sheathing glinting through a low morning fog. A prim gray effigy of the Swedish singer looked toward the shore like a fettered bird from its perch beneath the unfinished bowsprit.

Behind the outside ranks of mourners on the hill stood a slim, hunched-over figure. Having left his sky-blue wheelbarrow among the carriages on the cemetery road, Wiburd Penhallow stared mutely at the services while playing with a little gold coin—the three-dollar piece he had pried out of Nightingale's keel one moonstruck winter night.

That afternoon Matthew packed and took the coach to Boston, where he boarded a train to New York City. It was summer, and time he took a holiday. While clattering past Stonington on the New Haven Line at an astounding forty-five miles per hour, he took out a letter he'd received the week before.

New York, June 5th, 1851

Matthew Hadley, Esq.

Dear Matt:

Greetings from Gotham.

The yacht has been in the bay for a month and I have survived the ordeal of working with the upper classes. For want of a name, she has been christened the America. Mr. Steers gave her over to the syndicate for trials and we had aboard the Hon. George Schuyler as umpire.

Our first trial was against the sloop Maria, whose canvas is a quarter more than ours. Even with a seven ton ballast shortage, we beat them twice and lost once because our main gaff was carried away by mishandling.

Now I am happy to report that I have been designated master of this trim schooner, and will be in charge of the trip to Cowes as well as the regatta race we have every hope of entering. We think we have a good chance to win because of our new machine-cotton sails, which are cut in a different way from those of the usual rig. The Royal Yacht Squadron, as far as we know, has no boat thus equipped, due to the prejudice in favor of hemp canvas.

I have picked two mates and five seamen, as well as a cook and a boy, but we still have one berth open for a sailor who can handle a pilot schooner as well as you did the Mary Taylor last spring. In the event that your plans change because of the delay in building the Nightingale, consider this another way of attending the Great Exhibition in London. The pay is meager, but the liquor, bountiful.

We sail from Wm. Brown's yard at 12th Street on Saturday, June 21st. The regatta will be held during the 3rd week in August. As the yacht may

remain in England after the regatta for a period,
transportation back to New York will be provided.
We need you. Your country needs you!

Very Truly, your friend,
Dick Brown

CHAPTER EIGHT

Twenty days and six hours after leaving New York, the *America* anchored off Le Havre. The log showed five days becalmed, several days of drenching rain, and a best day's run of two hundred and seventy-two miles—an average of better than eleven knots. George Steers, the yacht's designer, was seasick much of the trip, as was one of his two sons and the second mate. Independence Day had been observed with minimum duty for all and several bottles of gin. Six hundred miles from landfall, a log entry reported: "Our liquor is all but gone." This explicit ship's document was kept by the designer's older brother, who, like the other non-sailors, was given a berth upon the "aristocratic" owners' decision to make the crossing in a comfortable steamer.

Syndicate Commodore John Stevens, his brother, and Colonel James Hamilton, son of the famed and unfortunate Alexander, came up from Paris and arranged to have the yacht put into a government dry-dock for a final coat of paint and a cleaning of her copper bottom. The borrowed sails were taken off and replaced with specially designed and crafted racing sails.

As the owners left for Cowes by channel steamer, *America* swept into the English Channel, gilding and brightwork glistening, under blinding bright new canvas, and set course for the Isle of Wight.

A Royal Yacht Squadron cutter of eighty tons, the *Lavrock* was sent out from Cowes to escort the challenger into harbor. Deemed a match for a schooner of *America's* size, it was also an advance examiner of the stranger's ability. *America* let the British yacht take a heady lead, then followed in her wake. Steadily, the schooner beat to windward and drew past her escort. In sailing four miles against the *Lavrock*, the *America* beat the cutter by some half a mile. As this occurred in full view of wharfs, houses and vessels in the harbor, the event did not bolster the Royal Yacht Squadron's confidence in the superiority of their craft.

After investigating the sailing waters around the Isle of Wight and discussing the various forms of rig indigenous to the course, the Stevens brothers decided to add a flying jib to the head. This required also that the bowsprit be doubled in length. Ignoring the objections of Captain Brown, the gentlemen sailors insisted, and the new sail and spar were made by the Ratsey loft of Cowes.

Entered in the final and most important contest of the week, which was "open to yachts of all rigs and nations," *America* received a numbing note from the Commodore of the host Yacht Club rescinding permission to enter the race, the first regatta of which was to take place on the following day. At the eleventh hour, a "standing rule" had been found. It required that every yacht entered had to be the property of one individual. *America* was disqualified because she had several owners. "Old Pig," as Commodore Stevens was known to the crew, got quite mad and went ashore to challenge the club's members to a separate $50,000 contest, but there were no takers.

Captain Brown, not one for protocol and club manners, asked Matthew to accompany him to a waterfront pub in West Cowes to tip a few while debating the predicament. Matthew watched the lights of Portsmouth blinking across the Solent through the pub's window.

"Damn," he slurred, "Here I'm sitting looking across the water at another Portsmouth, just like I did back home—and neither one looks hospitable. Three thousand miles I came to forget my bad fortune and girl at home. Turned away by my intended bride, and now rejected by the Queen of England. Bugger 'em all." Matthew pushed his empty whiskey glass toward the barmaid.

"Queen Victoria didn't write the rules."

"But it's called 'The Queen's Cup,' isn't it?"

"Also 'The Hundred Guinea Cup,' unofficially." Dick Brown leaned over the bar for a better look at the wench. "Don't we have an extra berth forward, Matt?"

"And more trouble yet?" laughed Matthew.

"Aye, that we don't need, my boy."

"Dick," Matthew's voice rose excitedly, "If the prize is called 'The Hundred Guinea Cup' unofficially, can we get into the race unoffically. Then we can win unofficially."

"I don't see why not. It's better than doing nothing,

and if we win, the periodicals will note it. That's the important thing—to prove an American vessel faster."

"We are scheduled for two races," Matthew said, draining his Irish whiskey with a grimace. "Tomorrow, the preliminary regatta—and a week from Friday, the important one. I say we should go out with the fleet tomorrow as if nothing had happened. The worst that can happen is that we will be disqualified officially."

"I'll drink to that, m' boy. We ain't come across the ocean to turn our tails an' run away. Let's talk to 'Old Pig'."

The *America* was ready: under foresail and jib only, she got under way and put after the Royal Yacht Squadron's schooners, all of which were under full canvas. The race had gotten off late because of lack of wind. For over an hour, *America* kept pace with the field with only half her 5,300 square feet of canvas set. At 4:30, after one and a half hours' sailing, *America* came about at the western point of the isle near the Needles and ran before the wind to her anchorage. The nine large schooners, including the *Brilliant,* of double *America's* tonnage, continued 'round the course, each captain regarding his full spread of canvas with disbelief and alarm.

On Friday, August 15th, the wind was right for a proper start. At about 10 o'clock, the entrants beat down to the Needles into a NW breeze. The *America,* standing off West Cowes, came about and made for the field, which was about three miles distant. At about 6 P.M. *America* dropped anchor—she had beaten the entire fleet of over thirty sail.

That evening, as the owners were cavorting in the

main saloon, Captain Brown and the crew sat disconsolately on the foredeck as a chorus of crickets sounded down from the wooded heights beyond the town of Ryde. Summer-night strollers could be seen on the pier, against the dancing lights of the Royal Victoria Clubhouse. A tinge of nostalgia descended on the gathered crew, and thoughts of home and family mingled with the stars of August and the rippling of water along the hull. Nelson Comstock, the first mate, leaned forward and called into the light of the galley hatch:

"Hey, doctor," he teased the Negro cook, "how 'bout an after dinner see-gar for us weary sailors. The jerked beef and spuds were passable, but the chicken was pitiful. There are six of us here who want to get the stinkin' taste out of our mouths."

"Massa Hamilton take all the see-gars and lock them up in his cabin. You go see the Colonel."

Comstock went aft and approached Colonel Hamilton. "Can you spare some see-gars for your crew, sir? Including Cap'n Brown and the pilot, I'll need six." The aristocrat went into his stateroom and came out with four Havanas. "You'll just have to divide them." Hamilton shrugged, then added: "The club ball is at 10 o'clock; I trust you'll have the gig ready and shipshape."

The next day, *The Times* of London ran a scathing article. It went, in part:

> "... she (America) *seemed as if she had a screw in her stern, and began to fly in the water.... She passed schooners and cutters, one after the other ... there was scarcely any foam at her bows, nor broken water before them.... The waves seemed to fall away ...*

offering a minimum of resistance. . . . 'This is all very well,' acknowledged one captain, 'for a schooner on this particular wind, but let us see how she'll come back, with the wind a point or two worse . . .'

"The America soon gave all an opportunity to judge. She went up to each sail in order, running to leeward as close as possible—then anchored at least two miles ahead of the vessel that was closest behind. . . . The shops and houses of the Isle of Wight echoed with excitement. . . ."

And in a later edition:

"Having landed the owners' representatives for the clubhouse ball, the America bowled away like a seagull . . . with a liberal display of stars and stripes flying . . . irritated with the 'gentlemen' for not accepting her challenge."

Such was the impact of *The Times'* article that the "standing rule" of individual ownership was not applied to the final and most important race of the series.

After a slow start at the gun, *America* over-ran her anchor and lowered sail for a second try. She went along easy under main and jib, between the steamers and sight-seeing yachts that lined the course. Though her opponents all carried more sail, she crept resolutely ahead and within an hour passed all but three of the seventeen sail. A small cutter, *Volante*, flying a huge jib, suddenly passed the leaders, to the delight of the partisan spectators. Then, with a freshening of the wind, *America* passed all but *Volante* and *Gypsy Queen*.

Into the wind at the next turn, *America* showed its

mettle. Sails cut to drumhead tightness when sheeted in, she drove ahead in a fashion unknown to traditional boats. Unschooled George Steers, the designer, had worked from observation and innate feel. He had drawn his inspiration from the New York pilot schooners that sliced through the narrows of their harbor into the teeth of gales. What forces abetted such performance could not be determined as yet by diagrams and mathematics—but the tautness worked. There were those who likened the phenomenon to the flitting of a lemon pit from between the fingers. *America* could point sharper into the wind than her adversaries—making narrower tacks, thus shortening distances from point to point. Her hull and sailplan had been called "a violation of naval architecture" by critics, but now they were quiet.

The secret of her sails lay in their composition and manufacture. Whereas the English sails were made of hand-woven flax, very loose in texture, and, in accordance with the universal theory of the day, cut with excessive fullness, *America's* sails were of machine-woven cotton, cut to fit as tight as possible.

While rounding Dunnose Point on the SE of the isle, Captain Brown noticed a sail gaining on them. It was a small cutter; from its looks through the glass, probably the *Aurora*. Brown had the jibs trimmed in, but to no avail. *America's* lead was steadily decreasing. There were about seven more hours to the finish at Cowes, and the pursuer was within two miles, and closing.

"Old Dick" Brown cussed into the wind at the flying jib. "It's no goddamn good to windward . . ." He could feel by the tiller that a force was working against the yacht—a strange force that he'd never felt aboard his beloved *Mary Taylor*. And this was Mary's younger sister, newer and livelier. He motioned to

Matthew to go forward and stand by on the flying jib halliard.

"Leave it be," thundered "Old Pig" from his sheltered niche in the companionway.

Brown shot a piercing glance at Matthew, who was manning the windlass. It was a signal between sailors that needed no words nor gestures. Born of storms and lee shores, of reefs and maelstroms, the look said, "Do what is necessary to save the boat—and to the devil with regulations and superiors."

Matthew had done it before—had slashed a line to let fly canvas, had cut away a spar to save the mast. "Heave," he called another seaman to the task and the windlass strained against its pawls, stretching the jib clewline till it thrummed.

Suddenly there was a sharp report as the extended jib-boom snapped and was wrenched aft into the head and forestay. Brown put the helm over and the yacht lost way, sails slatting and flying jib tearing and flapping violently.

Fifteen minutes later, with wreckage secured, *America* was back on course and picking up way. *Aurora*, taking advantage of the mishap, had closed to within a mile and a half. Nobody saw the wink given to Matthew by Captain Brown as *America*, without its flying jib, bolted ahead at a faster speed than before. After the turn at St. Catherine's Point, *America* headed for the Needles, where lay excursion steamers with spectators and the Royal yacht with Queen Victoria's party aboard. As Prince Albert and the ten-year-old Prince of Wales in his sailor suit watched the signal boat *Fairy* steaming by with semaphore flags wagging, the Queen summoned an officer: "Signal Master, are the yachts in sight?"

"Yes, may it please Your Majesty."

"Which is first?"

"The *America*."

"Which is second?"

"Ah, Your Majesty, there is no second."

The next day, Queen Victoria came aboard *America* after it anchored opposite Osborne House, the Royal summer residence. Her barge steamed once around the victor and came to the port gangway, where she and Albert were received by Commodore Stevens and shown to the quarterdeck while the rest of her party remained forward. The Queen was especially interested in the crew's quarters and the arrangement of ballast below. Colonel Hamilton was surprised at the informality shown by the monarch—only to find out later that, as hosts, the owners were put upon an equality with her Majesty.

"Old Dick" Brown, no lackey to royalty, showed Prince Albert the cabins and fo'c'sle, but not until the consort wiped the mud from his shoes. The Queen was so impressed with the tidiness of the yacht that she later presented Captain Brown with a gold pocket compass and gave each member of the crew a gold sovereign.

As a parting remark, she told Commodore Stevens that she would be interested in purchasing *America* for her son when he was a bit older.

That evening Matthew Hadley spun his gleaming sovereign in circles on the varnished saloon table before taking his turn on watch. The aristocrats were off to the club and most of the crew had gone into Cowes to spend their coins. As the sovereign spun, reflecting the glint of the saloon lamps, Matthew saw fleeting faces . . . ship's frames and mold lofts . . . gilded figureheads and familiar shorelines. His summer holiday was over. Now he would go back to the other Portsmouth—and try once again with Liz Mason.

Time and distance has been known to heal, he told himself. And, if he were not successful, there would be yet another way to turn. A choice. To be first mate aboard a clipper ship—or master of his own vessel. He spun the coin once more, and from it sprang the bright image of a sail. It sped toward him and he recognized the vessel.

It was the schooner, *Gemini*.

CHAPTER NINE

A day out of Liverpool the Collins' crack liner *Atlantic* throttled its engines down to half speed. Her position was some twenty miles south of Ireland's Cape Clear; the seas were rising and a squall ahead was laced with threads of quiet lightning.

Below, the first class dining saloon passengers looked up through the stained glass bordered skylight at the threatening and darkening sky as stewards cautiously balanced trays of *Filet of pigeon au Cronstaugh* and *Epigram d'agneau with sauce truppe*.

"David, this is such a great coincidence . . ." Matthew stopped his plate from sliding across the table. "I took this boat because my brother is second mate—but now, you!"

"Ah yes, the sensible twin," Montebianco joked.

"I travel on Collins' boats because I like luxury."
He stabbed at his leg of mutton, which had leapt off
the plate. "Cunard is now offering steerage accommodations—another good reason. Can you imagine
traveling on the same boat with farmers and sick
babies?"

"I spent twenty days coming across on *America*
with three seasick people aboard in a confined space.
I can understand."

"Matthew . . ." Montebianco watched indifferently
as his green peas rolled off his plate and cascaded
across the table onto the lap of an ashen-faced dowager.
"I'm sorry about the woodcarver."

"It was my fault," Matthew said, shrugging. "I
knew he'd been ill."

"Don't blame yourself. You had no choice—and
neither did I. His time was up. If it hadn't been the
Nightingale, it would have been the next one that
killed him."

Matthew clenched his fists below the table. He had
forgotten how ruthless shipbuilding could be—and
shiphandling. The images recurred fleetingly: rats
scurrying inside a dead man's shirt . . . a frozen
corpse lashed to the main yard . . .

"How I envy you," David changed the subject.
"You're going home as a hero. The victory at Cowes
was all the rage in London. It's a shame you didn't
get to see the Crystal Palace, but you did meet the
Queen. How extraordinary . . ." The financier prat-
tled on. "Had I known she was interested in buying
the yacht for the Prince of Wales I might have made
an offer first, and held it until the boy was of age."

"Did you see your family while in London?"

"Did I? Why, not only did I see them, but I'm
bringing my cousin home with me. Poor soul; he's in
a coffin." Montebianco pointed down to the deck.
"We came over together to see the fair. He came

down with a fever. It happened so fast. When we arrive, I shall send him by train to Philadelphia. I got a letter off on a previous steamer to his family.''

The *Atlantic* began to pitch and roll uncomfortably. Bottles and glasses rattled in the wall racks as entire suppers sloshed off the tables and diners tumbled from their benches.

Montebianco rose nervously to his feet. "Matthew, you'll have to excuse me. I feel sick and should go to my room." He staggered through the saloon, stumbling over furniture and falling against tables.

Once below in his stateroom, he took a small, portable oil lamp from a valise, lit it and made his way along the corridor to the stairway, where he descended to the lowest deck. Finding the cargo hatch padlocked, Montebianco accosted a seaman and demanded that the hatch be opened in order that he could inspect his most valuable cargo.

"You would have to speak to the Captain, sir."

"Call Mr. Hadley, please. I'm a personal acquaintance of his. Tell him that Mr. Montebianco has an urgent request. I'll wait here."

"Mind you, sir," the seaman addressed David's oil lamp, "careful with that down here."

Mark Hadley extended his hand as he came down the companionway. "Forgive me. My brother told me you were aboard, but I've been so busy. The boilers have been acting up again. Too much vibration for a wooden hull. But enough of our problems. On a Collins liner the passenger is always king."

"Mark, I don't mean to be such a nuisance, but I'm in a terrible state. I've never experienced such a difficult passage."

"Our apologies, David, but there's no ship that would fare any better in this storm. If it gets any worse, we'll heave to, but we'd like to get past Cape Clear first. What seems to be your problem at present?''

Montebianco steadied himself and assumed a solemn aura. "I have cargo in the hold. My dear cousin died suddenly in London and I'm bringing his remains back to New York to send on to his family in Philadelphia. The body was prepared well in London, and I just want to make sure that this excessive rolling doesn't disturb it. Perhaps I'll put some extra packing around it.''

"Understandable,'' Mark said. He took a ring of keys out of his coat pocket, selected one and snapped open the hatch padlock. "But I'll have to accompany you. Regulations, especially with that lamp. Do you have your claim ticket?''

Montebianco handed it to Mark as they descended into the luggage hold. The seaman appeared with a ship's lantern and held it as Mark read the location coordinates.

Mark watched as Montebianco unlocked the lid of a long wooden crate, then motioned the seaman to hold the lantern closer. Inside lay a polished black walnut coffin with ornate silver hinges and corners. Setting his portable lamp down on the lower lid, David slowly opened the other one. At the sight of the corpse's powdered face, Mark stepped back and the seaman turned away.

"I'll just be a moment.'' Montebianco picked up his lamp and the seaman nodded and waited with the second mate. Shining the light into the coffin, he reached under the lower lid, unbuttoned the corpse's jacket and pulled up the frilled shirt. There, in place of an abdomen was a cavity in which were set several soldered tin boxes. Montebianco snapped the catch of one and flicked open a felt wrapper within. His light beam blazed back, pocking his enraptured face with points of light—reflections from a cache of sparkling stones. Deftly he restored the subterfuge and closed the lids. What had commenced because of fear now became advantageous. Should a customs agent inquire of the coffin upon arrival at New York, the second mate's vouch would be forthcoming as to the contents.

CHAPTER TEN

After six weeks' lying at a wharf in Boston, *Nightingale*'s financial tangles were unraveled enough to allow her finally to be sold. The auction was held at Number 22, Long Wharf, on September 6, 1851, in the presence of a gathering of shipowners and merchants. A series of closed bids gave the vessel to Davis & Company of Boston for $43,500. The purchasers were ship brokers who had advanced money for the boat's completion. The auction set up a clear title to the ship and, shortly after, the brokers sold her to Sampson & Tappan, also of Boston, at a considerably higher price that set tongues wagging. There was talk of a silent partner—a New York financier who had engineered the proceedings and made a profit as well as retaining a controlling interest in the vessel, but it was soon forgotten as other ships were completed and sent on their ways.

The trim new clipper ship was thoroughly bolted and coppered, and well found in boats and tackle. Its main cabin contained ten staterooms with bedsteads instead of berths and it featured a ladies' cabin with eight staterooms. In all, there were accommodations for two hundred and fifty passengers.

Sampson & Tappan had plans for *Nightingale*, engendered several months earlier during a meeting with the mysterious partner before he left for England to attend to business and see the great international exhibition. Not the least of incentives were articles in the newspapers, such as this from Australia:

> "... the great gold discoveries in New South Wales are the all-absorbing subject of conversation here. Only fancy a man picking a hundredweight of pure gold out of one hole, putting it into his gig, driving to the bank, and receiving 4,500 Pounds for his morning's work! If this goes on, it must unsettle the whole monetary system of the world. California has produced nothing equal to this ..."

The new owners advertised *Nightingale* as the first clipper to clear for the gold fields down under, and she loaded under R.W. Cameron's "Pioneer Lines" with Captain John Fiske in command. The clipper was well-suited for passengers outward bound, and was to return by way of London with a cargo of tea.

Clearing on October 17th, 1851, for "Oceania and China," *Nightingale*'s first mate had made his decision. Matthew Hadley, upon returning with hope to Portsmouth, had found Elizabeth Mason engaged to a naval lieutenant from Kittery and the schooner *Gemini* still on the mould loft floor, with its building date uncertain.

As was the case with others sailing about the same time, *Nightingale* encountered unfavorable weather and winds in the North Atlantic and it was not until her thirty-ninth day out that she reached Cape St. Roque, land's end of Brazil and the first marker of the eastward passage to Australia. Able seaman Tommy Furlong, a man for words and chanteys in the fo'c'sle, gave the vessel an endearing sobriquet to describe her heavy weather qualities. Now, in light airs and out of the tropical doldrums, turning southeast toward the volcanic islands of Tristan da Cunha, the clipper was known to its crew as *Diving Bell*, regardless of the sea conditions.

Issachar Dew, a preacher from Salem, raised his arms over the gathered faithful of the passengers and crew. He spoke from the quarterdeck rail as if from a pulpit.

". . . and on this day of Thanksgiving, let me leave you with God's will, that it be done. Revel not . . . eat not . . . drink not in excess." The gaunt preacher, sweating under his black frock coat, took a note from out of his service book and adjusted his wire-rimmed glasses. "There has been no one who has said it better than the great clergyman from Boston, the reverend Cotton Mather:

'It is to be desired, that the sailors in our ships may not voluntarily drown themselves in drunkenness. Sirs, 'tis a mad thing to lie down drunk in the midst of the sea; to lie drunk on the top of a mast. Every time a sailor makes himself drunk,

the devil keelhauls him. Let thy tongue be well hung as with the strongest rudder-irons. Why shouldest thou not be as loath to take any obscure, smutty, bawdy talk into thy mouth, as to swallow so much filthy bilge water . . .' "

"SAIL HOOO. . . ." The torrid blue sky was shattered by a shout from the foretop.

"WHERE AWAY?" Matthew called back through a brass speaking-trumpet as a young woman in white crinolines and ribboned riding hat turned her radiant face toward him and closed her pocket Bible. She looked right and left at her seated companions and giggled.

"TWO POINTS OFF THE STARB'D BOW," came the reply from aloft.

"They seem to be in trouble; what do you make of it?" Captain Fiske handed his brass-trimmed telescope to Matthew, who edged out over the bowsprit with one hand on the forestay. He steadied the glass against his eye, crooked his elbow around the stay and focused on the vessel. She was an hermaphrodite brig, square-rigged on the foremast and schooner-rigged on the mizzen. Canvas furled and brailed, she was drifting slowly toward *Nightingale*'s path. Her gun'ls were lined with figures, waving and shouting. An American flag hung limply from the mizzen gaff.

"I make out women among the people on deck— ladies with parasols, and gentlemen with coats and hats . . ." Matthew studied her lines and rigging. "By the rig, I'd say she was a French-built boat."

Captain Fiske signaled the helm to wear over. "Mister Hadley, let's take a closer look. We're not breaking any records to Australia anyway."

Nightingale veered toward the wallowing boat and

came up to hailing distance on her port quarter. There was no name on the stranger's transom, nor port of call.

A man climbed up on the rail and doffed his top hat while clinging to the mizzen ratlines. Below him, several bonneted women, one holding an infant, waved excitedly.

"WATER . . . Could you please spare some water?" shouted the well-dressed passenger. "That's all we ask."

"Where is your captain?" called Fiske.

"The crew is down with fever. . . . just some water, please."

"Mister Hadley," ordered Fiske, "take her alongside and rig up the fenderboards. I don't want any scratches."

Taking a station on the quarterdeck behind the helmsman, Matthew called out orders to the bosun for boxing sail and easing the sleek, black clipper up to the brig. Below, the second mate, George Gerrish, was having water pumped into barrels from the fresh water tanks and hauled on deck for transfer.

Jenny Lind's polychrome effigy had pulled up parallel to the brig's counter, and just a pistol shot away, when Captain Fiske called out from the fo'c'sle deck: "What ship is that and where are you bound?" There was no answer, only grins and applause.

At that moment, a puff of wind streamed out the brig's ensign. Matthew, noticing it, suddenly grabbed the wheel and spun it sharply to port, to the surprise of the helmsman. *Nightingale* veered off as its backed sails filled and picked up way, while the spanker jibed—its boom crashing through the brig's mizzen shrouds. Suddenly the distressed vessel was alive with curdling screams and brandishing of weapons. Preacher Dew and his congregation were hurriedly ushered forward and below as a commotion erupted on *Nightingale*'s stern. A knot of unsavory sailors, knives in their flashing teeth, had made fast to the taffrail with grappling hooks as the boats brushed, and they had climbed up and over to advance on the quarterdeck with pistols leveled. The leader, in outlandish stocking cap with a hatchet tucked into his jeweled leather belt, raised his heavy pistol with flintlock cocked and aimed point blank at unarmed Captain Fiske as the other two waited gleefully beside him, ready to fire at Matthew Hadley next.

A cloud of smoke erupted from the quarterdeck hatch amidst a thunderous report. As the blue smoke lifted, second mate George Gerrish emerged, holding a bizarre brass weapon in his shaking hand. All three boarders lay on deck, blood running into the lead scuppers and on down to the ship's waist. The stockinged leader was dead, a ball through his right eye. Of the other two, one was writhing and clutching his stomach, while the second lay on his back, eyes glazed upward and hand fingering a silver cross on his bare, hairy chest as a trickle of red oozed from his bearded mouth.

"Well, ah'l be swived," Gerrish said, as he dangled his four-barreled duckfoot flintlock pistol by the trigger guard. One of the splayed-out barrels had burst like a steel banana. "Now where am I gonna get this fixed?"

"Mister Hadley, your astute action this day saved not only the ship, but the lives of our passengers as well," Captain Fiske said, as he poured three brandies on his day cabin table.

"But neither of us would be here if it hadn't been for Gerrish and his mutiny pistol." Matthew raised his glass toward the blond second mate.

"The gun's so old, it's a wonder we weren't all

blown up. I only fire it once before every trip, and then I load it with new powder and put it in an oilskin sack.''

''Aren't you afraid of it going off accidentally?'' joked Matthew, examining the huge pistol on the table.

''Not at all,'' replied Gerrish. ''Even if I cock the hammer—like this . . .'' He demonstrated. ''. . . there's still this safety latch.'' He pointed to a tiny metal lug behind the flintlock.

''Very clever,'' added the captain. ''I doubt that the average seaman would be familiar with that feature.''

''One of the reasons it's there,'' replied Gerrish.

''Matt . . .'' The captain swirled his brandy pensively. ''What made you suspect that the vessel was manned by pirates?''

''Their ensign. It was only at the last moment, when a puff of wind unfurled it. If it had really been an American boat, the flag would have been flown upside-down, as a distress signal. The practice is not used by any of the Atlantic maritime powers other than the United States because their flags are symmetrical and would look no different upside-down than the right way. It occurred to me that an American boat would be aware of the signal and hoist it properly. That, along with the brig's failure to announce her name and port.''

''They would have slaughtered us,'' Fiske said and up-ended his glass. ''Maybe I'm getting too old for this business, too trusting. Packet runs will do that to a man.''

Miss Ellen Russell was used to having her way. And why not? She was the grandniece of Samuel Russell and the favorite of the commission house clan. Old Sam Russell came out to China in the thirties and established American enterprise as competition for the octopus that called itself "The British East India Company" or, more simply, "The Company." Until the Revolution, the American colonies had been forbidden to trade with the Far East, lest they sap the interests that had been vested since 1600, when Queen Elizabeth incorporated it by royal charter. From a simple trading company, it grew into a monopoly—with the right to acquire territory, coin money, command forts and troops, make war, and exercise both civil and criminal jurisdiction. In 1833, The Company's monopoly of the China tea trade was rescinded by Great Britain—and Sam Russell was there to take up the slack. The Chinese *hongs*, or merchants, in turn, were eager to drive out British interests in favor of the Americans, who were not territorially motivated.

With the demise of The Company came the rise of a new breed of boat. The Company, driven to produce dividends for their investors, became the principal carrier of opium from India to the coast of China. In 1833, the last year of The Company's monopoly, they carried, in ponderous, slow ships, a greater value in opium to China than the total value of tea exported. As if this wasn't enough, the opening of China to free trade saw greedy British independent shippers arriving in 1834 via India to load tea at Canton. Opium sales soared, and China became weak with addiction.

Sam Russell watched as small but speedy schooners from England plied the opium routes to China and amassed enormous profits, without the encumbrances of the long return tea passages to London. One clipper-schooner sold almost two-million-dollars worth of the drug to Chinese agents in Foo Chow, Amoy and Ningpo.

Soon, Russell & Company was operating its own opium schooners that had been hurriedly built in Boston and New York. Even Portsmouth supplied two, the *Minna* and *Brenda*, of three hundred tons each.

Designed for speed to evade monsoons, bad tides and pirate junks propelled by oars as well as sail, the sharp little vessels created a new business for America's maritime interests, and precipitated the zenith of sailing commerce in the clipper ship.

During the next decade, Russell & Company, gaining favor with the dean of Chinese merchant princes, Houqua, became the richest and most powerful trading house in China. When, after the Opium Wars, the British were driven out, Russell was there. Retiring, he left his empire in charge of younger lions, one of whom was Robert Forbes, of Boston.

Ellie Russell was an heiress to all this—and a lioness to boot, behind her finishing school facade. Flaxen hair rippling, she stepped catlike-quiet from the companionway. White taffeta clinging from the breeze and pale mauve ribbons flying, she stopped unseen behind the first mate and watched as he aimed a complicated instrument toward the horizon. Waiting patiently until Matthew had lowered the instrument, Ellie interrupted his mental calculations.

"Excuse me, but what are those islands up ahead?"

The voice startled Matthew so that he juggled his sextant.

"Oh . . . er, Ma'am . . . Miss . . . I believe they might be the Tristan da Cunhas. In fact they must be." He laughed at his confusion. "If they aren't, we're lost."

"What is that?" She pointed at the sextant.

"It's for measuring the height of a heavenly—of

the sun, moon or a star." Matthew avoided Ellie's eyes.

"Is it like a sextant?" asked the young woman innocently.

"I believe that's what it's called, Miss . . ."

"Russell—Ellie Russell."

"Nice meeting you, Miss Russell; I'm Matthew Hadley."

"I know. You saved us all from the pirates."

Matthew fought against blushing and fiddled with the sextant's index bar. "Are you visiting or staying in Australia?"

"Neither—I'm staying in Macao, and I might visit Canton. The Chinese don't like Western women to stay in Canton."

"But they've relaxed those restrictions," replied Matthew.

"Not for single women. According to my great-uncle, Canton will always be an enormous gentleman's club."

"Does he live there?"

"Not now." Ellie grinned and skipped away.

CHAPTER ELEVEN

Crossing the Greenwich meridian, the next Australia passage touch-stone southwest of Africa's cape, after a commendable seventeen-day run from St. Roque, brought cheers from the passengers and a twinkle to Captain Fiske's eye. There was yet hope to make amends for the disastrous thirty-nine-day first leg.

"If it hadn't been for Lieutenant Maury's charts, we'd be in a worse fix yet," Fiske said. He tamped his pipe mixture into the bowl as Matthew spread out a chart of the Indian Ocean on the day cabin table. A volume titled *Wind and Current Charts* lay open. "I would have sworn," continued the captain, puffing his pipe, "that we would have been trapped at St. Roque, going in as far as we did, but no—there she was, the current set offshore, just like Maury said it might. No tellin' how many weeks I could have saved in my time with this book—that is, if it's as right for the rest of the trip. Too bad he can't tell us when the storms are due."

"We would have left Boston anyway." Matthew stepped a pair of brass dividers along the sailing route.

"I guess you're right, Matt. Where did you get this book?"

"My brother, Mark, is the scientific sailor. He gave it to me on my birthday—I should say 'our birthday.' We're twins."

"I don't believe there could be *two* of you, Matt," Fiske said, watching the younger man with fascination.

Matthew hesitated with the dividers. It suddenly felt wrong to be in the same room with the captain . . . alone. There had been hints and emanations before, but he had thought of them as peculiarities. Now, after almost two months at sea, patterns were forming. "My brother and I are very unlike; we're not identical twins," Matthew answered indifferently. "In fact, he is now a mate aboard the *Atlantic*, a Collins steamship."

"Then he has no need for Maury's book," laughed Fiske. "What are you doing now?"

"This is one of Maury's Abstract Logs. He offers a free, up-to-date *Winds and Currents* volume for filling in these blank pages with information about our passage. In that way, he gets more to include in his next edition."

"Clever man . . . why, it's almost private enterprise—he *is* in the United States Navy, isn't he?"

"He's in charge of the Depot of Charts and Instruments. As a midshipman, he traveled around the world in the *Vincennes*. Then, on leave, he broke his leg in a stagecoach accident. It didn't heal properly, so he was assigned to the depot, where he found thousands of naval records concerning wind, tide and weather from all parts of the world. He compiled them and noticed similarities of observations, then refined the information into his book." Matthew put aside the abstract and lined up his parallel rule with a small island in the Indian Ocean. "If we can average two hundred miles a day, we'll sight Desolation Island by New Year's Day. From there it's three weeks to Melbourne, at the same rate . . ."

* * *

Almost four thousand miles to the east, a trio of snow-crowned mountain peaks caught the first rays of morning. Nestled on a plateau between these peaks and above the snowline, stretched a field of ice in the shadow, crunching now and then against its boundaries and forcing itself, by its own weight, to seek room to expand. In gullies and crevices, valleys and extinct river beds, the ice crept—ever seeking, ever joining other frozen streams. Mounting, growing, hardening and carving out of the island a longer, deeper and wider path, the burgeoning glacier pushed inexorably down to the sea.

The glacier, a mile wide at the ocean, with palisades much higher than the loftiest clipper masts, nudged into the cold antarctic current on the eastern shore of Desolation Island where it pushed itself off the land and scoured the sea bottom of reefs and rocks. It moved slowly—too slowly to disturb the hordes of terns, penguins and albatrosses, or the languishing colonies of sea elephants lowing on their rock islands. Imperceptibly, the million-ton edge of ice was buoyed up by the sea—one foot, then two feet off the seabed, until a slight bend faulted its bulk. Now the forces aligned with fissures and faults result first in sharp snaps that send the terns screeching skyward and the penguins hobbling helter-skelter. Then sounds a deep rumble and the sea elephants slip into the safety of their element.

Abruptly, a crash as loud as thunder signals the breaking off of a half-mile section, and plunging into deep water from the island's volcanic tidal ledge, it raises a great speeding wave as the immense frozen chunk settles to its level of buoyancy—one hundred feet above water to nine hundred below. Now 'calved,' the icy mass drifts unerringly out to sea.

It came upon a midnight clear,
That glorious song of old,
From angels bending near the earth
To touch their harps of gold:
'Peace on the earth, good will to men . . .'

Issachar Dew led the faithful on a balmy Christmas Eve with a stirring song written only the year before by an American Unitarian clergyman.

Though not a churchgoer, Matthew was drawn to the service, as he had been every Christmas of his life. He remembered a church in Portsmouth where, as a child, he enjoyed singing in the balcony—unseen by his playmates in the pews below. Matthew fancied himself a better singer than most. Now here he was again, but with no balcony to hide him from the crew. He slipped around the passengers who were seated on boxes, hatches and hasty benches about the mainmast and forward of the deckhouse in his search for a secluded place. Sitting on a water cask beside the animal pen, Matthew lent his baritone to the chorus and was immediately accompanied by the bleating of a goat and the mournful lowing of a steer. This prompted a strident cackling and honking from the fowl coops. The combined cacaphony was such that Preacher Dew, illuminated by lanterns set along the quarterdeck rail, threw up his hands in dismay. Voices trailing off and accordion falling silent, the congregation turned toward the source of the disturbance and saw the apologetic first mate trying to silence his clamorous choir.

"Mr. Hadley, I simply adored your ensemble. I can see you at the Castle Garden next Christmas: Phineas T. Barnum presents an Evening of Carols, by Matthew Hadley and his . . ."

"Barnyard Baritones." Matthew concluded the sentence. Ellie had remained behind when the other passengers, including her chaperone aunt and a companion, had gone down below to their cabins.

"Well, it wasn't your fault," she consoled him, putting her hand on his. "Besides, I thought it was fun. This trip is getting to be a bore. There's just nothing to do." She withdrew her hand, fearing that Matthew would feel or hear her heart pounding. "Come, let's go up there," she said, and tugged at his coat sleeve.

Sitting on the skylight bench, Matthew kept a discreet distance from the ebullient young lady. He was grateful that there was no one but the helmsman on the quarterdeck and that it was his friend, Lano the Panamanian. He thought he saw the Negro grin by the light of the helm binnacle, and that made him even more uncomfortable. There were stringent laws concerning the crew's deportment with lady passengers—especially with ladies of tender age.

Matthew cleared his throat uneasily. "Shouldn't you go back to your cabin? It's past nine."

"But it's still a little light," Ellie said, pointing at the red glow over the taffrail. "Besides," she giggled, "Julie—she's my friend—told Aunt Clara that I was going to the ship's library to find a diverting book to read. I have at least half an hour before my aunt gets testy." Ellie shuffled closer to Matt and her crinolines rustled against his coat. A fragrant aroma had replaced the smell of varnish and brine.

"It feels funny to have warm weather for Christmas—but it's still Christmas, and I brought you a present. Sorry I didn't have time to wrap it." Ellie put her clenched fist into his hand and opened it slowly, suggestively, with a caress of his palm that sent shivers up his arm. "Do you like it?"

Matthew held the tiny object up to the skylight

behind the bench. "What is it?" He turned the polished wooden charm between his fingers. "It looks like a plum." He held it by a tiny metal loop.

"You're close. It's a peach, the Chinese symbol of longevity and immortality. It is thought that the peaches in China's heavenly orchard ripen only once every three thousand years. Merry Christmas, Matthew."

"I can't accept this. . . . Besides, I have nothing to give you in return." He fumbled in his coat pockets and, to his surprise, found something. Ellie took it out of his hand. It was a bone button.

"This will do for now." She held it up against the other buttons on his coat. "Where does it belong?" Ellie leaned across him to examine his other sleeve and he found his arm around her waist. He tried to withdraw, but she pressed his hand against her bosom and nuzzled her head under his chin. The privation of many months stirred within him until he was afraid that she'd notice. Matthew buttoned his coat and sprang up, hand in pocket. "Come on, I have a real present for you." He led her softly by the arm. "You're going to get a ship for Christmas."

"Lano," he called, as he swaggered up to the ship's wheel, "I'll take over till three bells." Matthew looked at the sand glass next to the lamp-lighted binnacle.

The helmsman nodded and took the glass with him. Each turn of the glass amounted to one-half hour—each turn to one more bell. There was still fifteen minutes' worth of sand left before the binnacle bell was to be rung. It was then the deck officer's task to make sure that the sand glass turns coincided with the ship's chronometer every change of watch—so much the easier if the deck officer possessed a dependable pocket timepiece.

Matthew handled the big spoked wheel as if it were a toy, turned it almost imperceptibly in rhythm with the boat to keep the sails taut and pulling to their maximum. A steady breeze from the northwest came over the port quarter and billowed Ellie's dress as she stood by the steering box admiring Matthew's skill.

"Now, you take the wheel with me," he offered.

Ellie hesitated, but Matthew took her hand in his and put it on the wheel. A feeling of elation swept over her as she felt the thrum of ocean against the rudder and the strain of canvas in the wind. Overhead, above the cloud of darkened sail, the southern constellations sparkled festively—Christmas candles among the booms and stays of the towering masts.

"You're doing fine." Matthew held up his hands to show Ellie she'd been handling the wheel alone. "My gift for you is the *Nightingale*, even if only for a few minutes." Matthew grabbed the wheel as Ellie, surprised, realized what had happened and swooned into him.

"My God, Matt . . . I could have wrecked your ship!" Ellie clung to his body, pressed between him and the massive brass-bolted oaken wheel. Captive of the ship and the man she'd desired ever since she first saw him on the pier in Boston, Ellie closed her eyes and imagined being lashed to the wheel and submitting to a man's—*this* man's—most impulsive desires.

CHAPTER TWELVE

"STOP," called out the second mate as the log glass sand ran out. Gerrish counted the knots as a seaman hauled in the line. Spaced at one about every forty-five feet, the knots had run overboard for twenty-eight seconds before being stopped. Two seconds of the half-minute glass had been allotted for erroneous spacing of the knots.

"Eleven . . . twelve . . . thirteen . . ." the lean Georgian squinted in the diminishing daylight. It was more than thirteen and less than fourteen. "Fourteen," he shouted decisively. There was no place aboard a ship for unlucky numbers.

Captain Fiske, apprised of the auspicious speed and progress of *Nightingale*, consulted his ivory-scaled mercury barometer and gave orders to carry full canvas for the night. With a visual bearing fix on the triple-peaked island called Desolation and with a fair wind, good easting was to be made. The charts showed clear sailing and no reefs, the closest landfall being well south and two days' run after Desolation Island.

At eight o'clock, when Matthew came on deck to relieve the second officer, he looked toward the hori-

zon in the wind's direction, then at the laboring
canvas and the main t'gallant sail which threatened to
blow away. Since nautical etiquette forbade the deck
officer to alter canvas while the Captain was on
deck—at least not without his Captain's command or
consent—the first mate observed: "Captain Fiske,
that main t'gallant is struggling hard . . ."

"It holds a good full, let it stand," was the reply.

Nicholas Miles held a disk of copper and rubbed
the silvered surface with fine pumice powder and
sweet oil on small balls of cotton wool. First he
rubbed the four-inch plate with a circular motion,
then with straight up-and-down strokes.

Next he mixed a solution of distilled water and
nitric acid in his cabin wash basin. Passing the plate
over a lamp flame, he heated it and washed it in the
prepared solution. After lowering the lamp flame,
and hanging his coat around it so the cabin was
almost pitch dark, Nicholas set the plate on a jar
containing iodine, its silvered face down to absorb
the fumes that were strained through a piece of muslin stretched over the volatile fluid. The plate, thus
prepared, was covered with a disk of opaque black
paper and slipped into a small, cylindrical, light-
proof cannister.

With the stateroom once more illuminated, Miles
replaced his chemicals in the velvet-padded cherry
case and extracted a polished brass barrel that was
five inches in diameter at the center and had both ends
tapered. One end contained a capped lens, and the
other a peephole ringed with a wooden insert. Miles
unscrewed the latter end and held it up to the light to
examine the ground glass screen. Satisfied, he replaced it and slid the three-element lens out of the
front of the instrument. Uncapping the lens, he dusted

the elements carefully before setting the unusual camera into a fitted and screw-adjustable pedestal. The artist was now ready.

Miles sat back on his berth and admired the instrument. He'd bought it in New Orleans after his trek and wagon train ordeal through the southwest territories. As an artist, he had been interested in the daquerreotype process earlier, but its limitations had discouraged him from using it. The poor lenses and slow-acting chemicals required exposures of almost twenty minutes, even in sunlight. He could sketch faster than that. Moreover, he was interested in recording flora and fauna of the nation's wilderness, and what animal would stay motionless for such a long time?

This camera represented a revolution in the art. Made by a German telescope and optical genius, Peter von Voigtländer, it incorporated a lens designed by Josef Petzval, a professor of mathematics at the University of Vienna. With no sacrifice of clarity, this lens gathered sixteen times more light than any other in existence. Exposure times dropped to under a minute, and Miles had perfected his chemistry, during a trip up the Mississippi, to enable exposures as short as eight seconds.

Giving up brush, crayons and watercolors for "nature's pencil," as it was dubbed by the famous English pioneer of the heliograph, Henry Fox Talbot, Nicholas Miles became the Audubon of the new medium. An exhibit of his wildlife daguerreotypes received wide acclaim in New York and resulted in an assignment from *Harper's Monthly* to travel to other countries and photograph the curiosities and wildlife there. The plan was to make duplicate exposures, when possible, so that one of the plates could be etched in galvanic baths and printed on a gravure press for reproduction and insertion in special editions of the monthly.

Miles put on his outrageous plaid coat, wrapped his camera and prepared film plate cannister in cloth, then locked his cabin door and climbed the companionway stairs up to the deck. There was a full moon and he was excited over the prospect of attempting a photograph to capture the romance of the night sea as seen from *Nightingale* on its way to exotic Cathay. He envisioned it as a frontispiece for his assignment.

"It looks like a telescope for observing stars. My brother had one in Portsmouth." Matthew watched as Miles lashed the instrument's pedestal to the port cathead timber, just inside the fo'c'sle rail. "I always liked to look at ships through it, except that they were upside-down. I'd swear that was a telescope."

"That's because it's round instead of a square box. It's logical, since lenses are round anyway—but boxes are easier to make. This camera was very expensive." Miles looked through the peephole at the low-hanging moon and its dazzling reflection on the rippling sea. Satisfied with what he saw in the ground glass, he tightened the pedestal set-screw. "Here, see what the lens sees before I put the plate in."

Matthew put his eye to the instrument. "Upside-down again."

"True," replied the artist, "but unlike our vision, we can simply turn the resulting picture around."

"Too complicated for me," Matthew said. He glanced at seaman Nickels, the forward lookout, then waved to Miles and went aft.

Miles looked through the peephole once more. Perfect. The composition was still centered—which proved that the boat was on a constant course. Good for an eight-second exposure. He slipped the lens cap back on and unscrewed the rear conical section. Taking out the ground glass disk, he put in its place one of the prepared copper plates—sliding out the opaque paper disk just before screwing the cone back in place. Taking off the cap once more, he counted:

"One . . . two . . ." Suddenly a dark pall descended. A cloud had obliterated the moon.

"Ruined . . . Ruined!" exclaimed the artist. His eyes straining into the blackness ahead and his hand ready to change plates, Miles waited impatiently for the moon to reappear.

There was a momentary break in the cloud which brightened the horizon, but soon all was black again. Only something remained on Miles' optic memory. It wasn't a cloud—nor an illuminated part of the sea. It was jagged, enormous . . . and white. And now it was gone. Was it an hallucination? No, he had great faith in his visual senses: shape, color, size.

Iceberg, he thought.

Then he shouted out the word.

"Where away?" Seaman Nickels had been drowsing.

"We're heading straight for it!" screamed Miles.

Nickels dashed to the foremast and rang the big ship's bell. "HARD ALEEEeee . . . !" The shout echoed throughout the ship in response to the clanging forward. Canvas slatting and spars groaning, the ship turned its head into the wind as it came sharply about—creating mayhem in the saloons and cabins. Passengers were flung from their bunks and steaming pots catapulted from the galley stove. Deep in the bilges, frenzied rats scurried up the frames and overran the rope lockers and cargo decks.

Captain Fiske, who had been enjoying his private commode, came storming to the quarterdeck with intention of upbraiding the deck watch, when the obscuring clouds parted to reveal the towering iceberg to starboard as *Nightingale* was wearing away.

"Six . . . seven . . . eight . . ." Miles triumphantly slipped the cap back on his celebrated lens.

CHAPTER THIRTEEN

"I'll be a wealthy man before I go back to Scotland, and when I return, I shall drive the usurpers from the rightful land of my ancestors. I'll buy them all out. Old Angus MacFergus will quadruple his fortune in China . . ." The whiskered passenger danced a short jig on the main hatch.

"Excuse the interruption, my friend—but who are the usurpers you speak of so violently?" Issachar Dew assumed the stance of a black praying mantis.

"Why the Dalriad Scots, of course, and their traitor king, Kenneth of Kintyre, who put his lot in with the Scandinavian pirates and slaughtered my people, the original landowners of the north of Scotland. It was my ancestor, whose name I bear, who was the King of Pictland. Now we are ridiculed as a mythical folk, hardly human, and credited only with building some ancient cathedrals."

"Pray, what business do you pursue in Cathay?" the prim preacher asked indifferently.

Angus slapped his striped breeches. "I'm afraid a man of the cloth would not agree with my pursuits, though there are some that would consider your interests equally habit-forming."

"My friend, it is not too late . . ."

"I'm beyond preaching to—Mr. Dew, is it? I waited a long time in Melbourne for a berth to Canton. I've sweated and bled in Ballarat, Yarra and the Plenty Ranges. The nuggets I found didn't come easy, and I ain't letting them go easy." Angus MacFergus waved his tam-o'-shanter vigorously at the receding heights of the town of Melbourne. "Farewell to ye," he sang out, "bleak land with all yer dingos, bats and aborigines."

Nightingale glided between Swan and Mud Islands, past the fishing port of Queenscliff and through the Port Phillip narrows. Sails abox, it put off the harbour pilot and stood out to sea.

Running in ballast, the clipper had unloaded its cargo of digging tools and most of the passengers in Melbourne—adding New Englanders to the influx of forty-niners, broken-down noblemen, continental rebels and Chinese that would swell the town's population within three years from 75,000 farmers to 300,000 gold seekers. In addition to Angus MacFergus, several Chinese had boarded at Melbourne, including a prosperous Cantonese merchant prince.

Following Maury's sailing directions, Captain Fiske took the clipper along the eastern shore of New Holland—as Australia was called on Maury's charts—and inside the Great Barrier Reef to the Arafura Sea. Turning north at Timor Island, *Nightingale* ran with the trades through the Molucca Sea, evading the monsoon-tossed China Sea in passing the Philippines by the Pacific route.

Averaging better than two hundred miles a day from Melbourne to Mindanao, a distance of more than four thousand miles, Captain Fiske's hopes for a record passage were crushed by strong headwinds north of the Equatorial Calms. On the Ides of March, Jenny Lind's glazed pine face finally looked into the setting sun toward Canton.

Crossing the South China Sea from the Babuyan Channel north of Luzon, *Nightingale* found on the coast as competitors the British clippers *Stornoway*, *Chrysolite* and *Challenger*, as well as the Yankees' *Challenge* and *Surprise*.

With a brisk north wind whistling up spindrift waves, the clipper beat its way up the western side of the Canton River estuary and anchored in the lee of the Portuguese peninsular settlement of Macao. Its name derived from *A-Ma-ngao*, or "Harbour of the Goddess A-Ma," the colony was built among rocky hills with flat-roofed houses painted blue, green and red. Along the east side of the peninsula, facing the river and anchorage, ran a white ribbon called the Praya Grande, or "great promenade," on which was built the governor's palace and the chief commercial establishments. Three hundred feet over the harbour loomed ancient churches and a fortress. Across the estuary, studded with shoals, lay a cluster of islands called the *Ladrones*, or Thieves—piratical retreats that, after being ceded to Britain as a result of the Opium War in 1842, were to be known as Hong-Kong, or "the Place of Sweet Lagoons."

Ellie Russell and her entourage stood with the other Macao-bound travelers at the waist gangway among trunks and boxes crammed with clothing and personal effects. Two tanka boats had come from Macao to ferry the passengers over the shoals; they were fat little craft, low in the choppy water, with seats wrapped in straw matting. This made them look like what the Chinese called them: "egg-house boats." Cantonese girls wearing loose nankeen pants and shirts handled the oars. Some wore red and white blossoms in their long black hair, and one had a baby strapped to her back.

"Hold on there," called Matthew Hadley to the bosun as the gangway ladder was being secured and lowered on the starboard side. "This is no sea for ladies and ladders. Rig up a chair and tackle from the main yard."

One by one, the score of passengers were swung over the rail and lowered into the arms of crewmen stationed on the tanka boats. The men went first, declining to be tied to the chair. The ladies, in addition to safety bridles, modestly accepted that their billowing skirts be tied below the knees.

As the egg-house boats pulled away, Ellie Russell stood up in the lead boat and threw a kiss at the clipper. Captain Fiske, leaning on the quarterdeck binnacle, chuckled at his first mate. "Matt, that kiss was for you, I take it."

"Do you refer to Miss Russell?" Matthew blushed.

"Too bad we have no business in Macao, eh?" Fiske pulled at his cheek whiskers as he puffed his pipe. "Have you heard of Russell and Company?"

"The biggest trading establishment in Canton . . ." Matthew's face turned color. "Do you mean that she . . . Ellie . . . Miss Russell . . ."

"She didn't tell you?"

"Miss Russell only mentioned her great-uncle. He used to live in Macao, but moved away."

"That's him, old Sam Russell. Even had a sharp clipper named after him—built by Brown and Bell, with Nat Palmer as master. She made Canton in one hundred and fourteen days on her first voyage. Beautiful vessel, heavily sparred, and with plenty of light canvas for the doldrums. Did a day's run of three hundred and twenty-eight miles last year outward from Canton. Sam Russell may have moved away, but he still owns Canton." Captain Fiske decided that he would not bring his first officer to the trading powwow at Suy Hong, the "Factory" of Russell & Co. As his forte was not women, he dared not exhibit his first mate for fear of complications. Even though women would not normally be found at the trading establishments, there was a chance that Russell's manager might initiate a rekindling of the shipboard friendliness between Miss Russell and Mr. Hadley. And what was there to stop the young lady from dealing directly with his first mate—or asking her uncle to show him favors? No, John Fiske needed Matt Hadley, but only as a subordinate—at least in the shipping business.

Nightingale weighed anchor and sailed with the tide up the broad harbour to the Bogue, a narrows commanded by five ancient forts atop sandstone heights, which marked the mouth of the great Pearl River, gateway to the riches of Cathay.

From the stone parapets, Manchu cannoneers looked out of loop-holes over their sixteenth-century Portuguese cast-iron barrels at the trim clipper far below. The cannon, obsolete by the day's standards, were fixed permanently in stone—incapable of traverse or elevation ranging. But a surveyor's transit, if applied to the axis of the cannon, would show that each weapon was fixed on its own spot in the narrow Bogue, which is a nautical term for a vessel "falling off the wind." What better place for fixed guns than a vantage from which heavy shot can be fired at enemy vessels as they wallow upon losing the wind and drift from one watery square to the next? An artillery chessboard.

*   *   *

Passing Tiger's Mouth Island, the clipper ghosted by the acacia and bamboo-lined sandbars of the Pearl River's tributaries to a sharp bend from which the foretop lookout saw a strange edifice.

"PAGODA HOOOooo. . . ."

A spindly ten-tiered column rose through the mist lying over Whampoa Island. As *Nightingale* drew closer, mast tops with pennants could be seen beyond the lowest hills.

The prosperous Chinese merchant, Yung Lo, wearing his winter tunic of various shades of blue, with a scarlet-crowned blue cap topped by a blue glass button, stood on the quarterdeck with Nicholas Miles. "As a painter," commented the mustached Oriental, "you must meet our illustrious artist-in-residence. He is an Irishman who has lived here twenty-five years. Mr. George Chinnery escaped an inconvenient wife, as well as his creditors, when he moved from Dublin to Macao. Several years ago, his wife sailed to Macao and Mr. Chinnery removed to Canton, where foreign women were not permitted. Today, even though the new treaties have decreed that women be allowed in the walled city, the situation is much the same. Traditions are not easily changed by the stroke of a pen."

"The Western woman is quite different from the Oriental," Miles snickered as he admired the view of Whampoa.

"That is because the Western man has allowed himself to become weaker. In China women are honored because of their submission to the wishes and will of the man. It seems that your women are more feared than honored, at least in the family realms."

"Do you fear the Western woman?"

"Ah, Mr. Miles, as a humble merchant, I keep my peacock in its pen and I feast on its beauty. When it is hungry, I bring it grain. Never do I let it find the place I keep the grain in. Canton is the grain house of

China. As an artist you may be familiar with our ancient symbol, the Yin and Yang. The first signifies darkness, water, cold and womanly submissiveness, as opposed to the Yang of light, earth, heat and masculine domination."

"Well, Mr. Yung," Nicholas Miles said, as he buttoned his flamboyant plaid jacket up at the neck, "I believe there is wisdom in both camps—as well as folly. As an observer of nature, I'm fascinated by certain parallels in man and beast, or bird, if you will. Would you consider man an animal?"

"Buddhism, as you may well know, regards the difference between human beings and animals as unimportant, and we believe that equal compassion should be extended to all. In this respect, I agree that man and animal are one."

"As an artist, I am enthralled with visual phenomena. In all forms of life, it seems—excepting man—the female is the least colorful. Lions, peacocks and lizards are continually demonstrating the dominance of the male. Not only does the male forage and fight for the sustenance of his brood in the wilds of jungle and plain, and in the sea, but he also stands out in plumage, gait and majesty in his territory. But, alas . . . in the human zoo it is not so. In my world, the female is now usurping that position that has been the male's since time began."

"Mr. Miles, you speak, no doubt, of the Western woman," Yung Lo said, ruffling his silk robes.

"That is true, Mr. Yung. The women of your Eastern culture wear drab feathers and do not speak up." Miles pondered his approach. "But it has happened in other countries—more and more are women rising from their secondary roles. In my country, colleges are now admitting women on the same basis as men. Soon, it will not only be that their feathers are brighter, but their occupations and pursuits as well."

"Mr. Miles." The Chinese merchant took slight umbrage. "Are you suggesting that the Chinese system of values will eventually evolve into something like your own? That it is inevitable that women will encroach upon man's domain?"

"Mr. Yung," Nicholas said, as he accepted a cup of tea from the merchant's servant, "I will offer that the further the male crow flies from the nest, the more the female will assume his role at the nest."

"Then, Mr. Miles, the male may have to feather yet another nest: the nest of power. But don't forget; it is not just the Occidental woman who is restricted. In Canton it is forbidden that a Chinese girl be seen with the *Fanqui*—forgive me; *Fanqui* is the term for your countrymen and the Europeans. Roughly translated, it means 'foreign devil.' "

"It seems that restricting a Chinese girl is for a different reason than . . ." Miles was interrupted by staccato voices and the creaking of oars in their thole pins.

"The *walla-walla* boats have arrived," exclaimed the resplendent merchant. "From now on we'll be harassed by the leeches who want our money and our garbage. These early birds come to be first at the gangway even before the ship is anchored. A nuisance, as they get in the way of navigation."

"The name sounds Indian," Miles said. He wished he'd had his sketchbook or, even better, his camera handy.

"No," laughed Yung Lo, "it comes from the incessant jabbering of women. Each sampan is owned by one family, all of whom live on the boat, with the possible exception of the adult males, who always seem to be employed elsewhere."

"Feathering nests ashore?" suggested the artist.

"Very possible, Mr. Miles."

"This first sampan has many children aboard—all

girls," observed Nicholas. A woman seated aft of the arched matting deckhouse was sculling a long, curved oar. One child, the smallest, was lashed to the mast; another, standing on the bow with a line, wore large gourds about her waist. Two more, with shaved heads, save a long, erect tuft of hair on top, sat peering out of the deckhouse.

"They are not *all* girls," corrected Yung Lo. "Since girls are not as important as boys in our society, the anxious mother and skillful master of the sampan seek to protect the male children from evil spirits. To do this, the mother dresses the boys as girls and even calls them by feminine names. The tufts of hair on the little ones are intended to interfere with the spirits' flight through the air. Aside from the babbling and bartering, the sampan families are very stable; each child has a task to perform while moored or under way, so consequently, the child, as well as developing a skill, also feels needed by the family."

Suddenly the decks of *Nightingale* sprang to life.

"Anchor catted, sir," the bosun called out as the two-ton bower was hung from its forward boom.

"Take in the main course. . . . Brail the standing jib. . . ."

The black-hulled clipper, waterline copper glinting, wore 'round Whampoa Island into the broad anchorage known as the "reach." Riding the flood current under shortened sail, Jenny Lind's namesake passed a series of brightly kept mastless hulls, moored fore and aft, sporting second levels above the rails, and covered with woven, pitched long roofs. Stars and stripes fluttered aft, and mercantile burgees forward on these latter-day arks.

Spotting a likely void among the moored clippers ahead, Captain Fiske directed the helmsman to ease in.

"DROP ANCHOOOoor . . ." A spume of white

spray rose over the bow as the heavy mass of iron hit the water.

"Over there," Fiske said, pointing at the mastless arks, "are the ships' chandlers. Tom Hunt out of Salem owns two of 'em. Makes more money selling goods to ships at high prices than we do hauling tea to London. Real Yankee enterprise, eh, Matt?"

The vessel glided ahead, precisely between its new neighbours, the rails and ratlines of which were speckled with waving figures. Veering, the clipper ran smartly past her anchor.

"BAG THE MIZZENnnn . . ."

The gaff-boomed sail was laid aback, slowing the boat's forward motion just as the anchor cable snubbed taut and its iron flukes dug into the bottom clay of Whampoa Reach.

"LET GO THE CABLE . . ." *Nightingale* picked up way again, ran a quarter mile, then dropped its port bower. Almost slack tide, the windlass was manned and the boat winched downstream as the second cable was secured to the stern and snubbed taut, mooring the vessel fore and aft—independent of tidal current changes.

Situated on the east bank of the Pearl River, Canton's waterfront was obscured by a floating city of small moored craft. Approaching in a sampan, rowed by children and sculled by their grandmother, the *Fanqui* passengers were captive to Yung Lo's tourism.

"That," pointed out Yung, "is the tower of a mosque built by Arabian voyagers over a thousand years ago. Commerce is not a new thing to us, as you can see. The other tower, octagonal, with nine stories, was built three hundred years earlier. It has guided many ships to our city, announced to our merchants the arrival of your trading boats and warned our people of aggressive fleets. Across the harbour is the splendid island of Honam, home of the city's *hongs*, including your humble guide. A quarter of a million people live on these sampans. Notice that, though they are packed together like the scales of a fish, there are still streets and lanes left open. One can buy anything from the vendor boats that ply these lanes. Kitchen boats sell hot foods, the barber rows his own boat and rings a bell, and the river doctor announces his approach by beating a drum. One can even avail himself of a floating mortuary."

A shrill, falsetto voice, accomanied by a clang of cymbal, pierced the calm harbour. "What boat is that?" asked Matthew. "The little sampan with the old man on the stern."

"That," whispered Yung Lo, "is a 'one-girl flowerboat.' "

"It sells flowers?" Nicholas Miles leaned over the rail.

The merchant shook his head. "For many centuries it has been the custom of Chinese gentlemen of leisure to find amusement on a warm summer evening by chartering a boat for himself and his friends, with music provided by singing girls. In the past, these girls were highly trained on various musical instruments as well as in voice, and they were well versed in literature. The height of this art was during the Six Dynasties, at the time of the building of that pagoda tower. Gradually the custom of hiring boats and singing girls became more general, and the ladies less educated. Also the boats became smaller, and are now the one-girl flowerboats. As a rule, the lower the talent of the flower girl, the brighter her boat is painted."

Blinding lights flashed from the rigging of a group of large junks anchored in mid-river. "They seem to be signaling; is it a form of semaphore?'' Captain Fiske shielded his squinty eyes.

"No, they are large mirrors set into the wind vanes,'' replied the merchant. "They now reflect the sun, but are intended to frighten off such nautical demons as the nine-tailed tortoise and the three-legged rain-calling frog. The demons are so ugly that they will fly from their own reflections."

"And the green flags?" Miles pointed at the sharply upturned bow of a medium-sized junk. Large fierce eyes of lacquered wood and porcelain leered down at the sampan as it sculled under the bow. Along the side could be seen square open ports, covered with matting. A black cannon muzzle protruded from one.

"*Nai Tzu* is the green force against sickness, disease and injury. Banners and strips of that color are commonly used by warships in port, especially when the crew has been given leave."

The child-propelled sampan, sail hanging limp against its mast, slid into the moored city and, deftly turning corners, came to a landing float in front of a tree-lined public square, behind which stood a row of white and pastel-colored two and three-storied buildings. Of Western design, they had been built by the British, Dutch and French during the preceding century, and were called *factories*, even though their function was to handle cargo and provide accommodations for the trading companies' personnel. In the square, before their respective buildings, stood four ships' masts, completely rigged with ratlines and maintops. From their pinnacles flew the colours of four nations, though it might well have been only one. The Dutch were long gone, and so were the French—maintaining only small 'token' offices. The British, with their monopoly broken and the ill feelings from the recent Opium Wars, had left a skeleton company and repaired to the "Thieves" or Ladrones Islands across from Macao, eighty miles downriver, where they'd established their new trading port of Hong Kong, or "the Place of Sweet Lagoons."

CHAPTER FOURTEEN

After accepting an invitation to visit Yung Lo's house on Honam Island during their stay in Canton, Matthew and Nicholas went their separate ways. Captain Fiske had already left the party to attend to the ship's cargo in the offices of Russell & Company, which occupied the largest group of buildings on the square. Matthew, in the capacity of supercargo for items other than tea, went around to the street beyond the factories to look in the shops for Kiangsi porcelain, a favorite and valuable commodity.

Nicholas Miles set up his eccentric brass camera on the edge of the square to photograph the bustling harbour. He had prepared a score of sensitized copper disks and looked forward to a unique portrayal of the ancient city and its inhabitants. To his knowledge, there had never been photographs taken of Canton and shown in America. He trembled so with excitement that he dropped the lens cap and caught it just before it rolled down an incline to the water. Passing laborers and boat people, upon seeing the strange device aimed at the harbour, walked behind the *Fanqui* rather than chance the glinty demon.

Miles doffed the lens cap at the decorative water-melon boat, so named because of its rounded sides and decks. With fingers crossed, he captured the Honam ferry, and was disappointed when a one-girl flowerboat did not come close enough.

The square was alive with hawking peddlers, cackling fowl, and the calling out of services such as ear cleaning, barbering and jolly toenail cutting. Portable kitchens spewed out tantalizing aromas of roast pig and goose. Jugglers kept an array of shapes and hues in the air, as lithe boys balanced atop poles and monkeys imitated their masters. Fortune tellers whispered secrets to their patrons and musicians plinked and rattled on primitive instruments.

At a far corner of the square, a circle of onlookers grew into a crowd. Thick as locusts, they pressed in on a hapless, ragged magician from the provinces— all of them eager to observe his sleight-of-hand and baffling nests of boxes.

Fearing pilferage and the confined spaces of an alien city, the tattered magician drew a string from his prop sack and twirled a musket bullet about his head in an ever-increasing radius. Eyes closed for fear of hitting someone, he relaxed as the crowd backed off from the whizzing missile. Once more he demonstrated his talents, then collected some coins from the ground and packed away his spheres, ribbons and boxes.

Fascinated, the photographer followed, carrying his own paraphernalia, and dangled a silver coin before the performer's eyes. With a happy nod, the magician set up his tools anew. After placing his boxes and spheres to best advantage and laying out his coloured strings and beads, he finally looked up at his patron. Only he saw not a foreign devil, but the black mouth of a brass cannon. With a curdling shriek, the ascetic Oriental threw his props into the air and bolted away. Miles, under the stares of merchants and peddlers alike, quickly disassembled his menacing instrument, boxed it, then collected the magician's scattered props in order to return them. Tying the pieces into the vermilion cloth on which they had been displayed, the photographer meekly waited for the claimant to return.

Finished bargaining for a sizeable cargo of various porcelains including dishes, bowls, tiles and figurines, Matthew arranged for their delivery to *Nightingale* and wearily made his way back to the foreign quarter. It was now late afternoon, a time when the *Fanqui* descended from their counting-houses and took their constitutionals, browsing along the teeming streets.

He stopped and waited as a procession of beggars staggered by, each tied to the next by pigtailed hair. Howling, they beat sticks together and clanged on iron pots. Encountering a group of foreign traders, they increased the din so that the merchants were forced to bribe them to leave.

Following the waterfront street, Matthew stumbled upon a crowd of Chinese sitting on a sloping grass hill. On the bottom, a large festive junk was moored alongside the river bank with a platform connecting its deck to the shore. It was soon apparent that he was watching a play in progress—the famous floating theater of Canton. Now and then, between sips of tea and rounds of nuts and sweets, the spectators grumbled and cheered at the demonstrative gyrations and grunts on the covered stage. Lanterns hung under the stage canopy gave a curious otherworldly aura as it was still daylight, the sun dipping behind the river valley hills.

A tea-seller wheeled his wagon down the incline and onto the junk to offer his wares to the actors as they performed. Now and then, a stagehand brought a prop into the scene and whisked one away. One of the principals, wearing a black lacquered mask, swung a huge ceremonial sword at his adversary, who fell to the matting. A stagehand walked briskly by and dropped a white cloth beside the casualty, who, despite being 'dead,' sprang up and walked offstage.

Confused, Matthew was about to leave when there was a commotion on the road above the slope. A group of the Emperor's soldiers, ancient matchlock rifles slung on their backs, came down and searched among the audience, row by row. As this was happening, a gray-masked actor sauntered from the junk and walked up the slope, gesticulating in cadence with the actors on the stage.

"Mr. Hadley," a friendly voice from behind the mask continued, "act as if I am not here. Your countryman, Mr. Miles, is on the stage. He wears a mask like mine. Those soldiers are looking for him. It seems he was taking a daguerreotype of some shrine inside the gates when the soldiers came along. Thinking he was desecrating their ancestors with a cannon, they were about to carry him off. Lucky for him I was watching. They believed my ruse and we escaped. Now I'm afraid they're looking for both of us. I suggest that your friend stay here for the evening. He is amenable to the idea. I'm sure there will be soldiers posted at the pier. By tomorrow they will be back with their regiments, but tonight I'm afraid of the effects of rice-wine."

"Are you an actor?" Matthew asked, puzzled.

"Only an avocation. I play Mrs. Malaprop in Macao occasionally, but I work as a portrait artist. I'm

George Chinnery, and I'm very excited at meeting a fellow artist such as Nicholas. You have no idea what an exile this life can be. By the way, Mr. Hadley, you must be tired of sleeping in a ship's bunk, and I have room in my house. Why don't you stay the night? I have a goodly supply of Irish whiskey.''

"No, thanks; I've got to get back. Perhaps another time." Matthew waved toward the junk, then left.

It was almost dark when Matthew climbed across several moored sampans toward the outside boat which had aboard some ships' officers and mates. As he stepped carefully over the deck of one, he heard what he thought was a faint scream from below. He hadn't meant to look, but a curtain had been pulled aside and he saw a terrifying sight. Silhouetted against a lantern in the cabin, a snake swayed slowly—poised to strike. On its hooded neck was a black spectacle marking. The dread cobra, although at home on land, was very much a creature of the rivers of China. Beyond the table upon which it swayed, hardly a yard away, a wide-eyed girl was singing—almost a high-pitched humming. Daring not to blink or move, lest the serpent strike, she seemed resigned to her fate.

"Hurry, mate," shouted a seaman from the sampan, "we ain't got all night." Matthew didn't answer. He stared at the black-haired young Chinese girl, and then at the swaying cobra. Feverishly looking about, he noticed an oar within arm's reach. Silently grasping it, Matthew undid the hemp seizing of the handle and fashioned it into a stout noose. Holding the oar by its blade, he thrust it slowly into the cabin toward the undulating serpent's head. Holding his breath, he summoned all his strength and slipped the noose over the cobra's head and pulled sharply. It was like fishing—like setting the hook—and he was a good fisherman.

The hissing, writhing coil of snake sunk its fangs deep into its assailant—tough close-grained wood. Carefully Matthew drew out the oar, then plunged its captive into the Pearl River and held it underwater until the oar stopped vibrating.

"Please to come in." The voice from inside the woven grass-covered deckhouse sounded like tinkling glass. Matthew leaned over and looked into the cabin. The girl was just lighting a large decorative lantern, and the light was reflected in numerous mirrors. Bulkheads and woodwork carvings gleamed with lavish, intricate inlays. Vermilion, ebony and green-veined marble accented the matting and screens. Wall-hangings of lustrous silk, with paintings and calligraphy, shimmered over a long, purple couch, upon which was set pillows covered with exotic furs.

"Please, I have good tea." The lantern highlighted the girl's white silk tunic as she poured tea from a delicately glazed pot. The translucent fabric stretched over her small breasts, roseate in the light. Satin blue slippers glistened under her flowing silk pantalets, and her long black hair blazed with the brilliant turquoise and aqua feather of a kingfisher, which hung down, its end almost touching her faintly carmined mouth.

Matthew stood up on deck again, and looked for the ferry sampan. Gone; only a mist on the darkening river. Ducking carefully, he took his boots off and stepped into the inviting cabin. The pungent-sweet aroma of camphor-laurel incense swirled from a dragon-shaped burner on the deep red lacquered table where, shortly before, the cobra had swayed. Next to the incense burner lay an enameled black and gold tray, upon which was propped a silver opium pipe in an ebony holder. Beside the pipe lay a shallow glass jar containing a molasses-like substance and a metal utensil.

Setting a curious lamp on the table, the girl lit it with a bamboo splinter. Inside a hemisphere of blue-tinted glass, a green flame flickered atop its whale oil repository as a wisp of smoke curled up through a circular opening of the outer shell. The flame's reflection danced in the girl's dark eyes.

"I am called Pao Ch'a. It means 'precious hairpins.' " She blew the feather away from her mouth. "It tickles."

Sitting gingerly across the table from the purple couch on a short wooden bench, with the girl to his right on a pillowed chair, Matthew suddenly realized that he might be aboard one of the boats described by the Chinese merchant. The couch that was a bed . . . the incense . . . the opium. Warily, he responded: "I'm Matthew Hadley; call me Matt. I'm first mate aboard the *Nightingale*, an American clipper out of Boston. I just missed the ferry sampan. That's why I'm here—having tea." He cleared his throat.

"Is very big boat . . . Matt?" Pao Ch'a pointed to the floor and giggled. "That *mat*, too? I call you Matt-wei, which means friend."

"Perhaps you would like to see the *Nightingale*?"

"What is Nightingale?"

"A songbird—the most celebrated of all songbirds."

"Pao Ch'a would like to see boat, but cannot go."

"Is your family ashore—your father and mother?"

"My family far away. Sampan belong to lady, to Kuan Nin—Lady Sincerity. She is famous *sing-song* girl. Tonight she entertains aboard big flower boat hired by famous *hong* Moqua for banquet. I will soon become apprentice to Lady Sincerity."

"Then you have not . . . entertained yet?" Matthew felt a glimmer of hope and concern.

"I shall entertain on my sixteenth birthday. Lady Sincerity is arranging a sampan for me. Tonight I watch the boat for the lady. I have also been practicing songs and poems. Will you stay and help me practice the art of conversation?"

Matthew sipped his tea. "Then I am here in friendship."

"There is no *laodah* to count the gentlemen or the money."

"*Laodah?*"

"He is the old man who clangs the cymbals and propels the sampan with his oar. The *laodah*, like this boat, belongs to the agent. He watches so the *sing-song* girl does not cheat the agent. I am not *sing-song* girl yet, so he go home."

"When is your birthday?"

Pao Ch'a held up three fingers. "Three day. Your Sunday."

Matthew looked around the cabin. "Is that Lady Sincerity?" He pointed at a portrait of an elaborately coiffured woman on one of the wall hangings.

"No," laughed Pao Ch'a, "that is P'an Chintien, the Goddess of Lady Sincerity's profession. She was a widow when her father-in-law murdered her to put an end to her disorderly behavior."

"Thieves have saints also," acknowledged Matthew.

"Matt-wei," the girl said, slipping onto the purple couch, where her new companion could not avoid her eyes, "I knew you would come. There is a legend from the faraway mountains of my father's people at the end of the mighty Yangtze. It tells of the demon's soul which lived in the serpent with twelve heads. The snake you slew had twelve such heads." Pao Ch'a moved her slim hand in a series of short gestures approximating a fan. "The cobra moves like so

. . . and appears to have many heads. In the legend, a warrior, Kök Chan, slew the twelve-headed serpent and gave the rescued maiden a golden ring which contained half his strength. Some time afterwards, the warrior in battle became very tired and was about to be slain. As a sword was raised over his body, a woman in the shape of a bird flew over and dropped the golden ring into Kök Chan's mouth. Inspired with new strength, he slew his enemy.''

"I have no golden ring to give you," Matthew said. He unbuttoned his shirt and took out the polished wood miniature peach. "Will this do?" He dangled the charm on its silver chain.

"Chinese girl give you? Very beautiful."

"No, it was a Christmas present given to me on the *Nightingale*—by a friend."

"You must not give away present." Pao Ch'a felt a touch of jealousy. The peach charm was exquisite and valuable. She wondered what rich mandarin's daughter it had belonged to. "The peach will make you live many years. It is better that you keep it."

Matthew poured more tea. "Very unusual taste."

"The Souchong tea grows in the mountains of Tibet. It is brought by river boats down the Yangtze to the lakes of Hupeh, then carried to the Chiang River where larger boats bring it to Canton. The Souchong tea is not favored by the English, so I practice with what I enjoy most." Pao Ch'a picked up the metal dipper from the tray and swirled it in the glass jar. With a large clump of soft opium adhered to the sharp end of the utensil, she held it, still twirling, over the opening of the blue lamp. Lowered closer to the flame, the clump sizzled and hissed, emitting a sweet aroma that mingled with the camphor incense

As Pao Ch'a roasted the opium gently, it became smaller and glazed, with the appearance of burnt worsted. Now and then she retracted the dipper, and rolled its product on the rim of the glass jar to form it into a perfect teardrop shape. Taking the opium pipe in her other hand, Pao Ch'a nimbly heated the bottom of the bowl, then thrust the opium-tipped dipper into the bowl's opening. After withdrawing the dipper, the clump of opium was firmly attached to the interior of the pipe's bowl.

"Please," Pao Ch'a entreated Matthew, smoothing down the purple fabric of the couch. "Sit next to me and we can enjoy together—and please to close the curtain against the night air."

This done, Matthew edged over to the couch and took the pipe from the girl, who had just inhaled. His eyes were watery and already the clouds of opium had affected him. His normal apprehension of the practice had weakened and he found himself wanting to be near this flower of the river, with her clinging tunic and her languorous movements—her naive trustfulness. She took his hand and guided the pipe down to the flame. "Hold it here," she instructed. "Now please to smoke a little at a time. We share, yes?"

"Yes," he agreed and drew deeply on the pipe as the girl leaned deliciously into him.

"Nice and cozy cabin, yes?"

"Very cozy, yes," Matthew said, and lay back on the pillows as Pao Ch'a unbuttoned his blouse.

The sound of drums woke him up. One small lantern was still alight, and he felt fur about his neck. It was a blanket, and he was under it—nude. His nose tickled, and he was about to scratch it when he grew aware of another body. Blinking and clearing his eyes, he saw a mass of black hair with something green in it. A feather had been tickling his face.

"Pao Ch'a?" he whispered.

"Matt-wei," she responded, and rolled over and pressed into him.

"The drums . . ."

"The hour of curfew has arrived." The girl was content that her partner had no previous knowledge of the Cantonese night; otherwise he would have recognized the significance of four drumbeats. "It is the hour of the horse. For the *Fanqui*, one o'clock." Pao Ch'a entwined her young body within his, wiggled her back into his front. She was small and fit perfectly. "This good; same as *yin-yang* picture." She clasped Matthew's hands to her breasts.

He remembered vaguely. They'd finished several pipefuls of opium, and he was woozy. She'd covered the purple couch with white linen. He was clumsy, but she was patient and submissive. For Matthew it was the first complete experience. There had been two occasions—somewhat unconsummated because of his strict family mores. But the opium had made him forget, as had the distance from home, the anonymity and the exotic surroundings. It was a dream— but there was the poem she recited. All he could remember were the last few lines:

'Alas and alas. Again alas.
So must a girl cry when she is in love
and she finds not a single heart
who will not leave her
till her hair is white.'

And there was the sign. Pao Ch'a had known no other man. Or was he dreaming? Had he only imagined the sign of chasteness? He would examine the linen again by the light of morning—quickly and discreetly. Here he had assumed that an apprentice concubine could not be other than . . .

*   *   *

Bells and vendors' shouts mingled with the bright sunshine that pierced the slatted forward window. Pao Ch'a was dressed and cooking rice and lamb cakes. Matthew waited until she turned away, then quickly threw the fur blanket aside. It was true. The sign was there. Re-covering the bed, he slipped into fresh linens that had miraculously appeared on the lacquered table.

"Lady Sincerity think of everything for the gentlemen. I wash your laundry already. You dry more on *Nightingale*." She set a tray of tea and cakes on the table.

"But I'll see you again," he protested.

"Only till Saturday, Matt-wei. I meet you someplace people no see maybe. After Saturday, no more. *Laodah* see, Lady Sincerity get mad. All tell agent. Better goodbye, Matt-wei."

"But this is ridiculous—crazy! Nobody can stop you."

"Agent can. He owns Pao Ch'a. See paper I have on sampan." She held up an official-looking document. "I read in English:

> *"PURCHASE OF A CONCUBINE*
> *The undersigned, Mei Chui—that's my father—from the village of Yung-pei-ting, has agreed to give his own daughter, Pao Ch'a, aged fifteen years, to the second party, Li Ying-tou, as a concubine, through the mediator, Wen Hsi.*
> *On this date the undersigned has received 200 taels of silver as payment. He agrees to give his daughter away on the date selected and will dare not cause any difficulties or extort more money. He also guarantees that the girl has not been previously betrothed, and there is no question as to her origin. Should such questions arise, or should the girl run away, the father*

will be held responsible. Should the girl die unexpectedly, it is her fate, and not the responsibility of the buyer."

"It is all over," Pao Ch'a tried to smile. "I honour my father's agreement. I will be good flowerboat girl . . ." A tear ran down her pale cheek.

"But it's unfair. A father should not be allowed . . ."

"This is not your country, Matt-wei. For many centuries in China, the daughter is sold. The daughter who becomes the mother is as a space in the air, but the son who becomes the father is as the mountain that touches the clouds. In our temples, the women pray that in the next life they will be sons and fathers." Pao Ch'a brushed off Matthew's coat. "You eat first please," she said, and sat across from him. "I practice cooking for you to be best flowerboat girl. Then it best for you to go before the hour of the rat, when *laodah* come back with Lady Sincerity."

Captain Fiske counted out the gold pieces. "Nineteen . . . twenty. That's a lot of money, Matt—just about all you will earn on this trip, including your share of the cargo. I'm sorry that we had to draw up an agreement, but one never knows when it comes to money. There's still a good distance to go and much to do before we get old 'Diving Bell' back to Boston."

"If I fall overboard or get run through by a Lascar, my family will reimburse the owners," Matthew said, putting the coins into a leather sack. "My father will simply deduct it from my inheritance."

"How you can joke about investing four hundred dollars in something you say will not bring you a monetary profit is beyond me. If I spent a half-year's wages buying something in China and bringing it halfway 'round the world, I would certainly expect a tidy profit.''

"I'm not bringing it back—at least not yet." Matthew tied up the sack and put it in his valise, next to an Ethan Allen pepperbox revolver.

CHAPTER FIFTEEN

The Mandarins were received with great ceremony at Chinqua's villa on the splendid isle of Honam, across the Pearl River from Canton. One, in particular, was fawned upon by merchants and government officials alike. Sharp-chinned and clean-shaven, he wore a magenta gown lined with white silk over his brocade robe, with sleeves flowing back from his manicured hands. An enormous star sapphire blazed on a finger, and long chains of lustrous jade hung from his shoulders and framed a square, embroidered gold panel on the gown's front. White-soled shoes were turned up at the toes, and his cap was topped with a bright blue button—symbol of his station and gauge of *Fanqui* behavior. It was customary that, should there be discord with the Western merchants, the cap would be unbuttoned, and the wearer in disgrace.

Nicholas Miles nudged his fellow artist on the elbow.

"*That*," confided dandified George Chinnery, "is Houqua, Jr. His father, the greatest *Cohong* of all, bought him the rank of Mandarin for the equivalent of 160,000 American dollars. I have painted several portraits of Houqua. While his son resembles him about the eyes and chin, he has little of Houqua's incomparable presence." The bespectacled Irishman plucked a stuffed plum from the tray of a passing servant boy.

"Houqua's fame is world-wide," Miles exclaimed. "What a coup it would be to photograph him. Benson Lossing could do a striking engraving for *Harper's* from a daguerreotype—that is, if the galvanic process cannot enlarge the original."

"You new-fangled artists will put me out of work with your electro-chemicals. I'm glad I won't be around to see calotypes in colour—and I don't mean the hand-tinted variety."

"George, could you arrange that Houqua sit for me?"

"He is frail and in retirement, but I'll see what I can do," Chinnery said. "The old man is quite adventurous, even at ninety. I think he still keeps a girl or two."

"It was certainly fortunate that I attempted to photograph a forbidden shrine; otherwise, I would have missed all of this. I can't get over these grounds—a veritable Xanadu." Nicholas looked through the marble-columned pavilion at the jewel-box landscape: gardens laced with streams and pools, decorated with mandarin ducks and slow-stepping ibises; the iridescent green dragonflies and brightly enameled birds; spindly bamboo bridges arching over miniature rivers with toy waterfalls and waterwheels; lush banks covered with geometrically placed chrysanthemums and flowering shrubs. "If this is Chinqua's villa, I don't think I could stand to see Houqua's." Miles drank green pea wine from a tiny silver cup. "Curious, that all the *Cohongs* have similar names, ending in 'qua.' Are they related? There's Maqua . . . and Puank-eiqua. . . ."

"The 'qua' means 'sir,' and the names are for business use only," Chinnery explained. "Think of Houqua as 'Sir Hou.' His real name is Wu Ping-ch'ein. The Chinese are very sensitive about involving their families and ancestors in the pursuit of profit."

Jovial, rotund Chinqua provided his varied guests with English, French and Chinese cuisine, each served in its proper ware. Thirty-course dinners were commonplace, the last three being desserts. These feasts lasted from three in the afternoon till ten, and they usually featured a company of actors and acrobats. Jugglers, tumblers and musicians performed between courses, while the actors offered a large repertoire of works. The finale was a pageant and circus consisting of tigers, mandarins and boys in bird costumes. Battles between demons and monsters were portrayed, the female roles played by boys impersonating quarrelsome mandarin women. A display of elaborate fireworks concluded the evening's fare—worlds apart from the grime and wantonness of the teeming city across the river.

Sitting at a well-provisioned table in a teahouse courtyard within sight of the main pavilion, Chinqua listened intently as Li Ying-tou related a story. The host savoured a spoonful of bird's nest jelly, and sucked it between his opium-yellowed teeth.

"Two hundred taels you paid for this provincial beauty—and then an American offers you thirty more? Only two dollars a pound, but still a good price for a wench to be resold. One day I shall realize that I pay thirty dollars a pound for Java birds' nests, and all I can do is eat them."

"Pure white birds' nests are fewer than virgins," observed Li Ying-tou as he sampled the delicacy.

"That's because of the difficulty of harvesting the nests," replied Chinqua. "Athletic Javanese boys descend steep cliffs by rope ladders despite the turbulent surf below, to pluck the swallow's house from its cave. A virgin is more easily found."

"But not in Canton," smirked the flower-boat mogul.

"Then why such a profit on used merchandise? The girl commanded a better price than a fresh virgin, according to my experiences—and I've had a few. Since when does a landlord like yourself purchase a young girl without being the first to sample her? It is the unwritten paragraph of the contract agreement, or . . ." Chinqua ran his whitened tongue over his wet lips. "Are you losing your manhood?"

"As surely as I partake of your favorite dish at this moment, so did I of the Tibetan child on the first night. Extraordinary girl, I am told. She learned the ways of the river and the *Fanqui* on her father's boat, a Yangtze trader."

"Why did you sell her?"

"I was in a selling mood, and amused at the offer."

"The American thought he was buying a white bird's nest, undefiled and never inhabited?"

"I'm sure he is convinced." Li Ying-tou smiled thinly. "Lady Sincerity is an advocate of the eel's blood technique."

Fits of laughter exploded from the host and, resounding through the lush green gardens, startled the hummingbirds from their blossoms and set off a flapping of white wings in the maze of streams and crystal pools.

*   *   *

Like a little boy with a new toy, Matthew skipped along the hemp-strewn shore till he found the row of sampans that included Lady Sincerity's flowerboat, conspicuous by its lavender mast. Bells in the unfinished spire of the new church in the merchants' square rang out, proclaiming Sunday morning services and casting a benevolent air over the crowded, tawny river.

Brandishing a white document before him like a pennant, Matthew scampered over the square bows of the moored and tethered boats until he arrived at the object of his quest. To be sure, he went aft on an adjacent sampan and looked for the curved nameplate on the stern that Pao Ch'a had translated for him. He recognized the calligraphic symbol for 'water' and was satisfied that the vessel was indeed the flowerboat known by the idiom,

WATER THAT SLEEPS IN THE MOONLIGHT.

Occupants of the various sampans that had been rocked by the intruder's exuberant passage popped their heads out, as neighbors do when the unusual is apt to occur. Sampan *Sincerity* was the talk of the waterway, a constant topic for conjecture and a pebble in the boat-wives' slippers.

"Pao Ch'a," shouted Sunday-dressed Matthew. There was no answer and he called again. About to jump aboard the end boat, he was confronted by a squat old man who assumed the position of a wrestler with sculling oar in hand. Holding up his writ, he stepped aboard the gaudy boat, only to dodge a blow from the *laodah's* oar. Sidestepping, he grabbed the wooden blade of the *yuloh* and twisted it sharply, throwing its wielder overboard. As the current carried the sputtering old man toward the adjoining row of boats, a dragon-faced apparition barged out of the cabin.

"Get off my boat," screamed the painted woman,

her white forehead crinkled in fierce lines. She looked
high and low for her oarsman, then backed away in
feigned terror.

"I bring an official *chop*," Matthew said, using
the Chinese word for directive. He held up the document and pointed at Chinqua's stamp as mediator.
The *sing-song* woman's eyebrows arched as she recognized the symbol, her frown changing to a practiced smile. "Are you the *Fanqui* called Matt-wei?"
Lady Sincerity primped at her towering coiffure and
promenaded haughtily on deck to snatch the document
from Matthew's hand. She read it quickly, holding it
at arm's length. "Take her then; I have no time anyway
to waste on apprentices . . ." She threw up her hands
and went below, secretly content. The fading flower
girl abhorred competition from young girls, especially in vying for the attention of Li Ying-tou. Amused
at the price of two hundred and thirty taels, Lady
Sincerity could hardly wait to tell her clique the tale.
It was a rare occasion when a man was caught by an eel.

With the last of his savings, Matthew hired a river
sampan to take Pao Ch'a to an inn on the River Li, a
four-day trip through the interlocking rivers and canals west of Canton. They moored at romantic and
picturesque points along the way. It was an idyllic
trip, the crew consisting of a man and his wife, who
did all the cooking, cleaning and piloting.

Tying up the sampan at the town of Zhaoging,
they hired a carriage and drove up a winding road to
the Inn of Forever Blue Jade. "Always," Pao Ch'a
confessed, "I have want to go here. Long ago, poet
write about Li River. Say 'river is green silk belt and
mountains are blue jade hairpins. . . .' "

The next day, they visited the "Thousand Year
Banyan Tree" and made wishes under its sprawling

branches. "I wait for Matt-wei till tree is *two* thousand year banyan tree," promised Pao Ch'a as their sampan turned back downriver.

Holiday over and *Nightingale* hull down with a full cargo of tea at Whampoa, the lovers chose Charcoal Bridge in Canton, near the herb market where Pao Ch'a was newly employed, to say goodbye. "Pao Ch'a work very hard. Save much dollars for Matt-wei come back." She took a white blossom from her hair and dropped it into the stream . . . and watched it float away.

Matthew kissed her on the forehead. "Precious Hairpins, I don't want you to save money. Promise me you'll stay in the room we've rented and buy nice things for yourself."

"But is so expensive . . ."

"Do you want me to worry about you?"

"Pao Ch'a stay; look like mandarin ladies for Matt-wei."

Matthew took the purchase agreement out of his pocket. "I would just as soon tear it up, but it's better that you keep it—just in case. The Taiping are getting dangerous. If the revolution gets to Canton . . ." He pressed the document into her hand as they embraced. "If there is any danger, bring this to the American *hong*."

They walked opposite ways on the arched stone bridge—neither looking back, and each with a tear in the eye.

Leaving Canton on July 31st, in the midst of the adverse monsoon season, *Nightingale* encountered several fierce storms from the southwest. Beating and tacking against the heavy weather and seas, it took her sixty-one days to clear the Sunda Strait, between Sumatra and Java. On September 30th, she wore 'round the tiny volcanic island of Krakatoa, near the center of the strait, and into the Indian Ocean. Her time thereafter, around Africa and to London, while good, was not enough to make up the deficit rendered by the South China Sea monsoons. The clipper arrived at Deal, an anchorage outside of London, on December 10th, some eight days later than her tardiest rival, *Challenger*, in an unofficial tea race from Canton.

Upon arrival, Captain John Fiske was so chagrined over the poor showing of *Nightingale* on his first voyage that he resigned and boarded a Cunard steamer to return to Boston. The owners sent out a replacement master, Captain John Mather, to take command while the boat lay at anchorage in the Thames. Mather, unfamiliar with the clipper ship, depended on the first mate to get the maximum out of the vessel on its return crossing.

Crowding on more canvas than he normally dared, Matthew was determined to better the east-to-west sailing record across the Atlantic. Running ahead of a northeaster, which persisted for almost a week, the vessel's log streamed to a high of almost twenty knots. The first mate, getting caught up in a frenzy, found himself acting like Jack Taggart on *Alchemist*'s voyage around the Horn to San Francisco. Matthew was doing it for Pao Ch'a. For the first time in his life, he wanted something bad enough to take it at any cost. A record passage would put him in line for command, if not of the *Nightingale*, then of some other sharp clipper on the Canton run. Despite the entreaties of the second mate to shorten sail, Matthew drove the ship and the men as only masters such as "Bully" Waterman and Josiah Creesy had accomplished earlier on record runs.

With minimum damage to her spars, and not a man lost, the clipper rounded Boston Light after a passage of less than fifteen days. The semaphores relayed news of the achievement and, upon docking, the vessel was met with a brass band and acclaimed by the owners and competitors alike.

Once ashore, Captain Mather accepted the accolades readily without a word of praise—even privately—for his first mate. This so enraged Matthew that he quit the clipper and rushed to Portsmouth, to put all his effort into the building of *Gemini*, the clipper-schooner that would carry him, as Master, back to Canton and Pao Ch'a.

CHAPTER SIXTEEN

Atop the flagpole, a green-edged copper windvane in the form of a sidewheeler steamship pointed north into a January gale with its sails furled. An ornate brass 'E' below the vane pointed toward the sprawling City of Brooklyn across the East River, while the counterpart 'W' lined up with 12th Street, a rural thoroughfare on the northern edge of New York City.

Below, on snow-rutted Dry Dock Street, a team of twelve dray horses snorted and strained as they pulled a wagon through the gateway of the Novelty Iron Works. Slung by cables from the beamed carriage, a ponderous riveted iron boiler was on its way to a shipyard further downtown.

The Novelty Iron Works was booming. Three high stacks belched black smoke from dawn till dusk over the complex of two and three-storied red brick buildings that housed foundries, finishing shops, pattern lofts and smiths' shops. The most prolific builder of marine steam engines in America, the facility employed over twelve hundred men and supported scores of sub-contractors in the area.

Inside the high-windowed main foundry building, huge clouds of dense gray smoke billowed up from a hissing mountain of moulding sand as a crew of workers waited with shovels in hand. In the center of this mass, a cylindrical iron barrel protruded from yet another larger tube. The inner barrel, four feet in diameter, had earlier been filled with molten iron for the casting of one of the two cylinders needed to power a side-lever marine engine, the latest variety being adapted by gearing to screw propulsion.

Looming over the smoldering scene, a gigantic derrick of thick oak beams and iron trusses waited—a lifting harness dangling on its cables. At a foreman's whistle, two dozen husky diggers swarmed over the hot sand and, enveloped in fumes, dug away until enough of the cylinder mold was clear to allow lifting of the unit from its ground-level pit.

Watching the procedure from a balcony a safe distance away, David Montebianco turned toward his client. "You can see, my dear Cleopatra, why a marine engine costs almost as much as the rest of the ship. The cylinder now has to be machined to a fine tolerance, and this is only one of a thousand pieces of the engine assembly. Since I am advancing you the capital to complete the *Javeline*, I must insist that it be built in New York rather than Boston. I happen to own an interest in Brown and Bells', it is true, but installing a screw engine demands the utmost of care. I have been in telegraphic communication with your engineer, Mr. Cook, in Boston, and he agrees that the Novelty Works can make a better engine than any concern in his fair city. It follows, then, that the enterprise should be accomplished in one locale.''

"Very well, David—but it must be ready by the end of this year. Jabez—that is, Mr. Cook—will have the hull ready by then, whether in Boston or New York."

"Now, shall we go and enjoy dinner, my dear?" The financier slipped a sable-trimmed pelisse over Cleo's shoulders. "Or is Mark Hadley in town again?"

"Must you always be so jealous, David? Sometimes I think you planned all this so I'd have to stay in New York."

"You must admit that Boston is a bore by comparison," Montebianco said, and escorted Cleo proudly down the stairs as many of the workmen looked up from their machines.

On Saturday, the fourth of July, 1853, the town of Portsmouth, New Hampshire, staged an industrial pageant in which shipbuilding was the dominant theme. Caulkers, painters, joiners and riggers—all attired in their working clothes and carrying tools of their trades—turned out in review. Ship's carpenters marched four abreast with brass-edged cherrywood squares on their shoulders, and boys swung buckets and mops, while rope makers wore coils of their product across their breasts. A line of timbermen marched with adzes, and coppersmiths with sheets of gleaming metal. Sailmakers, each carrying a small mast to which was affixed spars, a squaresail and a streaming pennant at the cap, followed, and bringing up the rear was a group of local shipcarvers, led by a wagon with Seth Mason at the reins. On it were lashed, left and right, figureheads in various stages of completion, from the raw trunk of pine to the final varnished product—including the original bust by Woodbury Mason of Jenny Lind, the Swedish Nightingale.

Next came a procession of the town's businessmen and shopkeepers, including George Raynes, the builder of several celebrated Portsmouth clippers, and his competitor, Will Hadley.

There was a cheer from the crowd as the last exhibit rolled by along Marcy Street—a wagon upon which was mounted full-rigged scale models of the clippers *Typhoon*, *Witch of the Wave* and *Nightingale*, each as tall as a man, as well as a group of clipper-schooners, including the *Minna* and *Brenda* from George Raynes' yard and the *Gemini*.

Matthew applauded enthusiastically—and stopped as he almost collided with a naval officer, on whose arm clung Liz Mason in summer gingham and parasol.

"Matt," she called out before he could avoid her, "I'd like you to meet my fiancé, Lieutenant Emory Potter. Emory . . . Matthew Hadley of Portsmouth."

"Lieutenant," responded Matthew, extending his hand, which was taken limply by the uniformed officer.

"Happy to make your acquaintance, Mr. Hadley. Liz has spoken well of you. You are of the Hadley & Company yards—sailing vessels, I believe, on the Eliot Shore."

"That's correct," replied Matthew sharply, "sailing vessels."

"Emory," Liz interceded, sensing discord, "Matthew has just come back from China, aboard the clipper *Nightingale*."

"Oh yes, that's the vessel that just set a new record from London. Captain Mather, wasn't it?"

"You are correct, Lieutenant," Matthew said,

amused. "And on what ship are you?" He eyed the officer's tailored uniform.

"I'm assigned to the sloop-of-war *St. Louis*, Captain Ingraham commanding," Potter said, then covered his nose with a handkerchief as a wagon rolling by raised dust.

"Emory is on leave now," added Liz. "His squadron is going to the Mediterranean when he gets back. It will be so exciting to see the ruins of Rome and Greece."

"Especially without a war," Matthew joked and incurred an arched eyebrow from his former amourette. "Are you going also?"

Liz ignored the *faux pas*. "We've decided to postpone the wedding until Emory is promoted to First Lieutenant."

"I hope to be stationed here in Portsmouth after my first tour of duty. We'll get married then. It's only right. Marriage should be togetherness, don't you think?"

"You're absolutely right. . . . By the way, the *St. Louis* is a steam-powered sloop, I take it."

"But of course, Mr. Hadley—with auxiliary sail, just in case. I don't know of a navy in the entire world that's building ordinary sailing vessels today. Those that we do have are being used for training purposes. But I do admire you traditional sailors— beating into a gale around Cape Horn and spending a year at sea at a time. I'm afraid that sort of life is not for me." Potter stroked his fiancée's hand lightly as the wagon with the schooner models aboard passed by, followed by a troupe of scraggly urchins and a disoriented thin man pushing a sky-blue wheelbarrow.

CHAPTER SEVENTEEN

India's sacred river, born of the Gangotri Glacier more than 13,000 feet high in the Himalayas, rushes past the fields of red poppy in the broad valleys of Uttah Province and carries the precious cargo in riverine craft to the government factories in Patna. On wagons, horseback and sturdy shoulders, the white poppy's produce converges on Patna from the plateaus and hills of Bihar Province.

The tons of poppy pods and petals are processed in the factories of Patna. Impoverished farmers, content with the fixed price received in sterling, set about planting the next year's crop. Wheat and rice pay only a sixth of what the farmers can realize from the same investment of land, money and work growing opium, so there is no question of the type of crop. Let the famished millions fare as best they can without rice. Profit is King, and the Queen's coffers in London are overflowing.

By late March, the February harvest has been converted into raw opium, granular and wet. Stored in boxes according to quality, it is dried for three weeks. The scraped-out pods have been mulched and the petals prepared for covering and packing of the finished product.

After testing and assaying, the thousands of small vats are poured into twenty-foot-long troughs and further kneaded by workers wading in them. Next, brass cups are lined with poppy petal layers and wetted down with opium mash to receive previously weighed balls of opium. Leafed over, the product, resembling a Dutch cheese, is set in an earthen cup and rotated for three days in the sun. Any distension noticed is then pierced to liberate the trapped gases. By the end of July, the opium is packed into one hundred and sixty-pound crates and stored in dry warehouses for a three-month curing period. In late October, the finished product is shipped down the Ganges, then along its western tributary, the Hooghly River, to the Kidderpore Docks in Calcutta.

An Indian diver broke through the surface of the fetid river at Princept Ghat, announcing the unshackling of *Gemini*'s anchor cable from its 'holdfast,' an underwater harbour mooring buoy that was secured to shore points.

"All clear forrard . . ." The cable ran through its hawse pipe and a block was fitted over the hole. Under main and inner jib, the rake-masted schooner paid off as it caught a breeze and headed for a channel between the dozens of moored ships and plying tenders.

Fores'l up and heeling, the schooner, copper showing, rounded the dangerous James and Mary Shoal at the juncture of the Rupnarain River. Wheeling river hawks swooped low over the shallows to dive at a bloated corpse, one of hundreds washed down the river daily. *Gemini's* bow, flanked by polychromed twin heads trailing gilded stars, slashed through a chop and scattered the bumboats full of greens, whiskies and ring-tailed monkeys for sale.

The two hundred and eighty-five-ton clipper-schooner, its hold packed with Patna opium, skimmed swiftly southward under the hands of a boisterous crew still relishing their last hours ashore. They talked and sang of Ballasteer Road with its hennaed Khanki girls and wiggling belly dancers and of the bazaars featuring white and half-caste girls, genuine French and English girls for as low as four *annas*, or six cents. They swore off Flag Street's groggeries for the rotgut swindles, the ensuing hangovers and the empty pockets—and they kept their fingers crossed against Cupid's itch and mercury.

On the quarterdeck, in the shadow of the immense mains'l with its long boom braced out and ensign stiff below the gaff, a Chinese girl stood behind the helmsman.

"You very good steerer in this river, Mr. Lano."

"It was Mr. Hadley who showed me, Ma'am, aboard the *Alchemist*. I've been sailing with him ever since."

"I am Pao Ch'a. No·call me Ma'am," she said, smiling at the hulking Negro and her long black hair streaming in the breeze.

"Captain's lady is always called Ma'am."

"But we not married yet," she said, as she moved closer to the big double wheel. Lano could feel her presence; he savoured her musty perfumes, her exotic ways . . . but he was afraid to look, lest he betray his passion. The Captain's lady, he felt, was more kin to him than to Matthew Hadley—or any other white man. Long fascinated by white women, Lano was resigned that they were unapproachable, but the Oriental woman was another matter. He had no qualms, and it was this knowledge that he feared aboard *Gemini*.

"Then allow me to practice for that day, *Ma'am*." He longed to reach out and touch her, show her his strength of arm and deep devotion. Now he dared look, as he watched for obstructions and debris to port. She did not see his burning eyes devour her, as the following breeze blew her hair forward and pressed her silk tunic and pantaloons against her back. Shivering in his knees, Lano was ashamed of his thoughts and gripped the wheel tighter.

"Lano," she entreated, putting her hand on a spoke, "what you think about opium cargo?"

The Panamanian wiped his brow with his powerful forearm. "The Russell Company pays good wages, and it's much better than carrying wheat or passengers, Ma'am." Lano craned left and right, careful of being observed talking with the Captain's lady. "Mr. Hadley was right when he told us about this. Much better than the *Nightingale*, and always warm weather. I don't like snow and ice."

"But think about Chinese people. Get too sleepy with opium. No more work. Whole country helpless." Pao Ch'a thought of her father, barely surviving because of his addiction and selling his daughter to buy opium.

"If they don't want to, they should stop smoking opium," Lano boomed. "I like rum, but I stop when I get sick."

"Opium not easy to stop like rum."

The glistening helmsman didn't answer. First mate Gerrish had emerged from the deckhouse hatch and was headed for the privy. As the door to the roundhouse shut, Lano looked quickly about.

The Captain's lady had vanished.

*   *   *

After eight days running with the northeast monsoons, the trim one hundred and five-foot craft sailed into the Malacca Strait, between the 'tail' of Asia and the long island of Sumatra. At noon on November 6th, *Gemini* had passed abreast of Kuala Lumpur, the jewel of Malaysia, and was entering the narrowest part of the strait at latitude 2 degrees, a hundred miles from the equator, when the wind slacked off. All sails hung limp and the searing tropical sun bore down mercilessly, as the impotent vessel drifted toward the savage green shores of Sumatra. After rigging up a spare jib for shade over the quarterdeck and another for the crew's comfort forward, Matthew ordered that the sails be wetted down by a bucket brigade up the ratlines every change of watch, in order to obtain the maximum from even the faintest air.

Hordes of huge purple and red Portuguese men-of-war mottled the tepid, flat sea, there being not the least breeze to support the kiting of petrels and red-tailed tropic-birds. The crew lay languid—sprawled and stripped to skivvies in the hot shade on the fo'c'sle deck—and the lookouts aloft and on the jib-boom had to be doused with water after fifteen-minute shifts.

"In Canton, on boat with Chinese sailors, lady can wear only pantaloons, too, like man when very hot," lamented Pao Ch'a, as she wielded a dragon-emblazoned ribbed fan, first on Matthew and then on herself. The helm was lashed and they sat on grass mats strewn on the deckhouse. Gerrish, the bosun, and two mates were playing a game of Boston, said to have been invented by officers of the French fleet which lay for a time off the town of Marblehead during the American Revolution. The first mate was anxious to master the card game, the tricks of which were called great independence and little independence, in order to 'whup' the New England abolitionists at their own table.

Noticing that *Gemini* was drifting dangerously close to some tidal flats, Matthew ordered the starboard bower catted and ready to drop, while soundings were taken at short intervals.

Sightings with azimuth vanes on the compass showed the vessel to be approaching the swampy island of Rupat in the narrowest part of the strait. The mangrove-lined island, an uninhabited part of Sumatra, occulted a harbour and several small fishing villages on the mainland shore. Consulting a book that contained descriptions of Sumatra as encountered during a Linnaean Society expedition in 1820, Matthew found that the lowland plains were inhabited by a forest tribe, the Orang-lubu, pure savages of whom nothing was known, and that the mangroves were host to large numbers of rhinoceros—reason enough to be wary of grounding.

Just as the order to drop anchor was about to be given, a light breeze sprang up and filled the wetted sails just enough for Matthew to take the helm and wear off. By sheeting out the main to port and fores'l to starboard, the schooner 'goosewinged' slowly ahead on the catspawed, flat water.

"Just a half-mile or so, Mr. Gerrish," Matthew said, as he coaxed the helm gently, "and we'll pick up a breeze once past that point. We're being blanketed by this island."

"Mr. Hadley," the first mate drawled, "those mangroves out there remind me of Savannah. Only thing is, they don't have nice ol' plantations and southern belles. I think when we've got a few more o' these cargoes under our belts, I'll jes' go on back to Georgia, buy me a plantation and some darkies, an' take my pick o' those belles. Whut you goin' to do

when you get back, Matt? That is, if yer goin' back—
you've got a real nice lady.''

"Thanks, George," said Matthew with a grin,
"but I know your feelings about Negroes and Chinese."

"Now heah, Matt, I never said that all coons were
bad—or coolies. It's jes' that most of 'em . . .''

The foremast bell suddenly clanged out. "STARBOARD!" shouted the forward lookout, "STARBOARD!"

The mangroves were alive, as if their sprawling
roots were in motion—a rhythmic white froth against
the dun shore.

"MAN THE CARRONADE!" shouted Matthew
as he uncased his spyglass. Bosun McLarty set a
detail to bringing up shot and powder for the thirty-
two-pound pivot cannon mounted aft of the foremast.

"Three Malaysian craft making for us," Matthew
said, focusing on the first and largest of them. It had
two banks of oars and a woven grass lug sail on a
tripod mast. There were also men paddling furiously
on the outriggers. Upwards of eighty oars were flailing the surface like a monstrous marine centipede.
Over the fo'c'sle was a barricade that projected several feet beyond the gun'ls. The bows were painted
blood-red and decorated with gleaming round shapes,
a large necklace running from the stem back along
the gun'ls.

There was a puff of blue smoke from the *prahu's*
bow. Then a muffled report and a spume of white
foam erupted fifty yards short of *Gemini*'s starboard
quarter.

The carronade, pivoted on its circular track and
bearing over the starboard rail, was sighted on the
lead boat. A ball and a bucket of grape shot had been
rammed in after the cartridge at the captain's cry of
"Fire when ready!" With the shot fuze clipped to

five seconds, McLarty yanked the percussion lanyard and his gun crew's hands shot up to their ears. Nothing happened. The Bostonian Irishman swore a streak and cut open a powder cannister with his knife. The contents did not flow out. The powder was wet.

There was no time for excuses. A case of Sharps breechloading rifles was broken out and issued to the crew. Pistols and sabers were passed around and a net stretched over the rails. The order was to fire at will. Matthew took another look through his glass. The lead *prahu* was a thousand yards away, and gaining. Aft, by the tiller, he spotted an imposing figure, dressed in scarlet and chain mail armour and wearing a feathered headdress. The boat was apparently being rowed by slaves, since a company of weapon-wielding warriors were visible above the rails. Matthew winced when he saw that the decorative necklace on the bow consisted of human skulls, strung like pearls from the stem. Casing his glass, he flipped the cylinder of a naval Colt revolver and took a position behind the starboard round house. Staccato small-arms fire could be heard from the attackers as well as occasional blood-curdling shrieks.

A shot from the *prahu's* eighteen-pounder tore through the mains'l as Pao Ch'a scrambled from the deckhouse hatch and crouched next to Matthew. "They Malay pirates?" She nuzzled close to him.

He nodded grimly and called a seaman to take her down below and watch her. "They're Dyaks . . . headhunters," he confided to Gerrish, "from Borneo. Twenty years ago they were driven away from the straits by an American warship. Only Dyaks collect skulls and hang them on their boats."

Another shot from the brass 18 came screaming in, splintering the starboard rail and leaving two crewmen moaning on the deck. Gerrish put down his

smoking rifle and crawled forward to pull one of the
wounded men to cover. Hauling the seaman down
through a hatch, he noticed the Indian steward closing a crate of carbines. The Moslem boy, white eyes
blazing, bolted up the companionway and dropped a
small package as he went. Gerrish picked it up; it
was a packet of percussion caps for the Sharps carbine.
Leaving the wounded seaman to the care of the
coloured cook, Gerrish opened the rifle crate. The
guns were still intact—but the percussion caps were
missing. Gerrish scrambled up on deck, brandishing
his revolver, but it was too late. The boy had just
dived off the stern. The southerner waited for him to
surface, then emptied his Colt at him. "Jes' cain't
trust any of 'em," he said to himself as the water
bubbled red.

Jawi roared his approval as the eighty-foot *prahu*
gained on the enemy's boat. He stood up and waved
his ancient musket. "Faster, faster! A prize for the
great Raga—and white men's heads!"

The son of Raga had almost realized his dream. In
the year of his birth, thirty-two years earlier, his
father was known as "The Prince of Pirates." Raga
was renowned for his cunning, intelligence and
barbarity, as well as for the extent and daring of his
enterprises. He was feared for his disregard of human
life, and his spies were everywhere. Raga's tribes
sailed in prahus, which were called *caracors* by the
Malaysians. The hulls were similar to those of the
Vikings, but were carvel-built and fitted with outriggers on both sides, a development from the Dutch
school of naval architecture.

Raga, in his prime, ranged with a hundred war-
boats, manned by scarlet tunic-clad warriors, from
his lair on the east coast of Borneo to the Philippines

in the north and the Indian Ocean. Having cleared the Macassar Straits of prizes, Raga sailed west with his fleet and ravaged the Malay Peninsula and the Straits. Unopposed, he sailed north around Sumatra and down through the Strait of Mantawi. Raga's misfortune was to attack a Salem brig, the *Friendship*, in the guise of pepper merchants. Boarding the ship while it was at anchor off Quallah Batu, a skirmish occurred in which the Americans, through treachery, were butchered. Raga fled with his fleet and $30,000 in gold and opium. The news of this misfortune so stirred the American people and excited the rough and ready Congress that a punitive expedition under Commodore Downes and the frigate *Potomac* was dispatched. The *Potomac*, disguised as an East Indiaman, landed three hundred marines at Batu, who reduced Raga's camp to ashes. Raga, who was charged with murdering the crews of more than forty European ships and with dispatching the captains to death by his own hand, was wounded, but escaped to the west coast of Borneo where he recovered and masterminded a new generation of marauders led by his son, Jawi. The warrior-pirates, descended from the Malays and the Dyaks, kept their forays close to the Borneo shores and preyed on Chinese junks and lorchas, rather than incur the wrath and fire-power of European and American vessels. The new camp was located on the Sarebas River, north of Kuching, and was inaccessible to deep draft boats. For twenty years, aging Raga pursued a relatively sedentary life, living off the booty of his previous conquests and bartering such items as astrolabes and European women's petticoats. Meanwhile, his son, fired with the same instincts as he, organized an ocean-going fleet and set out for Malacca to intercept the lucrative opium traders. It was a sacred crusade as well; for over three hundred years, starting with the Spaniards, Malaysia had been enslaved and pillaged by the European—and now by the American.

He had left his father's camp with glorious expectations of swift success in the Malacca Strait, but a week's waiting among the mangroves had only evoked cynicism among his chiefs. It was whispered that Jawi had not the heart of his father.

Now it had finally happened. *Vayu*, the god of winds, had heeded his Moslem brethren. Now the son of Raga would not return in shame, but with great riches to delight his dying father and to excite a new rampage against the white oppressors.

The new American breechloaders were deadly at a thousand yards; proud warriors crumpled and fell upon the slave rowers as if struck by invisible lightning. The *prahus* veered off, and the pirates threw the dead and wounded overboard as they commenced a bow attack with the protection of the athwartship hardwood barricades. Jawi was pleased that his attack had not been greeted with cannon, but he had not anticipated such deadly rifle fire. Was this one of the boats that had not been infiltrated by the faithful in Calcutta or Bombay? Were his offers of payment for sabotage of weapons too meager?

The feathered chieftain cocked his head. No longer were the crackling reports as numerous; no longer did the water spurt up about the boat. An eerie silence descended over the torrid sea. Even the faint breeze had stopped.

Jawi ordered his boats in for the kill.

The only ammunition left aboard *Gemini* was for the Colt .36 caliber Navy pistols—and that in short supply. There were balls, but no firing caps left for the Sharps rifles. The Indian steward had dived overboard with a sack of fifty containers which, being packed in paper, became waterlogged and sank. Each container held two hundred and fifty metal-lined percussion caps.

The lead *prahu* maneuvered toward *Gemini*'s stern, with the others flanking behind. Jawi's pride, the eighteen-pounder, was loaded with a solid shot and a charge of iron nails, then sighted for a raking shot over the schooner's transom, the most devastating shot of all because it travels the length of the boat. Now, within two hundred yards and out of pistol range, the ancient brass cannon belched its flaming death. A miss; too far to port. The second shot, several minutes later, tore off the starboard quarterdeck privy. The third splintered the rudder post and crashed through the stern counter.

With savage cries the skull-bedecked giant outrigger closed in on the immobilized schooner. Carcasses filled with putrified animal remains were set on a spring catapult, put to the torch and fired, one after the other, as the Dyak muskets concentrated their fire on the schooner's quarterdeck. Two of the rank, flaming missiles landed on *Gemini*'s deck—one amidships and the second just abaft the abandoned helm. A swirl of dense black smoke rose into the rigging, blinding and choking the pistol marksmen aloft in the ratlines. Taking advantage of the confusion on deck and the cover of smoke, Jawi's boat came under the schooner's stern with muskets blazing and grappling hooks flying, as the other two *prahus* sped by, port and starboard, to surround the prey.

The first wave of boarders were met and repulsed by point-blank pistol shot and pikes as they came over the forward port rail. Hidden behind the rattan sail, a Dyak emerged at the tripod mast-top and fired a blunderbuss down, only to be picked off by a Colt .36 from the schooner's foremast.

"Unship the carronade!" shouted Gerrish, and the two tons of iron rolled free and was pushed toward the rail where it crashed through the gangway to crush the *prahu* below as it was launching its second boarding party.

A barrel of scalding hot water was winched up on the main boom and swung out over the starboard attackers, then tripped amidst screams of pain from the boarders as they slashed at the nets.

With *Gemini*'s defenders occupied on port and starboard, Jawi and his fiercest warriors climbed up their boarding ropes and over the taffrail behind the billowing black smoke. Taking the defenders by surprise, they emptied their belted flintlocks with great effect, then charged with spears and cutlasses into the muzzles of the mates' smoking pistols. Turned back, the savages regrouped as fresh warriors came over the stern. There were no more pistol shots; the ammunition was gone. *Gemini*'s crew now faced the Dyaks with cutlasses and pikes. A sinister smile crossed the chieftan's bronzed face. He called for muskets and ordered his warriors to line up abreast, in three files—in the manner of the British formation. Slow-stepping past the helm, the first scarlet-tunicked line leveled their muskets as they chanted in unison, and the other ranks followed with weapons at the ready. Jawi raised his jeweled cutlass as a signal . . .

Suddenly, the march was stopped by the low-pitched, deafening blare of a steamship racing around the verdant island and bearing down on the smoking schooner. Breaking ranks, the Dyak warriors scrambled aft in terror, some diving overboard in their rush to get back to the *prahu*. Slashing the lines, the Dyaks pushed off and chopped at the fingers of frantic warriors trying to pull themselves aboard.

Oars thrashing under threatening spears, the war canoe made for the safety of the mangrove swamps.

Whistle blowing and black smoke trailing from her long funnel, the propeller-driven iron brig veered off and steamed straight for the crowded, flailing centipede at its maximum speed of eleven knots. The sharp iron bow cut through the *prahu*, split it like matchwood, and sent oars scattering and Dyaks screaming to either side. Discarding his chain mail armour, Jawi swam furiously and reached the tidal flats of Rupat along with several other survivors. Unfortunately, though, they disturbed a haunt of sleeping marsh crocodiles.

The chugging steamer, flying the colors of Augustine Heard & Company, was the *Javeline*, bound for Canton from Bombay. As she put a boat over, Matthew rushed below to his cabin to tell Pao Ch'a the good news. Bosun McLarty blocked his way.

"Don't go in there, Matt." McLarty stood grim. Behind him the cabin door and paneling was shattered. "Your cabin took a round of solid and nails when the rudder post was hit." He shook his head.

"Where's Simmons?"

"Also dead, 'e was standin' where I am now."

"*Also* dead?" With an animal wail, Matthew charged toward the door, but was restrained by McClarty and Gerrish.

The shot-weighted and pierced sandalwood coffin, a green jade hairpin nailed to its lid, slipped gently into the South China Sea from a sling let over *Javeline*'s waist. The service over, Cleopatra Smith and Mark Hadley went below to the day cabin, and left Matthew standing alone on deck—staring into the blinding tropical sunset.

"I hope your brother is well; the last time I saw anyone look like that was aboard the *Alchemist* after rounding the Horn."

"The famous curse of the albatross," added Mark, as he opened the brandy cabinet.

"You don't think . . ." Cleo gasped.

"Coincidence," Mark said, as he poured from a captain's decanter. "Besides, Matt was only following orders in getting the cook to set a line."

"Whatever did happen to Joe Lavender? The ship's boy who helped him catch that bird is probably dead in Mexico." Cleo stared into her brandy as if it could answer.

"I heard he went south and shipped aboard a slaver."

"Then nothing good has happened to those who caught that monstrous bird. When I last saw the albatross, it was in Wiburd's playroom. I could swear its eyes moved."

"I've never seen Matt like this either. He hardly recognized me. He's certainly in no condition to command a ship. Gerrish said he went so beserk that the crew is afraid to sail under him. He needs a rest." Mark opened the ship's log and pondered over the day's entries. "He'll get over the girl. . . ."

"Will he?" Cleo dangled a ball of madder violet yarn over her Siamese cat's prankish pale eyes.

Upon returning to the Pearl River, *Gemini* moored in a secluded cove off the smugglers' island of Linton and disposed of her "illicit" cargo, while the American State Department officials in China were trying to convince the Mandarins that President Pierce was indeed putting an end to opium traffic in Yankee ships. The damaged schooner then put into Hong Kong for repairs. Pockets bulging with dollars, the crew went off to the notorious institutions of Ship Street singing:

"We'll have our glass with a Chinese lass,
In Ship Street in old Hong Kong!"

Matthew, disconsolate, sought condolence in the Portuguese settlement of Macao, across the harbour. He called on Ellie Russell, but soon tired of the dilettantish community. The rich man's grand-niece did, however, in a moment of tenderness tell him that Russell & Company was building several more steamboats, and so would not long require the services of obsolete schooners.

He went to see Nicholas Miles, who was staying at Chinnery's villa, and was glad to leave after a few days of dodging the advances of the artist's hermaphroditic friends.

Dining alone one evening at an inn on the Praya Grande, Matthew was approached by a Portuguese gentleman who had the eyes of a Mandarin. By the time brandy was served, *Gemini* had been chartered for a lucrative and thriving new enterprise.

CHAPTER EIGHTEEN

No longer did he look like a Greek god. Two years of passages to the Sandwich Islands and the Chinchas, off the Peruvian coast, had changed Matt Hadley. In the bevel-edged looking glass of his opulent cabin, he saw a stranger: a mustache and beard darker than his fair and curly locks, his once bright cheeks leathern, the sparkling eyes now resolute and fixed.

He picked up a jade compact and snapped it open, as he always did before going on deck. The daguerreotype of Pao Ch'a smiled at him—giving him strength to face another day in a business that had become tedious and sometimes abhorrent.

The high-pitched jabbering of Chinese men wafted through the open scuttles of his cabin—exuberant and hopeful. They had been told by the agent in Macao that their destination was to be San Francisco and their destiny a life of luxury and opportunity in the bountiful New World. Some of them were captured Taiping rebels; others had been sold by their families. There were even men who, in the traditional Chinese practice of paying all debts by the new year, had sold themselves in order to save face. Shipping an "indentured laborer" to California cost about fifty dollars, the passage money usually paid by the agent who held the worker's contract. There were also those aboard who had been kidnapped, or *shanghaied*, by professional crimps. The unfortunate—often a visitor to the coastal city who had been lured into a glamorous gambling house or brothel—upon recovering his sobriety, would find himself held prisoner in a barracoon, or temporary cell. Where papers were needed, they were cleverly forged. The legal pretext of "indentures" prevented the British and American Navies from detaining emigrant ships as slavers. A naval officer who did stop a ship to examine its compliance to the law ran a risk of being sued. In 1856, twenty-three of the seventy ships carrying coolies were American. One of them was *Gemini*.

California's gold mines, burgeoning American railway construction, and Caribbean sugar plantations supplied the impetus to the coolie trade of the decade preceding the Civil War. In one year thirty thousand Chinese were shipped from the Canton area to California at a profit of almost two million dollars. The British bark *John Calvin*, named after the great religious reformer, made a profit in Havana, even though half of the three hundred coolies shipped had died en route.

There were only men transported aboard *Gemini* because Chinese law forbade the emigration of females. The plantations of the West Indies cried out for women in order to breed their own slaves, but to little avail, since such traffic could be managed only by kidnapping and was not easily hidden by subterfuge.

A week out of Macao, First Mate Gerrish hauled down The Stars and Stripes and raised the red and yellow stripes of Spain. When word was passed below of the change in destination, the indentured travelers, forgetting their personal wars, banded together and accosted the quarterdeck, only to be met with the massed weaponry of the crew. Several of the Chinese charged, unarmed, but were quickly shot down. Others jumped overboard in dismay. It was to be expected. Not only was Cuba a torrid, whip-snapping hell, but it meant a voyage almost three times as long as anticipated.

The crew of *Gemini*, however, was elated in being bound for Havana. The schooner was to be chartered by New York interests for the Atlantic trade.

In 1856, the phrase "Cotton is King," taken from a book on the economics of slavery, was often heard. The product from America's southern states amounted to one-half the total export of the Union. This was the year that a Massachusetts senator was severely caned and injured on the Senate floor by a South Carolina congressman for disparaging remarks about slavery and the Palmetto State.

It was the year in which John Ericsson's "caloric" engine was developed, and the steam calliope was patented and applied to merry-go-rounds. The marvel of the age was built by a Pennsylvania inventor. It was a miniature steam engine of gold and silver, containing one hundred fifty parts, 'invisible bolts,' and weighing a mere half-ounce.

First chartered, then bought by a Mr. Gardner of New York City, *Gemini*, still under command of Captain Matthew Hadley, made several trips to the Mediterranean, both as a private yacht and a fruit trader. During the summer of 1857, the failure of a New York City branch of an Ohio bank precipitated a dire national financial panic—primarily the result of over-speculation in western railway securities and real estate. Mr. Gardner, a member of the New York

Yacht Club, was intent on recouping his financial losses, regardless of the means, and chartered the schooner to a Savannah businessman. Along with another fast vessel, the *Wanderer*, it cleared Charleston for "Trinidad," and crossed the Atlantic to the Congo instead. Thus were Matt Hadley and his men initiated into the African slave trade. *Wanderer*'s owner, a man of versatility, shrewdly entertained the officers of the British warship *Medusa*, while flying the New York Yacht Club burgee. He invited the ship's company to inspect his ship to see whether she was equipped as a slaver. The reveling British departed, and *Wanderer*, under a Georgian sailing-master, led *Gemini* up a river to the barracoons.

Evading the American warship, USS *Vincennes* in Ambrizete Bay, south of the Congo River estuary, the swift schooners sped across the Atlantic and put off more than four hundred Africans at Jekyll Island, near the coast of Georgia. Under cover of night, the slaves were transported by steamer up the Altamaha River and under the guns of a Federal fort which had been "neutralized" by a grand ball set up by the slavers in honor of the garrison.

The slaves that had been purchased "for a few beads and bandana kerchiefs," brought seven hundred dollars each in the market, which meant a healthy profit for the owners and syndicate. As was usual in the South, the smugglers escaped, and the vessels were condemned, sold at auction, and bid for by the former owners at a fourth of their values.

Matthew brought the schooner back to New York with a cargo of cotton and molasses, and, while coasting past the piers of South Street, spied something dear to him: the familiar stern carving of a lady holding a nightingale on her finger. Finding the clipper working up under a new Brazilian owner, he applied for a berth for himself and those of his schooner crew that were of like mind. *Nightingale*'s master, Captain Francis Bowen, a "most learned and intelligent gentleman," offered him the position—by virtue of his previous experience with the vessel—of sailing master.

"I shall be so enmeshed in the intricacies of our consignments that the owner has agreed to the hiring of, shall we say, a sailing captain." Bowen sealed the letter of agreement and counted out a month's advance pay for Matthew and his five companions from the *Gemini*. "Enjoy yourselves in our fair city, and I trust you will be responsible in bringing your mates aboard healthy and in time for the tide one week from this day."

"It has been my dream to be master of *Nightingale*. There is a three-dollar gold piece in the keel scarfing that I set in nine years ago at Portsmouth." Matthew walked proudly about Bowen's cabin.

"Then *be* master. We shall share the accommodations, though I will retain the second mate's stateroom for my berth and certain of my papers and valuables. It is not often that a mariner of your ability walks in off the street, Mr. Hadley. Your accomplishment under Captain Fiske is well known. Fifteen days from Liverpool broke the *Yorkshire*'s record. Your gold coin may bring fortune to all of us." They shook hands and Bowen escorted Matthew to the quarterdeck and down to the gangway, where Gerrish and the others waited.

That evening, David Montebianco came aboard, and it was past midnight before the captain's cabin lights were extinguished.

* * *

By late 1859, over eight thousand businesses had failed as a result of the panic less than two years earlier. The nation was at a standstill. In 1854, the zenith year of shipbuilding, one hundred twenty-five clippers had gone down the ways. The next year's production had dwindled to sixty-nine. No new clippers were built after 1857, and the total tonnage of all ships built had declined from a half million tons to one-third of that annually. Great clippers, such as *Flying Cloud*, were laid up for as long as two years. The famous *Challenge*, only eight years old, was dismantled in Chinese waters and sold for a fraction of the original cost. The majority of Amerian vessels went into the India-to-England run, under British charters.

England, with a flowering of Victorian economy, regained its dominance of the world's trade routes and continued to build clipper ships while perfecting the iron steamship. In America's harbours, hundreds of once-proud vessels swung idly at their moorings, while others were "Sold British" and bought at bargain prices by slave traders, despite anti-slavery laws. It was practice for a vessel to be bought under pretenses of legitimate trade in order to obtain proper documents prior to entering the slave trade. To further the deception, the vessel would be "sold" to a country such as Brazil. In this way, the American owner profited exorbitantly from the "sale" without holding responsibility for the boat's misuse in Africa, and the Brazilian trader got protection from the American registry. Dummy ownership was common, and it would not be until the middle of the Civil War that the flimflam was crushed.

*   *   *

On February 18th, 1860, *Nightingale* slipped her cables and warped into the East River, where she picked up the tide and caught a following breeze through the narrows. She carried a cargo of grain, bound for London.

CHAPTER NINETEEN

"But I never agreed to be sailing master of a slaver!" Matthew was aghast as crates were opened on deck and spilled out leg irons, handcuffs and short lengths of chain. "You knew this when I signed on. Why didn't you tell me?"

"Simply because we needed an honorable man to complete the picture of a reputable venture. The name of Hadley on the ship's papers and cargo manifests is of utmost value to the principals involved in this enterprise. As far as London and New York are concerned, *Nightingale* has delivered a cargo of grain, and is presently bound for Rio with a consignment of firearms, powder, and cotton cloth." Francis Bowen, dressed and appearing more as a schoolmaster than a slaver, ticked off the entries on a bill of lading. "Ah, the romance of a pretty clipper ship; who would suspect us of such wicked deeds."

Matthew, eyeing Lano at the wheel, lowered his

voice. "Not *us*, Mr. Bowen. My mates are innocent of this, and any court of law—"

"Court of law, is it now? Have you talked to your former first mate? He feels differently. I understand this is not your first voyage to the Gold Coast."

"Gerrish is a southerner," Matthew said, clenching his fists.

"And I am a businessman. Look, Matt, this boat will make us all rich. Just think of it: a thousand head at five hundred dollars profit each—that's half a million dollars! With your share you can build another boat, or settle down on a farm. Didn't you tell me that your father's business needs shoring up? Well, man, here's your chance. In any case, Matt, you're in this as much as I am. Nobody will believe you, especially after your escapade with the *Wanderer*."

Shrugging with disgust, the young sailing master changed the subject. There was no arguing with Bowen, not at sea with inferior strength. "Going to Rio looks fine—except when a vessel turns southeast after passing Cape Verde."

"There are some chances we have to take."

"How long will we stay at Dahomey?"

"Only as long as it takes to bring the first batch aboard. You will mind the ship—with the help of my trusted first mate. I wouldn't want to see you try to . . . That is, I am of the cut of Blackbeard, the pirate, who is credited with the proverb about dead men."

Leaving the Benin Bight under a light breeze, *Nightingale* set course for Kabenda, near the mouth of the mighty Congo. Two hundred Nigerians were shackled on a plank shelf that ran around the 'tween decks level. They had been purchased from a native chief at his barracoon in the village of Whydah and delivered to the clipper in outriggers by the chief's warriors.

In rounding Cape Lopez, just below the equator and a day's sail to Kabenda, a thread of black smoke was spotted on the western horizon. Captain Bowen, upon being alerted, brought out his personal telescope and set it atop a tripod on the quarterdeck. Purchased at Mrs. Taylor's Nautical Shop in London, it featured a superb four-inch flint objective lens made by Fraunhofer. After a short observation against the lowering tropic sun, he snapped to action.

"Mr. Gerrish," he ordered, "have the bosun bring up the Africans for a bit of exercise—all of them. And Mr. Hadley, would you be good enough to have the port bower catted?"

Matthew was puzzled; the ocean's depth was beyond anchoring. Five hundred fathoms at least—and the longest cable was but two hundred in length. He passed on the order as a few seamen—veterans of the trade, who knew what was in the offing—closed their eyes in remorse.

Two by two, shackled at the ankles, the "black ivory" cargo shuffled along the deck, was prodded by pikes and cutlasses to positions by the rail, while the bosun's men hauled the anchor chain aft and outboard of the rail, then tied it at intervals with slender strings. The Africans were then forced to sit, in groups, on the rail, clear of ratlines and shrouds, where they were bound to the chain links with stout ropes from their shackles. Naïvely perched on and against the rail, the two hundred Nigerians broke into a rhythmic tonal chant, oblivious to the white captain's scheme and resigned to a life of misery across the sea.

* * *

Vermilion sun coruscating behind shortened sail, the three-masted steam sloop bore down on the gangway side of *Nightingale*. At a distance of five hundred yards, the USS *Mohican* fired a blank from one of her eleven-inch smoothbores as a signal for the clipper to heave to for boarding. Acknowledging the signal, Bowen raised his hand toward the anchor detail.

"You can't—" Matthew lunged at Bowen, but was felled by a blow from a carbine's butt. Stunned and bleeding, he watched helplessly as Bowen's hand flashed down. The two-ton cast iron anchor was slipped from its catting tackle and it crashed into the darkening sea, snapping the cable's tethers and catapulting the Africans in shrieking sequence over the side.

The *Mohican*'s search party found undisputed evidence that a number of slaves had been aboard, but it was not enough to detain, much less charge, the clipper with an infraction. The law was explicit, and demanded—as in a case of homicide—a body.

Exultant over his escape, yet lamenting a loss of five hundred dollars per head, Francis Bowen ordered his sailing master to crack on full canvas for Kabenda.

In New York City, Stephen Foster wrote "Old Black Joe," the last of his plantation songs, while battling alcoholism. In Chicago, haircuts went up two cents, to twelve, and the 7th-inning stretch was introduced to the game of baseball. The nation's population in 1860 was thirty-five million, of which four million were slaves. South Carolina became the first state to secede from the Union, on the basis of Lincoln's election, and Oliver Winchester started mass production on the first repeating rifle.

*   *   *

On April 15th, 1860, Commodore G.H. Perkins of the warship USS *Sumter* wrote in his diary:

> "The clipper ship Nightingale of Salem, shipped
> a cargo of 1000 Negroes and has gone clear
> with them. . . . She is a powerful vessel and is
> the property of Captain Bowen, who is called
> 'The Prince of Slavers.' "

A year later, Captain Taylor of the sloop-of-war *Saratoga*, described one of a score of captures in an accelerated campaign by the American African Squadron against slavers.

> USS Saratoga,
> Kabenda, April 21, 1861

To the Judge of the US District Court at New York City:

For some time the American ship, Nightingale
of Salem, Francis Bowen, master, has been
watched on this coast under the suspicion of
being engaged in the slave trade. Several times
we have fallen in with her, and although fully
assured that she was about to engage in this
illicit trade, she has had the benefit of the doubt.
A few days ago, observing her at anchor at
Kabenda, I came in and boarded her and was
induced to believe she was then preparing to
receive slaves. Under this impression, the Saratoga got under way and went some distance off,
but with the intention of returning under cover
of the night; which was done and at 10 PM we
anchored and sent two boats under Lieutenants
Guthrie and Hadley to surprise her and it was
found that she had 961 slaves on board and was

> *expecting more. Lieut. Guthrie took possession of her as a prize, and I have directed him to take her to New York. She is a clipper of 1000 tons and has* Nightingale *of Salem on her stern and flies American colors.*

> Alfred Taylor, Commander, USN

To complete the prize crew, Lieutenant Hayes of the Navy and Lieutenant Tyler of the Marines were ordered to report to Guthrie, in addition to six petty officers, six seamen, six landsmen, two boys and six marines. As the crew took up berths and stations, Francis Bowen was quick to break out the brandy with Guthrie.

"Lieutenant, your accent is decidedly southern."

"North Carolina, suh; Charlotte," he added proudly.

"That's cotton country," Bowen beamed.

"Yer damned right it is, Cap'n."

"I've always been an admirer of the South, Lieutenant. They know how to live," Bowen toadied up. "I don't see why the North just can't leave well enough alone. Those darkies are a lot better off in the Carolinas than in a godless jungle."

"Ah'l drink to that, Cap'n. Got a few slaves on m' family's farm m'self. Sure could use more." Guthrie rolled his eyes. "But God knows whut's happened in the States by now. Afore we sailed, Jeff Davis got elected and we—they—already got a new flag. Seven stripes n' three stars."

"Soon you just might be sailing under that new flag, Lieutenant; you never know."

"Suh, you are addressing an officer of the Yewnited States Navy. We'll have no rebellion aboard this vessel." Guthrie poured himself a generous dollop of brandy. Looking around the cabin cautiously, he added: "Except fo' Lieutenant Hadley, who is

reserve, we are all from south of the line. Shee-it,
Cap'n, if there was a good reason, I'd take this
floatin' toilet right on back t' Wilmington an' rig 'er
up as a Confederate privateer. . . ."

Lieutenant Mark Hadley, waiting until his co-officers
were asleep or drunk—more the former, since liquor
was prohibited aboard American men-of-war—went
forward to inquire about his brother. Finding Lano in
the fo'c'sle, he explained the situation to the surprised Negro, and was led to a cable locker, where
Matthew had been thrown in irons. In the light of
Lano's lantern, despite his entreaties, Mark was confronted by the ugly, hexagonal muzzle of a wide-bore
boot pistol, its hammer cocked. "Matt, it's me,"
Mark said, as he lifted his service cap off slowly, his
other hand high over his head. The gun wavered,
then steadied point blank at the blue-uniformed officer.

"When our supply ship, *Star of the West*, was
fired upon at Charleston in January, my squadron
was activated. When I heard about *Nightingale* and
Mohican, I transferred to Commodore Inman's squadron in the hope that I could find you.. Father's health
has been failing." Mark extended his hand to his
brother.

"I've been a fool," Matthew said, handing his
pistol to Lano. "How can I ask you to forgive me?
My faith in *Nightingale* has blinded me. I signed on
in good faith—and now I'm a slaver. . . ."

"Captain Bowen put Matt in irons yesterday,"
interceded Lano. "He was afraid that Matt signaled to
Mohican about slaves."

"You didn't have to, Matt. It was just a question
of catching him—and we did. The Navy is taking
new measures. Slavery is dead."

"But I'm implicated; Bowen is a viper."

"You're right, Matt," Mark replied. "He's told Guthrie that the real master has been put below in irons—and he's got papers to prove it. He means to leave you down here to die of the fever; then he'll be absolved."

"That's what he said," Matthew recalled, "*Dead men tell no tales*. He compared himself to Blackbeard, the pirate."

"We've got to get you off this boat. Lano, tonight's the last chance; we sail tomorrow for Liberia," whispered Mark. "I'll hire one of the Bantu boats to bring out produce and have it moored under the bow till after nightfall. At four bells, both of you go over the bow. When you get to shore, contact the Portuguese governor in Kabenda village. I'll give you a note for him and what money I have to arrange passage home if you can't find a working berth. I'll see you again just before ten o'clock."

Early the next morning Captain Bowen went forward to inspect his recalcitrant sailing master. Instead of finding him writhing with the fever and pleading, he found nothing. Cursing himself for not putting a guard on the man, he accosted Lieutenant Guthrie at breakfast.

"You must allow me to go to shore and find the rascal. Give me twenty-four hours, and I'll bring him back. Certainly it will not look good to your superiors that the master of a slaver escaped during your watch. I am but the previous commander, and I have papers to testify to that fact. Had I been the guilty one, it would have been I who is missing." Bowen slammed his fist on the cabin table.

"That makes sense, Cap'n—but ah won't care much about what looks good to my superiors when ah get back to New York. Ah'l make a report and then hand in my resignation. There ain't many south-erners gonna stay in this man's navy too long."

"Very well, Lieutenant, but perhaps I could in-duce you in another way." Bowen produced a sack and poured its contents on the table.

"Damn, I ain't seen that many Mexican gold pieces since I was a ship's boy at Vera Cruz!"

"Since there ain't any more buyin' to do, I don't think Captain Cortina will need these doubloons any more."

"Cap'n who, suh?"

"Captain Valentino Cortina," lied Bowen. "Can't trust these Latins. He's the sailing master who escaped." Bowen used a name that appeared on his duplicate set of ship's papers—the set that had been given to Lieutenant Hayes. A Brazilian subterfuge.

"Well, suh, now ah have a good bit o' musterin'-out pay. Ah sure hope you find that Spanish feller." Guthrie counted the gold pieces as he dropped them back into the sack. The Prince of Slavers gloated in his knowledge that another $25,000 in doubloons was safely secreted in the false bottom of his steamer trunk and would accompany him ashore.

Mooring at Monrovia, the clipper put off those eight hundred and one slaves that had survived a two-week scourge of fever. One hundred and sixty hadn't, and were thrown overboard en route from Kabenda. Guthrie and the Marine officer survived the fever, while one of the prize crew died. News of the attack on Fort Sumter and the declaration of Civil War was given to the crew at this port, and *Nightingale* sailed on May 13th. Lieutenant Guthrie spent the crossing polishing two papers: one, his resignation from the United States Navy, and the other, a report to the Secretary of the Navy, from which the follow-ing are extracts:

"I have the honor to report my arrival here today, June 13, 1861, in New York City, as

prize officer of the American ship, Nightingale,
32 days from Monrovia. . . . She was seized in
the act of receiving negroes aboard . . . and I
regret to say that an American named Francis
Bowen and a Spaniard named Valentino Cortina
effected their escape during my watch on deck
the night of April 22nd. . . . The first person
named was known to be commander of the ship
prior to capture and the latter was represented
as such at the time. . . . After filling up with
water and purifying the ship, we sailed for New
York. . . . Our crew had become so sick . . . that
it became difficult to carry sail. At one time
there were only 7 men fit for duty. . . ."

The case came before the district court in June, and
no defense being offered, the boat was condemned,
and purchased at a marshal's sale by the United
States Government for $13,000. Of the three ship's
mates on trial, the first mate, Sam Haynes, was
charged with brutality and acquitted for lack of proof
of citizenship. A second escaped charges on the same
basis, and a third, Minthorne Westervelt, scion of a
wealthy Staten Island family, was acquitted because
his lawyers argued that he'd known nothing about the
intended cargo when he signed on and had then had
no choice but to obey. The 'Prince of Slavers,' Francis Bowen, was never recaptured. Three years later,
a British Commodore met at Loanda, a port south of
Kabenda, "a most shrewd and intelligent person,
very gentlemanly, and with a perfect knowledge of
everybody and everything connected with this part of
the coast and the slave trade." The Commodore
learned later that the gentleman was Bowen, who had
just been released by the British after capture of his
schooner, the *Mariqueta*. At that moment Bowen

was living comfortably in the house of the agent recruiting contract laborers for the French West Indies.

Equipped with four thirty-two-pound guns, *Nightingale*, under command of Acting-master D.B. Horne, was ordered to report to the Gulf Blockading Squadron at Key West, Florida.

The Union had lost heavily at Bull Run and Wilson's Creek and there was a rush of enlistments by the young and patriotic of both sides. In both navies, ferries and merchant ships were hastily converted into warships and crews recruited while shipbuilding programs were laid down. Among those who enlisted for service aboard the clipper *Nightingale* was Matthew Hadley—eager to reap the promise of the gold piece in the keel and repentant for his folly.

In Washington, Lincoln's new Secretary of the Navy, Gideon Welles, reported: "No sailing vessels have been ordered, for steam as well as heavy ordnance has become an indispensible element of the most efficient naval power." In accordance with this theme, he was approached by Robert Forbes, the former partner at Russell & Co. in Canton, with an idea of great tactical merit. One of the major naval problems was to retake the Federal forts that had been seized by the southern states and thus regain control of the rivers, which were the lifeblood of the Confederacy. The United States Navy had been built for deep water operations and needed hard-hitting, swift, shallow draft gunboats. Boston naval architect Jabez Treat Cook was recommended by Forbes, and soon the plans were drawn up for a fleet of twenty-three vessels which came to be called the "ninety-day gunboats." It was decided to first build a prototype that could be duplicated easily in many northern shipyards.

New York's Novelty Iron Works had already developed an engine for a foreign gunboat, which was adapted to Cook's design. The engines, which took more time to build than the gunboats, were licensed to be duplicated in twelve different factories in the East.

Each vessel displaced seven hundred tons, was one hundred sixty feet long, and could make eleven knots under steam. They were rigged as schooners. Equipped with two engines and two boilers each, the boats could run on one while the other was being serviced, or on both for high speed. The hulls were braced by diagonal strap iron and drew only twelve feet.

Interestingly, the gunboats resembled a smaller vessel used by the American traders on the Calcutta-to-Canton run, specifically the *Javeline*—which Cook designed for Cleopatra Smith—to be leased by a company in which Forbes was a silent partner.

Two of the gunboats were assigned to be built in Portsmouth, at the newly reconditioned and incorporated yard of Hadley & Smith, largely through the lobbying of the new partner among the congressmen and naval attachés in the nation's capital. For the first time since Sam Hadley had left for the gold fields, never to return, the yard looked forward to a profitable year, albeit a result of war.

In the cloistered rectory of St. John's Episcopalian Church overlooking the Potomac at Georgetown, a nervous young reserve naval lieutenant and a raven-haired beauty exchanged marital vows. As befits war time, the wedding was an impromptu affair, attended by few, but distinguished, guests. Amongst the bemedaled uniforms, David Montebianco, in the latest Savile Row attire, blinked a welling tear. If Cleopatra Smith could not be his, at least her capture of the son of a shipbuilding firm would assure satisfaction of certain outstanding debts.

"Dear," Cleo purred, after allowing him the obligatory buss on the cheek, "I'm sure you won't mind watching Antonius while we take a short honeymoon. He is the most curious cat I've ever seen—especially when it comes to bedrooms. And I have the most marvelous news. When Mark leaves for the Gulf Coast Squadron, I shall go to Portsmouth and watch over our 'investments.' "

"I should have known," lamented David wistfully.

"Should have known what?" demurred the bride.

"Nothing. It would have made no difference." Montebianco grinned and changed his tone. "But of course I will take care of little Antonius. Better to have part of you than nothing at all."

CHAPTER TWENTY

In late September, 1861, a Northern flotilla of four warships had taken blockade positions at Head of the Passes, a widening of the Mississippi River just above the three-clawed foot that contained the navigable channels into that river. At the same time, the newly impressed armed supply clipper *Nightingale* had arrived at Fort Pickens, Pensacola—a day's sail away—to unload coal for the beleaguered outpost and its protecting flotilla—a show of force that stayed the hands of the Floridian and Alabaman militia.

Fifty miles upriver, in a shipyard across from New Orleans, a river towboat, the *Enoch Train*, was going through a transformation. The powerfully built steamer's topsides and masts had been stripped off and replaced with an iron "whale's back." Some would call it a "fat cigar" and others, "a smooth turtle."

Below her strengthened bow, catfish swam about an enormous cast-iron ram. Her back was smooth, except for one narrow smoke funnel and an "eyelid" on the bow, which housed a thirty-two-pounder, her only gun. Workers crawled over her like ants on a rock, in and out of the two flush hatches—installing an anti-boarding system designed to spray scalding water from the boilers over the whale's back. Oddly enough, the ironclad did not belong to a navy. It had been financed by a public subscription of merchants. The *Enoch Train*, named for a sailing packet builder, had been designed as an icebreaker in Bedford, Massachusetts, and sold to a New Orleans concern later for tugboat service. She had two powerful engines and twin screws. Her length was one hundred twenty-eight feet, her beam twenty-eight, and displacement, three hundred ninety tons.

The secret weapon, rechristened *Manassas*, after the Confederate term for Bull Run, was no longer secret. The story had broken in Northern newspapers about "an iron monster" being constructed in New Orleans that would "ram, grapnel, and scald the Yankee blockaders."

Early in October, the Commander of the Confederate Squadron of the lower Mississippi, Flag Officer Hollins, cast a covetous eye on the *Manassas* and ordered a gunboat to commandeer the ironclad. His six tiny wooden vessels, mounting a total of nineteen assorted guns, were no match for one Union sloop-of-war, let alone the fleet.

Lieutenant Alexander Warley, pistol in hand, boarded the ironclad and routed the ragtag crew of longshoremen who, in the words of a member of the boarding party, "took to their heels and like so many prairie dogs disappeared down the hole of a hatchway."

On the dark, moonless night of October 11th, one of the four Union blockaders, the steam sloop *Richmond*, armed with twenty Dahlgrens, was taking on coal from the *Nightingale*. Another steamer, the *Water Witch*, lay by waiting its turn, and two armed sailing sloops were moored nearby. Shrouded lanterns shone through the mist.

Just before dawn, the captain of the sloop *Preble*, roused from his berth, warned the *Richmond* of an "indescribable object" moving with great velocity toward her. Because of the coaling, the warning was not heard. The *Manassas* slammed into the *Richmond*, and glanced off the coaling clipper, then veered away onto a sandbar with part of its funnel sheared off by a hawser. The Union boats beat to quarters and fired blindly into the dark. Signaled by a rocket from the *Manassas*, the Confederate commander upstream loosed three fire rafts which were driven by the currents onto a shoal before reaching the blockaders.

At daybreak the *Manassas*, with help from the tide, powered off the sand bank, a damaged engine jury-repaired, and made for the grounded Union ships *Richmond* and *Vincennes*.

Concurrently, the gig had been lowered from *Nightingale*'s transom and rigged with a lateen sail. Grounded upriver from the ironclad, she cast loose the gig, which was equipped with a twenty-foot spar, lashed to its gun'l, on the tip of which was a torpedo.

The thirty-foot sailing gig, with Matthew Hadley at the tiller, cut diagonally across the river—a seemingly innocent fishing boat to the *Manassas'* helmsman, who ignored it as he bore down on the *Vincennes'* quarter with full steam up and with cannon and scalding water ready.

Picking up a beam wind, the gig accelerated into its final tack as Matthew lashed the helm and secured the explosive-tipped spar forward of the bow and under water. Waiting almost to the instant of impact, he dove off the gig's stern. A high geyser of water erupted from under the ironclad's starboard bow, staggering it and throwing one engine from its mount.

Regaining consciousness in the Squadron flagship's sick bay, Matthew was told that the *Manassas* had turned tail and retreated upriver after the torpedo attack, a pall of sooty smoke trailing from her stern hatch. Feeling a pain in his leg, Matthew cautiously ran his hand over his bandaged right thigh. One of the officers standing by his berth leaned closer. There was a silver caduceus on his uniform collar. "It's still there," he smiled. "You may limp a bit, but on a hero it will look distinguished."

"Hell," roared the long-bearded flag officer, "I'm real worried now. With that leg, he's to be sent home—and where am I going to find another rag-sailor in this iron-and-steam navy to wipe out the rest o' those rams?" Commander Porter produced a small box and plucked out a bronze medal, to which was attached a blue ribbon with thirteen white stars.

CHAPTER TWENTY-ONE

"When Johnny comes marchin' home again,
   Hurrah, hurrah,
   We'll give 'im a hearty welcome and,
   Hurrah, hurrah . . ."

The Boston & Maine's first-class car overshot the exuberant brass band, screeched to a stop, and the engineer threw the gears into reverse amidst a cloud of huffing steam and a whistle toot.

Portsmouth, New Hampshire, had turned out on a bright afternoon in early November to welcome a hero. Governor Nathaniel Berry presided over the day's festivities, which included a parade and a dinner at the town hall.

Everyone turned out except Elizabeth Mason, whose husband had been killed when a smoothbore burst aboard the USS *Wabash* during the shelling of Fort Hatteras in August.

By and by, Matthew called on Liz and their early romance was rekindled, but with a more mature and deeper understanding born of living, personal losses and solitude. After a cold winter that saw bloodshed and stand-offs at Shiloh and an indecisive battle between ironclads off Hampton Roads, they were married. Matthew joined his father and Cleo at Hadley & Smith's yard in the building of one of the ninety-day gunboats and an additional mortar schooner. Together, they planned the addition of a marine railway and a foundry to the yard, and wrote to Mark, who was on blockade duty in Mobile Bay, that he could concentrate on the war while they turned out boats.

In New York City, beneath a sidewalk on Broadway just a few doors from Bleecker Street, a Saturday night get-together was in progress, the first since the war began. The occasion was to mark the visit from Washington of Gotham's acclaimed poet and frequenter of Pfaff's beer cellar restaurant, Walt Whitman.

At the far end of the main room, a vaulted grotto had been built to house a long wooden table and a dozen chairs. As the revelers quaffed and exchanged stories, the clatter of carriages and shouts of newsboys drifted down through a grating. Pfaff's German-American proprietor had recreated a Bavarian brauhaus, and it had become, in the fifties, the haunt of a group of New York's scandalous rebels who called themselves "the Bohemians." They despised the stuffy dullness of Washington Square and were themselves denounced as a moral menace. The group of writers and artists listened in rapture as the gray-haired elder told of the valiant young wounded in Washington's army hospital where he worked as a nurse and of his brother's regiment and the beauty of the Potomac.

Ada Clare, the cigarette-rolling "Queen of the Bohemians," looked on with adulation, along with Frederick Church, the landscape artist, and Fitz-James O'Brien, the Irish writer and sportsman who had just donned a Union blue uniform.

Near the sacred grotto, at a solitary table, sat the

disillusioned shipcarver from Portsmouth, Seth Mason.
Thoughts tearing at his heart of weakness and failure
as a sculptor, words and phrases caromed from the
grotto as if meant for him. Women's voices . . .
readings of poems:

"I too have been bubbled up . . . and been washed
on your shores,
I too am but a trail of drift and debris . . ."

"I am drift and debris," repeated Seth into his
beer.

"Me and mine, loose windrows, little corpses,
Froth, snowy white, and bubbles,
See, from my dead lips the ooze exuding at last,
See the prismatic colors glistening and rolling . . ."

PRISMATIC COLORS . . . BUBBLES . . . DEAD
LIPS. Seth swung his scarf about his neck and clat-
tered his last coin on the table. Walking aimlessly
through the crowds, he was pulled by the magnetism of
ship's masts to South Street and the river. Windows
full of ivory and brass nautical instruments, binnacles,
lanterns and ropework taunted him. A shrill wind
touched him and he felt the urge to smash glass, to
steal. What had he now to barter with—for hasheesh,
for shelter. For warmth. A poster caught his woozy eye.

NATIONAL CONSCRIPTION ACT!
All Male Citizens
BETWEEN 20 and 45 YEARS OF AGE
Must enroll at . . .
. . . OR EXEMPTED BY A PAYMENT OF
$300 . . .

Almost nauseous from the effect of beer after having previously taken hasheesh, Seth stumbled to the
dock's edge, under the bow of a sailing packet.

Above him, a figurehead scowled down—its Greek helmet tossed back and sword on the neck of a dragon.

Saint George . . . Odysseus? Who?

No, it was his own father, long dead.

Gaunt-eyed Woodbury Mason, with his adz.

"Yes, father, I will," answered Seth, and he staggered out on the empty dock. Near the gangway lay some rigger's tools, abandoned for the warmth of a pot-belly stove in the pier shack. PRISMATIC COLORS . . . DRAGON . . . FATHER . . .

Awakening from his trance, Seth found himself climbing the stairs of a mercantile building. He looked out the landing window at the dizzying spars and river below. On the landing above him, a door beckoned, its shaded gold lettering proclaiming:

    GIBBS & CO.

    D. MONTEBIANCO

Hand hidden under his coat, it gripped a hard, metallic object—a sword, a marlin-spike, for the dragon.

CHAPTER TWENTY-TWO

On April 9th, 1865, General Robert E. Lee surrendered at Appomattox. The naval war had long since been over, as the remaining Confederate vessels were penned up by Union blockades of Southern harbors.

Lieutenant Mark Hadley, home on leave, and his wife Cleo were attending a birthday party in Portsmouth at the newly built house of Matthew and Liz, overlooking the harbor. The parents looked on proudly as their two-year-old twins were handed wrapped presents by their aunt and uncle.

Little Lucas Hadley squealed with delight as he tore the wrapping from a toy wooden boat. Painted silver, it had a low deck and a squat, cylindrical tower, from which protruded a toy cannon. Mark demonstrated for the child.

"See, it has wheels." He gave it a push and Lucas toddled after it to do the same.

Suddenly, Lucas' twin sister, Mary, broke out crying. An exquisitely detailed doll, dressed in the latest fashion, lay on its wrapping paper.

"I knew it," Cleo said. She shot a cynical glance at her husband, then rushed out of the parlor and returned with another package which she handed to the little girl. The adults waited breathlessly as little Mary unwrapped her new present. Smiling, she rubbed at her tears. It was another toy monitor steamboat. Soon the children were pushing and tooting all around the room, Lucas intent on ramming his "enemy."

"We'll get you a *Merrimac* for your birthday, Matt," Cleo said, dodging as one of the monitors rolled under her chair.

"I hear we have cause to celebrate something else," Mark said, setting two small candles on one side of a chocolate cake, then two on the other, under Cleo's scrutinizing gaze.

"I'm so glad it's all over," Liz sighed. "The judge said that Lano's testimony was enough to clear Matt. It would have been wrong to have it any other way."

"Medals never hurt, but I agree." Mark lit the

candles. "By the way, Matt . . . where is *Nightingale* now?"

Matthew walked over to the fireplace, stoked briskly at the embered logs and blew a cobweb from the rigging of the scale model clipper ship on the mantle. "She arrived from Key West at Boston infected with yellow fever, and was sold at auction to a Captain Mayo. He intends to refurbish her as a California trader. I hope he's more fortunate than Fiske and the others."

"Nothing that adding a little steam engine wouldn't fix," replied Mark, ducking as his brother threatened to throw a candlestick at him.

EPILOGUE

Col. H.C. Whitley
U.S. Secret Service
New York City

April 11, 1865

Dear Hiram:

I trust you will consider this an unofficial letter.

The Montebianco case has plagued me now for almost two years, and I seem no closer to a solution now than then. After interviewing all but one (deceased) of the debtors included on the original list, I am of the opinion that there were several who had other motives than were generated by the debts and usury. But there is no evidence against them.

Examination of the murder instrument by magnifying glass showed prints of a thumb and fingers, no doubt those of a male. When compared to prints taken from men of various occupations, the prints had the traits of a man who worked with his hands. Since the debtors are all gentlemen, there is an impasse—except in the case of a hired assassin, which is unlikely.

*The marlinspike, a well-used specimen, was sold
by the Boston firm of Bliss & Co., and bore no
serial number or other sign of owner.*

*As to the method of access to the victim's
premises, there were no signs of forcible entry,
which indicates that the murderer was known to
the deceased—or at least, expected. But I do not
rule out that a total stranger, upon seeing Mr.
Montebianco's gold nugget ring displayed at a
dance hall, may have followed him to the premises and later came back to the premises to lie in
wait for him to exit or use the hall water-closet,
thereafter overpowering the victim. The motive,
here, would be simple robbery.*

*My investigations have, at least, led to the
discovery of an ingenious, though grisly, method
of smuggling precious stones into this country,
the apprehension of which shall greatly enhance
the Bureau's posture. You will receive a report
shortly.*

*In summation, it is my theory that Mr. Monte-
bianco, scamp that he might have been, was a
victim of this city, hub as it is of destitute immi-
grants and wharf-rats of the world. Until such
time as further and contrary evidence comes
forth, I strongly recommend that the case be
discontinued.*

> *Respectfully,*
> *John C. Nettleship*
> *Operative*

ROMANCE LOVERS DELIGHT

Purchase any book for $2.95 plus $1.50 shipping & handling for each book.

_____ **LOVE'S SECRET JOURNEY** by Margaret Hunter. She found a man of mystery in an ancient land.

_____ **DISTANT THUNDER** by Karen A. Bale. While sheltering a burning love she fights for her honor.

_____ **DESTINY'S THUNDER** by Elizabeth Bright. She risks her life for her passionate captain.

_____ **DIAMOND OF DESIRE** by Candice Adams. On the eve of a fateful war she meets her true love.

_____ **A HERITAGE OF PASSION** by Elizabeth Bright. A wild beauty matches desires with a dangerous man.

_____ **SHINING NIGHTS** by Linda Trent. A handsome stranger, mystery & intrigue at Queen's table.

_____ **DESIRE'S LEGACY** by Elizabeth Bright. An unforgotten love amidst a war torn land.

_____ **THE BRAVE & THE LONELY** by R. Vaughn. Five families, their loves and passion against a war.

_____ **SHADOW OF LOVE** by Ivy St. David. Wealthy mine owner lost her love.

_____ **A LASTING SPLENDOR** by Elizabeth Bright. Imperial Beauty struggles to forget her amorous affairs.

_____ **ISLAND PROMISE** by W. Ware Lynch. Heiress escapes life of prostitution to find her island lover.

_____ **A BREATH OF PARADISE** by Carol Norris. Bronzed Fiji Island lover creates turbulent sea of love.

_____ **RUM COLONY** by Terry Nelson Bonner. Wild untamed woman bent on a passion for destructive love.

_____ **A SOUTHERN WIND** by Gene Lancour. Secret family passions bent on destruction.

_____ **CHINA CLIPPER** by John Van Zwienen. Story of sailing ships beautiful woman tantalizing love.

_____ **A DESTINY OF LOVE** by Ivy St. David. A coal miners daughter's desires and romantic dreams.